Praise for Laura Wright and the Mark of the Vampire Series

Eternal Beast

"Absorbing and edgy, darkly seductive—everything vampire romance should be! [A]n enthralling read, set in a rich world of blood wars and intrigue, complex characters and scorching sensuality. Laura Wright turns up the heat and takes you on a wild ride. I can't wait to see what's next!"
—*New York Times* bestselling author Lara Adrian

Eternal Captive

"Riveting. . . . There are plenty more stories to be told in this fascinating universe."　　　　—*Romantic Times*

"Excellent. . . . Continues to expound on [the] vampire genetics that make the Wright mythos the right stuff. Action-packed, with a powerful psychological obsession as its key base, [and] fans will relish this superb tale and series while hoping for future visits to the world of Laura Wright."　　　—The Merry Genre Go Round Reviews

"Sensual and compelling. . . .With action to spare and sensuality scorching nearly every page, Wright has created a fantastic paranormal series!"—Reader to Reader Reviews

"An action-packed read filled with intense scenes of intimacy and mysterious reveals that slowly add to the backgrounds of the myriad characters that people this world . . . enough twists that leave one anxious for the next in the series."　　　　　　　　　—Night Owl Reviews

"The story was very sexy. . . .The emotional strength of the story elevated this above other paranormals I've read of late."　　　　　　　　　　—Dear Author . . .

Eternal Kiss

"Complex and riveting."　　　—*Romantic Times* (4 stars)

continued . . .

"A super urban romantic fantasy due to the powerful Wright mythos that makes the realm of the Eternal Order seem genuine. . . . This author clearly has the Wright stuff with the complicated world of the Roman vampire brothers."   —The Merry Genre Go Round Reviews

"I fell in love with book one in this series, but this second addition moved me from innocent love to full-blown love addiction. . . . [I] could not put it down."
    —Shameless Romance Reviews (5 stars)

"The romance is rich in emotion and the plot infuses dangers and nail-biting action. The journey was so exciting! It was rife with chills and thrills, and altogether it never failed to keep my attention. . . . [This] was a great ride where a sweep-you-off-your-feet romance ignites within a high-risk plot. Laura Wright has found her niche in the paranormal romance genre with her larger-than-life Roman brothers!"   —Leontine's Book Realm

Eternal Hunger

"Dark, delicious, and sinfully good, *Eternal Hunger* is a stunning start to what promises to be an addictive new series. I can't wait for more from Laura Wright."
    —*New York Times* bestselling author Nalini Singh

"Action, passion, and dark suspense launch a riveting new series. Laura Wright knows how to lure you in and hold you captive until the last page."
    —*New York Times* bestselling author Larissa Ione

"Dark, sexy vampires with an urban bite make *Eternal Hunger* a must read."   —Jessica Andersen

"Paranormal fans with a penchant for vamps will find *Eternal Hunger* a must read, but be warned, you will quickly become hooked!"
    —The Romance Readers Connection (4½ stars)

"Deliciously dark while making you believe in the concept of soul mates."   —Fresh Fiction

"An exhilarating vampire romance . . . dark, passionate, and utterly intoxicating!"   —Reader to Reader Reviews

"In a field brimming with rehashes of the same theme, Wright has managed to create a sound, believable vampire culture with plenty of tension and interesting plot points. The pacing is smooth, with well-developed characters, and the satisfying conclusion leaves ample room for more from this strong new series."   —Monsters and Critics

"A bold new voice in vampire romance."
                    —*Romantic Times* (4 stars)

"Wright does an incredible job of wrapping everything up in a deeply satisfying conclusion while enticing readers to continue on. I know I'm looking forward to the next in the Mark of the Vampire series."   —*Sacramento Book Review*

"Wright has taken a common theme and transformed it into her own creation, a unique and intriguing world that stands out from the pack. A captivating take, *Eternal Hunger* is certain to make it onto your list of favorite books and will leave you thirsty for more."—Romance Reviews Today

"If you like testosterone-heavy man candy and sex scenes hot enough to curl your toes, you are going to kick yourself for not reading *Eternal Hunger*!"   —Bitten by Books

"In *Eternal Hunger* classic paranormal romance elements mesh with a fresh and exciting plot and characters. . . . [Wright] sure made an unforgettable impression with her storytelling."   —Leontine's Book Realm

"Just when it seems every possible vampire twist has been turned, Wright launches a powerful series with a rich mythology, page-turning tension, and blistering sensuality."
                    —*Publishers Weekly* (starred review)

Also by Laura Wright

The Mark of the Vampire Series

ETERNAL BEAST

MARK OF THE VAMPIRE

LAURA WRIGHT

A SIGNET ECLIPSE BOOK

SIGNET ECLIPSE
Published by New American Library, a division of
Penguin Group (USA) Inc., 375 Hudson Street,
New York, New York 10014, USA
Penguin Group (Canada), 90 Eglinton Avenue East, Suite 700, Toronto,
Ontario M4P 2Y3, Canada (a division of Pearson Penguin Canada Inc.)
Penguin Books Ltd., 80 Strand, London WC2R 0RL, England
Penguin Ireland, 25 St. Stephen's Green, Dublin 2,
Ireland (a division of Penguin Books Ltd.)
Penguin Group (Australia), 250 Camberwell Road, Camberwell, Victoria 3124,
Australia (a division of Pearson Australia Group Pty. Ltd.)
Penguin Books India Pvt. Ltd., 11 Community Centre, Panchsheel Park,
New Delhi - 110 017, India
Penguin Group (NZ), 67 Apollo Drive, Rosedale, Auckland 0632,
New Zealand (a division of Pearson New Zealand Ltd.)
Penguin Books (South Africa) (Pty.) Ltd., 24 Sturdee Avenue,
Rosebank, Johannesburg 2196, South Africa

Penguin Books Ltd., Registered Offices:
80 Strand, London WC2R 0RL, England

First published by Signet Eclipse, an imprint of New American Library,
a division of Penguin Group (USA) Inc.

First Printing, August 2012
10 9 8 7 6 5 4 3 2 1

SIGNET ECLIPSE and logo are trademarks of Penguin Group (USA) Inc.

Printed in the United States of America

PUBLISHER'S NOTE
This is a work of fiction. Names, characters, places, and incidents either are the
product of the author's imagination or are used fictitiously, and any resem-
blance to actual persons, living or dead, business establishments, events, or
locales is entirely coincidental.
    The publisher does not have any control over and does not assume any re-
sponsibility for author or third-party Web sites or their content.

For one amazing D, from the other . . .

GLOSSARY

Balas—Vampire child.

The Breeding Male—A *paven* of purest blood whose genetic code and structure has been altered by the Eternal Order. He has the ability to impregnate at will and decide the sex of the *balas*. He is brought in by Pureblood families and/or to repopulate one sex or the other in times of dire necessity. He is uncontrollable, near to an animal, and must be caged.

Credenti—A vampire community, ruled and protected by the Eternal Order. Both Purebloods and Impures live here. There are many all over the world, masked by the Order so that humans barely notice their existence.

Duro—Tender word for "brother."

Eternal Order—The ten Pureblood vampires who have passed on to the middle world, yet make the laws, punish the lawbreakers, and govern every vampire *credenti* on Earth.

Eyes—The New York City street rats who run the sales of drugs, blood, and body to both human and vampire.

Gemino—Twin.

Gravo—Poisoned vampire blood.

Imiti—An imitation vampire, one who can take on the characteristics of a vampire if he or she drinks blood regularly.

Impurebloods—Any combination of human and vampire. They have no powers, no heartbeat, and can live in the sun. They only have fangs when blood is consumed. Males are blood castrated, their sex drive removed through the blood by the Order. Females are blood sterilized and the inside of their thighs are branded with *I*'s.

Meta—The transition every Pureblood female makes into adulthood. Happens at fifty years of age. Though the female can still remain in sunlight, she needs and craves the blood and body of her true mate.

Mondrar—Vampire prison.

Morpho—The transition every Pureblood *paven* makes into adulthood. Happens at three hundred years of age. This state of being is as powerful as a *paven* can get. He is sunlight intolerant, and the need to find his true mate becomes impossible to deny.

Mutore—A Pureblood vampire shape-shifter. A Beast. A child of the Breeding Male gone wrong. Is considered less than trash, and a bad omen on the breed. Is usually killed right after birth when they shift for the first time.

Paleo—The Order's secret location where Impures are blood castrated.

Paven—A vampire male of pure blood.

Pureblood—Pure vampire. Powerful, no heartbeat, will go through morpho and meta and find their Pureblood true mate.

Puritita—One who is chaste.

Sacro—Dirty.

Similis—The Impure guards of Mondrar.

Swell—Vampire pregnancy.

Tegga—Nursemaid/nanny/governess.

True Mate—The one each Pureblood *veana* and *paven* is destined for. Each shares an identical or complementary mark somewhere on their skin.

Veana—A vampire female of pure blood.

Veracou—The mating ceremony between two Pureblood vampires.

Virgini—Virgin.

Witte—Animal.

The Impure

The private hospital located deep in the Maine woods was scented of antiseptic and bodily decay, despite the lack of patients residing in it.

Gray Donohue moved down the brightly lit hallway, his gaze ripping right and left as he took in each empty room, each perfectly made-up bed. Gray despised hospitals. And shit, after spending most of his life in them, nearly comatose and habitually restrained "for his own protection," it was little wonder. But this was no long-term stay he was walking into. This was just a visit—a quick trip down memory lane that would end in a very satisfying prize.

Gray spotted a maintenance worker exiting one of the rooms up ahead. Battling with an ancient mop bucket and wringer, the balding, middle-aged male came to a screeching halt when he saw Gray, his pale, watery eyes going wide, his mind kicking up a curse and a query.

"Oh, shit. What's this guy doing in here?"

Without another glance, Gray moved on, down the hall and toward his true goal.

But the foolish human decided to run after him.

"I'm sorry, sir," the man said, his heavy breathing suggesting his unease. "You can't go any farther. The hallway up ahead is being cleaned."

Gray didn't slow.

"Sir! Please!"

In the back of his mind, Gray heard the male's rapid-fire plans to call security. With a quick turn, he snatched him up and squeezed just enough breath from his wriggling body to knock him out. Then, after depositing him in one of the many empty rooms, Gray continued on. There was nothing, no one who would stop him from getting what he needed.

After rounding one corner, then another, he headed straight for the door at the end of the hall. Room 482. He hoped his spies were right about this one. After three false starts at three other care facilities over the past five months, his patience had grown thin.

As expected, a guard stood before the door. The male was tall, dark, and massive. In fact, he looked a hell of a lot like the Impure warrior Vincent, one of Gray's partners in the Resistance—the rogue band of four who were hell-bent on bringing equality to the Eternal Breed—but Gray was willing to bet this male carried no in-mouth bloodsucking hardware and was all human.

As Gray approached, the guard narrowed his black eyes and put up a meaty hand. *"What do you think you're doing, asshole?"* his mind growled. But aloud, he spoke in a calm voice. "Don't know how you got in here, but do yourself a favor and turn back around and walk out again."

Gray had no doubt that in a few minutes there would be more robo cops just like this one to contend with. He'd better be quick. Get in, take what he needed, and get out. Loss of life was always possible on these missions, but he didn't like it, didn't have a taste for it like the second male warrior in the Resistance, Rio. That ex-military Impure loved nothing better than to extinguish a heartbeat.

Gray was nearly to the door when the security guard pulled his gun. "Okay, buddy, I warned you. Take another step and you'll be on your—"

Before the man finished his threat, Gray reached out, snatched the gun, flipped it, and slammed the butt into the guard's head. Then, without missing a beat, he moved past him and opened the door.

No, he didn't have a taste for violence, but anyone guarding his prize was part of the Order's campaign to blood castrate Impures—and that was something Gray would kill for.

The room was large, achingly white and cold—as though the male lying on the hospital bed against the wall needed to be kept fresh. To Gray, the big bad senator from Maine looked anything but big and bad. His eyes were closed, his wrinkles deep-set, and his skin was frog-belly white. He was stretched out on the bed, his limbs locked in place by straps Gray remembered all too well. His muscles twitched beneath his skin as he moved to the side of the bed.

Get in, get out, Impure, Gray reminded himself as he

stood over the male and whispered a terse, "Open your eyes, Senator."

The man didn't move, didn't even flinch—but his mind came alive in a fit of alarm.

"Just lie still. Don't move. He'll go away."

A touch of a grin hit Gray's mouth. When Alexander Roman had unclogged his muddled brain so many months ago and left him with not only the knowledge that he was half vampire but with the gift of hearing the thoughts of others, he hadn't been all that thrilled. In fact, the onslaught of voices had nearly driven him mad. But in moments like this, he felt a deep surge of pleasure for his mental abilities.

He leaned down and whispered, "I'm not going anywhere, Senator. Not yet."

"Oh God."

The male's lids flickered.

"All the way open now," Gray instructed with deadly calm. "Or I cut the lids off with this very dull knife at my back. I suppose I should've sharpened it before coming. But what fun would that be, right?"

A gasp shot from the senator's throat, and his eyes opened and bulged like a fish. He stared up into Gray's face with undisguised terror.

"You've been very difficult to find, Senator," Gray said. "Even your wife has no idea where you are."

The male's lip quivered.

"They swore no one would find me."

Gray narrowed his eyes. "Who?"

The man's eyes widened further.

"Who swore no one would find you?" Gray repeated, moving another inch closer to the male's face.

Gray could sense the man's heart jumping, beating rapidly in his chest as his mind screamed the impossible truth. *"He heard me. Heard my thoughts."*

"Was it the Order?" Gray continued, undaunted.

"The Order. The vampires."

A growl of pleasure, of potential gain escaped Gray's throat. The lawmakers, the overlords, the elitist rulers of the Eternal Breed had indeed cloistered and used this human. "I want to know how you've been communicating with them. How do you call them? How do you receive their messages?"

The senator shook his head against the onslaught of questions.

Gray growled low in his throat. "You think *they* are something to fear? Then you don't understand what stands before you, human."

The senator's weak bladder released then, and Gray cursed. He needed to get this information and get out of here. It was hard enough standing over this man—this piece of shit who had been responsible for Dillon's beating. He wanted to slice him in half and leave him to bleed out as he screamed for help that would come too late. But he wasn't after revenge tonight. Tonight he wanted inside the male's blood, wanted to find his access into the Order's communication mainframe, their mental link with Purebloods, Impures, humans, and one another. He wanted inside the brain of the entire telepathic system, and if what the Impure male inmate at the vampire prison Mondrar had told Gray was true, this nearly dead fish lying before him was their conduit.

In the many months since the Resistance's inception,

Gray had found his calling, his purpose. After nearly being blood castrated, he'd joined with three other Impures to form a mental powerhouse. Now they were close to being able to hack into the Order's telepathic mainframe. If they could hijack that mainframe, they were pretty certain they could remain, intercept the messages to the Impures and send out their own, gather secret information to use as currency—perhaps even shut down the entire operation, if all else failed and the Order refused their call for freedom.

Below Gray, the senator shifted almost desperately, his eyes filling with tears.

"Please don't hurt me. Please."

Gray's lip curled. What a coward. He would see this man suffer, but not yet, not tonight. The Impure Resistance would need him longer.

He leaned in close. "I'll give you five seconds to tell me how you communicate with the Order and then I'm going in."

The male tried to scream, tried to open his mouth, but he couldn't. The Order had made it impossible for him to speak lies, truth, or anything in between, Gray realized. They had fused his lips together.

Christ.

Gray flashed his fangs, bent his head, and struck. He heard the senator's cry of pain and terror but shoved it away. This was his third blood memory grab in two weeks, and it was painful and fucked with his brain. But each one had gleaned him some important intel, not to mention made him a stronger mental force. Each member of the Impure Resistance was mentally at the top of his game and needed to stay that way to defeat the Order and take their first step toward self-rule.

Gray moved swiftly through the senator's mind, shuffling, sifting through memories to find the ones he needed. Any and all that connected him with the Order. Experience had made him shrewd, and it took him only a minute or two to find, gather, and file away what he needed. He was about to pull out when one memory, one dark and ugly scene, grabbed his mind and had him skidding to a halt.

Night, an abandoned lot, a few cars dotting the asphalt landscape, and a female—a *veana*, her expression pissed off, her face knocked around and bloody. The senator had thrown the first punch, but the cowardly piece of shit had stood back for the rest, watching with amusement and vindictive pleasure as several massive human males finished what he'd started.

Dillon.

Gray's pulse slammed against the skin of his wrists and neck as he watched the *veana* try to fight off her attackers. She was like a wildcat, filled with fury, hunger, and terror, but she was only one being. She was strong and a Pureblood vampire, but she was no match for that many males. She went down hard, and as the surrounding bastard males pummeled her with fists and with feet, Gray saw her change. One moment she was female; the next she was something else altogether. Something strange, cat and female mixed.

Gray thought later that maybe if he'd pulled out of the senator right then and there, the male would've gone on breathing another day. But he didn't. And what he heard next, saw next, sent him so far and so deeply into rage that he no longer cared about the Resistance or his future with them.

"Forget the face and tend to the body," said the senator from the safety of the sidelines. "Make that thing bleed. Make it incapable of breeding. Make it never want to fuck another thing for as long as it lives—make it always remember what happens when you say no to me."

Gray got as far as the first steel-tipped boot into Dillon's cheek when he snapped, pulled out of the man's temple in a rush and used his fangs like twin daggers across the senator's neck.

The Beast

Most cats despised the water.

But not the jaguar. Not Dillon the jaguar.

No, this was her salvation, her baptism. She was pure predator now, deeply integrated into the world of the animal for as long as it took her to claim her prey once and for all.

Rain pounded the black earth, her massive paws striking puddle after puddle as she ran at top speed through the Green Mountain region of Southern Vermont. She'd crossed the New York border thirty minutes ago, escaping the protective custody of the Romans, her *mutore* brothers, and the Impure male who had found and delivered her to safety for the last time—or so he'd said. She growled into the wet night. Didn't they understand? Didn't they all get it? She wasn't the one who needed protecting. It was the human who had sent her into this everlasting shift, the one who still breathed. He was the one in need of care.

Bounding out of the woods, she slowed just a hair as she came upon a children's playground. It was deep in the dark of night, and the shadows protected her golden fur and black rosettes from the curious gaze of any nocturnal humans who might be about. As she passed a merry-go-round that creaked a slow rotation in the wind, her belly clenched. She was hungry, for blood and for meat, but a true meal would have to wait. A cat must have its chase, its attack, its kill before it feasted, and there was no time for that now. Later. Much later. But when it did come, she vowed, it would be a celebratory feed. One that—if she got it right— would commemorate not only the death of the human senator who'd had her beaten, but the days and weeks and endless, restless, merciless nights she'd suffered ever since, trying to gain control over her shift from *veana* to Beast.

Granted, she didn't know where they were hiding this prey, this gutless human whom she'd worked for as a bodyguard for so many years. They'd moved him several times over the past six months. But she believed he was still somewhere in Maine, and she knew his scent.

Creeping under the overpass, where cars moved along at the frantic pace her cat's lithe body understood and craved, Dillon headed for another stretch of woods. By tomorrow, she'd be in Maine, where she knew the scents of every street, every brick—and if she was lucky, one very arrogant dick.

A car's headlights moved over her hips and tail just as she ducked into a patch of bracken, then darted off toward the woods again. Within minutes, she had the scent of a rabbit on the roof of her mouth, and, though her fangs hummed with the need for it, she pushed forward. She had to get to her human prey. She had to end his life—because only then could she live again. The rain continued to fall in heavy sheets, but she ran, mile after mile, focused and unfazed, all the way from the Green Mountains to Eastern Vermont, all the way until her feet were so caked in mud she was forced to slow— all the way until an aching thirst compelled her to stop. She hated stopping. When she stopped or slowed, she started to think. Maybe not think exactly, but feel— which was far more dangerous. Feeling made a body weak and foolish and vulnerable. It led to hope and a feral need to connect. It led to pain and potential ruin. In her vampire form, she wasn't as susceptible to it, but in her cat form, the need for connection, for the stroke of a kind, solid hand was, at times, unbearably strong.

Her lip curled. She was growing weaker with every breath, every thought. She needed to end this, find and kill the remaining member of the senator's assault team—the senator himself—so she could return to her vampire form, to the control over her shift that she'd once enjoyed, counted on, reveled in.

Survived by.

The rain ceased its endless torment, and scenting the cool, crispness of stream water somewhere to her right, Dillon darted off the path. Weaving between the heavy sugar maple trees, she ventured down into a gully and found a wide stream. Under the bleak light of a cloud-covered moon, she drank her fill, pausing only momentarily when she heard the sound of an animal in the distance. A mile or so away, she thought. Nothing to pose a threat. Again, she dropped her muzzle into the water and drank. The feel of it on her skin and tongue reminded her of the cold, clear water she'd run to as a *balas*, as a *mutore balas* so many years ago. The water had saved her, not from thirst as it did now, but from the one who had hunted her, the one who had worked for her adopted father, Cruen, and had stolen her innocence—the one who, with his sexually violent act, had turned her into a she-cat for the first time.

Suddenly the thought, the memory, was stolen away. A sound and a scent far too familiar for Dillon's liking rushed into her nostrils, and her eyes caught on something moving down the stream toward her. The light from the moon was still dim, but it was enough to see the creature. It was large, the size of a whale shark, but it was not a fish, not anything that naturally belonged in the water or the forest. Her limbs were frozen, the pads on the undersides of her paws pressed into the moist ground. This was an invader, and if he had tracked her there, others like him were surely close behind.

Her muzzle as dry as the inside of her mouth now, Dillon turned and raced from the stream. She was a jaguar, yes, and her speed, her sight, her instincts were strong, but the ones following her were just as strong, had the same keen instincts, and one of them could get at her from the sky.

Panic pricked at her skin, at her insides, and her breathing went labored. She wasn't afraid of them, of fighting them. No, that wasn't why she ran. She was afraid of being caught and returned, caged and forever fixed as this cat—afraid of never being in control of herself again.

Afraid that bastard senator would continue to breathe.

Yet another male who thought he could lay his hands on her without her consent and live. Live while she died just a little bit more.

Her sprint was tight as she weaved in and out of the trees, but soon she heard it behind her, closing in, then quickly matching her speed. The wolf. The dog chasing the cat. Her brain worked overtime. If she headed back toward the river, swam as her body was capable of doing, the creature that waited there, the water lord, would force her to shore. And if she climbed the massive tree directly in her path, it was the hawk who would halt her assent.

Fuck.

The scents of all three were coming at her fast and furious now. It was one thing to be chased as a vampire—as a grown *veana*. *That* she could handle. But being pursued as a Beast made her feel vulnerable, trapped, like a young *veana* again. She wanted to curl into a ball and wish it all away. But just as it had been the first time her jaguar emerged without her consent or control, the only way out of the weakness and fear was running straight through it.

They weren't taking her back.

They weren't deterring her from the vengeance that she had to believe would save her sanity, her life, and—shit—the soul that may still be lurking within her somewhere.

She leaped onto the base of the tree and began to climb, her nails digging into the sodden wood like fangs through flesh. She'd deal with whatever met her at the top. She'd fight as she always did, always had, to hold on to whatever freedoms she could claim. Because they—the control and the choice—were all she had. They were the only things left to fight for.

The growl, the bark of the wolf that sounded below her was menacing and all Lycos, but he wasn't the one who concerned her. It was the voice of another, the water lord, the one she'd suffered the most with—been found with as a *mutore balas*—had truly loved as a brother, that finally halted her.

"Stop running, Dilly."

Helo.

Her claws dug farther into the wood, ready to spring.

"We just found you again," he called, his voice cool as the water he'd just emerged from. "*I* just found you again."

Fucking Helo. The six-foot-six, skull-shaved, caramel-skinned water Beast had always been a bleeding-heart little bastard. She climbed another few feet and hissed. Unfortunately, he was her favorite bleeding-heart little bastard and he knew it. He was the one who always let her crawl into his bed at night when she was a scared *mutore* shit who'd belonged to no one but Cruen. The one she'd wanted so badly to run to the night Cruen had watched her shift for the first time with greedy, clinical eyes after his servant had raped her. The pretend father of them all had been interested only in the fact that the assault had caused her shift—not in protecting her. It was then that she'd realized no one could or would ever truly protect her. No one but herself.

Just a few feet above her, a massive snow-white hawk landed on a thick branch and trained his eyes, one brown, one green, upon her face. The panic within her threatened to steal her voice, but she pushed it back, as she pushed everything complicated and painful and terrifying back as far as it would go. Someday, all that suppressed shit was going to bubble to the surface and explode.

But not today.

The bird's beak lifted slightly into a sneer, and Dillon hissed at the thing. "Get out of my way, Phane, before you lose some of those pretty feathers."

"We want to help you, Dillon," Erion called from below. The flash of the eldest brother's arrival was lightning quick and brilliant next to his animal brothers, who had used their speed and scent to track their sister.

"If you want to help me, then walk, fly, swim, and flash the hell out of here," Dillon shouted down at the Beast, so massive in his demon state, his diamond eyes moon-bright in the dark forest. "Let me finish what I started."

"Killing the senator."

Her nostrils flared. "Yes."

"This isn't the way to get revenge, Dilly."

"This is the ultimate way!" she returned. Not to mention the only way she knew of to get control over her shift from vampire to jaguar back again. "Have you learned nothing from our adopted father? Or did Cruen teach you only to torture your prey?"

She saw Erion's eyes flash, Lycos's too. The demon Beast shook his head, as though he were attempting to remain calm. "You will only draw attention to yourself."

"You will get yourself killed," Helo added, his chest naked and wet from tracking Dillon in the river. "Get us all hunted."

Beside him, the wolf growled out an irritated, "She doesn't give a shit." Lycos looked at her with his narrowed canine eyes. "She didn't give a shit back then when she ran from us, and she doesn't give a shit now. There is no loyalty inside her. Look at her, brothers. She is an empty shell, selfish and without a conscience."

Strange bleats of pain shocked Dillon's insides. It was as though a knife were playing with her organs, making tiny cuts, attempting to make her feel anxious and slow and desperately alone. She wanted to feel angry at Lycos's words, wanted to shoot back with something equally stinging, but nothing surfaced for her to grab on to, to use as an emotional battering ram. Maybe because he was right or maybe because she didn't care about anything but herself in that moment—saving herself, getting control of herself.

But was that wrong? Shouldn't she care about herself first? It's how one survived—how she'd survived this long. Granted, they didn't know—the Beasts, her brothers—they didn't know what she had to run from, why she'd run from them. And they never would. Their memories of the past and her part in it were their own—not something she was ever going to correct.

She stared hard at Lycos, then Erion—then Helo. "Listen, Beasts. Return to your new family, your new lives, and forget the sister who so easily forgot you."

The words were effortless to say. Lies always flowed

from her tongue like blood from a gaping vein. It was the look in Helo's eyes that stopped her from punishing them further—that shattered the last bit of hope she had for a working soul.

Failure.

He'd thought he was going to bring her back, rescue her, carry her home on his back from an emotional or physical scrape like he'd done a hundred times when they were *balas*.

Dillon allowed herself a second of self-loathing and grief, but a second was too long. Above her, the hawk pushed from his branch and dove at her, landing on her shoulder and sinking his needle-sharp talons into her neck.

The jaguar screamed in pain, lost her grip on the tree trunk, and began to fall. Panic seized Dillon's muscles and she struggled to rotate, belly and feet down, as she stretched to catch branch after branch but missed every one. Fifteen feet. She hit the ground hard, paws slamming the dirt, back legs attempting to cushion, but something broke.

Something inside her.

A bone? Or was it her resolve? She couldn't tell by the pain—it was everywhere.

Her head came up, her fangs dropped, but she was in no position to fight. And even if she was, could she truly hurt these *paven*s? Any more than she already had?

Someone flashed directly beside her. He was tall, dark, had a closely shaved head and eyes the color of wine. Under the cool moon, she saw that he held a long silver object in his hand. Her instincts flared and she hissed and tried to snap at it, at him, one paw lifting, claws extended.

"It's all right, D," he whispered, his voice strained as pulled her against him. "Everything will be all right."

"No!" She struggled, desperation ripping at her insides. "Let me go. The senator. I have to kill him."

Alexander Roman's voice went hard as stone. "It's already done."

"What?" Clouded by pain and adrenaline overload, Dillon couldn't make out his words.

"The human male is dead. It's over."

"No!" she screamed into the cold forest air, barely hearing the concerned hum of the male voices surrounding her. "He's mine! Oh God. Oh shit! I'll never recover . . ."

"Calm down, Dilly, please." Helo. Or maybe it was Erion. She didn't know, didn't care.

They didn't understand. How could they? It was over. She was never going to be free.

Despair choked her and she cried out, "Who? Who did this?"

There was silence.

"Who?" she screamed. "Goddamn it! Tell me!"

There was a curse, then the word, the name. "Gray."

A growl exploded from Dillon's throat and she whirled to face Alexander. "I'm going to kill him."

Alexander's worried expression registered for only a second before he abandoned all mercy and plunged the needle straight into her neck, sending Dillon, the jaguar, to her knees, then into a sea of bitter nothingness.

1

The Paleo, the great oval space belowground that had for centuries been the Order's den of castration, where the sexual desires of Impure vampires were removed at a steady pace, hummed with the many sounds of blatant misery. Under the golden light of a thousand candles, Feeyan, the one who now led the Order, stilled over the wriggling Impure on the stone table, her fangs an inch deep within his vein. Information was bleeding into her mind at a frantic pace, and she suddenly ceased the bleeding of his body and lifted her snow-white head.

A few yards away, another member of the Order pulled his fangs from the groin of the Impure male he was castrating and glanced over his shoulder.

"The human politician has been found?" he queried, blood dripping from his bloodred fangs.

Feeyan nodded, a thread of anxiety moving through the already heavy feelings of irritation. It was what she had heard as well. "And our connection to him has been severed."

"How could that be?" the dark-haired Order member asked.

"I am not entirely certain," she told him. "He was well hidden, his location a secret within the Order."

"Perhaps someone inside the facility learned of his identity," the *paven* said tightly. "The Order would not betray itself."

Inside the Paleo, a hush had fallen. From those strapped on the stone tables to the many others locked inside the cages circumventing the arena, Feeyan noticed a keen interest in what was being said. This time she spoke to her colleague inside his mind. *"Think of Cruen. All he has done and continues to do. We are not perfect beings with pure intentions, no matter how we wish we were. We are flawed."*

The male Order member looked mildly insulted but didn't voice it. *"Shall I speak to the other members?"*

"Not yet. The senator's body is being brought to me. Along with the blood memories we've collected from his dead employees, we will piece together the truth."

"And the location of the mutore *female who has killed those employees."*

Feeyan nodded. The *mutore* female. The one called Dillon, who had somehow not only escaped death at birth, but had managed to live as a *veana* without detection. Still lived without detection. How had the Order not sensed her living among the vampire population? Perhaps they were truly flawed. It was a deeply humbling thought, but one that would serve as a reminder and as a fervent push to find this *mutore* and bring her in, comb her mind to see if there were more like her roaming free.

Feeyan glanced around at the faces of the Impures pressing through the bars of their cells. *"Impures breeding is problem enough. But those mutants, those animals who made it past their first breath would sully our bloodlines like nothing else."* Feeyan turned, her eyes narrowing on her fellow Order member. *"If we allow even one* mutore *to live, to breed, to think, to decide, it may change the way the Impures view their role and their place in society. We cannot have that."*

The *paven* nodded. *"Let us see what the senator's brain has to offer. He gave us the* mutore's *name, her face, her Beast."*

"Perhaps in death he can give us her location," Feeyan said aloud, returning to the Impure male before her—his puncture wounds calling to her razor-sharp fangs. "And the kind of bait we may need to draw her out."

Dillon the jaguar paced inside her cage. How could she have let this happen? How could she have allowed herself to get caught? Again?

Thirty minutes ago, she'd woken up in this same cage, Alexander's cage beneath his house in SoHo. A prisoner of the three Roman brothers, with a sore back leg and a knot the size of a penny on her neck from where the Pureblood Son of the Breeding Male had stabbed her with that needle.

Bastard. She hoped she'd granted him a few deep scratches with her claws before she'd passed the hell out. But the one she really wanted to see gutted was

Gray Donohue. Without his meddling, Alexander wouldn't have even known she'd escaped her cage until the deal was done. He never had her checked on until morning hours.

Her growl came quick and feral from her throat. Oh . . . all the ways she was going to rip the skin from that Impure's tight and formidable body. Her teeth and claws would work wonders, but the image she was having of a chain saw and a guillotine really made her grin. Of course, she'd need to shift back into her *veana* form to accomplish such a task. Paws did not have the sufficient dexterity to wield a machine like that.

But she wasn't shifting anytime soon now, was she? She'd been stuck with this fur suit for days, and before that—since Senator Slimeball and his pals had messed her up—she'd been unable to control the shift at all. Vampire, jaguar, and back again—anywhere, anytime. She'd thought she was almost there. With every attacker she killed, she felt stronger, more in control, and she'd come to believe that once the last member of the assault team was dead, her control would return. She would be what she was before the attack. Able to shift from Beast to *veana* at will. After all, it was violence that had brought out her cat to begin with, violence that had sent it into chaos. It had to be violence to bring the control over her shift back again. Shit. It had to be, she'd thought—because if it wasn't, she might as well just follow those human bastards into death.

Right or wrong, she'd never know now.

In killing the senator, Gray had robbed her of not only revenge, but of the hope that she could retrieve the control over her life.

Evans, the Romans' servant and her new jailer, moved suddenly in his seat outside her cage, and without blinking, without breathing, Dillon whirled on him and let loose a ferocious growl.

Outside the door, Gray watched the golden cat snarl at poor Evans through a four-by-four square of two-way mirror. Even under all that fur and fangs, he could sense her ire, her fear, her desperation to get out, get free. But that wasn't going to happen. Not after she'd killed several of the senator's henchmen, not with the Order no doubt looking for the culprit—not with that jaguar costume she was continuously sporting now.

Gray had hoped that the news of the senator's death would bring her some modicum of peace—the final check on the to-kill list she was working from these days—but it seemed she was feeling anything but peaceful. Alexander's call an hour ago asking him to come to the SoHo house, that Dillon had demanded to see him, had Gray thinking she wasn't all that pleased with what he'd done.

That *veana* had never really been one for appreciation. Giving or getting, he thought darkly. Once upon a time, she'd pulled his nearly castrated ass out of the Paleo; then he'd scraped her nearly passed-out ass off the concrete. Neither event had elicited a thoughtful comment.

Gray heard the heavy footfall of his brother-in-law coming toward him down the tunnel hallway. He didn't turn around. Just waited until the *paven* came to stand beside him at the window.

"Thanks for coming," Alexander said, his tone

smooth, but Gray could detect the thread of worry there. The *paven* and D went way back. To a war and a life debt Dillon had paid off a year ago by watching over Gray's sister, Sara.

"Of course. She calls, I come." Gray grunted. "Even when she's pissed."

"Yeah, well, just so we're clear, this isn't the normal pissed-off D we're dealing with anymore." Alexander sighed. "This is a balloon with way too much air in it."

"Explosive," Gray said, his gaze trained on the pacing cat. It was unfortunate that he liked her that way—was glad to see her that way. Because to Gray, anything was better than the desensitized Dillon she'd become after the senator's beating, the disconnected Dillon.

"Just watch yourself, all right?" Alexander said.

"Always do," Gray said, his hand reaching for the door handle.

"And don't think for a minute there's a heart there."

The words echoed in Gray's mind and he glanced over his shoulder at the *paven*. His eyes narrowed.

Alexander's brow lifted. *"No matter what she says."*

The scent of him hit her nostrils before he was even through the door. Feeling jaguar both inside and out in that moment, she stalked to the far side of the cage and pressed her muzzle through the bars. She took one long sniff, then growled low in her throat.

Yes. He had killed the senator.

Her prey.

Hers!

She bared her teeth as he shut the door and came

to stand directly in front of her. No fear in his scent, and his heartbeat pumped slow and calm. Bastard. Things would change pretty damn quick if she made Evans open the cage so they could stand face-to-face for real.

"Thinking up ways to kill me, D?" he asked, his eyes pinned to hers through the slats in the steel bars.

"Thought you couldn't read my mind," she returned with a dangerous purr.

"Can't. But I know you." His mouth twitched. His full mouth, which had a day or two's worth of stubble framing it. Dillon licked her chops.

"You don't know me, Gray," she said sharply. "Because if you did, you wouldn't have gone after something that belonged to me."

Gray turned, eyed Evans, who sat in a chair looking uncomfortable, ready to spring. "You can take a break, Evans."

The Impure looked unsure. "Sir?"

"Go," Gray told him with gentle force. "The cat will remain in her cage, I promise you."

With a quick, concerned glance in Dillon's direction, Evans got to his feet and swiftly made for the door.

"Good," Dillon said once the servant was gone. "Now let me out of this tuna can."

Gray turned back to face her. "I don't think that would be wise for either of us."

"Maybe you need to stop thinking, then," she snarled. "Or is that what had you screwing me over tonight?"

Gray shook his head. "I thought you'd be thanking me."

"For what? Fucking with my life?"

"Taking out the trash," he drawled. "That's a guy's job, isn't it?"

"Wasn't your trash to remove, Impure," she hissed, teeth bared. "That was my kill."

"You had your chance. In fact, over the past six months you've had several. You'd find him only to lose him again." He was tight in his response.

Anger slammed into her and she roared at him. "This time was different! I was on my way—"

"No. You couldn't get to him, D—you weren't going to get to him. Not in that getup. You would've failed. Again."

"Bullshit." This calm, cool act of his was really pissing her off. There he stood, outside her cage, free and easy and pretending he was her savior when really he'd just killed her future right along with the senator's. "Why do you seem to think this is your fight?"

He shrugged then, arrogance lighting his eyes. "Just keeps turning out that way."

"Does it?" she sneered, springing up against the metal bar so she was face-to-face with him. "Or do you seek it out, seek *me* out because you're so fucking obsessed with me you can't help yourself."

His eyes flashed then, fire and ice, and his jaw clenched. "Easy, pussy cat."

Her head dropped and she hissed at him. "Get a new hobby, Impure."

Their faces were just inches from each other, their breaths mingling in the cold air that ruled the tunnels below the Romans' home.

Dillon's nostrils flared, hating the male before her,

yet wanting to lap at him with her tongue. "You owe me."

He sniffed with disbelief. "For what?"

"Killing him was my only way out of this cat suit. Killing him was going to bring back my ability to control my shift."

His eyebrow lifted. "Says who?"

"I know it." Her gaze faltered, her resolve just a little bit, too. "Everything in me told me this was the way— that my cat wouldn't cede control back to the vampire inside me until it had its revenge. The beating brought it about, fucked up my control over my shift. It only makes sense that killing the males responsible would bring it back."

Gray grunted, said with easy sarcasm, "You're living in fantasy land with that one."

Fierce anger shot through Dillon and she lashed out, struck at his hand with her razor-sharp teeth.

Gray was quick to respond, flipping his hand down to get her fangs out of his flesh, then spinning it back and around until his palm was under her chin and his fingers closed around her muzzle.

Blood dripped from the wound in his fire-ravaged hands, but if he noticed, he sure as hell didn't seem to care. "You'll have to learn to control yourself some other way, Dillon," he said, his tone thick with impatience, "or this life behind bars is going to be a long one."

In any other scenario, Dillon would've tried again to bite him, used the claws pressing against the bars to slash open his neck or chest. But in that moment, all she was trying to do was breathe. Something was wrong.

Heavy, thick waves of feeling were rushing through her, over her. Ocean waves, high and consuming—a goddamn emotional tsunami. Then firecrackers erupted within her, popping inside her muscles and organs until she had to consciously take several deep breaths. What the hell? What was happening to her? The second the thought left her head, soothing heat, blistering and delicious, began to snake through her. It was the most addictive sensation she'd ever experienced and she wanted to drown in it. Saliva pooled her in mouth, and for a moment she thought it was her *veana*'s mouth again—not the jaguar's. Never in her life had she felt such internal intensity, such pressure in her mind, her lungs, every inch of muscle and skin—and she pushed away from the bars and from his touch.

The effect was instantaneous. Like stepping out of a sauna. Every feeling from a moment ago disappeared.

Her legs, both hind and fore, began to shake. She moved back into the corner of the cage where it was dark, pressed her long, muscled body into the rock wall, and tried to make sense of what had just happened. She wanted to blame it on desire, on needing a good fuck. But that would've been too easy. And wrong. Those waves, those firecrackers had gone bone deep and everywhere at once. And that wave of delicious heat—shit—that had curled around her cells, her DNA, and had hinted at a desire to change.

Not her cheery personality.

But jaguar to *veana*.

Her gaze flipped up, met Gray's. The tall, broad male gripped the bars of the cage, his chest splayed wide, his dark blond hair hitting his strained jaw, his gunmetal eyes narrowed as he watched her.

"What the hell was that?" she snarled at him, sheathing and unsheathing her claws.

For a long moment, Gray said nothing, but she could practically see him processing behind those soul-deep eyes of his. He couldn't read her mind, but fuck, in that moment she wished to God she could read his. Had he felt it? Had he felt that rush of volcanic lava leave his body and enter hers? Had he felt anything at all?

Then he pushed away from the cage, dropped the feral veneer, and said in a casual voice, "What was what?"

Her throat tightened. "You felt that," she sneered back at him. He had to have felt that. "Don't lie to me."

He shook his head. "No idea what you're talking about."

"Gray!"

"Sorry, baby," he said, turning away and walking to the door. "I think we're done here. I think *I'm* done here." Before he crossed the threshold, he offered her one last glance. "I've got a new and far more satisfying obsession these days."

Dillon stared after him, her breath coming quick and heavy inside her cat's lungs. This was insane, amazing— and far from over. With a growl, she turned away and headed for the dark corner of the cage. She dropped down and put her head on her paws. The intense feelings of a moment ago may have subsided somewhat, but the memory of them remained fresh as the kill her cat's belly screamed for.

Her gaze slid to the door, narrowed into two fierce slits. Perhaps her salvation wasn't as lost as she'd believed an hour ago. Perhaps it lay in the strong, damaged hands of a male who, up until a moment ago, had never been able to refuse her anything.

2

Had he felt it?
Shit.

Jaw brutally tight, Gray moved down the dark tunnels, his gaze focused on the pinprick of light that indicated the stairwell leading up to the subway. This was it. He wasn't coming back into the Romans' domain anymore. No need. No want. Regardless of the family they wanted to believe they were to him, his life belonged to the Impure Resistance, to the Cause, to all those who were having their sexual need bled out of them at that very moment—not to that she-beast back there.

Had he felt it?

His head clenched along with his jaw, and he picked up speed, nostrils flaring as a rogue blast of cold, unpurified air from the city above hit his face.

Fuck yeah, he'd felt it.

Granted, he always felt something when Dillon was

in his airspace. From curiosity to care, from desire to detonating something. But that, whatever it was back there . . .

Christ. It was as if pure, fluid energy had risen within him, then seen an escape route and shot directly into her. It was as if a tube linked them, allowing emotion, energy, and heat to pass back and forth like water. He'd touched her before—many times. But he'd never felt anything like that—nothing like that had ever happened. Sure, there had been heat between them, plenty of dangerously, irritatingly magnetic heat, but not like this.

Maybe it had something to do with all the blood-memory work he'd been doing lately. Taking memories from others, sharing it with his fellow Impure warriors, all in the name of infiltrating the Order's mainframe. Could the wires inside him have overheated and . . . ? And what?

He cursed into the cold, dank air of the tunnels. Maybe he needed to stop trying to figure it out and just forget it happened, forget Dillon altogether and accept the fact that she was always going to be a weakness he couldn't afford, a distraction to his true purpose.

Gray hit the stairwell and was about to climb when he heard something behind him. He turned and saw a female running toward him down the tunnel—a female he was truly grateful to see, a female he wished he could become closer to. But he worried they were too far apart now in their present lives, belief systems, and passions to allow for it.

"How you doing, Sis?"

Sara Donohue's blue eyes were warm as she came to

stand before him, but changed slightly as she noticed the wound on his hand. "You saw her."

"In the flesh." He raised a brow. "Or should I say, in the fur."

"Alexander told me she called for you. Told me she was very angry at you." His big sister's mouth formed a grim line. "What happened in there when you saw her? Did she tell you anything?"

"Just that I screwed her over, that she wants to take a chunk out of more than my hand."

Sara shook her head, laughed softly. But there was no humor in the sound. "She's just unreachable. She won't tell me anything about what happened that night she was hurt. She won't tell me about her shift, the process, the past with Cruen or her brothers. She won't even spar with me like she used to. I've never had a patient that hard to crack since—"

"Me?" he interrupted.

She smiled a little sadly.

He lifted his brow. "She's not your patient, Sara."

"I know. But she is my friend, and I want to help her."

Gray put a hand on the stairwell railing and sighed. "Have you ever considered that some people are beyond help?"

Sara lifted her chin and gave him a pointed look. "No."

His heart softened a fraction. Always trying to be the savior. That was why he equally loved and was frustrated by his sister. Whether it was her little brother who had lost his mind one day in the house fire that had killed their father or a *mutore veana* friend who had just lost her way, Sara Donohue Roman pushed, never gave up, annoyed the shit out of you—but it was all out of love, out of care. And, he thought, his gaze moving over her face, maybe he had that same impulse; maybe that was what had kept him coming back to Dillon. He pushed, never gave up because he cared. Because he wanted her. But where did that get you when the one you pushed, pushed you back, pushed you back so goddamn hard your ass hit the pavement and your head hit the wall and you forgot everything else in your life that mattered?

"Gray," Sara said, cutting in on his savage internal query. "What's going on? With you? I miss you, us, the family."

Gray's gaze faltered then. Family. It was what they were, and yet they both kept so much from each other. Gray had yet to tell her anything about his time in the Paleo, the Order's massive den of Impure blood castration. It was there that he'd met their father's best friend, Samuel. It was there that he'd learned that his father had not really been human at all, but an Impure. It was there that he'd learned about how Jeremy Donohue was no nine-to-five office dad, but a visionary and a soldier. It was he who had started the first Impure Resistance, he who had inspired many until he was captured by the Order and blood castrated.

Gray stared into those concerned, yearning blue eyes and questioned his silence once again. Shit. He'd truly wanted to tell his sister everything he'd learned—she deserved the truth just as much as he did—and yet he hadn't said a word. Still hadn't, and he wasn't sure why—wasn't sure what he was waiting for. More information to be revealed? Peace about it within himself? Or perhaps he wanted to fix that wrong first. Become what Jeremy Donohue never had a chance to.

"I miss you too," he said at long last.

Her smile brightened a touch. "You'll come around more? I know you're busy, but it's family . . ."

"I'll come around," he said. Then, hearing a thought within her head, he added, "Speaking of family, when are you due?"

Sara's eyes widened, and her hands slipped to her belly. "How did you know?"

Gray tapped his temple and smiled. "That mate of yours unblocked it all, remember? Made it so I can hear every damn thought." Except the ones in Dillon's head, his mind reminded him caustically. Her thoughts, feelings, all of it was blocked from him.

Why couldn't he be thankful for that, for small fucking favors like that?

"I haven't even told Alexander," Sara said, her cheeks stained with pink. "It's so early."

Gray put a hand in the air. "I won't say anything."

"Thanks." She smiled. "Uncle Gray."

He laughed, but it came out forced. He was in no mood to celebrate. "Congratulations, Sis." He leaned in and kissed her on the cheek. "I have to go."

"Back to the Impures." There was no malice in her tone, only a twinge of melancholy.

For a moment, he wondered if this was it—the time to tell her, when the discussion of family and new possibilities was fresh. But then again, would it only anger, confuse her, worry her . . . especially now with the *balas*? No. There would be time.

He touched her shoulder and said with deep conviction, "One day you will understand this fight. Maybe even join it."

Her other hand went to her belly as well. "My life is here."

Gray nodded. Yes, it was. And he wondered, as he progressed down this road of Impure equality, if he would be cutting one member of his family out to seek vengeance for another.

He granted her one last smile before heading up the stairs and into the subway.

Erion and his Beast brothers congregated in the tunnels just outside the room that held their sister hostage—the room they'd brought her back to just a few hours ago, after that chase-and-capture disaster in the frigid Vermont woods. Ever since, the four of them had been arguing about what to do with her, how to help her, who was going to have the iron balls to show his face to her first.

"You go in," Phane said to Helo.

"No," Helo snapped tersely in reply. "You go."

Phane's mismatched eyes and long, pale hair glowed in the candlelight of the tunnels. "She likes you better."

"That's when we were *balas*. I'm pretty sure she hates me now." Helo turned to Lycos, who was standing back from the rest, his ice-blue eyes wary. "What about you, Ly? A little cat and dog?"

Lycos sneered and said in a frosty voice, "Not a chance. I'm still pissed at her."

"For what?" Erion asked, stepping into the light, knowing his lion features and demon eyes looked especially distorted in the warm yellow flicker. "Running away? Choosing a different life? Get over it."

It was a truth, a fact they'd had to live with for decades. One of their own, a sibling, a *balas* of the Breeding Male, Titus, and one of the five who'd been plucked from death and raised by Cruen had, one day, turned tail and run away. Without a word. Leaving her young brothers to grieve, to search—and to think her dead until just a week ago, when she'd been carried into the Romans' house by Gray Donohue.

Erion still felt the shock of that moment within him, but he carried none of the anger or resentment his other Beast brothers did.

"Hey, she can run anytime she wants to," Lycos stated flatly. "But I refuse to sniff her out or chase her again, that's all."

Helo snorted, his grin anything but warm. "Who are you kidding? You love the chase."

"I love to chase females," Lycos corrected. "Not family."

"I'll try and remember that," Helo said with heavy sarcasm.

Erion released a breath. As the eldest, he had a natural sense of leadership within their tight family, and though he didn't choose to use that influence very often, he believed that tonight was as good a time as any. "Listen, brothers, no matter what happened in the past, no matter our personal feelings about it now"—he gave Lycos a tight glare—"our sister is in there, held in a cage because she cannot control her Beast. We have all feared such a fate, have we not?"

Helo, Phane, even Lycos fell silent, because, in truth,

there was nothing a *mutore* feared more than the inability to shift at will. And remaining a Beast for all time? Well, that was a fate worse than death.

"It is not something any one of us should go through alone," Erion continued. "We are here. Living in the Romans' house until we decide our next move, decide the fate of our father—"

"Cruen," Lycos corrected, deep disgust in his tone. "His name is Cruen."

Erion nodded. Yes, he felt that same bitterness for the Pureblood Order vampire who had raised them. And yet he also felt conflicted. He would not be in existence, would not breathe, choose, or feel at this very moment if that *paven* hadn't paid for his life. On the other hand, he would not have gone after his twin brother Nicholas's female and fathered an innocent child if his adopted father had seen him as an equal, had told him the truth about his ability to breed.

He pushed those thoughts aside. Now was not the time to think of Cruen, or for that matter, the *balas*—his *balas*—the young *paven* who was being raised by the brother Erion's mother had seen worthy to live. "Until we have made a decision regarding our future plans," he said to the three staring at him with steely gazes, "we must help our sister—help her escape this—"

"Don't tell me you're going to suggest letting her out," Lycos interrupted, his brow lowering over narrowed eyes.

"Control your temper," Erion warned. "Your ire isn't going to help—"

"And when we just caught and caged her!" Lycos continued undeterred.

"Fucking hell, Ly." Phane slammed the wolf with a dark glare. "You interrupt far too much. Perhaps it's time for a muzzle."

A warning growl came from Lycos. "If I get a muzzle, you get your wings clipped."

"Clip my wings and I'll clip your balls," Phane shot back, his mismatched hawk eyes flashing. Then a sudden grin split his features. "I know. We could let Dillon neuter Lycos! That would lift her spirits, eh?"

Erion began laughing first, and once he started, Phane got in on the action. Grinning broadly, Helo elbowed his wolf brother in the ribs, inching him toward the door to the cage. "Go on. Head in there, Ly. I'll make sure she uses the really sharp pair of hedge clippers."

"You're all a bunch of bastards, you know that?" Lycos put in drily.

"Yes, we do know," Erion said, sobering a little, though his diamond eyes glittered. "Just like the one in there. We're a family of bastard *balas*. An ugly, strange, mutant family, but a family. And we must take care of our own or we are no better than the Beasts the Purebloods of the Eternal Breed Order think we are."

Lycos sighed. "She won't talk to us."

Erion turned to Helo and raised one black eyebrow. "She'll talk to him."

The look Helo shot Erion said everything, said he loved their sister but didn't think he stood a chance of getting through to her. Even so, he tossed up his hands in defeat. "Fine. I'll go. But don't expect much."

Lycos turned, calling over his shoulder, "How 'bout I don't expect anything?"

"We'll be upstairs," Erion said.

"With our other brothers?" Helo added with a dry smile.

"With the *Romans*," Phane corrected, reminding them all that even though they shared a recent and mutual history with Alexander, Nicholas, and Lucian; temporary living quarters; and paternal DNA, the *paven*s who played host to them were in essence strangers.

Not to underestimate.

Not to romanticize.

And certainly not to trust, he mused darkly, turning away from Helo and his sister and following his true kin down the tunnel hallway.

Gray Donohue had left only an hour ago, but Dillon's Beast was already craving his touch.

It was shameful.

It was suckass.

Dillon padded around her cell, her brain working overtime, her jaguar's heart beating hard and fast. Goddamn it, she missed her *veana* self. Missed the cold, quiet inside her, the one-track existence her mind could follow in peace. This Beast she lived within was hot-blooded and hungry, emotional and capable of being hurt.

It was going on too long. She needed out before she imploded.

Her tail swished back and forth against the metal. Was it truly possible? Could Gray Donohue hold the key to her salvation? Or something close? The picture of his hand holding her muzzle was fuzzy, out of focus in her brain. After all, she could only imagine what it had looked like. But one thing she hadn't imagined was the feeling that had overtaken her. The closest she'd gotten to being a *veana* female in a week. But was it really him or simply the touch of another that had caused such a reaction? After all, she'd been touched by many in her cat's form, hadn't she? And there had been nothing—no heat, no tsunami. No sensation of change.

Maybe she just hadn't been aware.

Maybe she needed to try it again.

The sound of a door opening jarred her senses and she froze and hissed. For a split second, she thought Evans had come back to watch the cat again. But when the scent of an altogether different being wafted into the room, snaking through the bars of her cell and into her nostrils, her limbs relaxed and she caught herself grinning, purring.

"Helo, you little shit," she uttered, her gaze tracking the water Beast as he neared her cage.

"Not so little anymore, Dilly," he said with a grin of his own.

No, she mused, her gaze moving over him. That was true. The *paven* who stood before her was a good six inches taller than her, was no longer the skinny little *mutore balas* with the pale eyes and smooth, unblemished skin. This *paven* was handsome to a fault, with a broad chest that tapered into a slim waist and golden skin that sported a heavy share of tattoos, endless lines of black waves. But deep within the pair of eyes that seemed to change color every few seconds was a thread of unabashed familiarity, of one who had truly known her.

But that bond had been severed long ago. And the soft memories of it were best forgotten now. "Come to check on the prisoner?" she asked.

He nodded, his grin deepening. "We all drew straws and I—"

"Got the short end?" Dillon finished for him.

He shrugged. "Hey. I look at it as winning."

"Well, you've always been lucky, Helo."

"Not always."

His pointed words and expression hummed with an intimacy, an unmasked grief that tore at her insides. She shook her head. "I'm not going there. Back there. Ever. So if you came to chitchat about the past—"

"I don't chitchat; you know that. I just want to help you. We all want to help you."

For Dillon, the natural reaction to charity offered in any form was to question it with biting indifference. "Why?"

Helo's brow lifted. He looked incredulous. "Really? You have to ask that?"

"We were mutts together, Helo. For a short time. An experiment by a madman. We weren't a family."

His nostrils flared and he shook his head. "You're such a bitch."

She snorted. "Tell me something I don't know. I should've been the wolf *mutore*, not Lycos."

"He's pretty much a bitch, too." With that, Helo allowed a quick grin.

Dillon grinned back. She couldn't help herself. That fucker knew her. They may have been mutts, may have been together a short time, but in that time he'd really known her.

Growling with irritation, she turned away from him, walked in a circle, trying to clear her mind. Or maybe it was her unbeating heart. Helo had this way about him. He was one of those males who never had issues with showing his feelings, showing he had love for another. It never stole his masculinity and it never felt fake. Maybe that was why she'd gravitated toward him back then—that openness, that willingness to give had been fragrant as hell.

Still was, apparently.

Maybe that was one of the reasons why she hadn't gone to him after the rape. Besides dealing with her very first shift into feline form, she would've had to face what happened to her, feel the shame, talk about the act with this *paven* who cared about her. It had been better to shove it down and away and forget, go on. And damn, that had worked for a really long time. Until the night the senator and his assholes-for-hire had decided to teach her a lesson.

"Dilly," Helo said, his tone far too gentle. "Look at me."

Her gaze remained where it was. On the ground. Christ, this fucking cat was turning her into a full-fledged pussy.

Behind her, she heard the shift of the lock, quick fingers on the keypad. She whirled with a hiss to find Helo opening her cage, moving inside.

"How the hell," she uttered, her lithe body on alert, her mind humming with thoughts.

Helo shrugged. "Been watching Evans."

"Stealing from him, too, I guess," Dillon returned.

"Don't make me regret my thievery," he said, grinning.

Regret. Her eyes narrowed on him. No, she didn't regret him breaking into her cage, standing in front of her. Her gaze dropped to his hands.

"I don't like the way you're looking at me, D. Way too fucking hungry. Cool down or I'll have to head back—"

"Helo," she said abruptly, eyes up, her voice serious as a heart attack now. "I need you to do me a favor. I need you to touch me."

The *paven*'s eyebrows shot together as though this were the very last thing he'd expected her to say. "What?"

"Just put your hand on my head, on my fur. Just for a second." She knew she sounded insane, panicked, but unexplained phenomena did that to a *veana*. "Please."

There were questions behind Helo's eyes, which were now glowing a pale green. "I suppose you're not going to tell me what this is about."

"Little experiment, that's all."

"If you bite me, I'll be so pissed, Dilly."

"I hate seafood."

Helo raised one dark eyebrow.

She sniffed. "No biting. I swear." She dropped her head, giving him better access.

She stood there, eyes down, and waited. Nervous energy tingled within her, and she wished she could shake it off. She was truly growing weaker by the minute.

Come on, Helo, she wanted to scream. She had to know, had to see if she felt anything. She had to know if the change had been in her, inside her, and not from the Impure with the striking mouth and hazardous touch.

For a good minute she held herself still. She was just about to lift her head, give up, when she felt Helo's palm press down into the fur on the top of her head. A feeling did move through her in that moment, but it wasn't the one she'd hoped for. It was a soft breeze, that sweet rush of safety she remembered so well.

She released the breath she'd been holding and let the feeling of his skin, his fingers moving through her fur, sink into her senses. Helo. Her Helo. Goddamn it, why couldn't this have worked? Why couldn't it have been his touch, or anyone's touch, that made her *veana* flare to life within this cat suit? It would've been so fucking simple, so easy. She would've been back to walking on two legs within an hour, been in control of her shift once again.

She looked up then and regarded him with pleading eyes. "I need to get out of here, Helo. Will you help me?"

There was nothing in the world she despised more than begging. It was weak, humiliating, and vile. But remaining a jaguar for the rest of her long life, with no choice, with zero control over who and what she was every moment of every day was far more loathsome.

She asked him one last time. "Will you help me escape?"

Helo's eyes changed from pale green to muddied

onyx—the color of a bruise to match his bruised expression. "No."

"Then I'm sorry," she whispered.

"For what?" he asked, confused.

She was on him before he had a chance to shift.

3

Inside the circle, his body stretched over the blood symbol of the Impure Resistance, Gray allowed three sets of fangs to penetrate his skin and three Impure warriors to penetrate his mind.

It wasn't the first time and it wouldn't be the last. Riordon James, Piper Leigh, and Vincent Seal were his partners in freedom, had been for months now and would be until the Order destroyed the Paleo and ended blood castration. These three warriors who were poised above him now, feeding from his memories, were the most talented, most gifted Impures Gray had ever met. Each had a mental gift that complemented the other, each used the other to gain information—share information—anything that could get them inside the Order's mainframe, any avenue they could find to send out their tentacles and burrow deep into the Order and their dark secrets. Secrets they could use, perhaps a weak-minded Order member they could . . . control.

Then they could begin to infiltrate.

Vincent pulled out of Gray's vein with a growl, blood coating his teeth and lips, his dark brown dreads bracketing his fierce face. "Was that truly necessary?"

Piper retreated next, her lovely face ripe with frustration. "We could've used this human, Gray. Taken him from that hospital and brought him here. He could've been a conduit. Killing him was careless, reck—"

"No. It was justice," Gray said without passion as Riordon lifted his head and sniffed derisively.

"Let's not play games," Rio said, licking his lips. "That was for your girlfriend."

Inside Gray, a quick anger rushed over him, but as leader of this small band, thoughtful answers to bad-tempered accusations had to win out. He could not have them all fighting one another when the war that they had to win raged outside their tight circle.

He sat up, regarded the heavily muscled ex-military male. "I was quick to serve him justice. But the human male could never have been an instrument for our use. He was a beacon, a homing device that if we captured and brought here would only have attracted the Order. They are not fools—they would've had him bugged." The words, the clean explanation flowed from his lips with such ease. Problem was, while that was true, the reality was that he could not let the senator draw another breath after learning what he'd done, what he'd ordered to be done to Dillon. That had been the driving force behind his death sentence.

"Perhaps Gray's right," Piper said, her lavender eyes thoughtful. "Capturing him would've been foolish. We have his memories, his interactions with the

Order. We must comb through them and see if we can find the thread, the frequency the senator used to communicate with them. We must see if there is a member whose lock on their mainframe is not as tightly fused."

Vincent nodded, but Rio looked less than convinced. Which was nothing new. The ex-military badass couldn't help being continually suspicious.

"If we're done here"—Gray got to his feet—"I'm going to see Samuel."

"Good," Vincent said. "While you're there, have Uma check the frequency of visits from the Order on her next Paleo run."

Turning toward him, Piper asked, "You think they're slowing down castrations or speeding up?"

"I am hearing that more Impures are being taken to the Paleo than ever before. And I want to know why. I want to know if they're feeling our presence within the community."

Gray nodded. "I'll let you know."

He left the room, headed to his own to change. He'd met Samuel Kendrick and his son and daughter during his short stint at the Paleo. As they'd awaited blood castration, Gray had learned that the old Impure had been his father's best friend. He had learned through Samuel that his father had been no human, but an Impure and the secret head of the Resistance before he was found out and taken, then blood castrated by the Order. The shock of more lies within his family had cut Gray deep, and yet the knowledge had filled him with a sense of purpose. The truth combined with the visual nightmare of watching Samuel be dragged off—blood castrated in front of him—had changed Gray forever.

Dillon had rescued his sorry, naked ass from the Paleo that night, but Gray was determined to return. After weeks of using his new status, and the power of hearing others' thoughts, he had found a Pureblood willing to be bought and used. Days later, he'd executed his first search and rescue at the Paleo, gotten the entire Kendrick family out, and had them housed in the vacant apartments below the Resistance headquarters for several months now.

And there they would remain, for as long as they liked, Gray thought while moving down the hallway. His father's best friend would always have his help—regardless of how it may inconvenience or irritate one of the Resistance warriors.

Gray was nearly to his door when a sudden pain ripped through his skull. Dropping against the wood, he cursed and gritted his teeth against the intensity, against the blinding heat that shot up the base of his neck and spread like fingers of lightning. Flashbulbs behind his eyes, then images, memories flickering on the screen of his mind. The senator's, Vincent's, Piper's, and then his own. But they weren't his short-term memories. No. Fuck. These were from way back, from the days of the fire when he was a child.

With a groan, he barreled through the door and collapsed in a heap near the edge of his bed.

The Order had their blood extracted from their ancient veins every day. It was deposited in "banks" within the *credentis* for daily distribution among the Impures. It was how the nine remaining rulers of the Eternal Breed kept watch, kept control of their subspecies. They had been exercising this right for so long, they knew no other way.

Would accept no other way.

Within the bloodletting room in the Order's reality, a human body had been flashed and laid out on the pallet between two Order members. The pair hovered over the body, robes pooling around their feet, upper lips curled back to display their brick red fangs.

"Vile," said one.

"Must we have that thing in here?" said the other disgustedly.

Removing the needle from her wrists and neck, Feeyan sat up slowly on her pallet. She had just been drained, vials of her blood lined up in a neat row beside her. "That *thing*," she said pointedly, "may have the location of our missing *mutore*."

One of the Order *paven* looked confused. "I thought we had been monitoring this human. If my memory serves, he was able only to grant us images of her voice, her face, her animal."

Feeyan flashed from her pallet to the bedside of the dead senator. "Yes. But his killer may have more."

"You think the killer knows the *mutore*?" the second Order member asked.

"The guards at the hospital were in agreement that the perpetrator was not human. What reason would a vampire have for killing the senator?" She pressed his head to one side, revealing his temple. "I think one kills out of passion. That passion could be political, yes, but it could also be out of revenge." Feeyan inhaled deeply, lengthened her fangs. "I despise the cold blood of a dead human."

The Order members chuckled as she struck into the male's temple, but one—one who had only pretended to give his blood earlier that day and was now sitting in the very back of the room pretending to practice his meditation as he shook beneath his robes—did not.

Titus Evictus lowered his head and drank the newly pulled blood of the Order member, Feeyan. Too intent on what was happening with the human senator, no one noticed him, no one suspected. And why would they? They did not know that he was once a Breeding Male, a genetically altered Pureblood vampire who could breed on command and choose the sex of its off-spring. They did not know that when rogue Order leader Cruen had disappeared, his dark, magic-filled blood along with him, Titus had begun to decline. The Order's blood was strong and took the edge off his need, but just barely.

He snatched another vial, drank it down in one thick gulp. He needed to find Cruen, the creator of the Breeding Male program, or he was going to return to the ma-niacal Beast who thought only of rutting anything, anywhere. But what bargain could he strike with Cruen now? He had given him all he had. He was worthless, and he would not betray his sons, not anymore. Not ever again.

Down at the other end of the room, Feeyan pulled out of the senator's mind with a disgusted growl. "Vile indeed. But productive."

"Did you see the face of the killer?" one Order member asked.

"I did. And we have a problem." She released a weighty breath.

"You know this vampire?"

"He is no vampire," Feeyan said, "but an Impure—and the son of our greatest Impure enemy."

Both Order members gasped. "Jeremy Donohue."

She nodded. "This male must be handled just as his father was. Gray Donohue must be brought in and blood castrated before he has a chance to succeed where his father failed."

"You think he may be at the head of this newly formed Resistance?" an Order member said. "Behind these abductions from the Paleo?"

"Only when we have him before us will we know for certain." Feeyan's bloodred fangs descended rapidly. "We will bleed his thoughts first, then his body. A true son of the father."

"And will this Impure's life end in a fire as well?" the Order member asked drily.

Feeyan grinned. "Accidents do happen. It is part of the human experience when you are part human."

Gray didn't know how long he'd been passed out, but when he woke it was still night outside the wall of windows to his left, and a scent he knew all too well permeated the air around him—a delectable tang that made his fists clench against the sheets at his back and the cock resting between his legs pulse.

Eau d'equal parts frustration and the need to fuck.

Yeah, he knew who'd brought that in on her coat.

"Here, kitty, kitty, kitty," he uttered, pulling himself up to a sitting position.

Dillon sat at the foot of the bed, her gold head and fierce cat eyes trained on him, the dark night her backdrop. "Your security is shit, Impure. I believe I could've gotten in here with a blindfold and a collar made of bells."

Gray dropped back against the pillows. "You think you strolled in here without being detected? Come on, D." He clucked his tongue. "You got in because I okayed it."

Her eyes narrowed. "You knew I'd come."

"Eventually. You always come when you need something."

"Not true." She moved around the side of the bed, the strength in every feline movement almost hypnotic. "Maybe I just wanted to visit with an old friend."

"Yeah, that sounds like you," he said drily. To anyone sane, visiting was about relaxed conversation and a desire to see what the other person had been up to since you last saw them. For Dillon it was strictly about purpose: saving someone's ass, trading information, finding a way to get whatever it was she wanted in that moment.

Gray wondered how long it would be before she decided to start asking. Or maybe he'd make it begging.

"What happened here?" she asked, her eyes pinned to his. "Why were you passed out when I arrived? Partying too hard?"

"That's right. I'm a nineteen-year-old frat boy." He swung his legs off the bed and got up. He needed out of these clothes, into something clean, something that didn't smell like dried blood from the Impure warrior snack at his temples earlier. "It was nothing, just a little pain in the head." He knocked his chin her way. "Which is now being replaced with a pain in the ass."

"You're speaking metaphorically, right?" she hissed. "Because I don't think it was your ass I bit back at the Romans." She followed him to the closet, watched him as he pulled off his shirt.

"Listen, I have somewhere to be, so why don't you tell me why you've escaped your brothers again and come running to me."

"I didn't run," she said indignantly. "Though this neighborhood isn't the greatest for a lady to be walking around in at night."

Lady. He snorted. "What do you want, D? Patience is growing thin here."

"All right, fine." She came to sit near his feet and curled her tail around her body. Her cat's gaze roamed over his stomach, his chest, his shoulders, then finally they dropped to his hands. "I tried to have Helo touch me."

Gray turned away from the closet. "Come again?" He hadn't heard her right. Shit, he hoped he hadn't heard her right. But with Dillon you never knew. The *veana* could be a freak—a label she no doubt wore with pride.

"I thought, what the fuck? You know?" The jaguar gave a little shrug. "Any hands should be able to do it for me."

Freak flag flying.

Christ.

Wearing only jeans and a frown, Gray dropped onto his haunches and went face-to-face with her cat. "What are you talking about? The bull's-eye now, D, not this going-around-and-around-the-circle bullshit you're dishing."

Her muzzle twitched in irritation. "I'm talking about the effect of your hands on me earlier," she snarled, but the sound was soft and didn't contain much power behind it. "You felt it. When you held my muzzle in your hand, you felt that thing run between us like a live wire."

Gray didn't say a thing. Ever since he'd met Dillon, which was over a year ago, when she'd yanked his catatonic self from that hospital bed and brought him to the Romans, he'd wanted to explore the live wire that had been between them. But Dillon had always pushed him back—hell, pushed him on his ass. She'd made it damn clear she wasn't interested, and in turn he'd forced himself to listen and move the hell on. So right then, there was nothing in the world he wanted more than to deny he'd felt a thing back in her cage. In fact, he wanted to throw a big "no" back in her kitty-cat face. But how could he deny that sudden heat, that explosive sexual chemistry they'd tossed back and forth at each other—that deformed ball that had never landed anywhere? Frankly, he wasn't that good of a liar.

"What about it?" He got up, went back to digging in the closet, grabbed a T-shirt.

"This is so goddamn humiliating," she uttered to herself. Then, after a few deep breaths and two equally impressive exhales, she said, "Okay. Here it is. I've never felt like that before. Back in the cage. Your hand on me. What ran through my body . . . And it was you, all you. No one else can do that to me."

"Aww, well, that's really sweet, baby." He pulled the shirt over his head.

"No, you're not getting it," she continued with clear impatience. "That thing, that current, that whatever it was that ran between us made me feel—"

"Like a woman?" he finished drily.

"This isn't funny, Gray!"

He snorted.

"This is my life!" she snarled.

"No, this is *my* life." He didn't have time for this, for her—for another round of Dillon's game of Fucking-with-Your-Head. "And you can't seem to make up your mind if you want in it or not." He walked past her. "How 'bout I decide for the both of us?"

"Don't walk away from me, you Impure bastard," she growled. "We have business to discuss."

He ignored her. Sometimes it was the only way to deal with crazy. "The way out of here's even easier than the way in."

"Stop!"

"Later, D."

He was nearly out the door when the next words out of her mouth halted him.

"I think you can control my shift!"

Her words stuttered inside his mind, but he didn't turn around. Not yet. "Say that again."

"You, your touch. I think it might be able to turn me back into a *veana*."

There was a part of him that wanted to just keep walking, another part that was curious, and still another part of him that was pretty damn sure she was playing him. Again.

Curiosity won out, and he turned and faced her. "Why do you think that?"

She looked anxious, the fur on her back bristling. "I felt it, okay?"

"Where?"

"Jesus . . ."

"Where?" he repeated roughly. "Your tail? Your claws? Your wet, black nose?"

"Don't be an asshole, Gray."

"And don't fuck with me, Dillon, or I'm walking out that door and you can stay in the Romans' goddamn cage forever, as far as I'm concerned!"

Dillon felt shock in that moment, but it quickly morphed into anger. Anger soaked in desperation. And it clouded her mind so thickly that she was no longer in control of her actions. The jaguar was. In under a second, she sprang, like a bullet from a gun, across the room and onto Gray's chest, pinning him to the door.

He didn't flinch, didn't move, didn't try to get away. He just stared into her dark eyes with a potent cocktail of irritation, contempt, and barely masked desire.

"I fucking felt it," Dillon snarled at him. "Inside of me. Outside of me."

His gaze narrowed then. "Maybe you just thought you did."

"No."

"Could've been round four of that nasty attraction we have for each other."

Dillon fought for control, but this bastard was working her last nerve. She opened her mouth and ran her cat's tongue across his cheek. "*That* is the nasty attraction." She watched his eyes flash with undeniable heat. "What I felt last night was the change from Beast to *veana*. I know that feeling—I've had it a thousand times."

"Under your own control."

She nodded, her suspicious nature working to figure out what each comment, each observation meant to him. "I've been shifting under my own control since I was a *young veana*. From *veana* to jaguar whenever and wherever I felt like it. Up until that bastard senator beat the ability out of me. I'd hoped that taking his life might bring mine back. But it's too late to test that theory, isn't it?" Her voice dropped. "Listen, Impure, the sensation I felt when you were touching me is the very same one I used to be able to create within myself with just a goddamn thought."

She watched him process, watched his eyes turn from heat to wonder to skepticism. And just when she thought he was going to push her paws off him, tell her to fuck off and hit the road, he reached up and put his hand on her face.

Dillon felt the heat immediately, the rush of sensation in her cells. She leaned into the feeling like a junkie needing her next fix. In the back of her mind, she thought she heard him curse as he let his fingers sink into her fur, then spread out, but language seemed utterly unimportant in that moment. His gaze was locked on hers, probing deeply into her mind. But she knew she was the one being he couldn't hear. And then he trailed his thumb up the length of her jag's cheekbone and her mind went blank. Within seconds, the change from Beast to *veana* began.

"Holy shit," Gray uttered, his brow dropping low as he saw it too. He brought up his other hand and placed it on her other cheek.

Heat slammed into Dillon's face and she inhaled

sharply. It was as if the sensations she'd felt in her cage earlier had been somehow magnified. From one to ten in under a moment. Shifting had never felt like this—almost orgasmic, deliciously toxic. And she hated it as much as she loved it. Under the skin he touched, and only under the skin he touched, waves of heat and intensity tingled within her, suffusing her cells, altering her DNA. Then she felt Gray's warm breath on the skin of her face. Her *veana*'s face. It was a feeling so goddamn amazing, so rare, so prized to her, she would've given up anything she had to have the power within herself to create this change on her own once again.

"You owe me, Impure," she said, feeling her lips move for the first time in a week, knowing that as she stood there she was some vile-looking mutant with a cat's body and a *veana*'s head. "You stole my kill—the one thing that was going to give me back my control." Or so she'd believed—*had* to believe to stay sane.

"Apparently not," Gray uttered darkly. He dragged his thumb across her mouth. A sudden flash of heat registered in her eyes. "How the hell do I have the power to do this?"

"I don't know and I don't care."

"Sounds about right." His eyes lifted to hers. They'd lost some of their shock and awe and were hovering around suspicion.

"You'll help me," she said without even a thread of a query.

Gray didn't answer her, didn't confirm or deny. Just stared into her eyes.

"Why are you pretending to think about this?" she

hissed with annoyance, her cat's heart jumping with anxiety.

"I'm not pretending."

"You knew I was coming here. You knew there was something that had happened between us in that cage." She hated how desperate she sounded—hated that only her face was *veana* and the rest of her, where Gray's hands hadn't yet tread, remained jaguar. "Why allow me access to your Resistance Headquarter Barracks Safe House bullshit here if you were going to refuse me?"

His eyes lit with sudden and wicked amusement. "Maybe I just enjoy hearing you beg."

She growled at him.

"If you're going to do that properly, you'd better return to your previous form." Without a warning, Gray released his hold on her and moved away.

The sudden impact caused Dillon to drop to the ground on all fours. Her head shot up, her eyes narrowed on his—and her *veana*'s face slowly morphed back into the jaguar.

"You won't deny me, Impure," she snarled.

"You seem to think you have the upper hand here, D." He crossed his arms over his broad chest. "You seem to think I'll not only lie down and let you walk all over me with claws and fangs bared, but I'll be getting off while you're doing it."

Her snarl turned to a feline rumble in her chest. "Is that a metaphor or a suggestion for later?"

Gray pushed away from the wall and went at her, eyes blazing. Within seconds, his hands found her back. His fingers dug into her fur. Without saying a word, he stroked her—hard and delicious from nape to tail, back and forth until her nude *veana* body began to appear. Then he stopped—released her. For a moment he just stared, as if he needed to be fully convinced of this insane situation. As her back returned to that of a cat, as she gave a small whimper of frustration, he sniffed and said in the coldest of voices, "I will give you what you want, D. What you need. But it will not come for free."

Her gaze flipped up to meet his. "Nothing ever does."

"Nothing *good* ever does," he corrected sharply.

"What do you want?"

"Obedience."

Her head cocked to one side.

He grinned. "I know you heard me. You will stay here, in my room, and I will give you what you need, anytime you need it. But I will expect obedience and respect in return."

"Never!" she spat at him.

"Then you can leave."

Panic flooded her insides and her cat's jaw worked. Leave? As if. Christ . . . Right here in this room was the antidote to her disease. He might be acting like a power-hungry dickhead at the moment, but what if this was her only shot? *He* was her only shot? What if she could get him to change her completely? What if she could remain a *veana*? Oh God. What if she could teach herself to shift once again?

If she was a *veana*, she'd be able to truly walk away. From the Romans and their cage, from her brothers—and from this Impure male who thought he had a chance of owning her unbeating heart.

Walk away.

No.

Run.

"You want the control back?" Gray said, hijacking her thoughts, his gunmetal eyes the fiercest she'd ever seen them. "The only way you're going to get it is to give it up."

She had to know. "Why are you doing this?"

His eyes flared with sudden hunger. "Maybe because I can. Maybe because you need to be tamed."

"You might not like me that way."

"We'll see." His eyes closed for a second, and when he opened them again, they were far calmer. "I need the decision right now, baby."

"Call me 'baby' again and I'll bite your balls off," she uttered through gritted teeth.

"Maybe I'll let you try that," he said with an amused tone. "Later. One of my associates is on her way here to tell me that your brothers—all seven of them—are waiting in our gathering room."

Dillon's insides turned over. Fucking hell. This she did not need. The Romans and the four Beasts had found her. Well, of course they'd found her. Gray was right about that, about one thing—she did seem to run to him when she needed something.

"Answer now, Dillon."

She bared her teeth at him. "My obedience for a pair of magic hands."

He shrugged. "If that's how you want to see it."

She glanced down at his hands. "They're not very pretty."

"No. But they get the job done." His eyes glittered with wicked intent.

There was nothing she wanted more in that moment than to walk out, run away, but she couldn't, could she? Where would she go like this? Where could she go without having the control over her shift? Shit, maybe she could run around town looking for another body, another pair of hands who held such power over her cat. But was that even possible? Could she trust someone else with this secret—to not turn her in to the Order? Or Christ, the zoo? It had been months—she had no idea how long it would take to master her control again . . .

Her gaze drifted up, back to his. He was the lesser of all evils, wasn't he? And she could handle it—handle him. She could handle anything. Fuck—she already had.

"All right, Impure," she said. "Until I have control over my shift again, I will give it to you."

"Good," he said, his voice dark, his jaw tight. "And we'll begin with you calling me Gray."

She sniffed. "And if I don't?"

He stepped closer. "There is always a reaction to any action. Disrespect, disobedience, will always end with punishment."

Dillon's muzzle dropped open and she just stared at him.

"Now, follow me," he said. "Your family waits."

4

"*Fuck no! This is not happening!*"

"*The veana needs our protection!*"

"*Christ! In an Impure safe house. She doesn't belong here!*"

"*She's coming home with us!*"

As Lucian, Alexander, and Sara stood there in thoughtful silence, Gray listened inside his head to Dillon's four Beast brothers lose their shit, one after the other, over the news that their sister would be remaining with him at the Impure Resistance headquarters. He cared little for their response or their opinions on the matter, and yet he understood their confusion and frustration in the lack of details given. That being said, Gray wasn't about to reveal what he and Dillon now shared—this strange power he had over her jaguar. That was Dillon's choice to share—if she wanted to.

"What is your true concern, Lycos?" Dillon spoke

then, fully returned to her jaguar state now. "Because I'm guessing it's not about my well-being."

"It was," the wolf said, his blue eyes pure ice as he looked at her. "Long ago, it was, my sister. But you severed that feeling when you abandoned us."

"Abandoned you," she repeated caustically. "What should I have done? I wasn't your caretaker. I wasn't your mother."

"No," Phane put in with deadly quiet. "But you were our sister. We deserved better."

Beside him, Gray felt Dillon's anxiety swell, her confusion riddled with anger. "What are you all looking for from me? A reason?" She glanced quickly at Helo, then looked away. "I've given you one. It wasn't the life I wanted, so I left."

"Without a word," Phane sneered, his mismatched eyes flaring with heat. "Without a good-bye."

Dillon's ears twitched. "It wasn't possible."

"Maybe you couldn't tell us then," Helo said, his expression calm, though Gray heard the deep rumble of hurt inside the *paven*'s highly intelligent mind. "For whatever the reason, maybe you had to leave, but what about tonight, Dilly? Attacking your own blood."

Her growl was so fierce Gray almost put his hand on her back. Almost. "I did what I had to do, Helo," she spat at him. "I'm sorry, okay? Fuck! I needed to get out of there, out of that cage."

Helo nodded to Gray. "You think he will be your savior? An Impure?"

"Watch yourself," Gray warned the *paven* calmly. "Remember where you are. Whose home you're in."

"You think your weak, diluted blood frightens me?" Helo returned icily.

A slow, terrible smile crossed Gray's face. "No, but having all those thoughts about Nicholas Roman's mate shared with our group here might." He lifted his brow.

The *paven*'s eyes bugged and his lips curled. Behind him, Lucian said, "What the fuck, *Mutore*? You having dreams about my brother's *veana*?"

A few of the *pavens* chuckled softly, but Gray kept his gaze locked on the one before him, the one who looked ready to kill, his eyes black holes of rage.

"Gray." Sara, who stood in the curve of her *paven*'s arm, redirected the conversation. "I'm not making suggestions on where to put Dillon. But from what little you've told us, this arrangement sounds unhealthy for the both of you."

Leave it to his sister to go clinical on the situation. Gray lifted his brow. Where to put Dillon? As if she were a creature, a thing. "Living here in this home, with a proper bed and proper bathroom, sounds less healthy than a cage in the ground beneath the New York City streets?"

His jaw grim, Alexander acknowledged, "That was for her own protection. You know it was."

"Is that what your parents told you, Alex?" Gray asked simply.

The *paven* growled at him.

"Gray, please be thoughtful about this," Sara urged him, her hand on her mate's chest, trying to calm him.

They didn't seem to understand that there would be

no negotiations. "Dillon will make her own choice about where she goes."

"No," Helo said, shouldering his way forward, his gaze now locked on Dillon. "She can't. Not when she's in this state. It risks her life and ours."

Dillon's golden coat bristled and she snarled at him. "He's just pissed because I bit him and escaped again."

"Dilly . . ." Helo began through gritted teeth.

"Listen, all of you." Gray spoke to the group with ease, and a confidence born out of a power no one could strip from him. "I allowed you inside my home to explain the situation, ease your fears about where she is and if she is all right. It was a courtesy, not a request for permission."

All four *mutore* hissed at him, then, growling among themselves, started arguing about what to do and how best to kick Gray's ass. But one cool head with one calm question broke into Gray's mind.

"And if we force the issue?"

Gray's eyes flipped up and caught Alexander's dark gaze. The *paven* who had once broken into Gray's mind, stripped it of the memories that had held him hostage for so long, and saved him from a lifetime of hearing nothing but dead air, had—in his blood memory drain—given Gray the ability to hear the thoughts of others. But in this, he answered the *paven* aloud. "If you force the issue, then we will have a battle on our hands."

"With whom? Your Impure army? You believe them a match for Purebloods and mutore?"

Alexander's words held no threat, only question.

"Not in brawn, surely," Gray told him. "But strength in mind has surprising power.

"As you know, Alex."

"Don't talk inside heads," snapped Erion, who had stopped arguing with his *mutore* brothers long enough to see the mental and verbal exchange between Gray and Alexander and put two and two together. He turned his menacing stare on Gray. "You, how will you control her Beast? How will you keep her here when she wants to run?" His gaze shifted to Dillon. "Because she will run."

Beside him, Dillon flinched.

Gray didn't answer; he didn't have to. The bargain struck between him and Dillon was their own and it went beyond explanation. He went to the door, opened it. "Sun will be coming up soon, Pureblood *paven*. I think it's time to go. For now. We will remain in contact."

There was a moment when nobody moved, nobody breathed, and everybody stared at Gray. Then Erion released a weighty sigh and pushed past his brothers toward the door.

"We'd better," Erion said.

Phane shook his head but followed. "I don't like this."

"Shit, I don't like him."

The last dig was mental and came from Helo, and it made Gray smile. He didn't blame them, any of them, for equally loving, protecting, and being perpetually disappointed in Dillon. It was a disease they all seemed to suffer from.

As they all pushed toward the door, Gray saw Sara stop at Dillon's side, put her hand on the cat's shoulder, and whisper into her ear, "Is this what you want?"

"Wrong question," Dillon returned softly.

Sara continued. "Do you want to come home with us?"

Dillon's muscles rippled as she got up and padded over to Gray. She sat down near his feet and inclined her head. "I am home. For now."

Celestine Donohue lived in a modest house in the suburbs of Minneapolis, Minnesota. To everyone who knew her, her neighbors and friends, she was a simple, nonmaterialistic woman who liked to travel and had two children who had moved far away and rarely visited. This was exactly what Celestine wanted them to believe. It protected them and it protected her. Not merely from the fact that she was a Pureblood vampire, but that she had, for many years now, worked as an undercover agent for a European intelligence firm. She assisted not only human contacts, but vampire ones as well. It was very hush-hush, and she'd realized long ago when she'd accepted the position that if the Order ever found out about her exploits, she would be risking her present and her future.

But that had worried her little over the years, as the Order had seemed to spread their tentacles wide and deep into many other offenses far more worrisome than her perceived defection.

But now, as she stared at the message scrawled into the condensation-covered glass wall of her greenhouse, she wondered if that had been a simple, silly notion by a Pollyanna-like *veana*.

Gray Donohue harbors a mutore. *The Order requests the assistance of not only his mother but a very tal-*

ented spy to bring them both out of hiding and safely into the hands of justice.

Her insides quaked at the thought, at the demands before her. Was this possible? she wondered. Gray being involved with a *mutore*? A thing, a being so rare she hadn't come across one in all her years, both as a spy and a "human woman." And yet her son spoke to her so little, so rarely, and lately with such frigidity, that she really didn't know what was happening in his world. Ever since Alexander had healed his mind and Gray had found out the truth about his Impure side, he'd seemed to want nothing to do with her. His anger wasn't surprising, and she'd thought to give him time before she offered him the reasons that she and his father had for what they had done.

As the words, the threat of the Order, began to blur, drip down the glass, mere water droplets now, Celestine realized that time was up. There was no more waiting for his call anymore, or his forgiveness. She supposed the Order had seen to that.

Retreating from the warmth of the greenhouse and stepping out into the cold Minnesota night air of her backyard, Celestine headed up to the house. Her latest assignment would have to wait. She would flash to New York this evening and see if her son needed her protection and her counsel.

The cold cage with the bars and the stone had been replaced by a massive bedroom with a fireplace, bookshelves heavy with books, and exceptional views out the wall-to-wall windows. It was pretty damn lovely.

But it was still a cage.

Dillon stood at the entrance to Gray's room. No matter how much of a choice the Impure had felt he'd given her, there had really been no choice at all. She wasn't remaining a jaguar forever, and if she had to kiss ass and play the submissive, she would. For as long as it took to get the control back, get the power over her shift back. Hell, she was great at playing a part she despised—especially to get what she wanted in the end.

She just hoped she could do it with this one, this male. Things were never completely simple and easy with him. No matter how hard she'd tried, she'd never been able to drop his ass—forget about his eyes, pretend her blood wasn't inside his veins. From the moment she'd rescued him from Sara's stalker—hell, from the moment she'd seen him in that hospital, she'd found him compelling.

She walked past him into the bedroom—the same one she'd snuck into earlier when she'd found him passed out on the bed. She walked all the way to the fireplace—which was sporting an easy blaze—before she realized he wasn't following her. She glanced back over her shoulder and saw him still standing near the door watching her.

"You're not coming in?" she asked.

"I have something to do," he said. "But I'll be back in a few hours."

"You're kidding me, right? I want to start this thing. We didn't have time before with the entire Roman–*mutore* clan waiting on us, but now we do. Get your hands on me and let's see what happens." Her breath jumped in her lungs as her words fell rapidly from her lips. She knew she sounded manic as hell, but she didn't care. "Where are you going?"

"As I said, I'll be back soon. Make yourself comfortable. I'm having one of the staff bring you something to eat." He glanced down at his phone, his brow wrinkled. When he looked up again, he gave her a stern expression. "Don't scare them, snap at them, or berate them. I would suggest getting some rest." He gestured to the foot of the bed, where a thick, oval rug sat. "You can have that whole space to yourself."

"The floor?" Anger made her fur bristle. She padded toward him, almost stalking him. "I get a kitty pad to sleep on?"

He smiled, but it didn't reach his eyes. "Until the shift from Beast to *veana* is complete. Then we'll decide where to put you."

"You're going to drag this out, aren't you?" she accused. "Keep me here on a leash, waiting with bated breath for that next stroke?"

"Keep talking; you're making me hard." He sounded bored.

Her nostrils flared as she came to stand before him. "Who are you? And what have you done with Gray Donohue?"

"You mean that Impure who took you in a few months ago, tried to heal your wounds? That weak male who did nothing but lick your boots before you kicked him in the balls and told him to fuck off?"

"Yes," she purred, though she recalled no ball kicking, just a necessary reminder that she would never be the *veana* he wanted her to be. "Where is he?"

His gaze gentled. "That's not who you need, what you need."

"You're going to tell me what I need?"

"That is part of our agreement."

"You say jump and I say how high?"

"No." He reached down and placed a hand on her shoulder. The action screamed possession. "You say yes to everything I ask, and I say good little pussy cat."

She wanted to turn and bite a chunk out of the hand that held her steady, but heat was rushing over and through her like an ocean in a thunderstorm. She couldn't get her bearings, couldn't collect her thoughts—shit, she could barely breathe—and the shift that happened externally, from cat to female, was met with a nearly debilitating one on the inside. Total virgin territory: real lust, real need, real emotion—true bullshit.

He released her then, left her breathing hard, mewling hungrily, and staring after him as he headed for the door. "Rest now," he called back. "You're going to need all your strength for the days and nights ahead."

The moment he left the room, Dillon charged at the door. Leaping up, she used her mouth to crank open the handle. The wood dropped back easily. No lock, no key, no chains on this cage. She was free. She could leave at any time.

That fucker. Why did it have to be him . . . ?

Defeat swam in her blood as she padded over to the oval rug, circled it twice, and lay down. The thing was soft, she'd give him that—sort of unbearably, wonderfully soft, and she cursed him again. Before her, the fire began to warm her angry thoughts and cold soul, and she put her head down on her paws and exhaled the strain of the night. She was truly caught and held by a ready and enthusiastic master.

The thought made her suddenly bone weary, and she closed her eyes. Within moments, she was asleep.

"Purebloods in our headquarters. *Mutore* in our headquarters." In the warehouse's main room near the Resistance symbol, Riordon James got in Gray's path before he made it to the front door. He shook his head. "What makes you think that any of this is okay?"

"Easy, Rio," Gray warned.

"Are you trying to get us found out?"

"Yes. That's exactly what I'm doing."

"Don't be snide. I'm not busting your balls on this one. I'm trying to get you to see the potential problems in your choices."

Gray exhaled. The Impure warriors had every right to be pissed at him for bringing Dillon here—and her entire family for that matter—but it was what it was. There was no going back now. The decision had been made. *His* decision. The moment he'd chosen to become leader of the Impures, his word was law. No matter how much his frenemy here hated it. "Return to whatever it is you were doing, Rio. I need to go see Uma about the run tonight."

But the Impure didn't move, his night-black eyes resolute. "When is the *mutore* leaving?" he demanded.

Gray shrugged. "When she's ready.

"And when I'm ready to give her up."

Nostrils flaring with impatience, Rio crossed his arms over his chest. "I heard that."

"I know," Gray said pointedly.

"That's not a satisfactory answer."

"It's the only one you're getting, Rio." He pushed past the solid wall of male and headed for the door, but in seconds a slam of words—nasty and demanding— boomed inside his mind.

This wasn't like when he and Rio had first met, when he was green and cocky and knew nothing of his own power, much less Rio's. With a quick mental shake, he blocked the rest of the Impure's rant, then turned around and shot forward. He got in Rio's face so quickly the Impure barely had time to take a breath.

"I don't need to ask your permission," Gray warned with cool, black rage. "I'm the leader here, and I will keep whatever I want beside me: Impure, human, Pureblood or Beast." He raised a brow. "And if anyone dares to speak their displeasure to her, in front of her or inside her mind, you will be finding yourself a three-some looking for that missing piece again."

Unfazed by Gray's pluck, and at the memory of the three Impure warriors' insistence that Gray was the one, the only one, who would complete and exceed their power, make them a driving force with the Order, Rio lifted his chin and sniffed his disgust. "You're play-ing a dangerous game."

"I know."

Hearing Gray's thought, Rio snorted and took a step back. "I just hope when the time comes to choose be-tween the Impure Resistance and a *mutore* who has rejected you at every turn, treated you like shit on a wet boot, you'll choose wisely."

"Fuck you," Gray said with a snarl, but as he turned and walked out the door, he couldn't help but think, *So do I.*

He erased the thought before the male inside had a chance to hear it.

5

After flashing to the back door of the house in SoHo, the large party of Romans and Beasts filed into the house. With the not-so-gentle rumble of irritated voices, they headed straight for the library, where Nicholas and his true mate, Kate, were waiting.

Nicholas looked up expectantly. "Where is she? Back in the cage already?"

Erion gave his twin brother a frustrated sneer, then dropped into an armchair near the fire. "Not in our cage, no."

Nicholas turned to Alex. "What is my not-so-identical brother talking about?"

While turning on a second laptop, Alexander answered. "She wanted to stay with Gray."

Nicholas didn't even try to hide his shock. "Why?"

"Who knows."

"And you let her?"

"Let her?" Alex repeated with a snort, looking up

from the computer screen. "We're talking about Dillon here, not a rational *veana*."

As Sara went to stand beside her mate, Nicholas's brows drew together. "She keeps going back to that male. If I didn't know Dillon, I'd say she was seriously into him."

Lucian, who had been checking a text on his phone, glanced up at Helo and snorted. "Speaking of being into someone."

Helo's gaze flickered to Kate; then he growled at Lucian. "Shut up, dickhead."

Lucian chuckled. "Touchy, touchy."

"But we do know her," Alexander said quickly, his gaze narrowing on both idiot *paven*s, damning Gray for not only harboring Dillon but letting the entire family know that Helo thought Kate was an attractive *veana*. "Dillon needs him for something, maybe thinks he can protect her. I don't know."

"That male cannot protect her," Helo snarled, his eyes avoiding the couch and the true mate pair sitting on it. "He is an Impure."

Sara lifted her chin and regarded him with a tight smile. "Don't underestimate an Impure. Especially not that one."

Helo glanced at Alexander, who chuckled softly and added, "You heard the woman. Gray is different. He has gifts, deep and powerful mental gifts." He granted the *paven* a look that said, "You know what I'm talking about." "And we didn't just walk into his home earlier because we're Purebloods. I felt heavy magic around that warehouse space, as I'm sure you all did. It's as protected as this place, maybe more so."

"But how?" Erion asked him. "How could Impures have that kind of power? It's not possible."

"We are learning that power is not black-and-white, Erion. Not confined to Purebloods." He paused when Bronwyn walked into the library holding her infant daughter. Her face was flushed and her gaze went immediately to her mate, who jumped up to greet her. "And not defined by the old rules. Not anymore."

"We must convince her to return," Helo said, his tone no longer filled with ire but with the deep concern of a brother.

"Give her a few days," Sara said calmly. "Alex is right. Dillon makes her own choices, regardless of the consequences. I know you care deeply for her, but how much of a fight are you willing to take on to pull her out of there?" She looked at each Beast in turn. "A fight that will only end with her escaping again."

"The Order will find her there," Lycos growled, standing near a shelf of books, his wolf features unnerving in the dim light and shadows. "No matter how many charms they have unleashed. And if they get her, they get us."

Helo turned to the *paven*, said accusingly, "That's what you're really concerned with, aren't you, Ly?"

"You bet your water-loving ass, I am," he spat back. "I say we let Dillon be. She isn't one of us, not really—never wanted to be. I don't run after anything that doesn't wish to be caught—unless it's a food source." He looked to each *mutore* in turn. "I say we leave this house and get lost, find our own life."

Phane chuckled. "Shit, that sounds good."

"Too good to be true or wise," Erion finished. He

looked at Alexander, then Nicholas. "Do you want us out?"

"Yes," Lucian answered quickly, then looked up from his baby and nodded at Phane. "Especially that one. He snores. I can hear it all the way down the hall."

Erion chuckled. Alexander too.

"I'm surprised you can hear anything over the crying of your *balas*," Phane returned with a playful sneer. "What is that thing you have her in anyway?"

"Don't be making fun of my sling, bitch," Lucian countered.

"No," Alexander said, still laughing. "We don't want you to leave. Not when we've gotten so used to you being around."

Nicholas nodded his agreement. "And not when we finally have someone for Lucian to verbally assault."

Phane and Lucian started laughing first; then the others joined in. Lycos smirked. "You have a great risk with us being here—you know that."

Alexander and Nicholas nodded. The Beasts turned to Lucian, who gave them each a vulgar glare, but in the end nodded as well.

"We give our sister a few days, and ourselves a few days, too," Lycos said, pushing away from the bookcase and the shadows. "But then a decision must be made."

"Agreed," said Helo.

Erion nodded.

"In the meantime," Phane said, his mismatched eyes suddenly bright, his tone heavy with sarcasm, "Lucian needs to decide if he's going to change his *balas*'s diaper or let the rest of us pass out from the scent."

Bronwyn burst out laughing, but a growl emanated from Lucian's throat. "I'll change her diaper after I change yours, little birdie."

"My 'little birdie' isn't so little," Phane returned. "Want to see?"

Lucian sniffed. "And make my eyes bleed? Fuck no!"

The room exploded with laughter, male and female alike, and Alexander couldn't help but note that his house had never been filled with such a sound before, and he didn't want it changed. But that was a foolish wish. Lycos had been right when he said the Order would find Dillon, and in turn would find the Beasts, if they stuck around to watch. They were just biding time, all of them—waiting to see who was going to move the next chess piece and to where.

As if his very thoughts had commanded it, something flashed into the room.

A male.

Alex stared. *Titus!* The *paven* looked drawn, ill, ready to collapse, but purposeful as he searched the faces in the room until he found the one he sought.

His gaze pinned Sara where she stood. "Your brother is in grave danger."

In the apartment on the first level of the three-story warehouse, Gray sat in the good-sized kitchen around a rustic pine table with the man his father had called his best friend. "The male we need to retrieve tonight used to be an Impure consultant for the Order. Until they felt he was getting too powerful within the communities."

"Sounds about right. Not to mention familiar." Samuel Kendrick wore a pair of dark blue jeans and a red striped button-down shirt. He looked to be in his late fifties now. He had started aging rapidly after being blood castrated several months ago. "Where do we think the Impure is being held?"

Gray sat back in his chair. "Our informant says he's in the sixteenth cell, directly across from the secret entryway. It'll be a rough grab, but—"

"We'll get him out," came a sharp, confident female voice.

Gray looked up to see Samuel's daughter, Uma Kendrick, enter the room. As she walked over to the refrigerator, she tied her blond hair back into a ponytail at her nape.

"I'm starving," she said, yanking the door open and grabbing a glass of blood. After kicking the thing shut with her foot, she came to sit beside them at the table.

"I can't believe you drink that, Uma," Gray said, remembering the once-timid creature he'd met when they were both being held in the Paleo and the less timid creature he'd met when he'd returned to get her and her family out. "The Order's blood tastes like shit on a shingle."

She laughed. "I love it. I stole this batch on my last run and it's the best by far—like a really hard-core espresso to a human—that jolt gets me up and running." She downed the entire thing while they watched. "Now," she said when she'd finished. "I told Frankie to take the night off. I want to do this one alone. It's easier, nothing to slow me down."

Gray's gaze moved over the female—long, lean, and

tight. With a face like an angel and the strength and determination of a bull who constantly saw red. Shit, what was wrong with him? This was the kind of female he should be claiming—with his tongue and with his heart. Someone with purpose, someone with a drive like his to make things better for her kind.

Someone who ran into danger for the greater good, not away from it for her own selfish reasons.

This female would be a perfect mate.

"What's wrong, Son?" Samuel asked him, his tired eyes moving over Gray's face. "What's on your mind?"

It should've bothered him that Samuel called him "son," but it didn't. In fact, it was the opposite. It made him feel closer to his father—it made him feel purposeful and right. This was the closest he was ever going to get to the male who'd sired him and who'd shared his goal.

"How often did my father go into the Paleo for rescues before he was taken there for castration?" Gray asked, no strain in his tone, but he sure felt it within himself.

With a sudden, thoughtful smile, Samuel stretched out his hands. "More than I can count on these ancient things. He had a strong pull when it came to liberating his own."

Pride and purpose moved through Gray. He felt the same. He wasn't content to watch, wait, give orders—he wanted to participate. He wanted to feel the shock, the charge of heading into the action, to danger and coming out alive, his arms full of his brothers and sisters in blood.

He turned to Uma. "I'm going with you tonight."

Her brow lifted in surprise, but she didn't look displeased. "You sure? I'd love to have you along, but the other Impure warriors won't like it. Risking their leader."

Perhaps they were risking their leader by having objections to his actions at all. "I'm not built to sit behind a desk, if you know what I mean."

She smiled. "I do." Her eyes flashed with warmth, an interest, sexual and otherwise, that he'd seen a few times before. He didn't encourage it, but he sure as hell didn't discourage it. "Why don't you stay?" she offered. "We could strategize, leave for the Paleo together?"

"I'd like that."

She heard the "but" in his voice. "Got somewhere to be?"

He nodded. What an ungrateful, led-around-by-his-dick bastard. This beautiful, strong, intelligent female right in front of him, clearly interested, and all he wanted to do was get out of there and back to *her*. Get back and lay his hands on *her*, open her up like a goddamn birthday present and see what was inside.

He needed Alexander to stick those fangs back into his brain and remove this goddamn need inside him. Sometimes it was more debilitating than those trauma sessions his sister used to force on him in the hospital.

At least those sessions had ended with a happy pill.

"I'll see you both later," he said, standing up, pushing his chair back. "I have something waiting for me."

Some*one*.

A fierce kitty cat who wanted to become a *veana*, he mused, heading out the door. And he would see to it . . . give her what she craved. Slowly, very slowly.

But first, he had a stop to make.

*   *   *

Snow was falling outside the window, turning the afternoon light a dark, swirling gray. Dillon had abandoned her mat twenty minutes ago and, after eating the deer meat the nervous servant had brought for her, began stalking back and forth near the door, trying to decide if she was going to stay in the room or head out into the Impure Resistance headquarters. One choice made her curious; the other made her tremble like a little bitch.

She did not tremble.

She made others tremble.

And yet every goddamn time she thought about Gray returning to the room with those hands, those fire-ravaged hands, and the eyes that bulleted straight through her, well, she wanted to run.

Christ.

Running was the last thing she needed to do. And from his hands—the hands that warmed and soothed and changed molecules. Why couldn't she get it through her head that this male was her ticket out of here, out of the cat suit and into her *veana*'s thick skin?

A scent rolled toward her from the closet and she followed it. Among boxes, bags, and shoes, she found his clothing hanging from long, white rods, and she rubbed herself against them. First her body, then her face, back and forth, the material moving like calm ocean waves as she took deep inhales until her insides began to quiver.

"Starting without me?"

She stilled. "Wouldn't be the first time." She turned around to face him, though part of her body was still bound by his clothes. "Back so soon, Impure?"

"Now, what did I tell you about that?"

"I can't remember. I have a very bad memory."

"Well, maybe this will help." He held up something in his hands. "Maybe this will teach you obedience and who is truly in charge here."

Dillon stared at the collar in his hand, the animal's collar and a leash. "Clearly you've been drinking. Heavily. Or maybe you've been smoking something you shouldn't."

"What?" He ventured a quick glance at the objects in his hand. "It's pink."

"And that's supposed to tempt me?"

He grinned. "Just until we have you broken."

"No."

" 'No' isn't allowed here, Dillon," he warned.

She swallowed tightly and used her brain. "There will always be a 'no' in my world, *Gray*."

His brow lifted at that. "Well, since you used my name so nicely, and with such respect, maybe we'll put these aside. For now."

"Try forever," she nearly snarled, but she wasn't going to push it. She needed his touch more than she needed to lash out at him.

"Shall we get to work?" he said, his eyes flashing.

"Work?" she repeated.

"You got another name for it, D?" He didn't wait for her answer, just turned and walked away.

When she emerged from the closet, she found him sitting in a chair by the fire, which was all but dead now. "Are we really going to pretend you don't love this? Sitting there like a king, waiting for me to sidle up between your legs and beg for your hands on me." She moved toward him. "And let's not even start on the control trip thing."

As she came to sit between his splayed thighs, Gray's eyes moved over her cat's golden, fierce face. "I won't deny it, my unfortunate desire for you, the need to bend you to my will."

"Ha!"

His gaze pinned her. "But it's work. Just breathing the same air as you is hard, motherfucking work." His hand lifted, hovered over her head. "I wish to God I could quit."

"You can," she growled.

"Just shut up and sit still."

His hands found her muzzle first, his burned, destroyed hands, and he began to move them up and down her face in a steady rhythm. The heat surged into Dillon almost at once, but this time she didn't close her eyes and enjoy it. This time, as the breath caught in her throat and her fangs dropped, she watched. She watched his eyes searching her face. The hope, the wonder, the heat behind those gray orbs made her chest ache, and for just a second she understood what he meant—even joined him in his frustration. This *was* work. Work to not feel a connection to him as he changed her back into her truly female self. Work to not hate him for it, feel obliged to repay him for it. Work to not want this bond that was forming out of a chance to change her—the true her, the cynical, untrusting her— in any way.

And then the skin on her face began to transform, and she felt the heat of the dying fire and the breath of the male before her on her face.

"Oh God," she whispered.

Gray kept his hands where they were for several more moments, until Dillon breathed—completely and totally out of her mouth. Then his hands moved. His fingers went to her neck, and when that was a *veana*'s smooth skin, he moved to her shoulders and upper back. Little by little, inch by inch, the warm air of Gray's bedroom wafted over her skin. Until she carried no more fur from head to waist—just smooth, light *skin*. Dillon felt tears behind her eyes at the sensation. Though the change was only halfway complete, it felt so wonderful, so delicious—so freeing. She could stretch, move muscles and limbs in directions she hadn't in what felt like forever. Her shoulders smooth again, her neck, her spine, her collarbone, her breasts—

"Look at me," came the deep, male demand above her.

Dillon's head canted up. Gray's face was so close to hers, his mouth too. She hadn't even realized she had dropped eye contact. His eyes were fierce, looking into hers, his nostrils flared.

"What's wrong?" she asked.

"I don't know how this is happening," he rasped, his gaze moving down her body, from all *veana* to all cat. "It's like I'm taking in what I'm removing."

Dillon tensed at his words. "What?"

His fingers dug into her skin. "Your Beast . . . feels like it's in . . . me."

The last word was barely uttered aloud because he lowered his head and crushed his mouth against hers. Dillon cried out as he fed—fed from her breath and from her soul, if she could still claim to have one. The deep pulls of need were like heaven and hell, and she leaned into it and gave her lips over to him, hungry, impatient, possessive. For one brief second, a flash of herself, of the halfway state she was in, came into her mind. She'd never been touched, kissed, or felt true desire as an animal and as a *veana*—and there was no denying they both wanted this male. And it wasn't her body alone that craved him; it was also the unmoving organ within her chest, cradled and protected by her ribs—that thing that had never had a purpose, never beat with life or joy—it now suddenly ached, begged, cried out.

Dangerous. So dangerous. Not the wanting, the kissing or fucking or fondling, but the *needing*.

She had never needed another being in her life—not in this way.

"Stop!" she cried suddenly, pushing back, pushing away from him. "Stop it! Stay away from me!"

Gray's hands were off of her in seconds, but as he sat up in the chair, the throne beside the smoldering ashes in the fireplace, his gaze remained feral. Swallowing heavily, her entire body soaked with heat, with emotion, she backed away—this creature, this half *veana*, half Jaguar—this thing that couldn't breathe, couldn't think.

"Dillon."

She inched back all the way until she felt wall. There she curled herself into the corner and tried to get air.

"Dillon." His voice was calm, concerned now—it was the first time she'd heard him like that since the night in her house, the night she'd rescued him, let him touch her, drink from her. The night she'd pretended he meant less than nothing to her. "I'm not touching you. Look at me."

Her eyes flipped up as she moved away from the wall, awkward in her half-Beast movements, trying to get back toward the closet, the bathroom, out of sight.

"What's wrong, baby?" he whispered gently, though his eyes still retained the hot desire of a moment ago. "You're halfway there."

She felt too naked, oddly naked—a strange, foul sight. She couldn't seem to breathe right either, and everything within her was shaking so badly she wondered if she was dying. She cast around, looking for a reason to push back, to run, anything but having to reveal the truth about what she was feeling for this male. She saw his hands and bit down. "You can't touch me. Ever again. Your hands . . . The feel of them on my skin makes me sick. I hate them. I don't want them . . . They're . . ."

She was making no sense. She was prattling on like fool, a terrified fool.

But her words had cut deep and quick. Gray's eyes hardened into two steel-hued stones. "You don't have to say any more, baby." He sat there, unmoving, his tone ice cold. "My hands may be the ugliest motherfucking things you've ever seen, but they're also the key to your salvation."

Dillon couldn't bear it any longer—the lies, the truth, the sensations, his disgusted gaze. She got awkwardly to her hands and feet and ran into the bathroom, shut the door, and flipped the lock. Running. Goddamn it. She was always running.

She crawled into the massive shower and lay down

on the drain, wishing it would pull her in and send her off to where all dirty, unwanted things went.

Her throat felt scratchy and tight, and she squeezed her eyes together, trying to force the tears to come. But they didn't. They never did. Not since that night.

When her body was taken against her will, all the tears inside of her had dried up.

Gray's touch hadn't just brought out her *veana*; it had brought out her feelings, the real ones—the ones she'd thought dead and buried—and the emotions that came along for the ride.

As she slowly shifted from part *veana* to all jaguar again, she realized that maybe this was worse—feeling a *veana*'s emotion, pain, shame, and true longing. Maybe this was a far worse fate than remaining an animal.

6

Gray moved down the hall, slammed open the door to the stairwell, and hauled his ass downstairs. He had a raging hard-on, a black soul, and a need to slam his fists into something puny and sneering. Too bad Lucian Roman wasn't standing in front of him right now, barring his way.

Damn that *veana*.

Damn himself for being such a fucking fool, for allowing himself to enjoy even a moment of her transition from sleek animal to smooth and supple female. He'd just wanted to put his mouth on her for a moment, taste her. Christ, what was wrong with him that he couldn't give her up, let her go—kick her out?

Once he hit the basement level, he stalked down another long hallway, then rapped his fist against a metal door until it opened and an irritated Impure muttered, "Jesus! The house on fire or something?"

Gray gave Vincent Seal a fierce look, though the six-foot-four dark-skinned male was a veritable wall of muscle. "I need some weapons."

Vincent's eyebrows lifted in surprise. "Gotten tired of the cat already?"

"Tired's not the right word," he uttered tersely. "You going to let me in or what?"

"Shit, do I have a choice?" Vincent drew back, opened the door wide. "You're like a pissed-off bear."

"It's this female," Gray grumbled, stalking into the room. "Females are so impossible, irritating, frustrating, and sometimes unbearably . . ." He stopped when he saw that Vincent wasn't alone. "Oh, hey, Piper." Turning, he tossed Vincent a what-the-fuck look.

Behind him, Piper laughed. "You were saying, Donohue?"

Putting his hands up in surrender, Gray said, "Not talking about you."

"'Cause I'm not female?" she returned good-naturedly.

He snorted. "Not that kind of female."

"He means the kind with fur, Pip," Vincent said with a chuckle. "Why don't you put the poor thing out of her misery, G? I know a good vet. Cheap, fast, and discreet."

Gray cast the male a violent glare. He wasn't looking to off Dillon. Not today anyway. He hissed, "Weapons?"

Still chuckling, Vincent said, "I'll get them. Glock and a couple blades work?"

"Just blades. Those fixed Warriors you have locked away."

"The sweet sisters." He nodded, his gaze appreciative of Gray's choice. "I'll be right back."

When Vincent went into the other room, Gray turned his attention back on Piper. "Can I ask why you're down here lying on Vincent's bed?"

"You can ask." She fixed him with an imperious stare. "We're not rekindling that fool's errand we called a romance. We're actually sharing some notes about what we extracted from your pretty, pretty brain."

That got his attention. "Something worth sharing?"

"Looks like the senator had a direct line into the Order's mainframe. Like, able to call them up anytime—with just a thought."

The ancient clan of fools was constantly surprising him. Gray crossed his arms over his chest, the female upstairs momentarily and blissfully pushed aside for a moment. "Was that an implant, or did the Order gift him with a temporary power?"

She shrugged. "Not sure yet. But we're working on it." She gave him a knowing look. "If it is an implant, that's pretty useless."

"And if it's a gifted power," he reasoned with a sudden grin of satisfaction, "there may be a mental thread we can jump on and ride inside. The senator is lost to us now, but it stands to reason there are others hooked up to the Order's direct line."

Vincent returned with his hands full. "That's what we're counting on." He handed the weapons over to Gray. "Here ya go, buddy."

"Thanks." Gray started for the door. "Let me know when and if you get something useable."

"Wait a minute, fearless leader."

At the door, Gray glanced over his shoulder, eyebrow raised at Vincent. "Yeah?"

The male's dark eyes narrowed as he stood next to Piper on the bed. "You never said what those were for."

"No, I didn't," Gray answered before leaving the room.

Dillon was still in the bathroom when she heard Gray return. She felt like a hundred kinds of idiot—and then there was that shame thing she was working. For the first time in her life, she felt trapped. Really trapped. Not by a cage or a secret life, not by a past she'd been just freaking stellar at running from or a bathroom she'd run into, but by something she wanted. That feeling when Gray's mouth was on her, when his hands were on her, was terrifying—terrifyingly beautiful. A feeling she'd never allowed inside herself, maybe because she knew it could equally sustain and destroy her.

And she couldn't live with either one.

She got to her feet, her paws, and stalked out of the shower. God, she was thinking like a weak little bitch. This wasn't her; this wasn't how someone like her functioned. She was proactive, not whiny. She kicked ass, not kissed it—unless she initiated things and unless it got her what she wanted.

She stopped at the door and sniffed. Heady and tempting, his scent was pushing through the cracks, forcing her to deal with it, with him. Goddamn it, this should've been easy—an easy exchange of power. Hadn't she done something similar a hundred times before with a hundred different bodies?

Maybe that was the problem.

Releasing a breath, she pressed her head against the door. Gray Donohue wasn't just a body. Sure, she'd tried to make him that—shit, she'd really tried, over and over for a year—but the Impure wasn't having it. And, if she had to admit her weakness, maybe she wasn't having it either.

She lifted her head and closed her teeth around the handle. With a quick push, the wood went flying back, hitting the closet door. First thing she saw was Gray, standing over a table near the chair he'd occupied earlier. He was messing around with a couple of blades. Her insides twisted a fraction. The male who'd hurt her, the one who'd raped her in Cruen's laboratory so long ago, had used a blade like that—pressed tight against her throat.

She didn't like blades in Gray's hands.

He looked up then, his eyes hard, his expression harder. "She has emerged." His tone bordered on sarcasm.

"Nice bathroom."

He snorted, then turned back to the blades.

"Listen, Gray," she began.

His gaze never faltered from his work.

"It wasn't about your hands, okay?"

Those hands closed tighter around the handles of the blades.

She swallowed the unsettling feelings running through her. "It wasn't about the scars."

He grabbed a piece of leather and began to sharpen one of the already-sharp-looking blades. Back and forth, a rhythm of irritation.

"I don't know why I said that," she continued, her gaze following the movements of his hands. "Maybe I do. Fuck. I don't know. I just couldn't keep—"

"You know what, D?" he interrupted, turning his head, his gaze pinning her.

She didn't like that look in his eyes. It was too harsh, too disappointed. She was getting that a lot lately, and it wasn't as easy to blow off as it used to be. "What?"

"I don't care," Gray said plainly, the skin tight around his jaw. "I don't care what the reason is or what game you're playing now. I'm not forcing you into this, any of this." His eyes darkened as he pointed the tip of the blade in her direction. "You need to get in or get out."

Dillon flinched a little, the hair on the back of her neck standing up. Gray thought her run to the bathroom and that verbal diarrhea she'd spouted off at him regarding his hands was the petulant old Dillon rearing her massive cat's head. Of course he did . . . He had no idea what was going on within her, and she wasn't about to tell him. If she ever wanted to be free from the bonds of her jaguar, to control her shift once again, *ever* again—she would have to finish what she'd started.

What they'd started.

"I'm going out tonight," he said, returning the blade to the strip of leather. "When I get back, I'll expect your decision. You either want my help or you don't."

"If only it was that simple," she whispered to herself, heading for her mat, her eyes down.

"It is that simple," Gray said, his tone now even, lacking any stain of emotional hurt.

A fact that, as she put her head down on her mat and

heard his exit from the room, worried her more than it probably should.

Alexander attempted to gain control of the room, but the minute the Beasts had seen Titus appear, it was like trying to contain firecrackers inside a box. After the initial shocked rants, each *paven* began dropping one verbal bomb after another.

Lycos: "Bags are packed. We need to go."

Helo: "What the hell is he doing here?"

Phane: "We need to get the fuck out of here! Now!"

Only Erion seemed to contain his alarm as he turned to Alexander, Nicholas, and Lucian and said, "Do you know who this is? The goddamn Order. Inside your home."

"He's not just the Order," Lucian muttered under his breath, his large palm cradling his daughter's sleeping head—though his gaze was trained on the *paven* who had just flashed into their library and was looking a little worse for the journey.

"What the hell does that mean?" Lycos demanded, his wolf flickering in and out of his face.

Alexander met Nicholas's concerned gaze and silently cursed. They hadn't wanted to go there yet. The Beasts had just arrived a few weeks ago, and with all they'd had to deal with from Dillon—all they'd come from with their maniacal adoptive father, Cruen, all they'd learned about being a Roman brother, a son of the Breeding Male, they didn't need this dumped on them too.

"Whatever else he is," Erion stated calmly, though he moved closer to Titus, inspecting him, "he is Order and he has seen us. He will report back to them that there are *mutore* about."

"Oh, he isn't going back," Phane said, moving to the other side of Titus, ready to spring.

Lycos shifted closer to the *paven* as well. "The cage is free now."

Chuckling, Helo said, "Contain an Order member. Not possible. And even if it were, they'd find him here. All the magic in the world can't keep them from connecting with one another. It's like a goddamn beehive."

Erion nodded in agreement. "They find him, they find us. And know *mutore* are on the loose."

"They already know."

Alexander, Nicholas, Lucian, Sara, Kate, Bron, and the entire crew of Beasts turned to face Titus.

The ancient *paven* looked ill, pale, like he could barely keep himself upright. But somehow, he forced himself away from the chair that had carried his weight for the last five minutes and addressed them all. "That's why I came. The Order knows about Dillon, knows she's a *mutore*. And"—he looked directly at Sara—"they know Gray is harboring her."

He hadn't been inside the Paleo in months, ever since he'd led the mission to retrieve Samuel, Jacobi, and Uma. Not that he'd wanted to give up working in the field. In fact, there was nothing he enjoyed more— nothing that got his rocks off more than the adrenaline rush of search and rescue. Except maybe the high of escape. But as the leader of the Impure Resistance, he'd come to understand that his safety was top priority and had resisted the call, the innate desire to be inside the action. After her rescue, Uma had taken over leadership of the program, and had, over the past few months, retrieved more than a dozen Impures from the castration pit.

Slipping into the hole after Uma, Gray spider crawled his way down. The dirt smelled like danger and blood, and the scent got his own blood churning—it also pushed the thoughts of the Beast in his bedroom aside and allowed him to sink into action mode. God-damn, he'd missed that. Sometimes he felt like a paper pusher, scenting nothing but the stale memories of those connected with the Order.

Gray moved quickly, leaving the darkness of the sky above for another darkness in the tunnels leading to the Paleo. A few feet below him, Uma halted. She glanced up at him, her brows drawn together. Gray focused, listened, heard not only her thoughts, but the thoughts of a Pureblood guard several feet below. He motioned for Uma to press back against the dirt wall. When she did, he dropped, silent and quick, right onto the back of the surprised *paven*. He wasted no time, no breath. Grabbing for the male's neck, Gray executed a quick snap, let the *paven*'s body fall to the ground, then gave a soft whistle to let Uma know they were clear.

She dropped down beside him with a *whoosh* and gave him a troubled smile. "They know our way in."

"It was only a matter of time," Gray said, grabbing for both blades. "Weapons ready?"

She nodded. "Glad I had a partner today."

He grinned. "Let's go get our Impure," he said, then turned and took off down the hallway.

It was only seconds before they encountered more guards. Goddamn it, they really were compromised. Blades up, eyes peeled, his mind worked quickly. They were going to have to find a new way in next time.

Two Purebloods cut off their path. Without word or thought, Gray and Uma sprang into action. Back to back, they fought them off, their moments quick and complementary of each other. It was over in minutes, and when the guards were toe-up and no longer breathing, they continued down the hall, gazes vigilant.

"We're going to need to get around the center of the Paleo," Uma whispered when they hit the small opening into one of the cells.

"I'll retrieve the male." Gray pulled a Glock from his waistband and slipped it into her hand.

She gave him wry smile. "I'll cover you."

They were through the hole in seconds and giving each surprised Impure they encountered within the cell a quick sign of silence before they headed to the break in the cell bars.

Gray dipped into his mind, listening, focusing deep—trying to separate each voice, each thought, to get the ones he wanted. How many Order members were here? How many Impures were being blood castrated at this very moment? Where was the male they needed to find?

As he slipped through the cut in the bars, he shifted his focus, his eyes and mind working in tandem. *Where are you? Where are you?* He sifted through all the thoughts and conversations until he felt the call, heard the strain . . .

"Oh, shit," he uttered. He reached out and grabbed

Uma, pulled her to the side. Hiding behind a thick column that circumvented the massive oval, he turned to face her, whispered, "He's in there."

Uma looked up. Her eyes widened as she took in the two bodies strapped to the stone tables. "Goddamn it."

Gray's brow lifted. "No Order members around."

She sniffed. "How much does this feel like a—"

"Trap?" he whispered. "Too much. They may have guessed we'd try to rescue this particular male. Anything to stop the advancement of the Resistance."

"We're going to have to abort, come back for him."

"He's about to be blood castrated," Gray hissed angrily.

"We can't risk it." Her eyes didn't meet Gray's when she said those words.

"You mean risk me," Gray whispered back caustically.

"The Resistance can't exist without you," she said, her gaze lifting. "I thought this would be an easy grab."

Ire slammed into Gray, and his mind pounded with thought and with the pleading words of all those around him. *Easy grab.* That phrase was pretty much sitting in his gut like a rotten piece of flesh.

"All right," he said, giving Uma a quick nod. "Let's go."

For a split second, Uma looked at him as though she were surprised he'd acquiesced so quickly. But not wanting to upset her good fortune, she nodded and pushed away from the column, heading for the cell. Gray watched her go, and once she was through the bars and on her way toward the hole and the hallway beyond, he turned and, with a quick check of the voices near, jerked out from the shadows of the column. He sprinted into the very center of the Paleo, past unused tables dotted with dried blood. He knew Uma had turned around and was watching him now, no doubt pissed off and contemplating what to do next. But she couldn't yell for him, couldn't risk that.

Just as Gray couldn't stand back and risk the lives of the two males strapped to the tables before him. He'd come for one, but he was going to release both.

His blades out, he began cutting their bindings. He heard the panicked voices of guards in his mind, up and running, coming closer, but it just made him work faster.

Once he'd cut them both free, he shouted for them to run, to head for the cell straight ahead. He saw Uma waiting there, her eyes wide and angry, her breathing heavy as she ushered each Impure through.

"Go!" he shouted, feeling a guard come up behind him. He turned back just as the Pureblood struck him hard in the chest with his fist. Slamming back into the cell bars, Gray braced himself for the shock of pain, then pushed forward, blocking the *paven*'s next blow. Utilizing his blade, Gray ripped into the male's hand, then doubled back for a quick and deep strike across his throat. The *paven* dropped to the ground, but on his descent, pulled a dagger from his waistband and slashed it into Gray's side.

Electric pain shot through Gray, but he wasn't about to stick around to check the damage. Several guards were on their way down to the oval and the tables. His adrenaline high, he ran toward the cell. His mind

screamed with the voices of all the Impures around
him.

"Take us too."

"Breach! Security to the center of the Paleo."

"Don't leave us!"

"Take her," begged an Impure inside the cell, pushing a young Impure female toward him. "Please! We'll
hold them off."

This was bullshit, Gray thought as he caught the
woman with his arm. He wanted them all—no one deserved to be down here, a prisoner for blood, the Order
taking from them whatever it wanted.

With the female held against the side that wasn't
bleeding profusely, Gray scrambled through the hole.
He heard the Impures close the entryway as he hauled
ass down the hallway.

It took every ounce of strength he had to reach the
exit, then push the female up the hole in the ground.
Thankfully, Uma and the Impure males were at the top
and helped the female the rest of the way.

"Go!" Gray yelled at them. "The Pureblood can only
take four. Go!"

Uma shook her head. "You go with them. I'll stay."

"Not a chance." Gray eyed the Pureblood male who
for months had been helping the Resistance with flash
travel. A debt he'd insisted on paying when Uma had
rescued the Impure female he loved. "Do it," he ordered the Pureblood. "Take them to Resistance headquarters, then come back for me."

The Pureblood nodded, grabbed them all.

"Gray!" Uma yelled.

"I'm right behind you—go!"

As they flashed away, Gray crumpled to the ground, blood gushing from the wound in his side. But he refused to pass out, refused to return to his compound and his warriors a dead male, refused to not be the one who ended the nightmare belowground—refused to allow Dillon to remain a Beast forever.

7

Dillon heard the commotion outside her room and jumped to her feet, her jaguar's instincts kicking into high gear. The scent of fear, of blood snaked into the room through the walls and under the doorway, making her growl. She knew it probably wasn't the best idea to leave the room—be seen by anyone—but that blood she smelled? It was Gray's. She was certain of it. And whatever strange, unwelcome thing she had going on with that male, well, the scent of him inside her nostrils made her desperate to get out, get to him—then attack and kill whatever had brought his blood to the surface to begin with.

She opened the door and headed out into the hallway, her head down, nostrils splayed. She followed the scent, Gray's blood scent, into the open warehouse space that Gray and his Resistance buddies used as their workspace.

First thing she saw was the front door open, then a

Pureblood male ushering three Impures inside. One female and two males. A low growl emanated from Dillon. The female carried Gray's blood scent. Slipping behind a high-backed couch, Dillon watched, eyes narrowed into slits. Where was he? Screw these other Impures. Where the hell was *her* Impure?

Suddenly, a female rushed into the room. This one also carried his scent. This one was beautiful, appeared tough, intelligent, and capable, which made Dillon's jaguar's fur stand up in annoyance.

"You need to go back," the female said to the Pureblood, her tone demanding, insistent. "Now. Before he bleeds out."

Something moved through Dillon in those words. Something damn close to volatile possessiveness. She watched through narrowed eyes as the Pureblood nodded and walked out of the warehouse door. Dillon had meant to remain where she was. It was the smart thing—self-preservation and all that. But doing the right thing had never appealed to her.

Pushing forward off her powerful back legs, she padded into the room and demanded, "Who's bleeding out?"

The female looked up, caught sight of Dillon the jungle cat and gasped, as did the others at her side. "What the hell?"

"Speak, Impure," Dillon commanded. "Who is bleeding out?"

The female's eyes remained wide open, stunned at what was before her, this impossible creature who lived only in the nightmares of *balas*. But she soon recovered herself enough to speak, her tone a forced cool, calm, and protective. "The Impure Resistance is housing a *mutore*."

"*Mutore*," hissed the other Impure female, a mouse-brown thing with thin lips and an annoyingly rapid heartbeat. "It's not possible. They don't exist, don't live past birth. A *mutore*. Oh God, it's hideous." She and the males moved back, deep into a shadow on the far side of the room.

Dillon lifted her chin at the lot of them. "Don't faint, shake, or dissolve into tears, Impures. You'll only embarrass yourselves." She shifted her gaze back to the one who hadn't moved, the far too pretty one who seemed to wear the balls in this group. "Tell me who is bleeding or I'll rip out your throat—"

Before she finished her threat, the scent of Gray, of his blood, slammed into her nostrils. She had no time to react as the Pureblood *paven* burst through the door, someone affixed to his side. Someone tall, broad, stupid as hell, and bleeding like a stuck pig.

"Fuck," Dillon uttered, heading straight for him. "What the hell happened here?"

"Get back, *Mutore*," warned the very courageous, very stupid female, her hands already on Gray, her gaze assessing him. "We need a doctor."

Dillon's lip curled.

One of the Impure warriors ran into the room. Rio, Dillon believed his name was. He stopped short when he saw Gray and the blood. He closed his eyes, and Dillon saw his lips move. What was he doing? Calling to the rest of them? Gray didn't need a doctor—he needed a *veana*.

When the Impure was done, he walked over to Gray.

But instead of offering help, he starting barking. "You went to the Paleo," he accused gruffly.

"Eat shit, Rio," Gray rasped, barely conscious.

"You stupid motherfucker."

Dillon's fierce and feral growl stopped them both, and everyone in the room turned to stare at her.

"Speak that way again," she hissed at Rio, "and I'll rip open your stomach with these claws here and feast on your intestines."

Rio cocked his head. "I'd like to see you try it, *Mutore*."

"Would you?" Dillon would've sworn she heard Gray's soft, pained chuckle as she crouched down, ready to spring.

"Where is he?" Vincent and Piper ran into the room, her eyes panicked. When they spotted Gray, they headed straight for him. As Vincent shook his head, Piper cursed, "You endangered yourself and the Resistance. Goddamn it, Gray. Why would you do that?"

"I got him out," Gray uttered, his speech slurring now. "Got all of them out."

Piper cursed. "That's Uma's job, not yours."

Dillon's gaze shifted to the Impure female. So that was little Miss Tough-As-Nails. Uma. What a stupid name.

"There's too many," Gray whispered. "I can't sit around here and use my fucking mind, my fucking gift"—he said the last word as though it were poison on his tongue—"when there's blood being spilled every hour of every day." Suddenly, he gasped. "Ahhh . . . Shit!"

"He's losing major blood here," Rio said, more frustrated than concerned. "Call the doc, Piper."

"No," Dillon said. "Get him into our room."

They all turned to stare at her.

"Are you all deaf?" she shouted, her cat's eyes blazing with ferocity as she stalked back and forth. "Get him into our room and I will take care of this."

"Who is this *mutore*?" Uma asked Vincent.

"Gray's pet," the male answered.

"Fuck you, Impure," Dillon snarled. "I'm a Pureblood *veana* as well as a *mutore*. I'll be able to heal him." She narrowed her eyes at the Pureblood male who held him. "Follow me, if you value your life."

The *paven* didn't even pause to think. With Gray against him, he followed her down the hall, then past her into the room.

"Put him on the bed," she ordered, "then get out."

All three warriors and the female, Uma, stood in the doorway.

"How do we know you're not going to hurt him?" she asked, her eyes wary, protective.

"You don't," Dillon uttered. She stalked toward them, growled a sound so loud and fierce all four took a step back. "Now, get the fuck out of here."

She jumped up and slammed her paws against the door. It shut with such force it rattled the walls of the room. She didn't like the way she felt right now: obsessively protective and, hell . . . if she was forced to admit it, a little scared. And it didn't get any better when she crawled up onto the bed and saw Gray's face. Way too pale. Way too much blood.

Shit.

How was she going to get into her *veana* form? That was the only way she could heal him. Granted, she just needed part of the shift to happen, just her face, her mouth. Shoving aside the other queries in her head, she lay down beside him, against him, and tucked her head under one of his hands, pushed his arm so it was draping across her powerful shoulders.

Come on, come on, come on. Panic swept through her when nothing immediate happened—no warmth, no deep sense of shift within her. The scent of blood thickened in her nostrils. She'd brought him in here, cast down the idea of a doctor—scared the shit out of everyone who seemed to care about his welfare, and now he could die. Right here, right now. Because of her power play.

Her undead heart stuttered, a true and complicated fear tightening her chest. That she couldn't have. Couldn't let that happen to this male. Not ever. She didn't have to be in his life or see him after this was all over—hell, he didn't even have to return her to a motherfucking *veana*.

He just needed to keep breathing.

She dropped her head, scented for his wounds, then ripped the shirt off of him with her fangs and discarded it.

She didn't know what made her do it. Desperation? Inspiration? Who the fuck cared? It was something.

She starting licking him. Deep, powerful sweeps until Gray's blood saturated her cat's tongue. She tried not to think about how good he tasted, how she could drink from him all damn night. She just licked and licked until he was clean, until the wound no longer seeped, until his blood flowed into her, and the shift began.

Dillon didn't know, maybe would never know, if it was his blood that turned her that night or the close contact of their skin, but within seconds, she was a *veana* from the neck up. Quick as a blink, she blew her warm breath onto his wound. She blew, over and over against the deep gash until it started to close, then fuse, then disappear altogether.

When it did, when his skin looked tight and clean, she lifted her head and stared at his face. Her breath held, caught somewhere between her lungs and her throat, she waited. Seconds ticked by and time moved in an endless loop. "Come on, you Impure bastard," she whispered into his skin. *Please*, she begged deep in her mind. *I don't want to do this without you, any of this.* Dillon wasn't sure exactly what she was referring to, but it didn't matter. Gray let out a soft groan. She stared as his once pale and deathly skin turned pink and his breathing evened, slowed to a healthy rhythm, and then finally he slipped into a natural, healing sleep.

Dillon hadn't realized how heavily she'd been breathing, how anxious she felt, how exhausted the entire episode had made her until she felt it come over her in waves.

With a sigh of relief, she turned around and curled up beside him, against the now perfectly healed wound, and closed her eyes, letting the healthy rise and fall of his chest lull her to sleep.

Sometime later, she thought she felt his body stir, thought she felt him turn toward her and drape an arm over her, but she was too tired to lift her cat's head and see.

*   *   *

Per Alexander's request, which was really a thinly veiled demand, they were all sitting. A tough thing for seven Pureblood vampire males, and, Erion mused as he glanced over at Alex's female, Sara, not all that comfortable for their mates either.

Lycos spoke first. Seated at the very edge of his chair, he looked ready to spring. He growled fiercely at Titus. "Before we decide if we're going to kill you or just send you back to the Order without a tongue, I want to know why."

Beside the wolf, Helo picked up where the *paven* left off. "Why would you come here and warn us?"

"It's a trap," Phane offered, his upper lip curling, his hands fisting at his sides. "He's a spy."

"He's not goddamn spy," Lucian said, seated all the way back in his chair, immobile while his *balas* slept against his chest. "Not in the way you're thinking, anyway."

Lycos growled at him. "No one asked you, Daddy Palest."

Lucian turned to Alex. "Can we get this one a muzzle?"

"I'd love to see you try to put one on me," Lycos returned, nearly off his seat now. "My bite is a thousand times worse than my bark, and I haven't tasted dickhead for ages."

Lucian snorted. "Oh, there's way too many places I can go with that." Unable to stop himself, Lucian burst out laughing. "So you've haven't had dickhead. What about asshole? Have you tasted asshole?"

"Lucian," Alexander warned.

"Enough, brothers," Erion said, turning to Nicholas.

It was like looking in a mirror, save for the facial brands and the eye color. It was a shame, a tragedy that they'd had to meet the way they did—taking the *paven*'s sister-in-law and handing her over to Cruen. Erion's nostrils flared. That ancient bastard would have much to answer for when Erion stood before him again. And he would stand before him again. The lies told to him and the truth kept from him . . .

Pulling his mind back into the present, Erion asked his twin, "Who is this *paven*? Truly? He is not merely a member of the Order, yes?"

"He is my sire," Nicholas said tightly. "Our sire."

As a collective grumble of shock took over the room, Erion held firm, still. He hadn't been prepared for this. Perhaps he should've been. "A Breeding Male?" he hissed, his gaze shifting back to the elder *paven*, who sat deep within an armchair by the windows. "Then . . ." Erion looked back at Nicholas.

"He is the sire to us all," Phane finished for him.

All the mischievous jabs and posturing from a moment ago were now gone. The room felt cold, strange.

"I don't understand this," Erion said, first to Alex, then Nicholas. "It cannot be possible. He is Order. He cannot be a Breeding Male."

"It is possible to be more than what others believe you to be."

They all turned toward the ancient *paven*, each gaze set with their own particular brand of shocked unease.

"The Order sees what it wishes to see and ignores the rest," Titus said quietly, his skin as white as the moon outside the window. "Their only objective is to preserve the past—the old ways—because they fear what would happen to themselves if they did not. If things change, evolve, or are accepted, they wonder, does that mean we are no longer needed?" He lifted his chin. "They fear this more than anything—will do whatever they must to keep the old ways current and strong."

"Even kill," Sara said, leaning into her mate Alexander's shoulder.

Titus shrugged. "Castrate, kill, nothing is off-limits when it's framed with 'protecting the breed.'"

"Don't sound like you're innocent of either of these crimes, Order," Phane said tightly.

"I am not." Titus looked as if he wanted to elaborate, but wasn't sure how to go about it. "There is more. If Impures, *mutore*, anything that is not ideal or absolutely Pureblood gains in power, the Order is concerned that the entire breed will implode. They fear anarchy will ensue and we will be known to the humans—truly known for the first time in our existence."

"But why exterminate the *mutore* at birth?" Sara asked, her tone clinical, curious. "Why not castrate them like the Impures?"

Titus looked uncomfortable, his gaze avoiding the four Beasts seated around him. "Impures do not have mates, do not go through the intensity of that impulse to breed."

"Neither do *mutore*," Erion said, the taste of those words, that truth, bitter on his tongue. "We have no mates."

"Who told you that?" Titus asked him, looking even paler than a moment ago. "Cruen?"

"Yes."

Titus stood then, used the chair as support to move closer to the window. "You have true mates," he said to the night sky, the moon, to the view. "In fact, when you reach the age of your Beast's maturity, your need to find that mate is more uncontrolled than a morphed Pureblood *paven*."

Lucian, Nicholas, and Alexander all at once cried out, "What?"

"Dillon," Titus uttered. "She believes it was violence against her that set her Beast free, made it uncontrollable." He turned back to face them, shook his head. "Maybe there was a trigger, but this is a biological change the *mutore* undergo, something far beyond a Pureblood *veana*'s meta and a *paven*'s morpho. While a *veana* and *paven* reach their maturity and transition with the sun and their hunger and the driving force to find their mate, a *mutore*'s response to that same call for mating is at the base level of an animal." He glanced around to see if they understood. "A *veana* and *paven* would be damn uncomfortable if they couldn't find their mate, but they'd still remain themselves. A *mutore*? They become their animal forever."

The room exploded with sound.

"This can't be true," Erion said. "We would've known. He would've told us." He stopped himself there, because that was a proven lie. Cruen had told Erion and his brothers that they would never be able to sire a child—all because he didn't want them breeding, didn't want their dirty *mutore* blood within the breed. Erion snarled. They'd been good for protection, for fighting, for doing their "father's" bidding, but breeding was too far above their station.

A flash of Ladd, the *balas* he'd sired, came into his mind. Because of Cruen, he'd created a living, breathing *paven* who had no idea who his true father was.

"It was one of the ways Cruen created the Breeding Male," Titus was saying, his gaze moving from Beast to Beast. "One of the many ways. Experimenting with the strongest *paven* of the Purebloods, crossbreeding with animal DNA."

"For what?" Nicholas asked, shock and disgust lining his face as he realized that he could've just as easily been a *mutore* too.

"The ultimate vampire," Titus revealed. "A race he could control."

His body rigid, Lycos sneered. "So the Order had us exterminated at birth because they didn't want us to find our mates? Breed?"

Titus nodded. "Partly."

"What is the other part, Order?" Helo demanded, his fangs descending.

Titus sagged against the window, looking a century older than when he'd entered the room. "A *mutore* can become far more powerful, more dangerous than even the Order themselves."

"How do you know this?" It was Lucian this time. The nearly albino vampire asked the question softly, so as not to disturb his child—but there was a thread of ire in it.

Erion wondered if these two males shared a bond. Both being Breeding Males, there had to be something there, as Lucian had barely said a word since Titus's arrival. And the albino *paven* wasn't one for keeping his mouth shut.

Titus's hands shook, but his gaze lifted to his son. "It grieves me to say, but Cruen was my benefactor, too. Long ago, he gave me the blood to stop my Breeding Male desires and become Order. And with his blood came the knowledge of things he's done."

"Oh, shit," Lucian uttered, his tone shocked but strangely curious, too.

"You must find Cruen," Titus said to them all, his tone imploring.

"Why?" Alexander demanded. "Why would we want anything to do with that garbage now?"

"He is the one who can truly help Dillon." He looked at the other Beasts. "Help you all control what is coming for you until your mates arrive."

"And how would he know how to do that?" Phane asked blackly, disbelievingly.

Titus released a heavy breath. "Because he too is a Beast."

Every male in the room shot to their feet. The four *mutore* lunged. Sara shouted for them to stop. But it was too late.

Titus had already flashed away.

Gray woke to the delectable feel of skin on skin. Hard against smooth, white hot against blistering. Him against her. And he did the only thing a male could do in that moment: wrap his arm around her waist and yank her impossibly closer.

It took him a moment of the sun coming through the windows to wake his mind to the fact that Dillon lay nude and curled into him on his bed, and another moment to realize she wasn't a Beast anymore.

He opened his eyes and let the sun reveal all that his hands could not. The first thing he saw was her shoulder, her pale, silky skin just inches from his mouth. Hunger and thirst assaulted him like a bullet to the gut, and he felt his fangs extend, the tips nearly grazing her flesh. He'd bitten her there once before, in her bedroom inside the senator's guest cottage. Goddamn, he remembered his need to get to her, how his fangs had entered her back, slow, centimeter by centimeter, until he was all the way inside. Where he belonged. And he remembered the taste of her—blood so sweet he'd had a sugar high for weeks.

Shit, maybe he still had one.

His cock knocked hard and insistent against the waistband of his jeans. It wanted to be fed too, wanted to be suckled by the hot, wet walls of this *veana*'s cunt.

He brushed her hair back from her neck and kissed that spot, that bit of flesh that still called to him, still scented of him. He felt her stir in his arms, then seconds later, felt her back arch and her ass press hard against his cock.

"Hungry, baby?" he whispered.

She moaned softly, sweetly. "Yes."

Gray gave a groan of triumph. "Yeah, me too." For as long as he could remember. For as long as he'd known her. He let his hand drift from her stomach up to her breast, to the tight, hard nipple in the center. "For this." She fit so perfectly in his hand. "For you." Shit, she fit so perfectly against him. If they hadn't wanted to kill each other ninety-nine percent of the time, he might've believed in that moment that they were made for each other.

He lapped at her neck, ran his fangs down the curve of her shoulder as his fingers played with her nipple. Her sharp intake of breath had him grinning, had him desperate to strike into her hot skin—bite her hard and ravenous. His mouth watered at the thought. Goddamn, he could do this all day—hold her, stoke her, taste her, his hands playing her until she cried out, his mouth playing her until she screamed—slow and easy until neither one of them could stand it anymore.

"I love you like this, *Veana*," he whispered into her neck, pressing his fangs lightly against that spot—his spot. "Soft, hungry . . ." *Mine*.

She turned in his arms then, forcing him to release her, her hand reaching for his fly. In under three seconds, the metal was down and Gray's cock was out. Her eyes closed, Dillon felt her way down his stomach until she wrapped her hand around him, then placed her other hand under his balls.

Gray hissed at the possessive heat of her grip. "God. Dillon. Baby."

He wanted her mouth, wanted to taste her, wanted to touch her while she touched him, but when he pulled her close and drew her in for a kiss, she moved away from him and crawled between his legs.

Curious and completely amped up by her touch, Gray watched as she raked her nails down his abdomen, then yanked the waistband of his jeans to get better access. Gray cursed as she stared hungrily at his prick. There was nothing he wanted more in that moment than her mouth on his cock, her sweet, full lips taking him deep. Shit, he would've begged for it. Not that she ever would have made him. Not this D—this submissive creature before him with no attitude, no bark or bite.

The thought stilled him, made his mind work— made him wish like hell he could hear inside that brain of hers. He continued to watch her, her expression, her movement. Something wasn't right, wasn't right with her. Granted, everything she did, the way she gripped him, stroked him, the movement of her body—it was all hot as hell. Thing was, she hadn't looked at him once. Not even close. Her eyes stayed on her work, on his straining shaft, as though there was nothing attached to it.

He watched as she held the root of his cock in one hand and lowered her head, pressed her mouth against the tip. The sound she made in the back of her throat made cum bead at the head, and when she parted her lips and let her tongue lap at the salty wetness, he moaned.

Fucking hell, he wanted to force her eyes up, make her see him as she licked him back and forth, soft, feather-light sweeps. But then she opened her mouth wide and sucked him in deep. All doubts fled as heat shot through Gray's lower half, and his hands threaded in her hair, flexing and curling his fingers against her scalp.

"Yes, baby," he uttered as she gripped his thighs, his balls, and began slow, even thrusts in and out of her mouth. "My hungry D."

Gray jacked up his hips, meeting each stroke, his cock growing even harder as he touched the back of her throat. Nostrils flaring, he stared at her, at her raw hunger, at his prick, so wet and stiff moving between her lips. He was going come inside her, then flip her on her back and return the favor—eat and suckle and drown in that damp pussy he scented.

As if she'd heard him, she picked up speed, her mouth working him over until he thought he'd lose his mind. Fuck, he wanted to touch her—wanted his hands on her tits, his fingers playing her clit, easing through her lips until he could thrust them deep inside her cunt. But she'd positioned herself so far between his legs, positioned herself so he couldn't get to her. His mind spun. Heat and sexual need and logic all fought for dominion inside him. It meant something, how Dillon was acting, reacting, but he couldn't grab on to the thought. Could only feel the pleasure raging through him.

Shit, he was going to come—hard, deep, and uncontrolled. He was going to fuck her pretty pink mouth until he exploded—and then what? He fisted the sheets, gritted his teeth against the onslaught of aching heat climbing through his prick. Would Dillon even let him touch her? Let him stroke her into climax, let him lick her tight clit until she shuddered, suck her pussy lips until she lost her mind?

His mind took him there, let him see her on her back, legs spread, cunt begging for his mouth.

His hips jerked up then, and he cursed into the air. Fuck her and fuck her mouth, he snarled silently as he thrust deep again and again, all the way to the back of her throat, where he released a torrent of hot, pearly liquid.

Feeling her animal—or maybe it was his—seize control of his actions, his need, Gray gave her no time to think. When she released him and sat up, he went with her, capturing her mouth with his own, while his hand cupped her core.

"Oh God, my baby, you're soaking wet," he uttered against her lips. He bit the lower one and suckled it. "Let me take care of you, of that sweet, swollen cunt."

Dillon whimpered, pressed herself into his hand, and for one brief moment, Gray thought she was actually going to give herself to him. Let herself be taken, overpowered, loved, consumed.

Then he felt her stiffen, felt her go to ice beneath him, and he knew he'd lost.

Knew they'd both lost.

He didn't try to hold on to her. He knew her too well, knew she'd only bite his hand, scratch his face— and not in a way that would be mutually pleasurable.

As she scrambled off the bed, he dropped back against the pillows. With almost clinical eyes, he watched her. Watched her hurry toward the bathroom. Then watched her stop, turn, and slowly walk back. Watched as she came to the edge of the bed and tried to stand there, naked, with her eyes aimed somewhere near his chest, tried to be still and comfortable for one goddamn second.

"Thank you."

The two words were said in a quiet, tight voice, and Gray wanted to spring from the bed and shake her.

She lifted her hands, looked down at her body. "For this."

He tried to be casual, tried to stop his jaw from nearly cracking with all this new tension. "Hey, no problem. You saved me from bleeding out last night. So I guess we're even."

She chewed her lip. "Yeah. I guess so."

Then her gaze flickered up to his, and Gray hated what he saw there. Something hurting, down deep—a place inside this *veana* she'd never allow him access to, but he knew it was bad. His gut clenched as his mind became a dumping ground of ideas, of guesses as to what or who had created this *veana* before him. Maybe it shouldn't have come as a surprise that she'd found herself here—this bitter, impossible to crack, nearly broken feline. No. There was a reason Dillon remained on the surface of every situation, screwed anything and anyone who didn't challenge her—and kept the world, kept anyone who wanted to get close to her at arm's length with her cruelty. Right now, she stood naked before him, but he wondered if there would ever come a day when she allowed herself to truly be so.

His eyes fought to hold her gaze, hold on to her, but his instincts advised him to let go.

"Clothes are in the closet," he said. "Take anything you like, anything that'll fit you."

She glanced up, her eyes meeting his now. "What?"

He shrugged. "You're a *veana* again."

She stared at him.

"In control, ready to run."

She licked her lips, didn't move.

"That's what you want right now, isn't it?" he said, his tone tight as he tried to tamp down his frustration. "To get as far away from anything and anyone who could hold you down, hold you back." He opened his arms. "That collar and leash were only a joke, baby. You can run far, far away and I won't yank you back."

It was like she was frozen in place, her eyes locked to his, her beautiful pale body exposed, nipples a dark pink, cunt still glistening with a raw need she wouldn't allow him to soothe.

"Goddamn it, Dillon," he snapped, shaking his head. "What the fuck is this? What are you doing?"

She shook her head too, looked up at the ceiling.

"What the hell do you want?" he shouted. *What can I do to reach you?*

"I'm not ready, okay?" she cried out, her eyes dropping to his. They were wide, pissed, scared. "I still feel it . . . inside me. The cat. I need more time here. With you." Her gaze held his, but her shoulders sagged with unmasked defeat. "Okay?"

Gray's nostrils flared, his gaze roamed over her, and his mind worked. And goddamn her, his heart felt like it was being knocked around by an elephant. This had bullshit and danger and stupidity written all over it. And yet when he looked into her eyes, he couldn't help himself. He wanted her, and he wanted to know what the hell had turned her into *this*.

Gray nodded, then watched her turn and walk back into the bathroom. When he heard the shower water turn on, he grabbed one of the pillows off the bed and ripped the fucker in two.

8

She'd lied.

Dillon stood under the tepid spray and scrubbed the shit out of her skin until it felt raw.

She'd lied. She'd told him that her Beast was not fully contained when in truth—for the first time in months—she actually felt as though she had a choice in her shift. That her *veana* was, at long last, anchored in.

She turned around, put one foot up on the side of the tub and started scrubbing her legs, her inner thighs. There were many purposes for water: hydration, growth, sustained life. But to Dillon, water was a way to get things clean—cleaned up, cleaned out. Dirty things. Like the body, the soul—if you had one—and those thoughts you kept to yourself for a reason, thoughts that served only to make you crazy, thoughts that should never escape their cage.

She'd asked him if she could stay. Christ, she was a stupid bitch. *This is the part in the movie where the chick gets slashed, Dillon! The part where the guy sees his way in, sees the vulnerability and strikes.*

And she wasn't running.

She moved the sponge between her legs.

Still hot, still sensitive, still slick on the backs of her fingers. She wondered if he was still out there in the bed—the bed she wanted so badly to crawl into. Not as the cat this time, but as a female, a *veana* who remembered that feeling—that split-second feeling of awakening when Gray's hand held her breast—when his hand had cupped her pussy. Yes, she'd been touched before, fingered, fucked upside down and backward, but not in the way Gray Donohue managed it—not by those hands of his that outwardly displayed the very damage that wreaked havoc within her.

She shook her head, her hair, hoping the water that was released would take her thoughts along with it down the drain. In that moment, she had a sudden pang of grief for her jaguar. An insane thought after being held prisoner by it for so long. But she hadn't realized how protected she truly was within the confines of her Beast's fur. Soft emotions, vulnerable thoughts . . . they rarely got in, rarely made it past the ferocious predator's thick skin. And if they happened to, if they somehow squeezed their way in, those feelings manifested as a gentle rain.

Now she was exposed again and, Christ, it was a great, unrelenting torrent.

So, what did she do? Run? Stay? Keep him out? Let him in? That last thought sent shock waves of terror running through her. This was Gray. The more she allowed him access, the deeper he would want to go.

Sure, he couldn't read her thoughts the way he could with others. But, shit, that just made him dig with a different instrument. It was just his way. Like keeping her secrets buried under fifty sheets of icy glass was hers.

And yet that didn't stop her from wanting Gray Donohue. A male who had never given up on her, a male who needed her and had no qualms about admitting it. A male who had rescued her from the second worst night of her life and never asked for jack shit in return. A male she kept finding and saving over and over for reasons she'd refused to truly look at.

Her skin shivered beneath the spray. And now there was no denying, no pretending what he was physically capable of too. With just those few touches she'd allowed him, she knew how diabolically hot he was capable of making her. How crazy, how addicted. She wanted to know what it felt like to be taken by him. To be made love to by him.

But could she make it through such a thing? Her eyes on his as he hovered above her, ready to push inside? It was one thing to have sex—mindless, emotionless, faceless sex where her eyes remained as closed as her unbeating heart. She'd done that a hundred times. It was as caring and romantic and real as an hour on the treadmill. It was just taking what she wanted, accepting what was offered by a one-time lover she never had to see again—or hell, never even had to see while she was getting off.

But this wasn't mindless and detached. This was connecting on its truest level.

Suddenly it wasn't Gray's beautiful face in her mind,

but the face of a monster—one who'd relished the screams of a young *veana* as he took what he'd never been given.

Flinching, Dillon moved deeper under the downpour. She shook her head again, forcing the images from her mind. Water sprayed everywhere, and she hoped that once again it would take her thoughts and her increasing and uncontrollable need for Gray down the drain, to be lost forever.

But in Dillon's mind, forever was never more than a few hours at best.

Erion stood over a blanket of weapons. They were laid out on the bed he'd never used in the room the Romans had given him when he and his brothers had arrived on their doorstep a few weeks ago, after the epic battle at Cruen's laboratory—the one that had started off with the brothers as enemies and ended with them being family. Erion had never slept in a bed in his life. If he took rest at all, he preferred to do it on the floor, as he had in his *balashood*. In fact, he preferred the floor next to an open window. And if it was cold like tonight, all the better.

But there would be no rest tonight. He was on the hunt, and for the first time it would be with his brother, his twin, Nicholas. They were flashing out of town, searching for the one Erion had been fool enough to call "father." The one his supposed real father, Titus, had said was a Beast.

Erion's lip curled up in a sneer, and he grabbed a couple of blades and slipped them into the holders on either side of his torso.

"Father." What was the true meaning of that word?

He didn't know, maybe never would—maybe he needed to not give a shit.

He heard movement behind him. Two *pavens* entered the open door of his room. Erion glanced over his shoulder and gave the brothers a nod of acknowledgment.

"Phane and Lycos are off," said Alexander, coming to stand near the bed, his gaze taking in each weapon. "That just leaves Helo, Luca, and me. We'll be watching out for Dillon and working with the Eyes."

Erion had heard of the street rat informants called the Eyes, but he'd never used them. Hell, he barely trusted the males who shared his DNA.

Lucian moved to Erion's other side, picked up a machete, and grinned. "I have one like this. It can take the head off a sequoia."

"What about the head of an ex-Order member *mutore*?" Erion said drily.

Lucian eyed him, grinned. "Most definitely. And maybe every guard that stands in your way."

Erion took the machete from the pale *paven* and placed it behind his back in the waistband of his jeans. His gaze turned serious when he looked up at the brothers again. "I need to know before we continue on this journey, on this quest to find Cruen. Can we trust Titus?"

"No," Alexander said quickly, resolutely. "His own agenda is his first concern."

"Doesn't mean he isn't right," Lucian amended with sudden heat, and Erion knew that his earlier assessment of their relationship, their bond as Breeding Males was dead-on.

"Or that he isn't telling us the truth about all of this—about the *mutore* and Dillon," Lucian continued. "And what Cruen may be able to do for her, for all of you."

Alexander nodded with consideration. "Yes, but let's not pretend he doesn't want something out of this."

"Oh, he wants something," Lucian acquiesced with a sniff. "He didn't hide that fact. He told us about the bargain with Cruen—he didn't have to do that. And I want to wring his fucking neck for not revealing it to me—especially to me," he added with a dark curse. "But that matters not. Titus needs Cruen's blood like I need Bron's, if he wishes to remain on the Order. If he wishes to stay sane."

"And he wants us to do the work for him," Erion added with a low growl.

"He is a selfish *paven*," Lucian acknowledged. "But he's not overtly cruel, and there are times when his Order status has helped us." Alexander nodded, confirming this, then Lucian added, "And he's sure as hell not looking to get his nuts cut off and force-fed to him." He gave Erion a quick and deadly grin. "Which he knows would happen if he lied to you, to all of us about this."

"There you all are." Kate entered the room, her expression a little worn, anxious. Behind her came Ladd, looking very excited to be in Erion's room.

The *balas* had stopped being wary of him, of the Beasts, about a week ago and had become curious instead.

"What are you? Can you shift into your Beast form now? How about now?"

Erion grinned. He'd given the boy a few quick shifts from *paven* to demon and back again. Not in front of the

Romans or the females or the Beasts—just a scary little show for one.

He'd liked the way the *balas* had screeched with equal parts terror and pleasure.

Ladd's eyes grew saucer wide as he stared at all the weapons on the bed. "Are you taking all of those with you, Uncle Erion?"

Everyone in the room stilled, not at the question— but at the name the *balas* had called him. Their gazes shifted to Erion, all curious, all a little concerned. They wanted to see what he'd do, he thought, how he'd act with this *balas* that was supposedly his. Would he be gruff with the boy, tell him not to call him that?

Uncle Erion.

Or would he be irritated within his own black heart because he wasn't the boy's uncle at all but his father?

Christ, just the thought of it sent his body into tremors. Look at him. A *mutore*, an animal, he didn't have an ounce of true softness within him.

Uncle Erion.

He shouldn't care; he knew that. But the title got under his thick demon skin and scratched. This *balas* carried his genes, had *mutore* blood. And after what Titus had revealed earlier, Erion couldn't help but be concerned about that. What would it mean for the boy? Would his transition to *pavenhood* be a difficult one too? Would Cruen know how to ease it?

Erion's gut twisted. He looked up at Nicholas.

"Do you have something to say to the *balas*, Brother?" Nicholas said, no malice in his tone. "Here? Now? In this room?"

Erion's lips thinned.

Nicholas put his hands on Ladd's shoulders. "Just understand what that means." He glanced down at the boy. "And what that will mean to him."

No, Erion told himself quickly, resolutely. It wasn't time. Maybe never would be. The *balas* was happy, had a family here, a mother figure in Nicholas's mate, Kate. And, though he was starting to find it oddly frustrating, the boy had a father figure in Nicholas as well. After all, Ladd had not only been rescued from some maniac called Ethan Dare by Nicholas, but had forged a deep bond with the *paven*. How could Erion strip the boy of that, especially without any promise of care from his true sire?

He turned to the *balas* and stated, "I take only the weapons I can carry on my person, young *paven*."

The boy's riveted gaze traveled up and down Erion, at each weapon tucked against his body. "Are you going to fight?"

"Perhaps." He lowered his chin, gave the *balas* a grave look. "But only if I must, if there are no other options. Do you understand?"

Ladd nodded solemnly. "I could go with you." His eyes widened even further. "I am becoming a good fighter."

Erion felt a hitch of something within his chest. It was a strange sensation. He wasn't sure what it meant. If it was his demon at work or something else. "You will stay here and continue your training. I want to see your progression when I get back."

"I wish you both didn't have to go," Ladd said, looking from Erion to Nicholas, his lower lip pressed out.

A soft smile on her comely face, Nicholas's mate

came to stand beside the boy. She put her arms around him. "They won't be gone for long, Ladd." Kate's gaze lifted to Nicholas's. "Right, *Paven*?"

Nicholas grinned wickedly, intimately at her. "You know I cannot be away from you for more than a few days, sweetest one. My unbeating heart wouldn't allow it."

Kate returned his grin. "Nor mine, *Paven*. Nor any other part of me."

He chuckled, his expression tight, his nostrils flared. " 'Tis wicked to send me off like this, *Veana*."

"My poor Nicky," she said gently, sweetly. "I promise I will pay the price when you return."

"You will pay now," he said with a growl, taking her in his arms and giving her a tender kiss.

Ladd made a face at Erion, stuck out his tongue in disgust.

Erion chuckled, but within him there was a thread of envy for what his twin possessed with this *veana*. He imagined it wasn't in his future, romantic love, but he wondered at it all the same.

"Are we ready, Brother?" Erion said, moving away from the group and jumping up on the ledge, the cold air rushing his face.

"Let's go hunting." Nicholas gave Kate one last kiss and followed Erion out the window, their flashes two quick shots of lightning against the night sky.

After they were gone, after closing the window, Alexander turned and looked first at Kate, then at Ladd. "Never fear. They will be back soon."

"We know," Kate and Ladd said at the same time, then smiled at each other.

Behind them, something darted by in the hallway, then fell back, looking in the room. Evans. His face flushed, the servant entered with a breathless, "Excuse me, sir."

"Something wrong?" Alexander asked, coming to stand beside Kate and the boy.

"I was looking for Dr. Donohue," said the aged male. "There is a visitor just arrived."

"Who?" Alexander demanded, his tone suddenly fierce and protective. "Who is it?"

The male's eyes brightened. "Her mother."

"Cellie?" Alexander said, stunned. "Cellie's here?"

Evans nodded. "She says she must speak to Dr. Donohue immediately."

Under the brilliant light of a thousand candles, Feeyan inhaled deeply and opened her eyes, a sensation of triumph moving through her. One pawn down in this chess match. "She is there, at the Romans' compound."

The Order member seated across from her looked concerned. "We cannot track her there."

Several feet away, seated before an unmoving Impure male strapped to cold stone, another Order member lifted his head. "The Roman home is too secure, has too many enchantments protecting it." The *paven* sniffed with derision. "We are able to send messages within their walls, but we can't get inside. 'Tis very tiresome, indeed." He lifted one pale eyebrow. "Perhaps we should see to removing that obstacle."

Feeyan hesitated in answering the Order member's final statement. Though she would like total access to the Romans as well, the Order's relationship with them

was a vital one, a tenuous one, and she did not want
that unspoken truce compromised, not with something
like this. Not yet.

"Access to the Romans' home matters not at this
time," she said coolly. "The older *veana* will lead us to
her Impure son—and to the *mutore*."

"Both must be exterminated," the *paven* across from
her said. "The *mutore* for what she is and the male for
what he has done here."

They all ceased speaking for a moment as they gazed
at the Impures within the cells surrounding the center
of the Paleo. Feeyan could see the spirit in their eyes,
the burgeoning hope. Gray Donohue's rescue operation had given them all a belief that they too would
escape their destiny and be liberated.

Feeyan had seen it in their blood—and she'd seen
him in their blood.

First with the senator and now with the Impures.
This male was growing dangerous.

"We must speed up castrations," she said to the Order members surrounding her. "And when we have
this rebel Impure in our grasp, we will bring him here,
let them all watch their aspiring savior bleed out before
them."

Titus heard his leader's words and knew it was only a
matter of time before Gray Donohue lay on one of the
stones before him. Not only was the male harboring a
mutore, but he was attempting to bring about a revolt
within the Impure population.

The Order would be swift with their justice.

Titus stood beside his fellow Order member, who

was fang-deep within a male's upper thigh. He despised performing castrations, and Impure blood made him even weaker than he already was, so he had, once again, offered himself up as seeker. The one who chose which Impures would lie on the stone table next.

As the Impure male below him cried out in pain, in misery over a future he could no longer see, Titus couldn't help but recall his own history of torment and torture at the hands of the Order—long before they were even aware of it—back when he was taken from the Coliseum in Rome and sent to an experimental facility run by a new Order member named Cruen. There Titus was poked and prodded and changed into a Breeding Male monster who for decades lived in a cage and was released only to fuck and impregnate the cold, dry bodies of Pureblood *veana*s who hadn't found their true mates.

It had been a true hell on earth. If Cruen hadn't one day decided to offer him a vial of his magic-laced blood, he might have taken his own life. But the blood had turned out to be an elixir, and Titus had lived another several decades as a normal *paven*, with no urges, a member of the Order himself.

But everything was different now. Cruen had gone rogue and hadn't shown himself to Titus in weeks. He prayed that the Romans and the *mutore* found him. The *paven*'s blood was Titus's only hope for survival—his only hope to see a clear future. Because if they didn't, he wasn't altogether certain he could stop himself from offering up information on the whereabouts of a certain *mutore* female.

He didn't want to hurt his children, but the further

he slipped back into Breeding Male status, back into that depraved, uncontrollable rutting animal, the more ruthless he would become. For no one and nothing mattered to a Breeding Male animal but sex and survival.

9

The blood of the Impure male that Gray had rescued from the Paleo ran into his mouth and down his throat, but the memories he desired drifted up like a cache of balloons to his mind. He centered them there, then started popping each one in turn; first the Impure getting his virgin "call" from the Order, then his struggle to find that same frequency a second time. Gray pushed deeper, centered himself. He saw the Impure stretched out on a bed, felt his ease slipping into a relaxed mind state. This was the male's third go-round, and he obviously felt a keen strength as he called out to the Order. Gray watched him as he waited, as he remained open and eager with what he now knew and understood, all the way until the Order's hive answered him and welcomed this new bee inside.

The Impure had learned quickly, Gray mused. He opened his mouth wide, deepened his bite, then reached out and wrapped his thought stream around the male's perfect memory, over and over until it was cocooned. Then he squeezed like a python.

Gray heard the male's sharp intake of breath and he pulled out, then dropped his head into his hands and fought for peace, for his blood to slow, his pulse too.

"Take him downstairs," he ordered to no one in particular, his voice hoarse, his head pounding and swollen. "Get him food, water, blood if he wants it, and let him rest. It'll take a day or two for him to recover fully."

Shit, Gray thought, gritting his teeth against a sudden lightning strike inside his mind. How long would it take for him to recover? Or recover enough so that the three other Impure warriors could go inside and mine for gold, retrieve what Gray had pulled out of their Impure informant who'd been working so intimately with the Order.

A cup of water was shoved into his hand, and he drank it down with the fervor of a desert dweller. Then a second glass. He gulped it greedily. The warriors gave him only a few more minutes of peace before they pounced.

"Did you get it?"

Gray looked up at Rio and grinned through the pain.

Vincent walked back into the room after taking the male downstairs and placing him in the care of one of the Impure guards. His eyes gleamed, and he turned to Piper. "We're in. The Order's mainframe, baby!"

She nodded, gave them each a brilliant smile. "Now on to phase two. Listening in and one: seeing if there's a weak link among the nine members; two: gathering information, secrets, anything we can use as currency; and three: intercepting any and all messages to Impures."

"The listening and sorting information will be me and Pip." Vincent turned to Gray. "So after we take that memory from you, you should shut down for a while. Recharge."

"Yeah, I'll do that," Gray said passively, thinking about how to keep his little trip back to the Paleo tonight under mental lock and eye.

"Don't be a fool, Gray." Piper, with her blond hair and perfect face, looked as close to an angel as one could get, but that disguise hid one tough-as-concrete female. "After we drain you, you're going to be out of it for a while."

"I'll make sure I get a nap in," he uttered drily, his head clearing of the fog from a minute ago.

"You can't go back inside the Paleo, if that's what you're thinking."

Gray's head came up, his eyes narrowing on Rio. "Is that what I'm thinking, Rio?"

"I can't tell. You're too fucking talented at blocking me." Rio shifted to the edge of his seat. "You know there will be more guards in that place than ever before." *"It's impossible."* He cocked his head to one side and uttered caustically, "You going to risk getting taken by the Order? Blood castrated like Samuel, like all those others, like your dear old—"

Gray jacked to his feet, ignoring the shot of dizziness between his ears, and headed for Rio.

The male was on his feet too, meeting Gray nose to

nose, pissed-off male to pissed-off male. "Sometimes I think you just don't care enough about this cause."

A low growl rumbled in Gray's chest. "Are you fucking kidding me? Those Impures in the Paleo *are* the Cause—and don't you forget it!"

"No, they're the victims," Rio returned. "You need to learn the difference."

The urge to knock the male's head off was nearly irresistible, but Gray forced himself to back up. He found Piper's and Vincent's concerned gazes and said, "Are you two selling and drinking this swill too? Lose some bodies to win the war?"

Piper spoke first. "We're not suggesting abandoning the Impures at the Paleo."

"Good," Gray said tightly. "Because that's not going to happen."

"Doesn't have to be you getting them out though," Vincent said with the intelligent, calm thing he was always working. "Besides, I hear the old way into the Paleo ain't happening. Heard it's crawling with guards. It'd be like walking into a bank that's been hit three days in a row and expecting to get out with anything less than a shot in the leg and a pair of metal bracelets around your wrists."

Though the interior of his skull continued to scream, Gray's eyes narrowed. "Then I'll find another way in."

"How?" Vincent demanded, frustration pumping behind his eyes. "And how will you get there and back? The Pureblood who helped us out before has been taken. He's being questioned by the Order. No car, no gas, Brother."

"I'll help you."

They all turned to see Dillon standing there halfway between the hall and where the warriors stood in the main room.

Rio snorted. "So the cat's lost its fur," he said. "And its way, apparently."

Before Gray could shut the male down, Dillon did it for him.

"Listen, Impure," she said, eyeing the military bad-ass. "I'm here to stay. As a guest of your leader there."

Dropping into the chair he'd occupied earlier, Rio chuckled. "Just because Gray wants you around—or feels sorry for your kitty-cat ass—doesn't mean the rest of us do."

"Maybe save that newsflash for something sur-prising—and something I give a shit about," Dillon returned, walking into the room. Her eyes remained on Rio. "Now, unless you want to go a couple rounds with a Pureblood *veana* who's trained to stop a heartbeat in under five seconds—which I'm *totally* up for, by the way—then let's talk tactic."

"I don't talk tactic with the enemy," he returned.

Her brow lifted. "I thought the Order was the en-emy. Maybe you're the one who's forgetting why you're here and what you're fighting for."

"Fuck you, *Mutore*."

"No, fuck you and the high horse you rode in on." She gave him the finger, then smiled. "By the way, I had it for breakfast and it was damn tasty. Maybe you'll be next. I'd lock your door at night."

Gray grinned—at her, at Rio. He hadn't said a word through the whole back and forth, just sat and watched the show. Hell, the lady needed no help. Not when it came to picking up a cocky male by the nuts and tossing him off a cliff. In fact, he was pretty sure that to even suggest help at this point was an insult to her talent. And damn, the *veana* had talent. Her verbal takedown was a motherfucking thing of beauty—just like she was. Nothing better, nothing hotter than Death-Blow Dillon.

He stared at her long, lean body with the curves up top and down below, his mouth watering and his dick jerking to life inside his jeans. Oh, damn . . . And then there was the fact that she was wearing his clothes. A simple white T-shirt knotted against her small waist, showing off that flat, hard stomach. His jeans were way too big on her, but she'd cuffed them at the bottom and rolled the waist. He wondered if she was also wearing a pair of his boxers.

His nostrils flared, his hands closed around the sides of his chair. He didn't know which was sexier—his briefs on her hot little ass and cunt or nothing at all.

Knowing she'd shut up Rio, Dillon turned to face Gray then, her eyes narrowing at the expression on his face—which was no doubt a mask of desperate cavemanlike lust. "I want to help you," she said.

Gray wasn't fool enough to think this was in any way a question. "Me or the Resistance?" he asked.

Her lips parted and she smiled, flashing her fangs. "Whatever gets me out of here, gets my fists up and a gun in my hand." She shook her head. "I can't sit around here all day doing nothing."

Gray stared at her, into those steely hazel eyes. He got what she was saying, what she needed. She'd been caged too long, behind bars and under that animal fur. And not for nothing, but he wouldn't mind having her on the team. If she could manage to play ball.

"She's a *mutore*," Piper said, no malice to her tone. "If she shifts while she's in the field, the Order will be on it before you have a chance to take out anyone."

Dillon's gaze moved to the female. "I won't shift, honey."

"That easy, huh?" Piper said with a slight grin. "I thought you'd lost control of it."

"She has control," Gray said. He stood. He'd had enough of this play. Dillon had had her fun with Rio and the hostility with Piper was cute and all, but they were acting as though this was anyone else's decision but his.

"She will remain in control," Gray stated flatly. "Just as she will remain here with me." He gave each of his warriors a look that warned them to cease fire. Then he turned to Dillon. "I accept your help, but understand— my mission, my rules. Stray once and you're out, back to my room."

Back to my bed.

Celestine felt her daughter's presence before she saw her, and turned from the window she was staring out of. Blue eyes wide with surprise, cheeks flushed, Sara rushed into the room.

"Mom!"

Celestine opened her arms, and when the *veana* walked into them, she held her tightly. It felt so wonderful to touch her child. It had been too long.

"It's so good to see you," Sara said, pulling away

and guiding Celestine over to the couch. "I have so much to tell you."

Cellie's chest tightened. She was a sham of a *veana* in that moment, unworthy to even be called a parent. This young female wanted to sit and spend time talking, reflecting on the past or sharing stories of her life now with Alexander and his brothers. And Celestine could think only of Gray and what she must do.

"But first," Sara began, that trademark gleam of curiosity lighting her eyes as she sensed something. "What are you doing here? I mean, I'm glad you are—but no phone call, no warning?" Those beautiful eyes—her father's eyes—narrowed. "Is something wrong?"

Lying to one's children for their own protection was acceptable, had to be. It kept them safe, kept them alive. Celestine settled on the couch and took her daughter's hand in her own. "I've missed you, and I thought, why not come and surprise you with a visit."

For one moment it looked as though Sara was going to question that answer, but then she shook her head and smiled. "Well, I'm glad you did."

"I've tried to reach Gray as well," Celestine continued hurriedly. "I'd love to see him on this visit, if it's possible."

Sara's joy dimmed. "Yeah. It's not an easy endeavor getting through to Gray or pinning him down for anything social. He's good, though. Doing his own thing."

"For the Impures?" Celestine asked quickly. Perhaps too quickly.

A look of surprise moved over Sara's face. "How did you know?"

Celestine forced a laugh. "It wouldn't be all that

grand of a leap, my darling. He finds out he's a vampire, an Impure, and goes in search of what that means." She shrugged. "It's what I would've done."

Sara looked momentarily stricken. "Should I have done that too? Am I a bad Impure for not wanting to know more about what that means or jumping into that life, that cause, without truly—?"

"No, no, Sara. Please, honey." This was not how she'd wanted this to go.

"Perhaps I need to think about this some more," Sara said, her face tense with self-analysis. "You and Dad wanted to protect us from the Order, didn't want them to find your Impure offspring. I feel as though I completely understand that." She touched her stomach absentmindedly. "If I had a child someday . . . I would do the very same thing."

Guilt moved through Celestine like a fish through water, like a fish escaping a shark. Sara knew all she needed to know, all that was important. And she had Alexander and Nicholas and Lucian to protect her now.

But who protected Gray?

"I would really like to see your brother," she said again. "How do I do that? He won't return my phone calls, won't seek me out."

Sara put her hand over her mother's. "If it's that important to you, I'll take you to him myself."

"No, my dear," Cellie said quickly. There was no way she was having the Order on Sara's tail as well. "It's better if he and I meet somewhere. Somewhere private."

Suspicion clouded Sara's eyes. "Why?"

Something heavy and thick rested in Celestine's

throat. She thought for a moment about telling her daughter the truth about the Order, about them knowing that Gray was housing a *mutore*. But what was the point? A moment ago, Sara had been questioning herself, her feelings about the past and her choices regarding the present. She didn't need to know. It was only Gray who needed the truth.

Her gaze rested on her daughter's. "I don't wish to ambush him. Showing up on his doorstep without warning. I'm afraid it would make him even more distant and unforgiving."

The wariness in Sara's eyes worried Celestine. Her daughter had always been so protective, so proactive in regard to her brother. From the moment that fire had destroyed their family and Gray's mind, she'd taken his illness on herself. She'd become a psychiatrist for him, to heal him. Would she relax her cautious nature just this once?

"I think the tunnels below our home would do well for a meeting place," Sara said at last, her expression now impassive as she took control over the situation. "I'll contact him and set up a time."

Cellie smiled. "Perfect." She took a deep breath and squeezed her daughter's hand. "Shall we have that chat now?"

"Later," Sara said, her eyes just a little less bright now. "You go upstairs and get your things unpacked. I'll make us some tea."

"They drained the shit out of me."

"They did warn you about that."

"Not helping, D."

Dillon pulled Gray away from the wall. "Come on, now. Let's get you to bed."

"Fine. But don't think I'm going to be an easy lay," he uttered, leaning against her as they walked down the hall. "I'm not that out of it."

"I'll try to keep my hands to myself."

With a quick burst of energy, Gray took her hand and pulled her close, leaned back against the door to his room. His eyes found hers; his lips were just inches away. "Don't try too hard, okay?"

If Dillon's heart could beat, if it could thump against her ribs with girlish excitement, it would have in that moment—and at jackrabbit speed. She stood there, breathing in and out as he gazed into her eyes and contemplated kissing her.

Do it! she wanted to shout.

What are you waiting for, Impure?

For a second, she thought about leaning in and getting it done herself. Tasting him, maybe running her tongue across that full bottom lip, but then his knees buckled.

"Fuck," he grumbled, dropping his head back against the door. "Those greedy bastards. Took a good twenty pints at least."

"That'd be a clever trick," Dillon said with deep sarcasm, "since the body has, like, only twelve pints in it to start with."

"Don't get technical when I'm about to pass out, *Veana*."

Grinning, she hauled him toward her, then kicked the door closed behind herself. "Come on, blood boy," she said, helping him inside and easing him down on the bed. She made to stand, but Gray wasn't letting go—no how, no way—and she was forced to land on top of him.

Well, not exactly forced.

She rolled to the side—*her* side of the bed—and began to inspect his temples. She had watched both Piper and Vincent pull the memory from Gray's mind. It had taken no more than ten minutes, but it looked brutal, and she wondered how often Gray was having them do this.

She touched one of the bite marks. "Kind of a butchering mess here. An Impure's bite. Maybe I need to give some lessons in clean strikes."

"Yeah, they'd be all kinds of receptive to that."

Her thumb brushed against the wound. "Do you want me to give you a nice blow job?"

Gray's head turned, his eyes lifted, and a wicked grin broke on his face. "You already did, and for the record, it was way better than nice."

Dillon's insides stirred at his words, at the look in his eyes. "Doesn't have to be a one-time thing."

His smile softened, and the look in his eyes turned to something far more intimate than sex. "I appreciate that, but if anyone is getting blown tonight, baby, it's you."

She licked her lips. "I may act like a *paven*, talk like a *paven*, fight like a *paven*—I may even fuck like one. But there's no twig and berries down there to blow, Gray."

"No twig," he whispered, his gaze hungry, feral. "But there is a berry, sweet and ripe and buried within the hot, wet lips of your cunt." He gazed into her eyes, no doubt watching to see if there would be shock there, heat there, need there. If he was reading her right, he saw all three. "In fact," he continued, "I felt those lips against my palm not too long ago. Remember?"

She swallowed thickly. As if she could forget. That touch had started it all, cooled her shift while heating her body to a point of desire so worrisome she'd pulled away from him so she didn't have to examine the effect of his hands on her.

Remember? Ah. Yeah.

In fact, her lower half was getting a repeat performance right now. Bitch.

Gray rolled onto his side, which sent Dillon onto her back. He gazed down at her, growled possessively as he noticed what she was wearing. "I like you in my clothes. Shit, I like you in my bed."

Trying to ignore the warmth that moved through her at his words, Dillon nodded at the bit of blood seeping from the wound on his temple. "Let me close those bite marks. Come here."

Gray lowered his head, and Dillon leaned in. She was about to release her healing *veana*'s breath on his left temple when a sudden animal-like instinct took over her and she lapped at the excess blood instead.

Gray hissed.

"Hurts?" she asked, concerned.

"Like a wet dream," he said roguishly.

Dillon smiled, then licked him again.

"You lick me and I get to lick you," he uttered with dark hunger. "It's only fair."

"When have I ever cared about being fair?" But Dillon could hardly deny the lust, the need, the urgency rippling through her body at his words, at the images those words brought to her mind.

She opened her mouth then and blew. First on one side of his temple, then the other, until both wounds were closed nice and tight.

When she released him, Gray let his head drop down to her pillow. His eyes were closed and he looked tired and pale.

"You all right, Impure?" she asked, trying to keep her tone light. But the thread of concern she had for him—that she was having quite often lately—was back again and more intensified.

"I'll be fine in a few hours," he whispered against her ear.

Dillon chewed her lip. If she was smart—if she was the Dillon from a week ago, that hard-ass who cared about no one but herself—she'd get up out of this bed and let the guy sleep it off. He'd be fine; clearly he'd been through this before.

Problem was, she didn't want him fine.

She inhaled, exhaled, then whispered, "Drink from me."

"Oh, damn, D," he uttered, his lips just a millimeter away from her neck. "I don't know if I can handle Beast blood right now."

She shivered. "Don't be cute."

He chuckled softly. "I'm serious. Hot, rich, potent, and highly addictive. I may turn rabid." His hand came up, and he trailed one finger down the other side of her neck. "Do I get to pick the spot?"

"You're being cute again," she said, everything above and below her waist churning with heat.

Gray inhaled deeply, his nostrils flaring as though he could scent that heat. "No, baby, I'm just hungry."

Goddamn it, he needed to stop calling her "baby," and she needed to toughen the hell up. Panic was beginning to wrestle with the desire inside of her. The male needed blood, and she was cool with giving it to him. It was just . . . Shit. She turned and eyed him dangerously. "Take as much of my potent and highly addictive blood as you want, Impure—"

His brow rose severely.

"Gray," she amended with an eye roll. "But there's a condition."

He chuckled softly. "Tell me what you need."

"No memory grabs."

A surprised gleam flashed in his eyes and his mouth hardened just a touch, but he didn't question her. Instead, he lowered his head and whispered into her neck, "Agreed." Then he kissed the vein at her neck, and as he did his hand came to rest on her stomach. "I won't go back in time, D," he whispered into the curve of her ear, "but what about here? Can I go here?"

Dillon sucked in air as he eased his hand over the skin of her belly, down, down until his fingers touched the waistband of her jeans. His jeans.

Mimicking his hand, he grazed his fangs down her neck too, then circled the spot, the sweet spot where she would feed him. "While I take, will you let me give?"

Heat pooled inside her cunt, making her clit pulse with anticipation. She could say no. She could say no and he would take his hand away and leave her be. She could say no and he wouldn't be angry, wouldn't punish her.

She could say no.

So she said, "Yes."

She felt him smile against her neck, lap at it with his tongue; then, with the utmost gentleness, he pierced her skin and sank his fangs into her vein.

A sound escaped Dillon's throat, like pleasure and release and melancholy all wrapped up into one.

He uncurled the waistband of her jeans and pulled at the button. With deft fingers, he eased down the zipper and opened the fabric wide. She felt the air on her skin, on her shaved pussy, felt him shudder as his hand encountered nothing but smooth, hot skin. As he took slow, deep pulls at her vein, drank her rich, pure blood, his hand cupped her possessively.

There was something inside her brain that warned her not to take any pleasure from this male, but her body had other ideas. It craved Gray Donohue; it desired the touch of his long, fire-damaged fingers. It wanted to know what it would feel like to be completely without control. For just a little while. For one climax.

She released a breath, a soft moan of satisfaction and pleasure as his fingers played with her lips, first with the outside, so gently, so softly. She pressed her hips up, hoping he'd get the hint, wishing he could hear her thoughts in that moment. Then again, maybe he did. He dipped one long finger inside her wet slit and stroked her sensitive flesh back and forth. There wasn't anything hurried in his touch. Gray Donohue wasn't trying to get her off, then take off. He was an explorer, utterly gentle and highly erotic.

She didn't need to hear him say it to know that he

wanted to feel her, experience her movements, the shake of her lower half when he slid another finger between her soaking pussy lips and circled her clit, urging it to swell.

The slow-moving but powerfully shocking buildup of heat spread through every part of her, and Dillon grabbed the sheets at her sides and fisted them. Her eyes closed, her toes pointed, she listened to him suckle as he played her. For one brief second, the image of the monster, her monster, tickled the exterior of her mind, but she refused it entrance. Instead, she forced her mind on him, on Gray, the one with the magic hands and the fangs that belonged inside her vein and only her vein.

As Gray nursed at her neck, Dillon opened her eyes and looked down, watched as he pressed her lips open with his thumb and middle finger, then circled her shiny red clit with his slick index finger. Though it was highly erotic to watch, there was also something comfortable, stable in his hands. They were so big and scarred and yet they were the kind of hands that wanted to bring only pleasure to her body, never pain.

As his fingers feathered her clit, Dillon felt Gray's other hand tunnel behind her back, then move down over her ass to the slick wet trail that led to the opening of her body.

"Oh God," she uttered, feeling her body release even more moisture as she pumped against both of his palms, begging him to continue, begging him to come in, come in where it was warm and drenched and aching for his touch.

Gray groaned against her neck, pressed his fangs in

deeper, then entered her with one long finger, one delicious thrust. Dillon gasped, her fists tightening around the sheet. Shards of electric energy raced through her system. She wanted to move, wanted to attack, wanted to scream—and God, she wanted to touch him. But when she called upon her limbs to respond, they wouldn't. Her body, inside and out, was no longer her own—and yet she'd never felt more in control. She bucked, rolled her hips, moaned his name, and let her head thrash to the side.

Gray released her then, pulled from her vein. But as he did, he slipped another finger inside her.

"I'm inside you," he said hoarsely. "But you're inside me too. Not just your blood, but your jaguar. And it's screaming and clawing at me to give you more."

His thrusts grew quick and intense, and every time he drove up inside of her, he pressed the pads of his fingers against the sensitive spot of her clit.

"Oh God, yes, Gray," she cried out, then whimpered as he gave her clit another flick. "God, yes! Fuck me, Gray, please."

She couldn't keep her eyes open any longer, and she let her head drop back against the pillows. Knees bent, hips pulsing, Dillon let her thoughts evaporate. Gray's fingers were working her over like nothing ever had, thrusting, pistoning inside her as he circled her clit faster and faster.

"That's it, baby," he said, his tone a hoarse, hungry demand. "Come for me. Shit, no. Come for you—you and the tight, hot pussy that's riding my fingers, drenching them, suckling them."

She was dying—or was it living? She didn't know,

but whatever was slamming through her right now, spark after spark—whatever it was that had just made her mind and body connect for the first time—she wanted more of it. Her back arched off the bed, and as the walls of her pussy trembled, then clenched around his fingers, she cried out. Again and again. Climax ripped through her, sending wave after wave of delicious, bone-melting satisfaction to her limbs—hitting her from all sides, beating her against the smooth, unmoving rocks of impossible heat and wondrous pleasure. And as Gray rode them with her, his fingers still thrusting inside of her, her hips canted, again and again, as she stretched, trying to hold on, wanting more, until finally, the waves receded and she released a weak, shuddering sigh.

Her hips dropped to the cool sheet at her back, her breath hitched, and she just lay there. Then, through her exhaustion, her haze, she felt that old sense of doom creep in. It was that feeling she'd always had after sex, after orgasm. The need to run. To leave before anything got heavy, serious, intimate.

But she didn't, didn't move. Instead, she lay there, waiting for him to try to climb on top of her, take her, pull down her jeans and get something out of this encounter too.

Would she let him? she wondered, the doom inside her growing. Maybe.

Probably.

Her mind got fuzzy and her skin grew tense, and then Gray Donohue leaned in and kissed her neck, lapped at the spot where he'd bitten her and released her. Not pushed her away or acted as if she owed him something and she'd better get to it, but just released her. He lay against his pillow, opening his arms, letting her know she was the boss; she was in control.

Her breath caught somewhere in her throat, Dillon stayed where she was. She wasn't sure what to do with this, with him—with herself. Especially when the feelings of panic and doom receded and she was left only with a raw and honest need for intimacy. So instead of turning away, giving him her back, as was her nature, she moved closer and curled in to him.

For several minutes, she remained tightly pressed against his side, breathing in and out. It wasn't until she noticed his T-shirt was wet that she realized she'd been crying.

What a fucking pussy, she thought.

What a fucking loser.

And then he pulled her closer and kissed her hair, and she released a mighty breath from her aching throat, wrapped her arm around his waist, and pulled herself tighter against him.

10

Gray had a hard-on the size of New Jersey, but he wasn't going there. Not now, not yet—not until he knew she was ready. Sounded kind of nuts in his head, because ever since he'd met Dillon she'd been openly sexual, up for anything—with anyone.

But now he knew better.

He didn't know the details—but he knew better.

She pulled herself even closer, her core pressed against his thigh, her face buried in his side. For a second, he'd thought maybe she'd been crying. He didn't know . . . but maybe he'd heard something, and maybe his T-shirt was wet where her face was tucked in.

But that had to be sweat, right? D was no tear dropper. Hell, the *veana* got pissed, not sad. She got annoyed, not sad. It was her way.

"You got some seriously talented hands, Male." She glanced up, grinned. "You just said I couldn't call you 'Impure,' right?"

No tears, Gray thought, but those hazel eyes were glassy and a little red. Could be from climax. Shit, she'd come pretty damn hard a moment ago.

But even as he reasoned away the possibility that Dillon had gotten even the smallest bit emotional from their encounter, he couldn't stop himself from reaching out and brushing his thumb along the upper ridge of her cheekbone. The skin felt pliant, cool with the last shades of moisture. His chest hitched like he'd just had a blade thrust into it.

Her mouth thinned and her eyes hardened. "What are you looking for?"

"Just looking at you."

"You're staring. Thinking. I can feel it."

"Stop being so suspicious, D," he said, moving his hand down, running his fingers across her mouth. "Don't you recognize this? What we're doing here?"

"No."

He attempted a hurt-guy look. "Come on, baby. It's post-orgasm cuddling. Basking in the glow and all that shit."

She opened her mouth and swiped at his fingers with her fangs in play. "I don't do that."

"Well, now you do," he said, wishing every damn movement she made wouldn't keep cranking up his need for her to blistering. "I suggest you get used to it."

"Fine." She lifted up on her elbow and gazed down at him. "So. What are we supposed to do here? Share our feelings?"

He laughed at the look of utter disgust on her face. "How about we just talk?"

She shrugged. "You first."

His gaze locked with hers, and he took a risk. "What do you want to do after this? After you get complete control over your shift?"

The question surprised her, as he'd known it would, and her body stiffened a little. "We're getting deep, eh?"

"Dillon."

"I don't know, okay?"

She sounded defensive. What a shocker.

"You haven't even thought about it?" he said.

"Not really."

Annoyance on top of the defense, Gray mused drily. So much fucking fun.

"Maybe you need to," he said, his hand on her back. "Keeping out of the Order's way, off their radar, is going to require some strategy and planning."

Her jaw tightened. "I know."

It wasn't like he wanted to be thinking about this shit. He'd just touched her, made her cry out—wanted to again . . . and again—all night long if she'd let him— but like his gift of hearing the thoughts of others, these kinds of thoughts just weren't a choice. His brain went there too damn much. The thing wanted to know where his *veana* would be next week, next year—and if she saw him in any corner of her life.

"I can help if you want me to," he said, knowing he was a fool for offering, and yet . . . "Come up with a plan. Ask around about safe houses; if there—"

"What is this?" she said, sitting up, a scowl on her face.

"Just talking, D." He released her, dropped back on the pillows. "Back and forth, swapping info."

"Sounds more like an inquisition to me." Her body was going rigid, screaming its defense, total shutout. But the eyes, her hazel eyes told a different story. "Are you trying to get rid of me or something?"

Oh, baby, I'm trying to keep you.

"Get rid of you?" he said, keeping his tone light. "Not a chance. I need you."

Her mouth softened.

"You got the flash, D," he said, grinning. "The way into the Paleo."

"Nice," she muttered drily, but at least a thread of her defensive tackle was gone.

"Hey, you volunteered." He lifted his brow. "Which surprised me, you know. Since you don't really give a shit about the Impures."

"That's true," she said, all heat, all irritation—all D. "But I give a shit about you."

He grabbed her hand, threaded his fingers through hers. "Awww, baby, that's so sweet."

"Shut up," she snarled.

Grinning, he pulled her toward him. "I'm going to kiss you now."

"Thanks for the warning." She lifted her chin.

"Hard, wet, and lots of tongue."

"And for the play-by-play."

"Stop talking." His hand cupped the back of her head. "Or I'll put more than my tongue in your mouth."

"Promises, promises," she drawled, closing her eyes.

He chuckled as he captured her mouth. Groaned when she wrapped her arms around his neck and captured his mouth right back.

Goddamn, there was nothing in the world like Dillon's mouth. It could spew angry words, snap you in half with its sarcasm, suck you in and make you come—make you fly to the fucking moon and back—and kiss you like it was desperate to know every inch of you.

Kind of like now.

His fingers gripped her, and he growled as he sucked her tongue into his mouth. Dillon cocked her head, letting him take her deeper, then biting at his lower lip when he released her. Fuck, she tasted good. He went for a deeper angle and she followed him. Hot and heavy, they kissed, teeth knocking, *his* heart pounding, *her* fingers digging into his skin, their moans escaping hungry mouths.

When their lips parted, when she was breathing every bit as hard as he was, Gray found her gaze and whispered against her mouth, "Are we going to talk about what's happened, why you feel like you do—the memories you won't let me see?"

"No."

"Not today or ever?"

She drew back. "Why are you pushing me?"

He released a frustrated breath. "Shit, *Veana*. You know why."

Her eyes looked bruised, or maybe that was her expression, and she sat up again.

Gray stared at her back, released a frustrated breath. Why the hell couldn't he just leave this alone? Forget the pain and vulnerability he saw in her eyes every goddamn time he touched her? Maybe because he wasn't a dickhead—or maybe it was just simply that he cared way too damn much. Whatever had happened to her was brutal, something she couldn't control—no doubt sexual—and he was determined to find out what it was.

And who it involved.

Rage like he'd never felt before moved over him like a mudslide, threatening to consume him whole. He closed his eyes and inhaled—real fucking deep until there was no more air left in the room. His hand itched to hold his blades, to sharpen them until they cut pipe as if it were butter. Until they cut the skin off the one or ones who had hurt this *veana*, then the muscles, bones . . . His lip curled and his fangs descended. He'd ended the life of one male who'd thought he could touch this *veana*. Another death on his hands was nothing.

"We have work to do," he said, pushing that bloody fantasy into the back of his mind. For now. Struggling to keep the death march out of his tone, he added, "We need to go meet with Uma. Get a plan together for tonight."

"We don't need her," Dillon said with sudden heat, glancing over her shoulder. This was heat of a different variety.

Gray pulled back the sheets and got out of bed. "She's great in the field. Quick, smart, and has a killer rapport with the Impures." He tossed her a look that said no negotiation here. "*I* need her."

Dillon leaped to all fours on the rumpled bedding, growled at him.

Gray's cock twitched. Damn *veana*. Did she have to go there? Right now when he was barely able to stand up with the shaft of granite in his jeans? When she was all *veana* again, he lifted an eyebrow. "Was that your cat?"

"Yes," she hissed. "And totally controlled by me."

"Well, put it away before I strip, climb back in that bed, and teach it some manners."

Again, she flashed him her jaguar's face. Again, she growled.

"I'm not joking around here, D," he warned, knowing his eyes were as fierce as his face now. "A male can take only so much—Impure though he is."

For a moment she just stared at him, and though Gray couldn't hear her thoughts, he could see her thinking behind those eyes—no doubt wondering how far she could truly push him. Then she sat back on her haunches and sniffed, mewed. "My blood runs too wild through your veins, I think."

Damn right. Gray leaned on the bed, got in the cat's face. "There's no reason to be jealous, D."

She turned back into a *veana* in under a second. "You didn't just say that."

Laughing, shaking his head, Gray stood up and buttoned his jeans, tucked in his shirt. "Come on now. Out of bed."

She did as she was told, but the moment she stood up, her jeans—his jeans, fell to the floor and pooled around her ankles.

Gray stared at her legs—long, perfect, edible stems. Thank Christ his T-shirt covered her core or this would be done—he'd be done. They wouldn't be going anywhere—not for at least an hour. He cursed. "Are you trying to give me the worst case of blue balls in history?"

She attempted to look innocent. Didn't work on her. "They keep falling off. I need my own shit."

"We'll get that done. But in the meantime, I'm sure Uma has something she can loan you." *Like, immediately.*

She cocked her head. "Oh, now you're just asking for it," she growled, shifting into her jaguar state and leaping on him.

He went down with a thud. Cursing and laughing.

Twenty minutes later, dressed and back to her *veana* self, Dillon stood in Uma's kitchen and watched the Impure female bang some pots and pans around.

Or as the humans called it, cooking.

Sitting on a stool beside her, Gray sampled some vegetable thing in a sauce and made a noise far too close to the one he'd made when they were lip-locking earlier.

Blue balls. He was going to know *black and blue* balls if he kept this up.

"You didn't have to do this," he said to the tall, blond creature at the stove.

"I know, but that was a tough go down in the Paleo last night, and then the memory bleed today." She turned and gave him a brilliant smile.

Dillon sneered. It was like a freaking commercial for whitening toothpaste.

"With all the blood loss," she continued, "you need to eat to get your full strength back."

Oh, how Dillon would love to crush this female beneath her paws. Maybe rip out of few of those teeth with her claws. Didn't this bitch know what stood before her?

Yes, a killer *mutore*, but more important, the one who had given this male her blood—marked him deep in his veins. Fed him in the only way that mattered.

Uma turned then, her blond ponytail sweeping against her face and all that creamy skin, and with quick confidence, ushered the steaming ingredients onto a waiting plate. "This recipe is guaranteed to get your blood pumping again."

That's it! "Already taken care of, Female."

Both of them turned and looked at Dillon. Gray's eyes were glittering with twisted humor—*dickhead*—while the female had the balls to not appear scared, only strangely curious.

Maybe Dillon needed to snarl to get her to understand. One more time for the cheap seats. *Her* blood got his blood pumping. Not some freaking nasty-looking vegetable crap. She nearly said that aloud when the Impure decided to go all polite on her ass.

"Can I fix you a plate too, Dillon?" she asked, flashing that ten-watt again.

"I don't eat," she said.

"Oh, right; you're a *veana*. So you consume nothing but blood, then?"

"Unless I'm a jaguar," she returned. "Then I eat meat. Raw, and preferably still running away."

Uma stared at her, something close to humor in her eyes. "I'll keep that in mind."

"Good," Dillon said. "And Gray's right. You aren't as dumb as you look."

Uma's eyes widened, and Gray turned to glare at Dillon. "Remember what we talked about earlier? About keeping your mouth shut?"

"Or you'd put something in it," Dillon drawled, giving him an exaggerated wink. "Yeah, baby. I remember."

"Impossible *veana*." He narrowed his eyes, but Dillon saw the hitch in his chest, maybe even the pop of his zipper.

"Well, if you can't keep it closed," he said, "use it for something productive. Like telling us if you know of another way into the Paleo."

Dillon crossed her arms over her chest. "I do."

"Are you going to share it with us, or do we need to guess?" Gray asked, then quickly amended, "Don't make us guess."

"I've heard that there's another entrance below one of the nightclubs in the town nearby."

"And you can get us in there," Uma asked.

Dillon turned on the female and hissed. "Yes. I can get you in there."

"Very good." She sat down beside Gray and picked up her fork, then smiled again. This time she upped the wattage to blinding. "Shall we eat?"

Yes, Dillon thought, glaring at the female. Oh, she'd eat all right. Blond ponytail and all.

"He went under the bridge," Lucian called to Alex. "Fuck. Don't let him get away."

They ran through Central Park at top speed. That little bastard, Alexander thought. Even though it was night, he knew the brothers weren't about to flash, not in this heavy foot traffic. Lucian obviously thought the same thing as he kept pace alongside Alex. Helo, on the other hand, clearly didn't give a shit. Soon as water was in sight, the *mutore* slipped away from Alex and Luca, dove under the murky surface, and didn't come up again until Lucian and Alexander were around the corner.

And by then Helo had the Impure male by the back of his coat.

Impressive, Alexander mused as he eyed the dripping-wet *paven* with the sudden appearance of black lines, wavy tattoos shooting up his neck and spreading like tree limbs from beneath his shirt. Impressive, but not smart. If this member of the Eyes was even moderately intelligent, he was going to take one look at Helo, put two and two together, and come up *mutore*.

Deflecting attention, Alexander descended on the nervous-looking Eye. "What's with the running, Whistler?"

"Yes, Impure," Lucian added, his fangs dropping a threatening quarter inch. "You are never one to shy away from giving information for substantial monetary compensation."

"I have nothing for the Romans," he said quickly. "No news, no locations."

Lucian growled. "We didn't ask for locations. Hell, we haven't asked you anything yet."

Whistler looked at Lucian, then Helo. Something startled within him and he swallowed. "I don't have anything for the Romans," he repeated.

"Someone's shut you down," Alexander said, his eyes narrowing on the male. No question there.

Whistler didn't confirm. Or deny. Just kept acting nervous as hell.

"Who is it?" Lucian demanded. "The Order?"

"You're barking up the wrong tree here, fellas."

"Your Eye colleagues?" Alexander asked, taking a step forward.

Whistler sniffed. "We're done here. I have somewhere to be."

"Cruen?" Helo said, tattoos now gone, disappeared, and both his clothing and skin dry as concrete in summertime.

Whistler's gaze shot to the *paven*, his face ashen.

A cruel smile erupted on Helo's face. "You lie, you die."

Whistler's eyes closed, and before them, in the crowded park, the Impure disappeared—leaving no doubt in the minds of the *paven*s who remained just who he was working for.

The city had gone dark ten minutes ago and the sky was littered with stars.

Not that Gray could see and enjoy anything but bodies occupying seats and poles. He was belowground, inside the metal bullet, racing toward a location that was becoming way too familiar lately.

The subway car jerked to a stop, and Gray barely allowed the doors to open before he jumped off and headed toward the tight gap in the wall. He was through it in seconds, and took the stairs down into the tunnels two at a time. When his sister's message had found him, he'd been watching Vincent and Piper as they worked with the information they'd taken from his mind earlier—trying to sync up with the Order's mainframe. He'd wanted to stick around and see if they'd get anything, get anywhere, but family came before a mental exercise. He'd be a fool if he tried to pretend it didn't.

Once inside the stairwell, he headed into the passageway underneath the Romans' house. Before long, he saw her shadow in the distance and called out, "Hey, Sis. I can't stay long."

"I won't keep you."

Wasn't Sara. Wasn't someone he was expecting to see anytime soon. His guts twisted. *Family came first, eh?* Did that extend to this branch of family? After all he knew, all that Samuel had revealed to him?

With an irritated exhale, he came to stand before her in the torchlight of the Romans' tunnels. She looked as she always looked. Too young for her age, too gentle and kind for what she'd kept hidden from him and Sara. "Hello, Mom."

Celestine's eyes moved over every inch of his face. "It's so good to see you, Gray."

"Yeah. You too."

She smiled, and her eyes appeared hopeful. "That almost sounded like you meant it."

He did mean it. He had deep anger and resentment for this *veana*, true, but it hadn't killed the love. Not yet.

"Where's Sara?" he asked.

"I asked her if I could have a moment alone with you."

"Okay." His brows lifted. Waiting. Why was she here? What did she want? And more important, would there be anything said about the past—from her or from him?

Her eyes softened as she took in his face, as if she

were having a memory. "You weren't taking any of my calls. I got worried."

"No need to worry," he said simply.

She shrugged. "All right. I got offended, then."

The warmth of her voice snaked through him, tugged at the boy within. After all, she had been a loving mother, no doubt about that. Did she not deserve a chance to earn back his trust? Come clean and explain her actions?

"Well, as you can see, everything is fine," he said. "I'm good. Fully embraced my vampire side, the Impure I truly am." His gentle sarcasm in that last bit wasn't lost on her.

Her head cocked to the side in a sympathetic way. "Gray."

But he didn't need sympathy. He needed the truth, and he was going to give her a chance to offer it to him. Could be their way back to mother and son, maybe even friends. He crossed his arms over his chest. "Why don't you tell me why you're really here?"

The softness and familiarity evaporated, and she took a deep breath, nodded. "The Order knows about your *mutore*."

Shock slammed into him, and he replayed what she'd just said. Then again. Not at all what he'd expected. Not what he'd wanted. And definitely not good. There was no way he was discussing Dillon here, with her.

"What's a *mutore*?" he asked, his brows coming together.

"This isn't a game, Gray," she said with deep worry in her eyes now.

"That's good," he said calmly, evenly. "Because I don't play games." *Or play with the life and safety of that veana.*

"They know you have her; they know you killed for her."

His jaw tightened, and he ground his molars. "If this is what you came so far to tell me, you wasted a trip." Disappointment stung. She wasn't here simply for a visit with her children. This was either a warning from her or a message delivered from the Order.

Either one sucked.

"I've got to go," he said. "Good seeing you. Have a safe trip back home." He turned to leave, head down the tunnel and back where he belonged. But her next words halted him.

"You think she wouldn't turn on you in a second?" She sniffed. "If the Order gave her a chance to remain free?"

Gray turned back ever so slowly, his nostrils flaring. "Like you turned on Dad?"

Sudden shock registered in her eyes, stealing away the concern from a moment ago. "What are you talking about? Why would you even say something like that?"

"I met someone in the Paleo," he said.

She paled, ghostly white under the glow of the torches. "The castration hole? You were in there?"

"Was nearly blood castrated. Would've been if that *mutore* hadn't gotten me out." His voice went low, dangerous—a warning he hoped she'd understand and heed. *Do not screw me over with that bit of information or we're done.* "Unfortunately, Samuel Kendrick wasn't so lucky."

His mother gasped. Shook her head. "No."

In that reaction, Gray knew that everything Samuel had told him in the Paleo was true. It wasn't that he hadn't believed him; it was more that he hadn't wanted to.

Gray shook his head. "He told me everything. About Dad, the Resistance, the Paleo." His voice dropped. "And afterward, when he came home."

"You don't understand," she said weakly.

"No," he said tightly. "That's true. How can anyone understand when they're continually lied to their entire life?"

She just stood there, tears in her eyes, defeat in her expression. Gray waited for her to say something, give him something that might possibly repair this collapsed bridge before them.

"You weren't supposed to know," she cried softly, "any of this—goddamn it. I did everything . . . Oh God—"

She turned and ran from him.

And he let her.

Standing in the shadows of the tunnel, Sara watched her mother retreating in tears. Then she heard Gray's footsteps, going back toward the stairs to the subway.

All that about their father, the Resistance, the Paleo—what didn't she know?

Goddamn them both, what didn't she know?

11

Dillon hadn't memorized the lay of the land in the Impure Resistance compound yet, but one thing she had memorized was Gray Donohue's scent.

She was a Beast after all.

And he was sweating.

She'd followed her nose all the way to the basement, and after a sharp right and a stroll down the dark hallway, she hit the door that caged the Impure—the male.

Gray.

She turned the handle and pushed. Inside she found a stark-white room—except for the black and red targets affixed to the wall—and two nude-colored dummies hanging from the ceiling. One was taking a killer beating, slashed and penetrated by two fierce and shiny blades.

She knew those blades, knew the fire-ravaged hands that worked them.

She licked her lips. Terrorizing the poor, defenseless

dummy was a six-foot-tall, profusely sweating, shirt-less male with a six-pack for a belly and a killer wing-span for shoulders.

For a moment she forgot why she was there. Had to have a reason, right? Coming to stare at the Impure meat candy wasn't going to cut it when he asked. Which was about to happen any second now—

"Need something, D? Or did you just come to watch?"

She narrowed her eyes at him, wondering for a moment if he truly couldn't hear her thoughts as he claimed. "No," she said. "There was a reason."

He raised his brow.

What the hell was the reason?

He flipped both blades in his hands and plunged them into the dummy, one through the neck, one through the heart.

Dillon swallowed. *Yum.*

"Wanted to see how your meeting with Sara went." The words tumbled out of her mouth effortlessly. *Ah, there it was. Thank you, brain.*

"Pretty damn bad." He executed a sharp turn and slammed a hard kick into the dummy's abdomen.

She leaned back against the wall. "What happened?"

He glanced over his shoulder, gave her dark grin. "You're not going pretend you care about this shit, are you, D?"

"Excuse me?" she asked, attempting to look of-fended.

"Because, damn," he said, his eyes registering severe frustration even with the all the high-speed, sweaty deathblow action he was wielding. "I'm really needing a female to be totally honest with me right now. Even if it tears my ass up."

What the hell had gone on over there? Dillon thought, a little taken aback by his ferocity, and maybe a bit concerned too.

"Hand me the blades," she said, going up to him, putting her hands out. When he hesitated and had the nerve to look suspicious, she added, "Hand me the blades or I'll tear that ass up." She grinned. "You want honest? I got honest."

Instead of placing the blades in her hands, he tossed them past her shoulder without even looking, his gaze locked on hers. Dillon glanced back, saw that both had landed in the eye sockets of the dummy.

She turned to face him again. "Damn," she said, her nostrils flaring with heat.

He moved closer to her. "You said if I didn't hand them over, you'd tear my ass up." One sharp eyebrow arched. "Liar."

He was close now, so close she could watch each individual sweat bead travel down his pectoral, up and over each ridge of his impressive abdomen, down to catch in his navel, then south to paradise.

Inside her, the cat scratched to get out. A feeling that surprised her. Never had her shift—her animal life—cared for anything or anyone she bedded. Not that she'd bedded this male.

Yet.

Her gaze flipped up to his, saw the challenge, the demand. She grinned. She'd give him the fight he was looking for.

She was quick, *veana* quick—Beast quick. She whipped

her body to the side, slashed her leg out and behind his, then shoved him back hard. He went down like a one-hundred-and-eighty-pound brick onto the massive gym mat, and she was right there on top of him when he landed.

"No one calls me a liar," she whispered, feeling the sweat on his chest soak through her shirt.

"Not unless they want you on top of them," he said.

Dillon's skin went hot, jumpy, and below her waist, the muscles inside her cunt tightened. She brought her hands to the sides of his face, tried to look fierce as he gazed up at her like there was nothing in the world he'd rather do at that moment than fuck the shit out of her.

And she wanted it too. Every damn inch of her screamed for it—for him. And yet she hesitated.

Goddamn it. Why was he different? Why was this any different than fucking anyone else? Yes, she liked him—but she'd liked many others. Why did this seem to mean more?

She felt his cock stir against her pelvis, felt the magnetic pull of his mouth, his neck, his blood.

She drew in a breath. She didn't want him to have this kind of power over her—it wasn't good. In the end—because there would be an end, had to be—no one was going to come out unscathed.

Her expression must've changed, because so did his. From hungry, hot male to all concern all the time.

"What's wrong?" he asked.

She shook her head, to clear it and to get herself back on track. "You," she said. "And Sara. Tell me what happened."

He heaved out a breath, let his head drop back to the mat. "Wasn't Sara."

She inched up his body, so they were face-to-face again. "What do you mean? Who was it, then? The Romans?"

"My mother."

Dillon felt him tense up. She said, "All the way from Minnesota? What's that about? A little vacation to see the family?"

Ice formed in his gaze. The tenseness of a moment ago turned into impenetrable steel. "She came to warn me."

"Warn you about what?"

He wrapped his arms around her and flipped her to her back. He loomed, his gaze warrior hard. "You." He snapped out the word almost like an accusation. "She said the Order knows I'm keeping you."

His eyes were pinned to hers, his tawny hair bracketing his sharply angled face, his now rock-hard cock pressed into the top of her pelvis and his thickly muscled thigh rooted between her legs.

A hum of anxiety moved through Dillon. She didn't like being trapped, feeling trapped. And yet this was Gray. Was she really desperate to get away from him, or was it that fierce accusatory glare he was throwing her way?

She lifted her chin. "She wanted you to turn me in."

He nodded, his expression blank now. She hated that—she needed to be able to read him.

"You going to do it?" she asked, despising herself for the thread of true fear that ran though her voice.

He glanced up, past her. "I would, but we have to leave soon."

It took her a moment to process his answer. And another to recognize the trace of humor behind it. She reached out and grabbed his ass, squeezed the rock-hard globes, then dug her fingers into his flesh. "I'll flash you anywhere you want to go if . . ."

He dropped his head and kissed her—kissed her almost covetously. Then pulled back a fragment and bit her lower lip. "If what?"

Dillon felt breathless, turned on, and for a moment—one brief moment—unconcerned with lying on her back, pinned by this male. She looked up at him. "If we leave Chef Blondie at home."

Gray laughed. "Someday you're going to have to follow through on that jealousy trip you keep riding. But for now, for the next few minutes anyway . . ." He dropped his head again and fed off her lips.

On the third floor of an abandoned warehouse blocks away, Celestine crouched beside a huge picture window and watched the building that housed Gray and the *mutore*. She may have been an emotional *veana* with secrets she didn't want to reveal—and reasons for them that were too complicated to sort through in the seconds her grown *balas* had given her—but she was also a spy. Trained in the art of tracking a subject without being followed.

And tonight her subject had been Gray.

She moved the high-powered lens to each window, hoping for a glimpse of him or the Beast. But the building was locked up pretty tight, shades drawn. It was a good site they'd chosen, right neighborhood too—lots of warehouses, both in use and up for lease.

She sighed. She wasn't looking to take down these Impure warriors or their fight; she just wanted to protect Gray.

She didn't trust *mutore*.

The one she'd known, the one she'd had the unfortunate luck to fall in love with once upon a time, had turned out to be nothing but a demon. Maybe worse than a demon. And his "children" couldn't be that far behind. She wasn't going to have one of his aberrations hurting her son. Even if it meant Gray would never forgive her.

Her mind traveled back to the tunnels below the Romans' house. With all Gray knew now, all that Samuel Kendrick had revealed, odds were Gray wasn't going to forgive her anyway.

She focused the lens on the front door and waited. All she needed was a picture or two, and if the Order was her last resort to put an end to this Beast, she would have what she needed.

"Your flash is different than the other Pureblood we've been with," Uma remarked the moment they touched down in the back parking lot of what used to be a Trenton nightclub. "Smoother."

Dillon rolled her eyes and released the pair. She was way too jacked up from the mutual heat thing she and Gray had been working earlier. And with the quick get-up-and-go combined with the zero-release, she was cranky in the extreme. And it was this chick's fault. Dillon was pretty sure she could've convinced Gray to stay on top of her and play a round of strip and lick, but they had a commitment to meet Blondie here.

"Thank you for flying Pureblood *Veana* Airlines," she muttered. "Please don't come again."

Uma laughed. "You're funny." She glanced at Gray. "She's funny."

"Sidesplitting. Literally," Gray said drily. "Let's go." He nodded to Dillon. "You lead the way, Chuckles."

The parking lot was deader than Dillon, and they crossed over it quickly and headed for the back door. Dillon didn't even check to see if it was locked, just kicked the thing in and walked inside. With a quick heartbeat check, she knew they were alone. Except for the roaches and a few spiders as big as her palm hanging from lines of thin, silky rope in the corners of the room.

"How do you know about this entryway?" Gray asked as they bypassed the bar, a few upended tables, and headed toward the back of the building.

"I heard about it somewhere," she said, ducking down the short hallway and into what must have been the manager's office. "You know, Purebloods talk."

"They talk about where Impures are kept to be castrated?" Uma said, the disgust in her tone unmasked.

"It's not a Pureblood's main concern," Dillon said, shoving a massive desk back toward the wall. "Impures serve the Pureblood communities. They don't need their sex drive to do that."

"Christ, D," Gray uttered blackly.

She hated that tone on him, hated it directed straight at her. "I'm not saying it's right or that I agree with it," she returned defensively. "In fact, I think it's total bullshit and another tool by the Order to control anything and anyone." She pulled back the rug that had lain beneath the desk, and a massive dust cloud shot into the air. "Come on; help me with the trapdoor."

"But you don't push to stop it," Uma said, crouching down, ready.

Dillon glanced up and snarled at the female who thought it was in any way okay to lecture her. "Hey— I'm here tonight, aren't I? That's doing something to stop it."

Gray yanked up the thick trapdoor. "Let's go. We're wasting time." He shot her a fierce look. "We don't have all night to listen to you defend the indefensible."

"I don't need to defend anything, Gray," Dillon said caustically, jumping onto the ladder and beginning her decent. "Now, you on the other hand . . ."

"Christ," he hissed, helping Uma onto the ladder, then jumping on it himself. "This is going to be a long goddamn night."

Uma snorted softly. "You two are like an old mated couple."

"One that continually wants to off each other," Dillon said.

"How much farther?" Gray asked as they jumped down to the dirt floor beneath.

"Just a few floors," Dillon said, flicking on her flashlight and leading them to an elevator. The thing was old, metal, and had strange purple markings on the doors. She pressed the button marked "down."

When the doors opened and they were all inside, Gray said, "How long has this secret passage been here? It's so calculated."

"I have no idea," Dillon returned. Irritation snaked through her veins. How was what the breed and the Order did for kicks suddenly all her fault? If they kept this up, she was going to give them exactly what they seemed to expect from her. Zero help and a whole lot of not-my-problem.

When they hit bottom and the doors opened, all three took their positions. Gray went first. On the alert, his blades out, he searched the long corridor for any sign of life.

"I hear heartbeats, and they're not yours," Dillon said, coming up beside him, Glock in hand. "Maybe a few yards up."

"Remember," Gray reminded them. "Goal is to get as many out as we can without endangering their lives."

"Or ours," Dillon added.

Gray ignored her. "This tunnel seems to drag out farther than we had anticipated," he said, moving quickly down the dark corridor.

"You still think this tunnel comes out between two cages, right?" Uma asked, taking up the rear with two small pistols.

Jogging beside them both, Dillon said, "That's what I remember hearing, but like I told you—it was at a club a hundred years ago, and I haven't made this trip myself. At some point, we'll just have to man up and take it as it comes."

"I see a door up ahead," Gray whispered, and they quickened their pace. "Weapons ready, eyes vigilant."

"There's something," Dillon whispered, her nostrils flaring as she tried to figure out what she was sensing, hearing. Gray had to hear it too. What the hell? "Massive heartbeats . . . Something's wrong—"

But if Gray heard something, he didn't hesitate, his need to rescue driving him to open the door. The sounds of a full-blown riot met their ears, while the intense metallic scent of blood flooded their nostrils.

Gray pulled back, grabbed Uma, motioned for Dillon, and they all moved into the shadows away from the arena. They'd come out between two massive cells just like Dillon's memory had recalled, cells that housed at least fifty Impures each. Hiding behind a stone pylon, they assessed the situation.

"This is out of control," Dillon whispered loudly over the din. "We've got to go back."

"No," Gray said, his gaze watchful.

"Gray, there's no order here—and I'm not talking about the nine idiots who try to rule us all." She nodded to the cells surrounding the Paleo, where males and females were screaming and banging things on the bars caging them.

"Oh God," Uma cried, her eyes wide and horror filled.

Dillon followed her gaze. In the center of the arena, all eight stone tables were occupied with bound and writhing Impures.

"Look at the ground," Uma said.

Like puzzle pieces, ten or so Impures lay at different angles on the ground surrounding the stone tables. They were moaning, crying as though they'd already felt the fangs of the Order.

"What's happened?" Uma said, shaking her head, the noise nearly deafening now. "I've never seen it like this. It's chaos."

"They're speeding up castrations," Gray shouted over the madness with blatant bitterness. "Fucking Order. We need to get to the ones on the table before the Order members return."

Dillon grabbed his arm. "You've lost your mind. You'll be a dead male the moment you step foot in there. You think they're not watching, not waiting for you?"

He turned, his eyes blazing. "I don't care."

She saw the passion burning there, the blind determination. Christ, he wasn't kidding. He would die for this cause. How could he think that was how this war would be won? She had to reach him. "That's not strategy, Gray—that's suicide. You need to think."

Uma laid her hand on his other arm. "I'll go with you."

Dillon fought down her jaguar's growl and held on to her *veana* common sense—because truly, she appeared to be the only one with a functioning brain here. "I'm not watching you die."

He jerked his arm from her, his eyes flashing with a fire Dillon wondered if she'd ever understand. Or ever want to. "Then go and wait for us near the exit."

He turned away from her and took off, down the rest of the corridor, then out of sight, Uma after him. Dillon left the shadows of the pylon and stalked back to the door. Goddamn stupid, motherfucking Impures. This wasn't bravery—this was just plain stupid.

She paced by the door, not ready to walk through it, every second ticking off in her head.

Goddamn it! She couldn't just stand here doing nothing while Gray was being captured or killed. Not happy about it, but her decision made, she whipped around and headed back in the direction of the pylon, but she got only five steps when the pair came running at her with two Impures.

"Go!" Gray called out harshly.

No one spoke as they broke through the door and hauled ass down the tunnel. No one looked at one another as they piled in the elevator and shot upward. It was only when they were out of the metal box and hustling down the second tunnel heading for the club that Gray let loose.

"You just don't get it," he said with deep menace as they crawled up through the trapdoor. "What we're doing here."

"I was just supposed to be your ride," Dillon returned sharply.

"Bullshit." He slammed the trapdoor shut and kicked the rug into place. "You wanted in on this job and you choked."

Dillon glared at him. "Because I didn't want to embark on a suicide mission?"

"We're still alive."

"Then you're damn lucky."

His nostrils flared, Gray glanced down at his hands, then back up at her with eyes frozen over with ire. "Yeah, D. Luck and me? We're tight."

"No pity parties, all right?" Dillon snarled. "Everyone's got one to go to. This was stupid and fruitless. What did you manage? A couple bodies. You could've put together something that would've removed a dozen or more."

"With what army?" he yelled back. "We're just lowly

Impures, remember? And if we can out one or two, we've done something." Gray turned away from her and led the terrified Impures out of the office and through the nightclub. He burst out of the back door and into the cold night air. "You and me." He shook his head at her. "We're from two different sides of the street."

"Try two different worlds," she bit back.

Barely noticing that there were others present, Gray descended on her, his fangs dropping. "You don't care about anyone but yourself."

"Not true and you know it."

"Right. You care about me."

She stuck a finger in his chest. "That's something."

"That's not enough."

Dillon froze, his words moving like ice water through her veins.

"All right," Uma said behind them. "Easy now. Both of you."

Ignoring her, Gray shook his head, his eyes blazing into Dillon's. "I'm such a fucking fool. Thinking there was something there."

"Like what?" Dillon shot back. "A relationship? Do you not know me at all?" She threw up her hands. "I'm the witch in those fairy tales, Gray—not the princess. There's no happily ever after, no Prince Charming, no true mate lover for life coming for me."

"Well, she's right about that."

Both Gray and Dillon whirled to face Uma. The female stood beside both Impures, who looked confused and exhausted and ready to get the hell out of there. She took a step forward, grabbed Gray's hand and rubbed her thumb over the top.

He hissed.

Dillon snarled. "Touch him again and die."

Uma dropped Gray's hand but didn't step back. Her gaze found Dillon's, and she said with complete calm, "Your true mate's not coming for you, *Veana*. Because he's already here." She clicked on her flashlight and positioned it over the top of Gray's hand. "I wondered about this, thought I had seen something within your scars. But tonight I saw it flicker under the lights of the Paleo when you were cutting one of the Impures free."

Both Dillon and Gray looked up, confused.

"You're both such idiots," Uma said, shaking her head. "Look!"

Dillon narrowed her eyes on the skin of his hand. "Oh, shit. The mark."

Gray looked up. "It looks like a jaguar."

Uma snorted. "It looks like Dillon. Now can we get the hell out of here?"

12

Gray couldn't remain still. His mind or his body. He paced in the shadows of the car parked in the lot behind the club and wished for the first time since finding out his true vampire status that he was a Pureblood *paven*. Then he could flash. Like Dillon had a few moments ago. He could take the two Impures and Uma back to the warehouse so they could connect back with family, then get that hardheaded *veana* locked in a room and figure out what he'd just heard. Shit—what he'd just seen.

Cursing, he halted in a panel of cool moonlight and raised his hand into the light. He stared at the mark on top, squinted.

There was no mistaking it now. The outline of the jaguar was clearly stamped into the web of burn scars, even down to the rosette pattern on its fur. How hadn't he seen this lurking beneath all that ravaged skin? Maybe because the mark was the same color as his skin. Maybe because he so rarely looked at his scars—his deformity—at the ever-present reminder of the past? A past that was now called into question by what he'd learned in the Paleo from Samuel.

He ran his thumb over the mark, hissed at the strange sensation that ran through his body. Like feathers one moment and fingernails the next.

Around him, the air seemed to drop ten degrees in temperature, and when he opened his mouth he saw his breath. His pulse kicked up.

He and Dillon—true mates.

The idea was as improbable as it was unfortunate. Yes, he had a thing for Dillon. He wanted Dillon—wanted inside Dillon. But to be bound to her forever? That thought made his blood run as cold as the frigid air he existed within.

Dillon could never be anyone's true mate. She trusted no one. And if Gray was honest with himself, he wasn't completely convinced he could trust her either. After what had just happened in the Paleo—how she'd run in the other direction when lives were on the line. Run away instead of toward him, toward his cause.

That could never be the mate for him. For the leader of the Impure Resistance. If he ever wanted to get serious with a female, she would have to be a true partner, like-minded, someone who would allow him to see all of her, even the shit from her past, the scars that never healed.

There was a sudden flash in the center of the parking lot and Gray looked up. Dillon. As beautiful as ever. As impossible to love as ever. His heart stuttered, then stalled. Something was wrong. Her eyes were wide and she was running—balls out—toward him.

"We have to go now!" she shouted.

"What the hell—"

Gray heard the sound of another flash. Then another. *Pop. Pop.* Instinct gripped him and he leaped onto the hood of the car in front of him. Drawing out his blades, he dropped into fighting stance.

"No!" Dillon screamed. In one lithe movement, she jumped up on the hood of the car to meet him and wrapped her arms around his waist just as two Pureblood males came barreling toward them.

Gray drew back and sent both knives straight at their heads.

The moment steel entered skull, Gray and Dillon flashed away.

The Order sat at their long table in their desert reality presiding over a case regarding the thievery of several Pureblood homesteads within a large *credenti* in Ann Arbor, Michigan. So when Feeyan raised her head and declared, "Damn those fools! We will see each one laid out in the sun and dried until they are nothing but dust!" both Pureblood *veana*s who stood before the table gasped, one clutching her neck, the other rendered completely immobile with panic.

Feeyan sneered at them. "I do not speak of you." She sniffed. "Although the crimes with which you have been accused certainly could make you eligible for such a fate."

One of the *veana*s began to cry. Feeyan lifted her

hand in one smooth arching movement, blocking the Pureblood *veana*s from hearing her next words.

"We have failed, Order members."

The *paven* to her right looked confused. "The trap we set at the Paleo was a success, was it not? The *mutore* accompanied Gray Donohue to the raid, and two of the Impures we're taken."

Her nostrils flared as she pressed her bride-white hair behind her shoulders. "Yes, but when the *mutore* flashed them back to the Impure Resistance safe house, our guards could not get ahold of her mid-flight. Only when she flashed back alone, and even then she fought them off like a wildcat. They could not contain her, and she and Gray Donohue got away."

Several members of the Order released sounds of irritation, even a call for severe punishment against the guards.

Feeyan raised her chin. "They have already been destroyed."

The *paven* beside her nodded, pleased. "You have made quick work with their lives, Feeyan. That is justice."

For a moment Feeyan wrestled with the idea of telling the true cause of the guards' deaths, but she knew it would come out eventually, and she wouldn't want to look like a liar and a braggart when it did. Especially when she was seeking the leadership position within the Order.

"Gray Donohue killed the guards," she stated simply, then took in the fierce sounds from each member of the Order. "We must contact Celestine Donohue again," she said over the din. "Press her further. We will have the location of the Impure Resistance headquarters and her help with bringing in her son, or she will be joining these two simpering, thieving Purebloods before us in a cell at Mondrar."

Before any member had the chance to respond, she raised her hand and swept it across in a rainbow curve, then trained her eyes on the lawbreakers before her.

Dillon was no fool. She wasn't about to let anyone take her out mid-flight. She didn't flash and remain at one location for more than a few seconds. Instead she quick-flashed from one place to the next—one country, one state, one city to the next, mountaintop, Disneyland, desert cave, ocean liner. It was manic, a total brain seizure, and when she finally touched down near the river in Eastern Vermont where her Beast brothers had found her, she dropped like a stone against the very maple tree she'd tried to hide within.

Her head spinning, she squinted up at Gray, at the blur of him as he walked toward her, seemingly unfazed.

"Why aren't you puking?" she uttered, holding her head steady.

"When you deal with hundreds of voices and conversations in your head every minute of the day, you learn how to stabilize." He crouched down beside her, utterly calm, collected, and clear. "Just breathe for a few seconds, *Veana*."

Dillon dropped her head back against the tree trunk and inhaled deeply through her nostrils until the spinning stopped and the stars overhead stuck in their proper places.

"What the hell happened, D?" His tone was tense, intense and demanding.

She swallowed, her throat ached. "They found me mid-flash."

"Who? Those Purebloods I lost my blades to back there?"

Her gaze shot to his. "You took them down?"

"Fucking right, I took them down. They're bleeding out on the blacktop behind the club."

"Oh good," she breathed, feeling relieved, though far from secure. "At least we weren't followed."

As Gray stared at her, his mind working the questions behind his eyes, the sounds of the night, of the forest, of the river began to swell. "You gotta give me something here, D," Gray said. "Something to fill in the blanks, a reason why were not in the Bronx headquarters right now. Who were those *pavens*?"

A problem. A big one that would no doubt be part of her present and future. "Sent by the Order, I think. They tried to lock on and capture me mid-flight."

Gray's face paled. "Before or after you dropped the Impures?"

The question bothered her more than she wanted to admit. He cared deeply about those Impures, and if his intense, scrutinizing gaze were anything to go by, he cared about them more than her.

She arched one brow. "After."

"Shit," he breathed, a sigh of relief.

She wanted to punch him. Actually, she wanted to bite him, then punch him.

"How do you think those Pureblood pirates knew where you were?" Gray asked, all business now that his kind were back home safe and sound. "How to get to you at the exact moment?"

"The Order must be able to track the flashes of Purebloods," she said, sitting up.

"Then we can no longer flash."

She nodded. She'd been the thinking the same thing. "That's going to be a problem if we ever want to leave here."

He glanced around at the river, the dark forest. "Do you know where we are?"

"Vermont."

He stood. "Too bad we don't have a cell. We could've called the Romans for a ride." He eyed her. "Or maybe not. If you're being tracked, I think there's only one way of getting home. On foot."

"Getting home?" she repeated, her eyes narrowing, her body tensing. She'd been exhausted a moment ago, but now, with what Gray had just said, she felt a second wind coming on.

And it wasn't blowing her back to New York City.

"We can rest for a while," he said, his gaze moving to the river. "Then we should get going."

She shook her head. "Are you insane?"

His gaze swept over her. "Maybe. But not about this. I have to make sure the Impures are all right and the warriors are warned."

She leaned forward. "The Order doesn't know anything about the Impures or the safe house." She lifted her hands. "They want me. And if I'm not there, there's nothing to go after."

"You're a smart *veana*, Dillon. Think." He crossed his arms, the moonlight falling over his shoulder like a shroud. "The Order will do whatever it takes to find out where you are. They'll question, torture, or kill the Impures who knew you were staying there."

"All the more reason to stay lost."

"For you maybe, but not for me. I need to be there to help them and fight, if that's what it takes."

She stared at him. "You really love walking into certain death and/or imprisonment, don't you?"

He didn't answer that. "I won't allow anything to happen to them—or to you," he said resolutely. "Rest. We leave as soon as it's light."

When he walked away, headed down to the river, Dillon dropped back against the tree trunk again. She couldn't believe it. He wanted her to go back to the very place where the Order would be looking for her. He didn't care if she was captured—he only cared if the Impures were. Frustration screamed through her. She should've just taken off on her own instead of flashing back to him. She wasn't a priority to him—even with the mark of her jaguar riding his hand.

The mark neither one of them had said anything about.

13

"After we are finished here, will you show me where you lived?" Erion asked as they moved down the uneven cobblestone street, lit only by the early-evening moonlight.

"It's not much of anything to look at," Nicholas told him, his gaze searching for their final destination.

"Perhaps not, but it is something of value to me," Erion returned, veering to the right, toward an ancient furnishings shop. "Here we are."

A small bell jingled over the shop door as Erion entered, Nicholas behind him. Lycos and Phane had broken off from the group a few hours ago and had headed to Norway on a lead they'd received from a Pureblood who had worked as a guard in Cruen's laboratory, while Erion and Nicholas had flashed on to this small French village to follow up on a rumor a member of the international sect of the Eyes had sold them for ten grand. But being in France, so close to where he'd been born, Erion was finding it difficult to remain focused on their task.

He moved through the deserted shop. "I want to see where my mother gave birth to me."

"To us," Nicholas amended.

Glancing over his shoulder, Erion saw that his twin brother wore a cautious smile. "Us. Yes." He nodded. "One who she kept inside in a cradle and the other who she brought outside and disposed of."

"Exactly," Nicholas said, his eyes now sympathetic. "Not kind memories, Brother. So why would you want to revisit them?"

Erion never got the chance the answer—and even if he had, he wasn't sure what that answer would have been. Out of the shadows, a man—no, a *paven*—came toward them. He was short, thin, and very old, deep lines carved into his tired, suspicious features. He was no doubt a vampire, and yet he had aged like a human.

"How can I help?" the male asked in gruff French.

Nicholas spoke first, utilizing his own keen mastery of the language. "Are you Raine?"

The male's brown eyes narrowed, and his jaw twitched. "Perhaps I am and perhaps I am not."

"We seek information and will pay well for it," Erion said, his own grasp of French not nearly as impressive as his twin's.

"I do not sell information here," he said, his entire body scenting of anxiety. "I sell furnishings. If that is not something you are interested in, then I suggest—"

Nicholas lowered his voice. "We seek Cruen."

The scent of anxiety was quickly replaced with the scent of fear. "Don't know who or what that is," he said quickly, turning around and scuttling back behind his long wooden desk. "I am about to close for the night, so if you don't mind—"

"We have heard that you may know this *paven*," Nicholas pressed, moving closer to the desk. His voice dropped to a whisper, though there was no one inside the shop but them. "That you may be related to this *paven*."

Raine's gaze was downcast as he pretended to be focused on his ledger, but his hand shook as he held his pencil. "I am sorry. There is nothing I can do for you. Good day to you now."

Erion's gaze narrowed on the *paven*'s hand. On his fingers, his nails. There was something his peripheral vision had picked up on. What was it— Suddenly, a low, slow growl leaked from his throat, and it caused the old *paven* to look up.

Erion's nostrils flared with understanding as he saw the *paven*'s eyes, saw the quick shift from *paven* to Beast.

His own Beast perfectly in control, Erion flashed the *paven* a quick look at his demon self. Instinctually, Raine gripped the counter, claws digging into the wood.

"A *mutore* knows a *mutore*, monsieur," Erion said softly.

The *paven* leaned forward. "And a relation of a mad *paven* knows one of his many *mutore* children."

Nicholas cursed. "You knew."

The *paven* sniffed. "From the moment you walked through that door. But there is still nothing I can offer you."

"What about what we can offer you?" Nicholas said with calm, cool ease.

"What does that mean?" Raine asked with an air of apathy—though Erion could see the *paven*'s almost desperate curiosity leaking through. "I don't want your money or your silence. I have remained in the shadows for a long time—and will continue to do so."

"It appears as though your time is running out," Erion remarked, his gaze trained on the male's aged features.

Raine nodded, said begrudgingly, "Yes. We seem to age faster than a normal Pureblood, and more painfully."

"Why?" Nicholas asked.

"Our line was used as an experiment," Raine explained. "We were never meant to breed with another race."

"Only to breed with one another?"

"Yes."

"What line are you talking about?" Erion pressed, his skin prickling.

"The shifter," Raine said in a hushed whisper. "The animal within. It is how we all began—"

"How your brother began," Nicholas said quickly.

Raine gave a small gasp, as though he'd never expected them to know this. "No. He is not my brother. Whoever gave you that information was wrong."

"But you are related," Nicholas said.

The *paven*'s mouth thinned. "He is my uncle. He forced one of those Breeding Males he created onto my mother. She was a true shifter." His shoulders sagged.

"But you look so much older . . ." Nicholas shook his head.

Raine nodded sadly. "I told you. It was not meant to

be. In a way, the Order is right about that. About the *mutores*." His eyes shifted to Erion. "You will know. And if you are truly unfortunate, you will someday be faced with the horror of leaving your family, your mate, and your *balas* before you have even had a chance to watch them grow."

Nicholas turned to Erion, lifted his brow. Erion could almost hear his twin's thoughts. Family, *balas*— Erion hadn't embraced either, and according to this *paven* that was a good thing. Jesus, this *paven* . . . He could barely swallow all that Raine had just offered him. There was a true shifter lineage, a breed unto itself—and Cruen had decided to mess with it. For what? His master race? Or were the *mutore* exactly what the Order, the Purebloods, the vampire breed had always believed them to be?

A mistake.

"What if we could offer you that?" Nicholas said, turning back to face Raine. "A life extended."

The *paven* sniffed, shook his head. "A magical cure? If there was such a thing, I would know of it."

"Because your uncle would have offered it to you?" Erion said. "You truly think there is some kind of family loyalty within that monster?"

The *mutore* in Raine hissed, his reptile eyes blinking furiously, his body sagging with misery.

"We believe Cruen may have many treatments and antidotes in his possession," Nicholas said. "If you help us find him, if he has this elixir, we will bring it to you."

"Why should I trust you?" Raine asked bitterly.

Erion shook his head. "You shouldn't." Then he

caught and held the *paven's* gaze. "But what choice do you have? What choice do any of us who managed to live past our birth have?"

She was running through the woods, past barren trees—toward something. Within her, she knew it was something vital and hopeful, something that would give her peace at long last. Tears streaked down her face, her jaguar's face, soaking the golden fur. She wanted it so desperately. She could taste the sweet essence of happiness, and she believed herself so close to it that she quickened her pace.

Down a hill she ran, darting to the right to follow the river. It rushed quickly, over stones and into deep pools, where small fish and frogs gathered. Just a little farther, beneath that footbridge.

There it was. Salvation. Rebirth.

And then suddenly the scene shifted—both in structure and in feeling—and she was no longer running toward her freedom, but away from certain capture.

Her muscles twitched in panic, and she felt a bullet hit the back of her skull. She plunged into the river. Rolling over and over in the current, she tried to dig it out, but it was no use. She wasn't meant to live, to taste that sweet essence of happiness she'd scented earlier. This was her destiny—to lose herself beneath the water.

"Dillon! Wake up."

Her eyes opened and she gasped at the sudden cold invading her senses. All around her, the world was a moon-coated black, not the stark sunlight that had a moment ago been her reality.

She glanced around, down. She was standing in the river.

"Oh God," she uttered as the icy water slapped at her thighs.

"What was that?"

Gray. She looked up. Had he been there the whole time? Why hadn't she seen him? He was staring at her like she was crazy. And no doubt he was right. She wobbled and stepped back against a slippery stone.

Gray put his hands on her shoulders, holding her steady in the heavy current. "Are you all right?"

She forced herself to nod. "It's nothing. Just a nightmare."

His eyes blazed with the heat of wanting more, wanting to push her for answers that he knew she'd always refuse him. Then he bent down and lifted her into his arms.

"Let's get you to shore," he said as river water dripped from her pant legs. "Get you dry."

Dillon's first instinct was to wriggle out of his grasp, remind him—and herself—that she was fine and could walk on her own. That she needed no one and nothing. But the jaguar inside of her curled into him, into his heat and the steady rhythm of his heart.

Gray placed her beside the tree that had held her weight earlier and started removing her boots and socks. Her teeth chattering, she watched him. Was this what she wanted? she asked herself. A male who took care of her when she was lost and when she'd lost it for a moment? Was this a good idea? With how different they were, how impossible was it for them to find common ground?

Fooling around—fucking around—that was one thing. That she could easily walk away from. She knew how to do that, manage that kind of "relationship." This familiarity, this unwise intimacy that had grown between them was a problem, especially when she let him down—especially when she was planning to leave him.

"I'll go as far as the New York State border," she blurted out. Timing had never been her strong suit, but what was the point? Neither one of them believed this was a long-term situation.

Gray didn't look up. Instead he took her feet in his hands and started to rub them. "And then what?"

She tried not to sigh at the warmth of his hands and the pressure of his strokes. "I'll go my own way."

His hands continued their work, but his gaze lifted to meet hers. "Sounds about right."

Goddamn it, she hated this pseudo-relationship bullshit. "You're not going to make me feel guilty."

Heat flared in his gaze. Beneath that tousled bed-head he was working, he looked far too sexy for his own good. "I've never been able to make you feel anything, D."

"Well, we both know that's not true."

"I'm not talking about getting off here. I'm talking about the real shit—the down-deep, connecting, understanding shit."

She sniffed. So was she. He'd made her feel all of those things, but she wasn't about to admit it. "Listen, Gray, this isn't my fight. I get what you're doing and I respect it."

His fingers continued to work her soles—his charcoal gaze continued to work her insides.

"But I'm not going back into that fray just to get captured or killed," she continued. "Though you seem to be asking it of me pretty often lately."

The heat in his gaze changed to anger. "You really think I'd allow you to get taken or hurt by the Order? Do you really think so little of me?"

There used to be a time when she could look at this male's face and think only of having it beneath her own, or turned to the side as she bit into his neck and drank from him, or strained with passion as she rode him hard until he exploded. But things had changed since that night he'd rescued her and her jaguar from the senator and his thugs, from near death and discovery on the abandoned streets of that small town in Maine, all that time he'd spent trying to reach her in her massively depressed state. When she looked at Gray Donohue now, she saw a male she wanted at her side as well as beneath her, a male she wanted to listen to and be advised by, a male she might even fight her own kind for—a male she wanted to allow herself to trust.

The problem was, trust in her world equaled abuse and emotional ruin. And there wasn't much left of her to ruin anymore . . .

"What I think," she began, forcing an edge to her tone as she jerked her feet away from his grasp and underneath herself where they belonged, "is that the Impure Resistance is your number-one priority."

He didn't refute that. "And what is your number-one priority, D?" His brow lifted. "You?"

A sudden wind blew around them, but it didn't take away her feelings of defensiveness. "Why shouldn't it be? I'm the cause I fight for. I'm the one and only member."

He shook his head, released a bitter chuckle. "Don't go the poor Dillon route. Doesn't work on you."

"Listen, *Impure*," she said through gritted teeth, a heavy stress on the latter word.

"I'm not going to follow behind you like a little lost puppy dog because you happen to have some wavy lines on your hand that have been misconstrued as a true mate mark." It was the first time either one of them had mentioned it, and maybe it shouldn't have been tossed out so crassly. But Dillon was over it. She was cutting through the bullshit and getting to the true issue that hung between them.

Gray's entire being changed. The calm, cool male with hands that had offered pleasure and comfort a moment ago turned into a ferocious beast who couldn't be contained. "Wavy lines?" he raged, ratcheting his hand up and into her face. "Are you fucking kidding me?"

"Put your hand down," she snapped.

"Make me," he snarled back.

Infuriation mingled with the scent of his skin and Dillon lost control over herself for a moment. She bared her teeth and bit him. Her fangs. Right into the mark.

Gray cursed, yanked back his hand, and grabbed her. His eyes were fierce as he hauled her onto his lap. "You'd better blow on that."

"No," she spat back. "I like you bloody. And so does my cat."

"You like me every goddamn way, just like I like you. That's why we have this problem. That's why we can't seem to let go of each other." He felt his cock straining against his jeans, straining to get to her. He held up his bloody hand, the jaguar mark only partly hidden. "And this has got to be the reason. Otherwise I'm a total pathetic idiot who loves to keep ramming his head up against a brick wall."

"Am I supposed to be the brick wall in this scenario?" she hissed.

His nostrils flared as he stared into her eyes. He breathed in and out like a bull, and then suddenly his ire dissipated and his devastatingly beautiful eyes closed. When he opened them again, they hummed with melancholy. "No. You're what's on the other side of that wall, baby."

Jeez. Dillon let her shoulders fall, out of fight for a moment. "I am a *mutore*, Gray. There is no mating. Genetics pretty much ruled out my happily ever after."

"As if you ever wanted a happily ever after." He shook his head. "You're the only one who stands in the way of that happiness, D."

Her jaw tightened, but she felt devoid of fight in that moment. "You think you know me so well."

"I do," he said, wrapping his arms around her waist even as he looked miserable. "I wish I didn't. I wish I didn't know you at all. You make life suck. You make life impossible."

Inside herself, deep down, where the last dregs of good remained, an ache pulsed. Maybe because those words hadn't been said in anger, but in regret. Maybe because she didn't have the heart to keep telling him what he just wouldn't hear—wouldn't accept. God, she wanted to shout at him and pull away. That would feel like her, feel familiar. But the truth was, she felt safe and comforted in his arms—even if that feeling came with his disappointment in what could never be.

"Why are you like this?" His eyes claimed her then, searched hers for that bit of good she couldn't ever let him see. "Really. Why are you—"

"Such a bitch?" She smiled.

He didn't. Instead he gripped her tighter, as if she might slither away as all snakes do. "No. Why are you so tormented, so constantly miserable in your own skin—whichever one that may be?"

Dillon's smile faltered.

"Why are you having nightmares and refusing to let anyone get close to you?" he continued. "Why are you fucking anything that moves, but have no interest in making love to someone who'll stay? There's got to be a reason." His mouth was so close to hers. "How long have you been this way?"

"Forever," she bit out.

He shook his head. "I don't think so."

Her protective shell coiled around her. "Are you going to read me now, Kreskin?"

"Read you, your skin, maybe your blood." He lifted his chin and she saw his fangs drop. "Let's go back in time, D. Let's see what's really there."

Panic swarmed her like a thousand angry bees and she pressed back. "No! You promised me."

Gray held her tightly. Breathing heavily, he stared at her. Then, as if on cue, the sky began to change all around them—black dome to a sea of gray-blue etched with pink.

"Saved by the dawn," he said, his fangs slowly retracting, his hold too, his eyes once again simmering with regret.

As she scrambled off his lap, Dillon felt anything but saved. It was as if she were being buried, this part of herself she'd relied on for so long. The part she always thought was her true self. The bitch, the unfeeling *veana*. But maybe it was the cat who was pushing that Dillon aside.

Dillon grabbed her boots and tugged them on. She knew that part of her would be able to run from Gray when they hit the border, but she wasn't so sure about her cat—the jaguar that was at this very moment scratching to get out and get at him.

The hunger of an Impure was an odd one. You could live consuming only food forever, but once you decided to taste blood—and more important, the blood of someone you desire—well, you begin to crave both. And at times, the hunger for blood will be an even stronger need.

As the day wore on, and they walked mile after mile toward their destination, Gray's hunger intensified. He knew he would need to consume something soon, and as they'd followed the river, it might very well need to be fish.

He fucking hated fish.

"You need me to carry you?" Dillon asked, stopping when he did, giving him a mocking expression.

"If I did, would you?"

"No. Not me." She grinned. "But the jaguar might."

"Good," he said. "I like her best anyway."

It was quick and gone in an instant, but Gray saw the sting of his words within her gaze. It surprised him, her sensitivity sometimes. Wouldn't that kind of reaction come from deep care, both about the other person and what they thought of you? She was such a damn mystery, all she kept hidden inside that mind of hers— all he couldn't hear, couldn't crack.

"So, what's the problem?" she asked, placing her foot on a tree stump, pretending to get comfortable. "You need to take a leak or something?" She tossed him a mock look of understanding. "Don't worry. I won't look over your shoulder."

He shook his head, chuckled softly. "You're so damn classy, D." And always covering your true thoughts and feelings with a fresh coat of humor. But how long before that coat wore out . . . Shit, it seemed to be fraying already.

He bent down, grabbed a couple of sticks.

"What are you doing?" she asked.

"Looking for a pole."

"Really?" she purred. "I'd say you have a mighty fine one already."

"Fishing pole," he amended drily. And sex—she used that too. Thing was, he wasn't about to walk away from that offer. Ever. He wouldn't allow it, and neither would that thing on the back of his hand that hummed her name even now.

She mistook the depraved gleam in his eyes for needing to eat. "You're hungry."

"I am an Impure, lest you forget."

"And lest you forget, I have blood on tap. Today's

special is Veinilla Spice." She smiled and wiggled her eyebrows. "Get it?"

Yeah, he got it. The joke, the cover-up, the offer, the deflection. "I'll stick with fish."

She shrugged. "Suit yourself." She sat down on the bank. "What are you going to use for a hook? Or are you planning on hitting them over the head with that smooth, long pole of yours?"

His cock twitched. Traitorous bastard. He pulled his shoelace loose, tied it around the pole. Then he picked at the small silver grommet that circumvented the lace hole. He slipped the lace through the hole and tied it off. With quick fingers, he worked the silver circle back and forth until the one side broke, then pressed one side back until the other resembled a thick hook.

"Not bad," she said.

He glanced up into those cocky hazel eyes. "You sound surprised."

She shook her head. "Impressed. But you've always been good with your hands."

"You going to keep flirting with me?"

She shrugged. "It's harmless."

He dropped the hook in the water and turned away. She just didn't get it—how what she said, did, implied, and bitched about was anything but harmless. It affected the shit out of him. He'd thought once upon time that he could save her, rescue her from whatever reel-from-hell played in her mind, whatever was trying to yank her back into the past—but he was starting to wonder if she was a lost cause.

What did that fortune cookie say last time he ate

Chinese? *No one can walk backward into the future.* Dillon had to want to move forward. He wasn't going to push her. Not anymore.

"How long do you think this is going to take?" she asked. "Like ballpark. Twenty minutes?"

He couldn't help the grin that touched his lips. How long would it take? "No idea. Maybe you could go gather some wood. I'm going to need to build a fire so I can cook this thing."

She made a sound that resembled a small explosion. "Will you just have some blood? It's way faster and less work."

He looked directly at her. "No, it's not."

She growled at him.

Or he thought it was her. Until she uttered the word "Shit" and began to back up from the river, her eyes wide with fear.

Gray turned and spotted a large shape on the bank across the water. His skin jerked and he eased his pole to the ground.

"Don't move," he whispered, knowing exactly what that shape was. "And don't make eye contact."

"Can't. Help. It."

Gasping for air, Dillon began to shift into her jaguar state, and Gray knew this wasn't going to end well. Sensing danger, a threat, the bear cocked its head and sniffed the air. With one massive growl, the black bundle of fur, teeth, and claws came barreling out of the woods toward them.

It had its front paws in the water when Dillon's jaguar attacked. She jumped on the bear's back and tried to sink her teeth in its neck. It was a crash of fur and fury, and at first, Dillon seemed to have the upper hand. But the bear quickly recovered and shook her off, then started pounding on her cat's head.

Adrenaline rushed through Gray's veins. He looked around for anything he could use as a weapon. Goddamn blades still rooted in the heads of those Purebloods. Shit. What was he going to use? He stooped and grabbed some rocks. He started chucking them at the bear's body—anything to distract it. And for a moment it did. Then Dillon's jaguar reared up and ripped into the side of the bear with her teeth and claws. Furious, the massive black bear howled and slapped her back. With a yelp, the jaguar went flying a few feet, landing on a rock, still and bleeding.

The sound that erupted from Gray as he saw her go down made the bear freeze. Gray moved based on instinct and possessiveness, because no sensible Impure would've taken on a snarling black bear if they'd wanted to get out of the situation alive.

As the scent of Dillon's blood wafted into his nostrils, Gray let loose a series of terrible howls, and going completely mad, he took off. Fangs down and flashing, he ran at top speed toward the bear, no care for his own life.

Only for hers.

14

Lucy Roman was the perfect *balas*. She was soft, sweet, and scented of heaven, and as Sara cradled her in her arms and rocked her slow and steady, she wondered what her own little bundle would look like, sound like, smell like.

It would be only seven months until she knew, but that seemed like a lifetime away.

Especially when she hadn't had the guts to tell the baby's father yet.

"You look good with her. Natural."

Sara glanced up and smiled at Bronwyn as the dark-haired beauty came out of the bathroom, showered and looking as radiant as ever.

"I can take her if it's getting to be too much," Bronwyn said.

"No," Sara assured her. "I love it. She's sweet. You're so lucky."

Brushing out her wet hair, Bronwyn sat on the edge of the bed. "I know. Times have changed—and become wonderful." She shook her head. "Seems like yesterday I was going into labor, scared, totally alone."

"Not totally alone," Sara reminded her with a gentle smile.

A smile Bronwyn returned. "I didn't mean that. I was incredibly thankful you were there. I just mean without Lucian seeing . . ."

"I know. I get it." And she truly did.

"He'll be there for the next one though," Bronwyn said, placing her brush down on the bed.

Sara's eyes widened. "You're not . . ."

Bron laughed. "No! God, no. Not now. But someday, I hope. And he'll be there." Her eyes held a gentle melancholy. "I know it really bothers him that he wasn't there to see her enter the world."

Maybe it was the smell of the baby or the intimacy of the conversation; maybe it was the sad fact that after overhearing Gray and their mother earlier, Sara felt more alone and in need of a friend than she ever had before. Suddenly she found herself blurting out her secret. "I'm pregnant."

"What?" Bron stared at her; then a brilliant smile crossed her face. "Oh my goodness, Sara. Congratulations!"

"Thanks." God, it felt good to say it out loud, tell someone.

"Alexander must be over the moon."

And then again, maybe not. Sara's heart dipped. "I haven't told him."

"What? Why?"

She sighed, shook her head. "I want to tell him. I want to tell him so badly, but . . ."

Bronwyn leaned forward. "What's wrong?"

Yes, what was wrong? She struggled for the right words. "I think I'm afraid he won't be excited about it."

"Oh, Sara, that's impossible," Bronwyn assured her.

Her heart clenched. Her eyes lifted to meet her sister-in-law's. "He didn't want to be a father. With how he was brought up, he's afraid. He agreed to try, but . . . I don't know . . ." She stilled at Bronwyn's concerned gaze. "The thing is, I don't want him to feel like Luca and regret not seeing his *balas* enter the world."

Bronwyn smiled gently. "Look at the males we have chosen, my sister. Look where they've come from and what they've endured. It is little wonder they feel as they do and fear as they do."

The bedroom door shot open then, and decked out in fighting gear, looking fierce and deadly, his left eye black-and-blue from his practice bout with Alexander earlier, Lucian entered. First he went to his *veana* and planted a devilishly passionate kiss on her mouth; then he lifted his head and sniffed the air.

"Where is my little bloodsucker?" he snarled playfully.

"Lucian," Bronwyn chided, though her eyes were lit with overwhelming love. "You know I don't like when you call her that."

He growled and kissed her again. "She loves it, *Veana*. Laughs every bloody time." He turned toward Sara, spotted the wee babe in her arms, and grinned. "Damn fine specimen of a she-*balas*, isn't she, Doc?"

Sara grinned and repeated, "Damn fine."

Bronwyn rolled her eyes. "Don't encourage him, my sister."

"Not as beautiful as her mama, but close." Lucian scooped up the baby from Sara's arms and started for the door.

Bronwyn called after him, "Where are you taking her?"

"Helo believes he saw some moths by the light at the back door. I want to show her before we head out to hunt and decapitate that bastard Cruen."

Bronwyn shook her head as he left the room. "Lovely."

Sara laughed, and after a moment Bronwyn joined in.

"So you see," Bronwyn said, her eyes bright. "They may start out as *paven*s who believe themselves incapable of fatherhood. But they soon become the very ones who rush in to get their wee beloveds just to show them a creepy white bug in the lamplight."

When Dillon woke, she knew she was in her jaguar state, but she had no idea what cage she had ended up in this time. She lifted her head, narrowed her eyes at the stone surrounding her and at the condensation dripping down the boulder to her right. Then the ground moved beneath her, and she realized she was resting on someone's lap. Gray's lap.

She sat up, and after a moment of dizziness, took in the cave that sheltered them and the small curved doorway several feet away that opened to the black woods outside.

"What happened?" she asked, her head heavy.

"The bear," Gray said. "Do you remember?"

Her mind shuffled through thoughts and images. "A bear came out of the woods . . . attacked us . . ."

"Technically, you attacked it first."

She turned, narrowed her cat eyes on him. "You know how much I love it when you get technical."

One tawny eyebrow lifted. "Gets you hot?"

"It's like an oven inside here, baby," she growled back.

He smiled, but his gray eyes moved over her, every inch of her fur, her muzzle, as though he were looking for anything out of place. It was so strange to have a male, have anyone, look at her jaguar and see the *veana* inside. Know the *veana* inside.

"Are you all right?" he asked, the humor no longer apparent in his gaze. "That animal was pretty brutal."

"Which animal?" she asked, trying to bring it back. "Me or the bear?"

He laughed softly. And she felt better.

"Anything broken?" he asked. "Eyesight okay? Memories intact?"

She nodded. She was okay, nothing felt broken. Maybe just a little banged up. And the memories, well, they would always remain intact no matter what massive creature tried to shake them out of her.

"A good night's rest will help," he said. "We'll head out first thing in the morning."

She nodded, then noticed the drawn look on his face. "You didn't get any fish."

He shook his head. "I'm fine."

"No, you're not," she said with sudden determination. He had helped her, fought for her, taken care of her.

"You're hungry and you'll have my blood." She closed her eyes and concentrated on shifting back to a *veana*.

"I don't think that's a good idea," he said.

"Why not?"

"I don't think we should get any more bonded than we already are."

Her eyes opened. Not because of what he'd said, but because of something she felt—or didn't feel. That easy shift she'd been enjoying lately was gone, access denied. Panic bubbled within her.

Gray's eyes narrowed on her. "What is it?"

She didn't answer; she couldn't. She closed her eyes and again attempted to shift. Her breathing ticked away the seconds. Why was this happening? Her shift had been fixed. And one good swipe from a bear and she was—what? Locked up tight again. Fucking bear. Her eyes shot open and she jumped to all fours, into fighting stance. She was going hunting right now. Vengeance and a good meal for her Impure male here, and if she was lucky the battle would set her shift to rights again.

"Dillon."

Gray's harsh tone made her pause. She turned to look at him. And the moment she did, all the fight inside her dissolved.

He sat on his very fine ass before her, his handsome face a mask of sharp angles, his mouth parted and ready to speak. "You can't shift back, can you?" he said.

Dillon felt tears behind her cat's eyes, but there was no way she was allowing them to fall. She wouldn't give him that, give anyone that. She lifted her massive head and said plainly, "I need you."

His eyes darkened to near charcoal and the cords of muscle in his neck bulged. "With what?"

"I need your hands on my fur. Again."

Gray sat there for a moment, surrounded by the stillness of the rock cave; in the distance, the many sounds of the night seeped into their cozy space. She wondered if he was going to deny her, allow her to remain as an animal—use it to keep her by his side as he returned to New York City.

But then he put his hand on her back, and Dillon forgot everything and just sighed with relief. The heat his touch provided was instantaneous. Standing before him like a blue ribbon feline, she purred as he stroked her from head to nape, shoulders to tail. Again and again, back and forth, down each leg until she felt herself shifting.

Her mind spun with questions and she tried to block them out, but it was impossible. What did this mean? she wondered as delicious shivers broke out on each square inch of skin his hands came in contact with. Was she forever stuck in this cycle? Jaguar to *veana*, *veana* to jaguar? And would she always need this male to use his damaged and utterly wonderful hands to bring her back to vampire life?

No answers came, only more questions. And she didn't have time for them. The fur was gone and she was all feeling. *Veana* once again, naked and on all fours in front of this hungry-eyed male.

"You're no longer a Beast," he said, his hand stilling on her lower back.

She arched and purred. "Yes, I am."

His curse echoed throughout the cave. "Oh, my impossible, irresistible kitty cat," he whispered, his tone heady with lust. "There is nothing I enjoy more than stroking you. Inside and out. If that's what you want."

His words made her skin tighten, made her breasts tingle, made her insides quake. Yes, she wanted him to touch her. Yes, she wanted him inside of her. But she was afraid of how badly she wanted it—the big, bad, biting jaguar was really just a helpless kitten crying out for affection and warmth.

"Tell me," he said, moving his hand from her lower back down the curve of her buttocks.

"Tell you what?"

"If this is what you want."

She hissed. "Why? Why do I have to say anything?"

"Because it's good for you." He gave her backside a gentle slap. "You need to learn that both taking and giving are important in a relationship."

Dillon let her head drop. "We don't have a relationship." Her cunt was on fire, leaking moisture. "We have sex."

"Bullshit." Gray gave her another slap on the ass. "You won't remain quiet on this subject, not when you have so much to say." Again, he spanked her—harder this time. "Your body is speaking for you, D. Christ, my palm is nearly soaked."

He gave her two hard slaps, and she cried out in ecstasy, her clit aching with sharp swirls of heat. *Don't stop*, she wanted to scream at him. *Keep at it—keep at it until I burst. Because I will. Someday I won't be able to keep it all locked inside.*

But the words would not release from her throat. What was wrong with her? Why couldn't she breathe, speak, beg? It didn't make her weak, goddamn it. It didn't make him all-powerful either . . .

She shook her head because everything inside her warned her that giving in to him and to the pleasure of his touch would make him just that.

A power over her.

His other hand tunneled beneath her belly and moved up until he cupped her breast. "Still nothing to say to me, D?" he whispered as he began to play with her nipple. Light, teasing strokes as his other hand held firm, his fingers splayed on her tender buttocks.

She released a breath, nearly whimpered. "What do you want?"

"I want to hear you cry out, say what you want from me and where you want my hands to go. You're going to be a part of this or it's not going happen." He moved his hand down her ass, one finger slipping between her cheeks and sliding down the damp pathway to the opening of her body. "I want to hear you say that this cunt I'm playing with is mine. That the hand tunneling through your slick and delectably hot lips, the hand hovering at the swollen and so-goddamn-pink entrance to your body bares the mark of your jaguar."

She couldn't think, couldn't reason. Her mind swarmed with warning, but her body refused to listen. His fingers played with her nipple, tugging, making her skin tight around her muscles while his hand circled the opening to her pussy.

"I'm waiting, D," he said, his voice sounding strained. "And it's not an easy thing to do. Not when I want to watch my fingers disappear inside that pretty pink cunt of yours."

Dillon pressed herself back against his hand.

"That's right," he said hungrily. "Arch your back, but you're going to have to tell me where you want to be scratched."

"There." It was one word, but she'd managed it.

"More," he commanded, sliding his fingers through her wet lips to the hot, tight bud of her clit.

The sublime heat, the aching need, the willingness to beg, and inevitability of surrender all slammed into her at once.

"Christ, I don't want to beg, but I will—I fucking will!" she cried out, utterly lost to her desire, nearly in tears she was so desperate. "Put your hands inside me and fuck me, Gray. Fuck me until I scream." She moaned, hissed, pressed back against his hand. Oh God . . . His hand. "That's *my* jaguar. It belongs inside *me*."

She heard his sharp intake of breath, felt his hand still. "Inside you, outside you, beneath you." His fingers eased back. "You want this," he whispered, circling his finger at the wet entrance to her cunt.

"Yes," she uttered, the anticipation driving her insane.

"Just one?" He slid one finger inside of her, stretching her.

She gasped.

"How about two?"

"Yes!" she cried breathlessly, hungrily. "God, yes. Please, Gray."

He slipped a second finger inside her.

Her hips jerked and she moaned. This was madness. Delicious, intense, overwrought, wondrous madness.

And she didn't want it to stop. Ever. Because if it did, her mind would take over—that part of it that refused to allow lust, real lust in—the kind that came with feeling and connection.

"The other fingers are getting lonely, D," he groaned, his voice rabid and raw. "They want to be together. They want to fuck you too. They want inside your silky wet pussy so badly. Can they all come to the party, baby?"

"Yes," she gasped, arching her back even further, giving him the access he needed to enter her good and hard and deep. "Yes, goddamn it. Yes!"

When all five of his fingers entered her, Gray cursed. "The way your cunt took me in, inch by inch of drenched heat. Fuck, and the way it's suckling my fingers."

"More," Dillon begged, pumping against him, sending his fingers as deep as they could go. "I want more; you want more."

"Dillon."

The warning in his voice nearly made her come. "I know your cock is screaming to get out and inside me—feel what your fingers are feeling."

He growled like a Beast and drove his fingers up hard within her slick channel.

Dillon sucked in air. "Get behind me, Gray! Take me. Ride me so fucking hard, we both black out." She bucked against his hand, the burning sensation rioting within her. "Now, please. I need you. Only you."

He cursed again, then again—but kept thrusting his fingers inside of her, so deep, playing with the sensitive flesh of her clit. "Goddamn it, D."

The cave scented of her heat and echoed with the sounds of her pleading cries. "Why is that wrong?"

She heard him unzipping, then felt his hand slip from her cunt. "Mounting you like a fucking animal—"

"I am an animal!" she cried out, feeling him behind her. "And you love it. Don't pretend you don't."

He gripped her hips, spread her wide. "Look at you. Even in this dim light, I can see how your pussy glistens for me."

She could feel the head of his cock against the wet entrance to her body. "Gray, please," she begged.

He entered her slowly, one inch at a time. "God, baby, you're so beautiful. So wet, so tight. The way your pussy sucks me in." He cursed, moaned. "Oh, shit. I knew you would feel like this. The perfect fit, your candy walls fisting around me."

Shards of white-hot pleasure assaulted her as he pushed all the way home. She didn't want to think. No, it was a bad idea. And yet she couldn't stop herself from agreeing. Yes, it was the perfect fit. She'd never experienced anything like it. And maybe she never should again if she wanted to a live a moderately happy existence on the run, without him.

She canted her hips, trying to draw him in deeper. But he withdrew, and for a moment she wondered if he was going to leave her in misery. But he only gripped her hips tighter and slammed his way home. She gasped at the delicious brutality and cried out for more, her muscles convulsing.

Sensing what she wanted, what she needed, Gray withdrew again, then thrust back inside of her. Dillon's clit ached with the pain of wanting release. She wanted it so desperately, and yet as Gray moved inside her, hitting the very spot that throbbed and pulsed, she prayed she could hold out. Never had she felt such pleasure or such pain in the empty wasteland where her heart should be.

The sudden need to connect with him made her sit up, made her press her back to his chest. Oh God, yes. The angle of his thrust hit a new and wondrous spot inside of her and she wrapped her arms around his neck and looked over her shoulder.

Her entire body clenched with desire at the sight of him.

Gray Donohue was a fierce and hungry beast. His hair was wild, his eyes narrowed, his face contorted into a mask of diabolical intensity. And then that face descended on hers and his mouth claimed her in a ravenous kiss.

As his cock worked in and out of her pussy, as his tongue fucked the inside of her mouth, Dillon knew this was something beyond what she was capable of, beyond what her tiny scrap of an unbeating heart could ever hold on to.

This was her true mate, her perfect fit. And yet there was nothing perfect about either one of them or this up-and-down, push-and-pull thing that was going on between them.

Dillon felt the rising heat of imminent orgasm and she allowed her thoughts to flee. Her thighs trembled, her nipples were hard and aching, her belly clenched, and then Gray's hand—the one that was marked by her jaguar—moved over her pelvis and claimed her cunt. She was soaking wet, her lips, her inner thighs, and

Gray groaned into her mouth as he slipped his fingers between her folds and found her clit.

The feeling of his fingers on her sensitive flesh had Dillon crying out and dropping back down to her hands. Gray pounded into her so hard she was afraid he would rip her in two. And yet she arched her back and pressed against him for more. She felt like her mind was unhinged, that her body was working on its own. Her hips jerked and shook as he rubbed her clit. The heat building inside her was about to spill over. She wasn't ready. She couldn't hold on and yet she was afraid to climax. Afraid to look at him. Goddamn it, she was just fucking afraid period.

"Oh, yes," he uttered hoarsely, savagely. "There it is. The walls of your pussy . . . Shit, it's like an earthquake. Come for me, baby."

His breathing went rabid, and she felt his cock swell. Or, God, maybe that was her, but she was gone, done for. His fingers played her clit in a heavy burst of movement and she screamed into the cold air of the cave as she came. Light, heat, rocking waves of unbearable beauty coursed through her as she shook, shuddered.

Behind her, Gray groaned and slammed into her with five possessive thrusts. She felt his hot seed pour into her body, lapped up by the convulsing walls of her pussy, and she wanted to die. This was how it was supposed to be. This was how it was supposed to feel when someone cared about you, connected with you, wanted to give you everything and then some. This was how it felt when someone wanted more than just a mindless fuck from a faceless cunt.

Tears blurred her vision and she let them fall because he couldn't see her in the dim light of the cave.

Now she knew. Now she would know the truth and have to live every day without it because she was too afraid to give herself over to it.

To him.

To a life with her true mate.

Blinking away her tears, she lay back against him, shaking, his cock still inside her, his arms wrapped around her.

"Gray?" she whispered, forcing back the weight of emotions running through her and down her cheeks.

"Yeah?"

She didn't know what made her ask it or what made it come to her mind, but as she asked, she put her hand over his hand—over the mark. "What happened to the bear? After it knocked me out?"

There was a pause, and for a moment she heard only the sound of his breathing. "I chased it away."

Her insides clenched. Not from sexual heat, but from something far more worrisome. "How?"

"It was afraid of me," he said, his mouth close to her neck, her ear. "How I sounded, how I acted."

She shivered. "And how was that?"

He tightened his hold on her. "Vicious, uncompromising, ready to take death, ready to face it."

She felt something on her neck—sharp, blades. No. Fangs. And then he whispered, "Like a male who was protecting his true mate."

Dillon stilled. She waited for the feeling of apprehension, of trepidation to come over her at his words.

But it wasn't there, never came. In that brief instant, all she felt was safe.

"You can deny this all you want," he said softly, gently. "But you and your pussy belong to me."

Heat spread within her, and for a moment she thought that Gray was going to press her forward, back onto her hands and knees and take her again. But instead he cursed and gripped her possessively, protectively.

"Hey." Concern pulsed within her. "What is it? What's going on?"

"I can hear them."

"Who?" She lifted her head so she could see his face, his eyes. Both were strained, confused. "Gray, what's happening?"

"The Impure warriors," he uttered, shaking his head. "I can hear them in my head. It's not possible. How I can hear them from so far away?"

The cave felt suddenly colder, and Dillon pressed herself even closer to him. "I don't know. What are they saying?"

He didn't answer her immediately. His gaze seemed unfocused, as though he was listening. Then his gunmetal eyes flickered down and pinned her with their intensity. "They've found the way into the Order's frequency, their mainframe." A low curse bled from his throat. "And it seems as though the Order has found its way to them."

15

The night air crackled with raw energy as each *paven* flashed to the exterior deck of Alexander's lighthouse in Montauk. Lucian and Helo, then Erion and Nicholas, then Phane. Below them, the sea was angry and crashed against the rocks with curls of white spray.

"Come inside, brothers," Alexander said, holding the door open.

Erion was the first to enter, his gaze taking in the sparsely furnished room and the dim lighting. There were seven chairs set around an oval black marble table. Each place was set with a glass of blood.

As each brother took a seat around the table, Erion noticed that one of their brood was missing.

He turned to Phane, who had dropped into the chair beside him. "Where's Lycos?"

The hawklike *paven* turned his gaze to Erion. "He said he'd be along in a few minutes. He was finishing up with an uncooperative source."

"In Norway?" Erion asked.

"No. That was a dead end." Phane grinned. "Literally."

Damn wolf and his kills. Did that *paven* have to act like a Beast as well as look like one? Erion narrowed his gaze. "I hope you didn't make a mess, and if you did, I hope you cleaned it up."

Phane's grin widened, his fangs dropping low. "Always."

Turning back to the assembled brothers around the table, Erion said, "Lycos will be here soon. Shall we begin?"

Across from him, Alexander nodded. "Helo, Lucian, and I met with the Eyes. With Whistler."

To his brother's left, Lucian snorted. "Who wasn't very cooperative, but your sea-loving boy over here was pretty damn impressive with him."

Beside Lucian, Helo shook his head. "Not so impressive. The male got away."

"No," Alexander amended. "Whistler was *flashed* away."

Something hummed inside of Erion, and he reached for his cup of blood. He didn't drink it, but just his hand around the thick glass steadied him for what was coming next.

"We think Cruen pulled him in," Lucian said, reaching for his own glass of blood and knocking it back in one quick swig. His nostrils flared and he made a face. "This is chicken piss compared to my Bronwyn's blood."

"Why would Cruen be using the Eyes?" Phane asked, ignoring Lucian's comment. "Especially when they can be bought so easily."

"Perhaps Cruen *is* paying," Helo said, glancing out the massive windows to the dark sea.

"Or Whistler is," Alexander remarked. "In his hide. Torture, fear . . . sometimes a stronger motivator than cash."

Lucian pointed at Helo's glass of blood. "You going to drink that?"

Helo turned and snorted at him. "Thought it tasted like chicken piss?"

"It could taste like your piss right now, *Mutore*. That's how thirsty I am." He grumbled softly, "Damn Breeding Male gene. Never-ending hunger for blood, for sex—"

"Ease up now, Luca," Nicholas said from the other side of Alexander. Then, while Helo pushed his glass toward Lucian with a grin, Nicholas turned and addressed the group. "We have news as well. Erion and I found Cruen's nephew."

Silence gripped the table, and every brother turned to Erion.

"He is a *mutore*," Erion told them, the words still strange on his lips. "Made from a shifter mother and a Breeding Male."

"A shifter mother?" Helo repeated, moving forward in his chair. "As in an actual race of pure shifters?"

Erion nodded. "Seems to be."

"Where are they? Do they have a compound?"

"No idea, Helo. Didn't ask." They were looking for only one mysterious creature at the moment. "And that's not even the big reveal, brothers."

Helo narrowed his eyes. "What does that mean?"

Erion glanced at Nicholas, then back to the three

others. "The *paven* said that his uncle, that Cruen, is a *mutore* too."

"Bullshit," Lucian hissed, his face thick with shock.

"Like Luca said," Helo growled. "That can't be. We would've known. Right? We would've sensed it."

Erion shrugged. He'd asked himself that a hundred times since leaving France. "Would we? That bastard kept everything real and true from us. How would this be any different?"

Phane, whose chiseled jaw looked tense as steel, said in a deathly whisper, "Does this *mutore* know where his uncle is hiding?"

"He said he has heard that Cruen retains multiple hideouts," Erion answered. "He gave us the only location he knows."

"Have either of you gone to check it out?" Helo asked them.

As the sea crashed against the rocks below them, Erion looked at Nicholas. "There's a problem."

"Another one?" Phane said drily.

"Or perhaps it is more of a challenge."

"What?" Phane asked, his eyes narrowing.

"It's inside a *credenti*," Erion said.

Lucian placed Helo's empty glass back in front of him with a little too much force. "That's no challenge."

Helo agreed. "That should be an easy task."

Nicholas turned to Alexander, his face grave. "Your *credenti*."

Hunger assaulted him, made his thinking unclear and his draws on her vein greedy. He pulled out of her wrist, then growled his way up to her neck and entered the thin, succulent vein there too. Honey sweet and warm, the blood flowed down his throat. Fuck, there was nothing better in the world—nothing he wanted more on his tongue.

Except perhaps the ripe, pink cunt he'd played in earlier.

"Ah." She sucked in air. "No smiling when you're feeding, Gray Donohue."

After three or four massive gulps, he pulled out. His grin was wide as he looked at her.

"Yes, like that." She narrowed her eyes playfully. "Causes your fangs to open me wider."

The heat of desire shred his body. "We're talking about your vein, right?"

"For now," she murmured.

Gray's nostrils flared, and he watched her blow on her wrist—watched her mouth form a perfect O. "Hope I didn't drain you."

Her eyes flickered up. "Likewise."

"Not possible," he said, trying like hell not to stare at her naked frame, her shoulders, breasts, navel, legs, what was between her legs . . .

"Besides, you needed it," she said, her voice calling him back from the edge of damn near hellish need. "We'll be able to move much faster with pure blood in your veins."

Her words halted him, reined in the lust and reminded him he needed to get his head out of this blood haze and into the trip home. The Impure warriors' call last night concerned him; it hadn't included any specifics on what was happening. Gray had tried to mentally connect with them, but there had been no answer. The sooner he could return to New York, the better. He wished they could flash, but with the Order so closely monitoring Dillon, he wasn't going to risk it. And it wasn't just the threat of her getting nabbed by those bastards anymore—but him as well.

Dillon stood, her head just touching the ceiling of the cave. Gray couldn't help but stare at that sweet perfection, those long limbs, that curved waist in the pale morning light filtering in through the small opening of the cave. But within seconds, Dillon had closed her eyes and shifted into her jaguar state.

"Moving faster with your blood in my veins and the jaguar's fur on your back?" Gray asked.

"That's right."

His gaze moved over her, missing her *veana* form, and yet his hands itched to touch her sleek, golden coat. "Risky as hell running through the woods like that. Hope we don't meet with a hunter. I'll have to pretend you're my pet."

"You do, and I'll be forced to bite the both of you," she returned with a halfhearted snarl.

"Well, at least one of us will get to enjoy being blown afterward," he said, then slipped out the hole in the rock.

She followed him, out of the cave and into the weak, early-morning sunshine. "Besides, what choice do I have? I'm not running through the woods naked."

Gray stretched, feeling strong, nearly predatory. "I told you I wouldn't have minded, that I'd carry you all the way home if you wanted me to."

Her jaguar's eyes glittered with heat. "'Carry me.' That's a new name for it."

Gray grunted, then turned toward the river. "I've got a hundred names for it, and we can discuss them all as we travel."

He felt ready to spring, knew he could be as fast as the Beast beside him, and his desire to get home to his warriors beat strong within him.

Without a word, he took off, sprinting toward the water and the forest beyond, Dillon keeping pace beside him.

"Do you wish for your son to remain alive after capture?"

"I wish for my son to never be captured." Celestine stood before the Order's long wooden table, her feet covered in sand, her body clad in a long, off-white jumpsuit. Moments ago, she'd been wearing black pants and a black jacket as she'd entered a shop called New Baby on Manhattan's Upper West Side. Her daughter hadn't revealed her pregnancy yet, but Celestine had scented the new life within her almost immediately—a scent only a mother could recognize. She'd wanted to pick out something special for when Sara announced her *swell*, but she'd never even touched the pale yellow chenille blanket.

The Order had pulled her out of one reality and into another, humbling her by stripping away her clothing mid-flash and replacing it with their own choice of dress. Celestine's gaze moved down the line, from one Order member to the next. They all looked the same, cranberry-colored robes and a single black circle around their left eyes. They all felt the same too, one mind, a solitary ruling. She couldn't believe how brazen they had been. Grabbing and transporting her in broad daylight, in front of a small crowd of humans.

Her gaze fell on the *veana* leader, Feeyan, with her snow-white hair and skin the color of clay. The female's eyes burned with impatience. Yes, Celestine thought, they were indeed desperate for information.

"Your son cannot avoid capture," Feeyan said. "But he will live if you give us the location of the Impures' safe house."

Celestine held her ground, her tone as calm as she could make it. "What makes you think I would know it? My son does not confide in me. He never has."

The *veana*'s eyes narrowed and her lips parted, revealing those bloodred fangs the Order was famous for—their united symbol that demonstrated they were beyond an earthly vampire's needs, that they no longer needed to consume blood.

Celestine sniffed with irritation, felt a sudden understanding and kinship with her son and with his cause—the same one his father had fought for. No, the Order didn't need blood to survive, but they certainly used it to control, to maim.

"Your son may not want you, *Veana*," Feeyan said, her eyes intense. "But that hasn't stopped you from trying to get to him."

She knew, Celestine thought, her skin prickling with nerves now. Cellie didn't know how this *veana* knew she'd found Gray's safe house, but the knowledge was clear and threatening and hovered just behind the Order member's eyes. And if Celestine planned to get out of this with her veins intact, she had to think, devise a plan—utilize the skills that kept her protected in the field.

Adopting a melancholy facade, Cellie sighed. "Yes, I tried to get to him," she said thickly and with the deep anguish of a foolish mother who was close to losing her child. And maybe she didn't have to pretend that was true. "I just wanted to know if he was all right."

Feeyan's nostrils flared. "And was he?"

"I didn't see him," Cellie admitted. "I didn't go inside."

Her eyes narrowed venomously. "Tell us the location of this safe house and we will send you back to your shopping expedition."

Celestine hesitated. She could think like a spy, give the truth, then get the hell out of there and try to get to Gray in time. Or she could think like a mother and say anything in that moment to protect her child. Just the thought brought up images of both her children as *balas*, the fire, the loss of Jeremy, Gray's damaged hands—all those years Sara could see nothing more than healing Gray.

The ache inside her grew until it felt as though it would burst. She'd lost her son to the lies she'd told to protect him; perhaps now she'd be able to save him.

"It's 2622 Herkimer Street," she said quickly. "Remember your promise not to hurt him."

Feeyan turned her head to look at her neighbor. The *paven* had his eyes closed. After a moment, he opened them, looked at Feeyan, and shook his head.

A low growl sounded in the *veana*'s throat as she turned back to face Celestine. "Foolish *veana*. We will get all the information we seek, and you will go to Mondrar for lying to me."

Celestine barely had time to blink before the *veana* flashed directly in front of her, grabbed her head, and plunged her brick-red fangs into Celestine's temple.

16

By nightfall they had nearly reached the border. Dillon couldn't believe Gray's speed. His movements were light and quick and intense. It was Gray juiced up on pure blood, and she found it sexy as hell. She also found his obsessive drive to get home, back to New York City, admirable even though she didn't share or understand it.

He was the leader of the Impure Resistance, and his first concern was protecting his own.

"We follow the highway now," she said as they stopped beside a massive boulder overlooking the speeding cars, their lights flickering like oversized fireflies.

Gray turned to face her, his eyes near charcoal under the dome of sleepy sky. "We?"

As the wind blew her fur and coated the insides of her nostrils with the scent of small prey, Dillon knew the time had come for choices to become decisions. Her mind had swirled with them for hours as she ran through the forest. She glanced to the west. One path would lead to the unknown, to an open field where she could run and continue running until she wished to stop and take a breath.

The other way was by this Impure's side.

He moved then, and a shard of moonlight hit the back of his hand, illuminating the mark of the jaguar.

Her cat purred deep in its throat.

"Lead on," she said, pressing her head into the small of his back. "I will follow."

The moment the world had gone dark and the shades had lifted, the *paven* came out. Not to play, but to plan. They were gathered in the Romans' library, some on computers, others kicking back on the couches and chairs, and one on the floor with Kate and Ladd playing a board game.

Sara stood near the fire, wishing her mother were back from her holiday shopping to see this family assembled here. It was a lovely sight, no matter what had brought them all together, and it made her feel nostalgic.

In a few short months, there would be another joining them.

The heat from the fire stroked her insides. She'd thought maybe she'd try and grab a few moments alone with her mate before she had to leave for the hospital in an hour. But that looked as though it wasn't going to happen. The Romans and the Beasts had returned with some pretty staggering news and were trying to negotiate a plan of attack. Her announcement would have to wait.

She despised the thread of relief that played within her, evidence of her fear in Alex's response. Because, in truth, no matter what he said aloud when she told him, she would know how he really felt inside. The true mate bond was a wonder and a curse.

"Alex is going to have to go first, since he can enter with his blood," said Helo, who sat behind a computer screen.

"Right," Alexander said with a dark chuckle. "Pretty amazing how one's home *credenti* welcomes them and their blood, even though the vampires inside do not."

Sara glanced at her mate, saw the fierce expression on his face as he continued to clean his gun and knew that the news of Cruen's hideout had hit him hard and that he wanted nothing less than to return to that place of horrible abuse from his *balashood*.

Beside Helo, also engrossed in whatever was on his laptop, Nicholas said, "There has to be a way to know if Cruen is there without actually having to send anyone."

"Does the *credenti* know he's there?" Phane asked, sprawled out on the couch. "Do you think they allow it?"

"I can't imagine that," Sara said. "Can you, Alex?"

Continuing to polish his gun, Alexander spoke softly. "Anything can go on behind those walls. Good things can be celebrated; terrible things can be hidden."

Sara's heart squeezed painfully. She hated seeing him this way, wished she could do something for him—wished she could go instead of him. Maybe it was a blessing that she hadn't told him about her *swell*. One less pressure for him to take on.

"Do you think he may be hidden within the *credenti*?" Helo asked, his brows coming together. "Do you think he may have created his own hidden compound within a protected one?"

"Only one way to know," said Lucian, watching Ladd move his game piece five spaces past his own. "You'd better not be cheating, little *paven*."

Ladd giggled.

"There may be someone who could find out," Nicholas said, pressing the cover of his laptop down an inch or two so he could see Alex clearly. "Your sister. Any interest in contacting her? She may wish to help you."

Even though Alexander was across the room, Sara could feel his anger pierce the air. "Never. She can never be brought into this mission."

"What about me?" Ladd said, scrambling to his feet. "I could help. I want to go on a mission."

Alex's gaze rested on the boy, and instantly Sara felt his tension ease. "You are brave, young *balas*. And someday soon you will be out there with us."

"But not tonight," Erion said resolutely. The demon-eyed *paven* had remained quiet and thoughtful near the fire as he watched Lucian play a game with his son.

Sara wondered what went on in his mind regarding Ladd. Did he want to be the boy's father? Or, like the rest of the sons of the Breeding Male, did fear keep him at arm's length and his mouth shut tight to the truth?

With a burst of sound, the doors to the library opened and the wolf *mutore* entered. Sara would be lying if she didn't acknowledge that this *paven* had something special. Thing was, she wasn't sure exactly what it was. Lycos was tall and broad like all the Breeding

Male *paven*s, but he had an unpredictable wildness about him, from his hair to his eyes to the way he seemed to always be in predator mode.

"About time," Erion said flatly. "Where the hell have you been?"

"And more important," Helo added, "what did you gain from this contact of yours? What did the male say?"

"Wasn't a male," Lycos growled, heading over to the couch, yanking Phane's booted feet off the end and plunking down beside him.

"You truly are a dog," Phane muttered. "In every damn sense of the word."

Lycos chuckled. "Every sense? You don't see me humping your leg, do you?"

"Not yet," Phane returned with a grunt. "But give it a minute or two."

Lycos released a wild, feral howl, and Kate put her hands over Ladd's ears. "*Gentlepaven*, watch your language and your audio levels please." She eyed every *paven* in the room, and they all seemed to shrink a little beneath her fierce gaze.

Shifting to his knees, Ladd pushed Kate's hands away and did a howl of his own.

The room broke with laughter, the tension from a moment ago eased somewhat.

Kate lifted her chin. "The least you could all do is set a good example for him."

Trying to suppress his laughter, Nicholas addressed them all. "I'd do as she says, brothers. You don't want my mate whipping out that blade she carries at her ankle. It only feels good when she's trying to get herself a meal."

"Nicholas Roman," Kate scolded, then looked up at Sara and shook her head. "Why do we even try?"

"Because these *paven*s need us," Sara said with a bright-eyed smile. "Whether they deserve our care is up for debate."

"I know I deserve it," Alexander stated roguishly. "Twenty-four-seven, if she'll have me."

Sara rolled her eyes at her mate. "Boys."

"We apologize, *veana*s," Phane said with more affected manners than Sara had ever seen from him. "We'll try and keep it down."

"Keep it appropriate," Helo added. "You know, we're not used to—well, all of this."

"He means a family atmosphere," Erion finished, his gaze shifting to Ladd.

"Yeah, yeah. We'll all be very good little boys, Mummy," Lucian drawled, his gaze completely focused on Lycos. "Now, come on, wolfie, give us the story. Just keep it G-rated so the females here don't have a reason to knock us about."

As Lycos told of the female he had encountered, attempting to keep it as G-rated as he could manage, Sara looked over at Alexander again. This time his gaze was trained on her. In it, she saw the great love he had for her and the deep sorrow of a *paven* who would be returning to the one place on earth he never wanted to go to again. And her heart lurched. She wished she could be by his side as she'd been the last time he'd gone home.

For Gray, entering the city was like auditory overload on steroids. In the woods, in the cave, he'd been exposed only to the sounds of nature and animals—nothing with words and nothing that had entered his mind.

Except for his own thoughts, which at times were nearly as tough to take.

With Dillon in her jaguar state walking beside him, Gray moved through the parts of the Bronx he knew were less populated. According to a digital display on one of the banks they passed, it was nearly four a.m. There was no perfect time to traverse the city with a jaguar by your side, but this was about the best, and least conspicuous, it was going to get.

Turning down an alleyway, Gray sought out the shadows, trying to keep Dillon as hidden as possible. Granted, she could shift back and be the naked chick running up the city street, which might actually be better than an uncontained feral wild animal, but they'd cross that bridge when they were forced to.

As if she'd read his mind, she grumbled, "I need clothes."

"Or a leash and collar," he said, crossing into another alleyway.

Her eyes darted around; then she stalked past him. "Let's not start that again."

"Just trying to get you to blend in, D."

"Never have, never will."

"Besides," he said, stopping near the edge of the alleyway to wait for a garbage truck to pass. "Your jag likes the idea of a collar. She wants to be contained by me."

Dillon's large head shifted to face him. "What?"

His back against the brick wall, Gray kept his eyes

on the world around him. "I can feel it. Every time I mention it, the cat purrs."

"You're cracked." Though the words exited her jaguar's mouth, the fierce outrage was all Dillon.

Gray turned and looked directly into her eyes. "I will put a black collar around your neck and a leash to keep you close to me."

On cue, Dillon's jaguar purred. She gasped, trying to stop it—the sound, the deep rumble within her. She backed up a few steps.

The heat in his eyes pounded through her. "You may not be mine, D, but she is."

He saw her start, her fur bristle, but he gave her no time to respond. "Let's go. Just a few blocks away now."

As the scent of smoke pushed into his nostrils, Gray moved in silence, staying deep in the shadows, under fire escapes, away from entrances and exits, until they came out on the street lined with warehouses. Immediately he sensed that something wasn't right. Dread moved through him as the scent of smoke grew stronger, more intense, and he quickened his pace. A moment ago, he'd been thinking about taming her Beast—his Beast—and now, as he placed his arm over his mouth to keep from coughing, he heard only panic in his mind.

Shock, horror, and disbelief gripped him by the balls as he came to a halt a few yards from the Impure Resistance headquarters.

Or what was left of it.

"Oh God," Dillon breathed as they both stayed back. "What the hell happened here?"

Gray felt as though he'd been emptied of all air. As he stood there and witnessed the smoking pile of rubble that used to be the Impure Resistance—that was now being treated by several firefighters with some kind of chemical retardant—his mind churned with images of the warriors, of Samuel and Uma, and of another fire so long ago.

His hands twitched. His true mate mark throbbed.

"The Order did this," he uttered, his voice sounding destroyed even to his own ears. It had to be them. The Impure warriors' message was still playing in his head. The Order was coming after them. Gray sniffed. He didn't believe in coincidences.

"We need to go," he said flatly.

"Go," Dillon repeated. "Go where?"

"They could be watching us, waiting for us—for you." He grabbed her by the scruff of the neck. "Move. Into the shadows and down the street."

She didn't argue with him. Not then. They ran, side by side in silence. Back into alleyways, heading out of the Bronx. Overhead, the sky was beginning to change, lighten. When they were far enough away, when the scent of smoke dissipated, she came at him.

"Where are we going?" she called out to him. "We can't just run around the city."

Gray kept his eyes forward and his speed even—and his direction spot-on. "We're going to a secret location."

"It's getting light out," she said. "Let me flash us there."

"No," he said harshly. He couldn't seem to stop the heat in his tone or the grip of hatred that was rolling through him with every step he took. The Order would pay dearly for this, he mused. "It's too dangerous to flash."

"Maybe it's more dangerous not to."

Gray darted into an alley between two buildings and came to an abrupt halt in the shadows of a massive trash can. Breathing hard, gaze flaring with intensity, he dropped down on his haunches and stared straight into those green cat eyes. "You need to make a decision. Right here, right now." His nostrils flared. "This isn't playtime anymore—shit, it never was—but this is the end of the road for pulling you along, pulling you into something that has nothing to do with you. You were right about that. This isn't your fight. But, true mates or not, I have the Resistance to lead, warriors to find, Impures to rescue and protect. And right now, that's more important than us, than you."

"Why?"

Her overtly simple reaction stunned him. "What do you mean why?"

She made a grunting sound and her expression turned hostile. "I don't understand your utterly blind passion for this. Forget the danger you're always in or the constant battles you seem to get into with that jerk-off Rio—what have any of these Impures ever done for you, Gray? And the warriors. They bleed you dry, accept your role as leader, then constantly question it." She inched closer to him. "Let's go. Let's get out of here, forget the war and the bad blood and the Order's bullshit rules and go make our own."

There was a moment, a flicker inside Gray that responded to her words, her passion. There was a moment when he wanted to leap and run just as she'd suggested. That was the part of him that loved this *veana*, craved this *veana*, had always hoped there could really be something between them. But a true mate's bond wasn't enough for him to turn his back on an entire group of suffering Impures and a dictatorial rule that needed to be taken apart and left like the Resistance Headquarters—in ashes.

His guts clenched. Just the fact that she'd suggested running made it all the more clear how important this uprising was to him—and how they could never be a true part of each other's lives.

She was watching him, her lip curling. "You blame me for this, don't you? The fire, the misplaced Impure warriors?"

Gray's eyes searched hers for something close to humanity. The Order may have come looking for her, may have put a match to that building to send a message. But this was so much bigger than her, than him. Looking into her gaze, he knew she didn't see it, couldn't see it. Her eyes were devoid of concern for anyone but herself, her future, including having him in it.

He shook his head. "Shit. You're right. You don't get this."

Dillon pulled back from him, shook her massive head. "It goes against every survival instinct I have. And those instincts have kept me alive and breathing and sane."

A few seconds passed between them, a few emotions and several heavy regrets. It seemed as though she were waiting for him to grab her and pull her close, tell her she was coming with him whether she wanted to or not.

But Gray stood his ground and kept his damaged hands at his sides.

As the sun rose further, the bond between them started to sink like a stone in the water. Dillon released a breath, gave him one last look and turned around, ran away down the alley.

Pain like he'd never felt before coursed through his veins, and the mark on his hand burned with a fire that would never die.

She was his love, his true mate, and as he watched the last flick of her tail before it disappeared behind the building, he felt the deep pull of grief within him.

Grief, but not surprise.

17

She'd run all the way to the ocean. She'd stood before the dark, churning sea. She'd shifted into her *veana* form, then raced into the frigid water and dived beneath the waves. As her skin turned to ice, she'd wondered what it felt like to drown—and what it felt like to live.

With him.

Without him.

She'd be wondering that every day of her life from now on because she'd walked away from him. Not only him, but all that he believed in.

The icy water hardened her blood, but it couldn't reach the cat inside her, who burned to be with its master—would perhaps even try to return to its master without her consent. Dillon knew the control over her shift wasn't guaranteed anymore. Shit, Gray had more control of it than she did . . . That male soothed her savage Beast something fierce and cleared the way for her *veana* to come through.

He gave her body peace, her mind too. So why couldn't she give him what he needed? Why was it so hard for her to watch him fight for his Impures? Support him in that fight? Because, goddamn it! She slapped the water with her fists. *He* was one of them— an Impure. Why couldn't she understand that fighting for them was fighting for him too?

She swam close to shore, then walked out of the sea and shifted back into her jaguar once more.

Without another thought, she bolted from the sand and ran. She ran for miles in full daylight, praying she wouldn't be seen. But it was impossible. Back in the city, though careful to remain in the shadows, she ran into several shocked and terrified souls on their way to work. It was only when she hit a familiar street and stole around the side of the massive house and through the back door that she felt as if she could breathe again.

Luckily, the first person she ran into was the very one she sought, and she whimpered and rubbed up against the female's side.

"Dillon," Sara exclaimed, surprise unmasked in her tone as she left her nearly unpeeled orange on the counter and came to stand before the massive cat.

"I need help," Dillon said, hating the desperation in her voice. Knowing she probably reeked with it, there was no point in pretending. "I need clothes, somewhere to stay until it gets dark."

Sara glanced around, no doubt looking for the many *paven*s in the house, and whispered, "Follow me."

Dillon moved silently behind her, up the stairs and down the hall to the room she knew by scent was Sara and Alexander's. As soon as Sara opened the door, Dillon raced inside and immediately shifted into her *veana* form.

Sara's eyes widened as she took in Dillon's naked form. It was funny. Just a few months ago, Dillon had thought herself attracted to this female. But now she knew what that minor obsession had been about. Going after a person who was already taken—whose heart belonged to someone else. She'd thought it had made life uncomplicated, free of vulnerability and the pain of losing control.

"Give me a sec," Sara said. "I'll be right back."

That all seemed so stupid now, Dillon thought as the female hurried out the room. And based on nothing more than a way to keep herself tied to unhappiness and emotional deception.

She was learning, it seemed. Slowly and painfully, but she was learning.

A few minutes later, Sara returned with an armload of clothes—undergarments, jeans, shirts, sweaters. She tossed them on the bed, and Dillon grabbed whatever looked like her size and threw it on. Each piece felt warm and smelled sweet, fresh from the laundry, and when Dillon was completely geared out and stood before Sara again, she released the breath she'd been holding for what seemed like hours and said, "Thanks."

Sara sat on a chair beside the empty fireplace, her expression tight with concern. "What's going on, Dillon? Where's Gray?"

Just hearing his name ripped at her insides. "His safe house was destroyed tonight."

Sara's eyes went wide with horror. "What?"

"Fire."

"Oh God." She stood up, started pacing, her tone, her expression heavy with worry. "How did it happen? Is he okay?"

"He's fine," Dillon assured her. "Pissed off and planning his next move, but fine. He thinks it was the Order."

Sara blanched. "Why would he think that?"

Gray had never asked her not to reveal what was going on inside the Resistance Headquarters, and Sara was family. "The Impure warriors have been hacking into the Order's mainframe—their central command, how they communicate with each other. Gray thinks the warriors got caught, traced, and the Order executed some payback."

Sara's eyes narrowed. "But you don't."

Dillon shook her head. "Maybe that was part of it, but the Order wants me. They've made no secret of it. They want to capture and kill the *mutore* who managed to make it past her birth day. And, hey, if she knows of any more Beasts that may be lurking around town, all the better." She sighed, tired all of a sudden. "After seeing that building gone, reduced to ash, Gray was pretty devastated—and worried about the Impures who'd been inside. He wanted to go find them, in some secret place."

"And you?" Sara asked, hovering near her chair again.

"Well—" Dillon stumbled, not sure exactly what to say, how much to say. "I came here."

Sara's eyes softened then. "Why didn't you go with him, Dillon?"

Because I'm an asshole. A scared, stupid asshole. "I couldn't."

"Because you wanted to protect him?"

"No," Dillon said quickly. " 'Course not. I wanted to protect myself."

"Well, that does sound more like the Dillon I know, but . . ."

"But what?" Dillon wished she could stick a foot in her mouth and stop engaging in this back and forth.

"I just don't think that's the Dillon you've become," Sara said.

Dillon released a heavy breath. "Don't start analyzing me, Doc. There's nothing altruistic here."

"Oh, I agree. You didn't walk away from him for nothing."

"Fine," she acquiesced. "I didn't want the Order to go after him, okay? Is that what you want to hear?"

"Partly."

Dillon snarled at the grin on the female's face. "What?"

Sara's grin widened. "You're falling in love with him, aren't you?"

"No!"

Sara's eyes widened too. "Oh God, you already have."

Dillon was about to tell the pink-cheeked and far-too-satisfied female just where she could stick that theory when Alexander burst into the room. He saw Dillon, muttered a terse and confused, "What the hell," then shook his head and directed his attention to Sara. "When was your mother here last?"

"What do you mean?" Sara stood up. "She's still sleeping, I'm sure. She went shopping all day yesterday and into the evening."

He looked momentarily relieved. "You saw her come home then, talked to her last night?"

Sara's face drained of color. "Well, no. I was at the hospital until early this morning. There was a shortage in the nursing staff. I just assumed she . . . Alex, what's going on?"

His mouth thinned into a grim line. "The Order claims to have her, my love."

Panic flared fast and hot in her gaze. "Where is it?"

"Library wall."

Sara tore past him, ran down the hall and the stairs. Dillon followed closely behind, entered the library just in time to see all of her brothers staring at words etched into the wall.

Celestine Donohue is a traitor to the Eternal Breed. She has kept the whereabouts of a mutore *from the Order. She is being held in Mondrar.*

Sara made a sound like an injured animal. "I've got to do something." Her hand went to her belly. "Shit. I've got to get to Gray. I've got to tell him."

"You're not going anywhere," Alexander said, coming up behind her, putting his arms around her. "I'll take the message."

"No," she said. "You're leaving for your *credenti*."

"That can wait," he declared hotly. "I'll go to Gray."

Tears welled in her eyes, and she tried like hell to shake them off, but it didn't work. She broke out crying, and all the *paven*s in the room looked helpless.

"It'll take hours, days," she said, swiping at her tears with irritation. "We don't know where he is. Besides, I need you and Nicky and Luca to help find a way to get my mother out of that hellhole."

"We will help as well," Erion stated. "Any way you need."

Sara turned to him and nodded. "Thank you. But I've got to go, got to do this."

"You're not going to find Gray," Alex said, his tone resolute, his nostrils flaring. "It's dangerous."

Tears still glistening in her eyes, Sara whirled on her true mate. "You will not tell me what I can and cannot do, *Paven*. I am not a child."

"No, but you are carrying one and I cannot have either one of you—"

Her gasp of shock and outrage brought his lecture to a screeching halt. "Oh my God. How did you know? Who told you?"

Alexander's jaw clenched, and his gaze seemed to flick in Lucian's direction. Clearly Sara saw it too, because she turned around and glared at the white-blond *paven*. "I don't have time to kill you right now, Luca. I want to. Really, really badly. But lucky for you, I want to find my brother more."

"No." The single word popped out of Dillon's mouth. When everyone turned to look at her, she lifted her chin and said, "I'll go."

Sara shook her head. "Dillon, you don't know where he is either."

"I can find him. His blood is inside me." Her gaze held tightly to Sara's. "A true mate can find the one who bares her mark."

* * *

One year ago, he had been driven out of the Eternal Order.

One year ago, he had been deemed a criminal.

Cruen sneered. That's what premorphing a few Pureblood *paven*s who may or may not have carried the Breeding Male gene got you. The Eternal Order had no love or respect for advancements in science, for change, for a better vampire race. But Cruen did, and he wouldn't stop his experiments no matter who got in the way.

And over the past months, several had gotten in the way. His *mutore* children, the Breeding Female. It would be a lie to say their loss in his life wasn't felt, but he wasn't one to dwell. Wasn't one to remain in the past.

Even when the past came calling.

Perhaps it was because the Order member standing beside him had always respected him—or feared him. Perhaps it was her desire for advice on taking over leadership of the Order. Whatever it was, it had caused her to go in search of him—resolutely and persistently within her mind until he'd finally answered.

Cautious but curious, Cruen had begun meeting with her at a mutually agreed upon reality that allowed them both to shut down their respective mental frequencies and share information. Most meetings had been fruitless for Cruen, but, he mused as he stood on the snowy Aspen mountaintop and watched skiers race down the slopes below, this one had the potential to turn out to be more than significant.

"This is surprising, Feeyan," he said to the white-haired female beside him.

"No," she said tightly. "This is a grave problem."

"And you wish to know how I would solve it?"

"Indeed."

Cruen grinned, his fangs no longer red—but white, bride white, and needle sharp. "If I give you the answers you seek, would you welcome me back to the Order?"

She turned to him, surprise alight in her clay-colored eyes. "Would you want to come back to the Order?"

"And be contained again?" He chuckled. "Never."

"That is what I thought. So what do you want for your advisement?"

His tone went grave. "I want the *mutore*."

She glared at him. As he'd known she would. "No, Cruen, I want the *mutore*. It is why I am here."

"You want to catch her, Feeyan, have the rest of the Order see you do it." He turned back to face the mountains. "I want to keep her after you do."

There was silence, save for the whoosh of skis on powder. Then the *veana* said, "Agreed. But even with the dark magic that backs your power, she will not be easy to obtain. There is an Impure who protects her."

Cruen laughed. "An Impure. You cannot be serious?"

"He is no ordinary Impure. He has gifts, superior mental strength I've never seen before. He and his three warriors have broken into the Order's collective."

This news was equally shocking and impressive. "Who is this male?" Cruen asked.

"Gray Donohue. He is the son of the Impure who began the Resistance. Don't you remember?"

Yes, Cruen remembered. His lip curled and his fists

pressed against his sides. No, he did not dwell in the past, but this was a very singular and vital memory to keep. The *veana* who had come to him, begging to have her husband's castration stopped. Cruen had never seen such beauty, such intelligence, such passion. He had never wanted a female more than he had wanted her. The bargain they'd struck that day had surely haunted them both, maybe even destroyed them both a little.

"I have laid a trap for this Impure," Feeyan continued, her words tripping over his memory. "His mother has been placed in Mondrar. He will attempt to rescue her. It is in his nature."

Inside Cruen, a flood of vile anger was beginning to churn. He refused to release it. But in truth, he could kill this *veana* who stood beside him with one thought for what she had just said to him. And yet he mustn't act hastily. Celestine would not be harmed. She was only bait for the son, and he was only a trade for the *mutore*.

The *mutore*.

He would start with her, and perhaps that would bring the others back home where they belonged, where their blood and skin samples could be of true use.

He turned to the *veana* and kept his disgust for her actions hidden. "I will give you my council on how to proceed with the Impure, how to interrogate him, how to make certain you get the result you are looking for, but once you have caught the *mutore*, have showed her around to the rest of the Order like the prize cat that she is, you will give her to me."

A flash of heat moved over Feeyan's face, but she clipped him a nod and said, "Very well."

It had taken Gray twice as long as it should have because he'd doubled back, made sure he wasn't followed, then headed for the shore. As he jogged up the beach, filtering out the sounds of combers and families inside their lavish homes, he wondered what he was going to find within the newly constructed *credenti*. If he'd find it empty or humming with Impure life. The Resistance had only started building it a few months ago, but most of the main structures and homes were up and ready. It had been their understanding—he, Piper, Rio, and Vincent—that if anything went down at the Bronx warehouse, if it was no longer safe to remain there and he hadn't heard anything from them via text, e-mail, or inside his head, they would meet at the *credenti*.

Gray left the sand and the water behind and shot up a small hill that led to a path. He ran at high speed, Dillon's pure blood still working within him, until he came to another section of beach. Utterly beautiful, utterly deserted—or so any human life would believe.

The same as it was at the gates of the Pureblood *credentis*, here too blood acted as a key. But for this new *credenti*, it was only Impure blood that gained one access.

Gray bit into his wrist and let the blood run for a moment before he lifted it and pressed it up against a solitary and strangely placed lamppost. The tall structure appeared beach weathered and seemingly forgotten, but it was everything—the very start of a new life for the Impures, a self-contained, self-ruling society dedicated to freedom.

Gray waited, the seconds ticking by, nothing shifting dramatically before him, the landscape remaining the same. And then in the distance it was as if the fog lifted and he could see the sprawling village ahead, or the beginnings of one.

He started toward it, got about twenty feet when he heard voices. His mouth twitched with relief and maybe even a smile if he could manage it. They were here. They were all here. Warriors, the Kendricks, staff from the headquarters. Within his mind, he heard Uma ask about him, heard Samuel assure her he'd be there soon.

No guilt swam in his veins as he moved toward the main building, only a deep sense of relief that his Impures were well and safe. And yet, as he saw Vincent emerge from the front entrance and look his way, shielding his eyes from the sun, Gray had the strange and foolish wish that D was beside him. As if her mark had heard him, felt him and his desire, it heated up like a goddamn candle was being held to it.

"Damn good to see you," Vincent said, his face tight with concern.

"Are they all here?" Gray demanded, slapping the male's outstretched hand, then moving inside the main building. "Warriors? Impures? The Kendricks? Did you get everyone out?"

"Everyone escaped before the fire took hold," Vincent said, moving through the hallway.

"Did you see who started it?"

Vincent chuckled. "No. But we have a pretty good guess."

"Yeah, me too."

"The Order doesn't take kindly to those who hack their server." He lifted a brow. "You got that mental text we sent, yes?"

"Long reaching and clear as crystal." Gray glanced sideways at the massive Impure. Of course that's what they all thought. That the Order was punishing them for breaking into their frequency and listening in. Hell, maybe that was part of the reason, but there was more. And Gray was going to have to tell them all about it.

When they pulled open the doors leading into the main hall, the space that would serve as a meeting place for all Impures in residence, Gray scented her. Not Piper or Uma or any of the other females who were standing around talking inside the large rectangle space—but *her*.

His nostrils flared and he cocked his head to the side. No, no, no. Not possible. Had to be her scent lingering on him—his clothes. There was no way—

"Hi."

She moved out from behind Rio then, her gaze locked on his. The cat was caged. She was a *veana* again, and she made his fucking heart stop.

The room went dead silent.

"What is she doing here?" he demanded of Rio.

The male looked at him like he was crazy. "She came with you, didn't she? Two seconds before you came in here."

Gray felt as though he were about to explode. He wanted to run at her, grab her and haul her against him, take her mouth as he wanted to take her body, then shake her until she told him why she kept running back instead of away. Why the hell was she playing with him? Was that all she knew how to do? Shred someone's heart into pieces because she didn't have one of her own? He was done—so goddamn done.

"Fuck you," he uttered, then turned around and walked out of the hall. Inside his head, he heard the room explode into thought, but out loud he heard her say, "I guess I'll follow him."

He'd known she would. Shit, maybe he'd even wanted her too. Maybe he'd just needed to unload his anger, his fear, his relief.

When they were alone in his office and she'd closed the door behind herself, Gray rounded on her. "How did you find me?"

She nodded at the back of his hand. "True mates."

"No," he said, his voice like steel. "You need Impure blood to get in here. Who'd you con into helping you?"

"I have Impure blood inside me, Gray. Yours."

That fact, that delectable fact, clipped his wings for a moment, maybe even punched the shit out of his heart. "Well, maybe the important question should be why. Why did you come? What? Do you need me to bring the jaguar back again? Or did you need—"

"Stop," Dillon interrupted, her eyes suddenly grave. "It's your mother. She was taken by the Order."

A low growl of warning erupted within him. "What did you say?"

Dillon moved a step closer to him. "She's in Mondrar, Gray."

18

"Where are you going?" Dillon followed him out of the office and down the hall, back toward the main gathering room.

His jaw set, his eyes blazing, Gray refused to slow. "If my mother's in Mondrar, I need to find a way to get her the hell out."

"You can't just walk into Mondrar. Trust me. You need to plan." She quickened her pace to keep up with him. "And you need help, especially of the Pureblood variety."

"You know Mondrar, huh?"

"Yes. And it's a total labyrinth. Impossible to find what you're looking for without a tour guide."

He was at the door to the main hall, his hand—the one that held the mark of the jaguar—wrapped around the silver knob. "Thanks for the advice."

"Wait," she cried out.

"No time, D."

"But I can help you!"

He paused for only a second, his chin cocked, his eyes evading hers. "This ain't your fight, remember?"

He was through the doors in an instant, leaving Dillon behind, her cat scratching to get out and run after its mate.

Alexander stalked the tunnels below the SoHo house, following his nose to a room of rock and iron that had once contained the animal inside himself, and most recently, the one inside of Dillon. He found the cage door open and his true mate sitting inside, clutching her cell phone.

"Here you are," he said with relief. He leaned against the side of the rock wall and took in her hunched shoulders and grim mouth.

"I'm not hiding, I swear," she said, her gaze remaining on her cell. "It's just quiet down here, in here."

"It is that. Always felt too quiet for me, though." He walked in, looked around. "In fact, I'm beginning to enjoy the sounds of family around me."

She didn't respond to his gentle push to talk about the life growing inside her, the life she hadn't wanted to share with him. And he needed to know why. He sat in front of her, their knees touching.

"Nicky and I went to the Hollow of Shadows," he said, thankful when her eyes lifted hopefully. He shook his head. "The Order wouldn't see us, didn't even acknowledge our presence."

She growled out a breath. "Why are they doing this? She didn't even know where Gray was."

Alex reached for her hands. "Don't worry, Sara. We'll get her out."

"Do you think Dillon got to Gray?"

He nodded. "If they really are true mates." He shifted closer. He wanted to pull her onto his lap, but she looked like she still needed her space. "I can't believe those two."

"I can." Her eyes found his and they glistened. "I knew they were falling for each other back when she found him whoring it up at the nightclub. She didn't like him with other women."

He tilted his head and joked, "Another secret you've been keeping from me?"

He'd made sure his tone was anything but accusatory, but her lower lip began to tremble.

"Sara, come here."

She didn't move, but burst out with an intense apology. "I'm sorry for not telling you."

This time he did pull her onto his lap, and held her close and tight and safe. "Don't be sorry for that."

She looked up into his eyes, not understanding his meaning.

He touched her face. Her beautiful, intelligent face that always made his gut ache with love—and that might very well be replicated on the wee one who grew within her. "Did you really think I'd react badly to this?"

Sara closed her eyes and sighed. "I know the thought of being a parent scares you."

"Damn right. Like nothing ever has or could."

"Then you understand why. All the changes this brings, a little life that's all ours. I couldn't bear it if you were disappointed, if I looked into your eyes and didn't see pleasure and excitement."

She was scared too, he realized. Not of the *balas*, but of losing his love. He had to make sure she understood that his love was always for her, would never wane, and was inside of her right now, growing strong and healthy.

"Look in my eyes, *Veana*," he demanded, tilting her chin with his fingers. "Tell me what you see."

Sara gave him a small smile before she took in his gaze. For several moments, she truly studied him; his eyes, his expression, and when he broke into a wide and happy smile, she did too.

He leaned in and kissed her. "Can't wait, my love. Can't wait to meet this *balas*." The sudden appearance of tears in her eyes brought him to his knees emotionally. "I don't know how I got this lucky. From a prisoner in this very cage to a mate and a father." His mouth was so close to hers. "From we to three. Oh, my dear, I love you so."

The round, red Impure Resistance symbol was painted into the entire length of floor in the room off the main hall. The four coiled snakes with fangs extended was permanent and a reminder of why this *credenti* was built, and for whom, and that the Impures would always fight for choice and freedom.

Rio pulled back from the small vampire circle that stood around the painted one. "We're blocked again."

"We were too quick going in," Piper added.

"Or too sloppy," Rio remarked.

Piper tossed him a testy glare. "Let's try again. We'll go slower this time."

Gray felt the power of the warriors recede inside of

him and the hum of unease saturate his organs. "This isn't going to happen. The Order has severed all known links into the mainframe. What are our other options? I need to get into Mondrar tonight."

"I'll give our contact a call," Piper said. "The one who gave us information on the senator. But something like this . . . It's going to cost big-time."

"Do it," Gray said without hesitation. "I'll cover it— whatever the cost."

Piper nodded. "Give me a couple of hours, okay?"

"If I have to," Gray grumbled.

"Better to go in under the cover of night anyway."

When she walked away, no doubt heading to her office within the main hall, Vincent dropped a hand on Gray's shoulder. "Go back to your place," he said, and Rio gave a nod of agreement. "Get some rest; get some food. You're going to need serious muscle if you expect to pull this off."

There was no point in arguing, and no other options at the moment. Vin and Rio were right. He needed to unplug, get something to eat, and get himself right before he went into the Order's jail and took what belonged to him and his family.

He left the main building and walked down the path to the private strip of beach. The anger that swelled within him every time he thought about his mother and the lies she'd just kept spewing over the years was still there, deep inside him. He didn't think it would ever truly go away. But shit, just the thought of her in that hole. It made him want to rip off the heads of every Order member, then refasten them and do it all over again.

Betraying the Breed. Fuck them. His mother was innocent. It was the Order—they'd been betraying the Breed since the beginning of time.

As he neared his cottage, the scent of *veana* and jaguar rushed into his nostrils and dropped three feet, giving him an instant hard-on.

So she hadn't bolted. She'd found her way to his home and invaded it like the delectable plague she was. His chest swelled; the back of his hand went hot. He could fight this need all goddamn day and night, but it went far beyond a response he could control now.

The small house he'd designed stood sturdy and welcoming, but instead of going inside, Gray headed around the side to the back. Her scent became heavy and lush there, and he wasn't surprised to find her in the small hot spring that had once been connected to the ocean in the distance.

She looked to be sitting on a rock beneath the water, her arms outstretched on the bank. The sight shook him up something fierce. Not because she was naked, her breasts and ripe nipples floating deliciously at eye level with the water. But because he'd imagined her here, just like this.

Waiting for him.

"How did you get in here?" he demanded. "How did you find this place?"

"Followed my nose," she said with irritating simplicity. "Been working really well so far."

He didn't appreciate this game she was playing. Not after she'd run out on him in the alley this morning. "Making yourself at home."

She shrugged, which only managed to show off her

incredible breasts even more. "You don't have a shower. I was pretty filthy, so I thought I'd take a bath." She looked around herself. "What is this place? A new Resistance Headquarters?"

"The new Impure *credenti*," he told her. "We've been building it for several months. Should be ready in a few weeks."

Dillon's soft gaze hardened. In fact, she was looking at him like he was crazy.

"An Impure *credenti*?" she repeated with disdain. "You offer this to a significant portion of the vampire population and it's like waging war on the Order."

He moved closer to her, closer to the heat. "If they wish to make it so."

Dillon rolled her eyes and scoffed. "They'll make it so—they'll make it a huge motherfucking death sentence."

"We'll see." He walked past her, his gaze on the ocean in the distance, pulling its weight to shore.

"You really ready to fight to the death over this?" she called to his back. "And before you answer, let me say it won't be just your death. Everyone you take on this trip into battle will go down with you."

Go down. Why was she always ready to admit defeat? Run in the other direction when something got hard and daunting? He turned back to face her. "The problem is, D, you think the Order is indestructible."

She turned too, rested her arms on the bank. "I know the Order, Gray. I know one of their ex-members so well I could scent him at a thousand feet. They are ruthless, unsympathetic devil vampires. They'll never surrender to Impures—no matter how just the Cause."

Her passion, her fear burst from her features. This wasn't just about winning an argument or losing a battle with the Order. This was about her feelings for him. She cared, maybe even more than she knew. And right now, with the moon lighting up her face, he could see it all, an unmasked expression of care, desire, maybe even love.

And it was irresistible.

He stripped out of his clothes as he walked toward her, then dove over her head into the pool. When he surfaced, he found her just a few feet away.

"They're everything you say and more, D," he said, watching the steam rise around her. "And that's just one of the reasons they must be dealt with. Not reasoned with—but dealt with. The warriors and I will exhaust all avenues until we have a place of equality within this society."

Her gaze moved over his shoulders, his chest. "Why not just live outside the *credenti*, your own rule, under the radar, running if you need to—"

"We shouldn't have to run," he said, adding pointedly, "No one should." He swam toward her, and she backed up until the curve of the bank stopped her. Gray placed one hand on either side of her shoulders, blocking her in. "Not from our pain, our past—or a future we refuse to fight for because we're scared."

"I'm not scared," she assured him.

But he didn't stop. "Or because we don't think we deserve it."

"Gray, please stop this. You're not listening to me. This isn't the way to fight them—"

He leaned in and kissed her. One soft, hungry kiss. And when he pulled back, he said, "You deserve it."

His words cut her. He could see it in her eyes, her face. She shook her head. She looked exhausted, and for the first time strangely vulnerable. He didn't want to care, but that was bullshit—he cared. He cared like a foolish, head-up-his-ass male.

"Why do you think this happened?" she whispered.

"The true mates thing?" he asked.

She nodded. "It's so unfair, so wrong. I don't know what to do with it."

He frowned, his guts tightening, but he said with a thread of dark humor, "Nothing in the world that disgusts you more than to be bound to me, huh?"

"Yes."

His frown deepened. "Christ." He started to move away, but she grabbed his hand, the hand that bore her mark.

Her eyes caught his and held. They were desperate, miserable. "I would rather be bound to anyone else."

"Stop," he snarled brutally. "Just stop talking now."

But she wouldn't. "Being bound to someone you love is the worst fate in the world for someone like me," she cried out.

Gray stilled with shock. "What?"

She shook her head.

Blood pounded in his ears and his cock was hard as steel. He wasn't having any more of this horseshit. He gathered her up and held her to him. "What did you just say? And for fuck's sake, say it loud because I can't tell if it's just me hearing shit or you just told me you loved me."

Seawater dripped from her shoulders, her neck, the

tips of her nipples, but what glistened in her eyes came from a very different place. "I love you, Gray. I do."

He went completely and utterly mad with hunger. Crushing her to him, he stole her mouth and kissed her hard and deep. She moaned against him and gave him her tongue to suckle. He drew it in and savored it. She tasted like the ocean, like tears, and he drank from her, his arms pressing her sides, his hands raking up into her hair to hold her scalp.

He tipped her chin back and kissed her neck, her jaw, one side of her mouth, then the other. Her eyes opened and she stared at him through dark, wet lashes. Her gaze was searching, intensely vulnerable, as though she were asking herself if she'd done the right thing admitting her true feelings to him. Gray offered her a small smile of gratitude, and instantly her expression changed, softened, and she surged toward him and captured his mouth again.

It was like a rush of honey, and his fingers fisted in her wet hair as he sucked her tongue into his mouth. She moaned and pressed her core against his hip. Steam rose up all around them like a screen, protecting them, encasing them in heat and scent and hunger.

As he kissed her, he moved, dragged her to the other side of the spring. He was lost in the headiness of the moment, felt like a drugged human who would die if he didn't get his fix. When his back hit the bank, he gripped her waist and lifted her so he could see her breasts in the shaft of moonlight. Nostrils flaring, he stared. She was so goddamn perfect. Full and round with a hint of slope that would lead him straight to heaven. He growled, calling out to her jaguar, warning the protective feline that her true mate was hungry and would be fed.

He lowered his head and took as much of the soft flesh of her breast into his mouth as possible. She gripped his shoulders, her nails digging into his skin, and keened into the cold air. He released her and just nuzzled the wet, heavy globe until he heard the cat purr. A grin hit his mouth and he flicked the bud with his nose once before suckling it again, first with his tongue, then gently scraping at the tip with his fangs. Above him, Dillon moaned and bucked her hips, and the steam around them began to scent of her, wet heat and hungry *veana*.

Gray's cock pulsed against his belly, ached, begged him to lower Dillon right onto his shaft, but he wasn't ready for dessert yet.

Shit, he hadn't even had dinner.

With a snarl of demonlike possessiveness, Gray whirled around and placed her on the very edge of the bank.

"Open up for me, D," he commanded with rough hunger. "As wide as you can."

Dillon whimpered from her perch and slowly spread her thighs. They shook. Goddamn, she shook.

"Not nearly enough," he uttered wickedly. "My tongue aches and my throat is so dry, baby. I need to drink you down."

She tore in a breath, wiggled her backside.

"Feet up now, baby, knees bent. That's right." When she was completely exposed to him, he reached around and grabbed her ass, slid her forward. "This is how I like it." He watched, his skin on fire, as pearly moisture leaked from her cunt. "Baby, you're crying for me."

"Oh God, Gray, please," she begged above him, dropping her hands behind her so he could have even more access.

Gray lowered his head and licked her.

Just once.

One lap from cunt to clit.

Dillon cried out.

The sound that echoed within him, rumbled through him was all pain, pleasure, and decadent torture. "You have the sweetest goddamn tears in the world, D."

And then he buried his head between her legs and feasted on her sweet syrup. The taste of her went straight to his cock. The thing jumped and pulsed against his belly, beading with precum, but he told it to fuck off, to be patient, and he drank deep until her swollen clit called to him. Raking his tongue from the opening of her body straight up between her drenched pussy lips, he circled around the hot bud, then suckled it into his mouth.

Dillon quaked and writhed in his arms, but he held on, suckled until he felt her clit swell against his tongue. Then he released one hand from her buttocks and brought it to her clit. While his fingers feathered the pulsing bud, he fucked her with his tongue.

"Oh God, yes! Gray. Please. I can't take any more."

But even as she said it, he gave her more. His thumb working her clit, tugging at the swollen flesh, dragging it up and down as his tongue went so deep he had to open his mouth wider, let his fangs rest on the head of her pussy.

And then he pressed them down gently, the hard, sharp tips just piercing a millimeter of her flesh.

It was like an earthquake against his mouth, against his tongue, as the walls of her pussy clenched and soaked the back of his throat in cream. Fuck yes! God, this *veana* was his, every inch, every drop. Dillon bucked and cried out as she came, and Gray just let her ride his mouth and tongue until the waves of pleasure receded.

He could've stayed there all day, camped out between her trembling thighs, licking her nice and slow and gentle until she came again, but Dillon wasn't having it. She wriggled down into the water, her skin pink and dusted with sweat. Or was it mist from the spring? Either way, he wanted a taste as she rode a different part of his anatomy.

But before he could get his hands around her waist, she turned and gave him her back. "Fuck me, Gray. Please."

Gray tensed. Her hands were spread, her legs too, and she was leaning over, using the bank to hold her weight. All he had to do was slip inside and take what he wanted—what his dick was screaming for.

He took a step closer, his thighs against the backs of hers, his hands itching to wrap around the curves of her hips.

"What's wrong?" she uttered, sudden tension in her voice. But she didn't look at him, didn't even glance over her shoulder. "You don't want me."

"Shit, D." His voice was gravel rough. "You feel my cock against your back. It's ready to explode. I'm ready to explode. But this isn't cutting it. You love me and I

love you, and yet you'll only let me fuck you from behind."

Her head dropped forward. "What's wrong with
that?" she nearly whimpered. "Most males would be
very happy for a fuck—"

"Stop right there." He grabbed her hips, but only to
turn her around to face him. His rock-hard glare
slammed into her soft, green one. "When are you going
to get it? I'm not most males. I'm not looking to screw
you and walk, fuck you, then watch you walk away."

"I know that."

But he didn't believe she did. Hell, he was pretty
sure she believed the opposite. His hands went to her
face. "How do I get you to look at me?"

"Stop," she uttered, trying to pull free.

As much as he hated seeing her struggle, both with
him and with her insides, Gray knew this had to happen or they couldn't be, couldn't go any further than
fucking like animals. "How do I get you to face me, let
me hold you, let me look into your eyes as I kiss you,
as I move inside of you?"

Her eyes were wide; her fangs scraped at her lower
lip. "You don't."

"I want to look at you, goddamn it!"

"And I just want you to fuck me!"

"What is it? What stops you from having even the
smallest bit of intimacy?"

"I let you into my body," she cried. "That's pretty
damn intimate."

He put one hand, the very one that held her mark,
on her left breast. "I want to get into your heart, not just
your cunt, Dillon. Christ."

Her lips trembled. "I can't."

"Why?" he rasped, his guts ripping apart inside him.

"I can't. I won't be able to . . . It won't work . . ."

He had a pretty good idea what was going on here, the fear inside her, the past creeping between them. He wasn't going to allow it. "What won't work?"

She tried to turn toward the bank. "I'm done here."

"No." He wouldn't let her go. This was it. They gave themselves over to each other or they gave up.

She glared at him. "I'm a hundred times stronger than you, Gray! I could snap you like a fucking twig!"

He held her firm. "Do what you gotta do, baby."

"You won't hold me against my will!" she screamed. "EVER!"

Pure misery and purer love wrapped around Gray in that moment. She wasn't perfect, and shit, he was far from perfect, but there was love there, a long-term and consistent fight within both of them that kept this flame alive.

Slowly, gently, he eased a wayward hair from her face and curled it around her ear. "If you need to beat the shit out of me to release some of what's holding you hostage, then do it."

She broke then. Crumpling in his arms, she cried, "Why are you doing this? Why won't you just run like everyone else in my sorry motherfucking life?"

He was really going to make the male responsible for this scream in agony. He kissed her cheek, the crease of her eye where one sad tear tried to escape. "No one ran from you, D. Take a good look back and you'll see it was you—you who did all the running." His eyebrow lifted a fraction. "I'm not saying there wasn't a good reason. But it's done. No one is ever going to hurt you again. Stop running, baby, and stand still with me."

"Oh, Gray . . ."

He picked her up and gently placed her down on his shaft, but instead of pumping inside her, he pulled her against his chest and just held her to him. Held her strong and supportive until he felt her limbs relax, until her breathing slowed.

Dillon felt as though she were being carried. Not by his body or his arms, but by his love for her and his unflinching belief in them as a couple. Her insides warmed and her cunt squeezed around his shaft and she held on tight. God, she wanted to believe in them too, so much. If she could just let go now, right now, and trust that this male she loved wouldn't let her fall.

Leaving the safety of his warm chest and steady heartbeat wasn't easy, but she lifted her head and looked into his eyes.

He smiled. "There's my baby."

One of his hands remained around her while the other traveled down to cup her backside. It was the most difficult, most wonderful, most gut-wrenching feeling to look into Gray's eyes while he began to slowly thrust inside of her.

She felt impaled, both in her core and in her unbeating heart. Dillon, the Beast, the *mutore*, the one who survived on shame, loved and was loved.

"Don't close your eyes, D," he said with fierce, possessive hunger. "Not for this ride."

She nodded, quivering in his arms as heat spread within her.

"Keep looking at me. Even when you come." He kissed her, suckled her lower lip. "Especially when you come."

His words sent another shock of heat to her core, and her cunt clenched mercilessly. She wanted to come so badly, and yet she didn't want this intimacy, this intensity between them to end.

Water jumped and sprayed around them as Gray ground his cock inside her, circling his hips, pistoning inside her. But his eyes never left hers and his arms remained strong around her.

"You belong to me now," he growled possessively. "Never forget that." His nostrils flared and he looked like he could eat her raw.

He bent his knees and thrust deeply, battering her cunt again and again until Dillon lost her breath completely and gripped his back, his shoulders, her nails digging into his flesh.

"Oh God, Dillon," he uttered, his gaze fierce and his voice strained. "Baby, you're sucking me so deep, from the head to the base of my cock—I'm drenched in your cream."

Shaking, on the verge of exploding, Dillon wrapped her legs tighter around his waist and bucked her hips, moving with him, taking blow after blow as she held his gaze and tears spilled down her cheeks.

"I love you, D," he whispered, so pained. "I love you so fucking much I think I'll die from it."

"No," she whispered. "You'll live. Just like me, with me—over me, night after night, your eyes on mine."

Gray grabbed her hips, settled his cock deep inside her, then executed a series of wondrous, breath-shattering, earth-shaking blows to her cunt. One, two, three—until Dillon cried out. Shaking uncontrollably, her eyes wide, she lifted her chin and howled her release. Then Gray too fell, delivering one final thrust before he answered her call with one of his own.

It wasn't her first fuck, Dillon thought through the haze, through the heat.

But it was the first time she'd ever made love.

19

As Gray carried her out of the water and up to the house, one emotion after another slammed through Dillon. Love, connection, anxiety, questions, doom. She hated the onslaught, wanted to run from it, but she wasn't going to do that anymore. She'd made a promise—to him and to herself—when she'd looked into his eyes and allowed herself to be taken.

She didn't go back on her word.

She wasn't that *veana* anymore.

It was dark inside the cottage when Gray burst through the double door, but the half dozen skylights in the ceiling welcomed the twilight inside. Gray didn't slow. He moved through the main room and into a bedroom that was utterly beautiful and all him. White, gray, and black, uncluttered and clean lines. Dillon couldn't help but smile.

Under the pale light of the young moon streaming in through another set of six wide skylights, Gray placed her on the large bed and crawled in with her. He covered them both with sheets and blankets, then gathered her close and kissed her until her skin warmed and dried.

"I want this," he whispered close to her ear. "Not just you, but this."

Dillon couldn't help herself. She wrapped her leg around his waist and squeezed. "Me too." God, more than anything.

"Then I need you to tell me, D."

Her throat tightened painfully, and a current of unease moved through her. She didn't need to ask him what he meant.

"Just me, okay?"

She released her hold on him and rolled onto her back.

Gray lifted his head. His eyes were gentle, but firm. "Remember the love thing."

"Don't remind me of that," she said drily.

"Fuck you, D. I'm going to remind you of it every goddamn second until you tell me what happened that turned you inside out and backward."

He stared down at her, waiting. Only Gray Donohue. No one ever spoke to her the way he did. No anger, but the fierce heat of love and care. Was it possible to have a relationship, the real kind, when one person kept a part of herself hidden? She'd never even thought about it until this male dropped into her life. She'd never wanted to think about it until he'd placed her down on his cock, forced her to look at him, deep inside him, and made love to her.

What was she so afraid of? she wondered. That he

would be disgusted by her, ashamed of her—that he'd think she brought it on herself? No. That wasn't Gray.

She took a deep breath and a huge leap of faith, then reached up and brought his mouth to her temple. "Do it."

"Like this? Through the blood?" His breath was warm on her skin.

"Yes," she whispered, her muscles tensing, her head dizzy. She couldn't say the words . . . all those words. It was too much. "But you have to promise me something, Gray."

"Anything, D."

She swallowed. This was it. No going back. "No matter what you see, how it makes you feel, you won't go after anyone."

He sighed.

"Promise me," she said.

"All right."

She braced herself, fisting the sheets at her sides, and whispered, "Go."

Gray bit hard into Dillon's temple and, with the confidence of someone who had accrued much experience navigating memories, he fast-forwarded through the near present, through the past several decades, slowing down only when he started to see a younger and younger *veana*. Then he stopped altogether when he saw her surrounded by her young Beast brothers and a face Gray recognized as the vile demon among vampires, Cruen.

For the briefest of moments Gray just stared at the face of a young Dillon as she kicked a blue ball back and forth with her brothers in what looked to be a basement. No windows, cement floor, brick on the walls. But they didn't seem to mind the lack of light and decor. In fact, they were all laughing, enjoying themselves, but none more than her. Gray's heart pinged with longing. That long tawny hair swinging around near her waist, those bright and happy hazel eyes, and that smile. When had he ever seen her smile like that?

He heard her moan softly, and the sound kick-started him into action. He propelled himself forward, clip after clip, image after image. Fight training, blood samples, more play, less play, a swim in the river—

He stopped. He'd nearly run over it. It was the swim that made him slam on the brakes. Fear, shame, and unimaginable pain clung to this memory as it hadn't with any of the others. In fact, the memory almost resisted his call to view it. Gray had never experienced such a thing, such a brick wall.

Fighting to keep the swell of anger that was threatening to rise further, he pushed back hard, a few frames at a time, until he had the beginning of the scene.

Which, no doubt, was the beginning of the end for a happy, laughing young *veana*.

Dillon was inside a room, a laboratory. There were no windows, so he couldn't tell if it was day or night— just that the room was empty, save for her. She was standing over a metal table, looking into a microscope. She appeared to be around fifteen, and the way she was handling the placement and care of the slides she was observing made Gray think she was far more serious at this age than she had been as a carefree *balas* playing with her brothers.

"It's late."

Gray's heart stuttered as Dillon glanced up and smiled at the guard in the doorway. He was built like a short linebacker, with round, dark eyes that seemed to take in everything. It was clear that Dillon knew him well, that he was one of Cruen's best and most loyal sentries.

"I'll be done in a few minutes," she told him. "Just checking a blood sample of mine."

He walked into the room, came to stand beside her. "Can I see?"

"Sure." Dillon felt no fear, no strangeness at this action. She trusted him. She had no reason not to.

He looked up, grinned at her. "Pretty blood for a pretty female."

Something quick and strange moved within her, but she cast it aside. "Thanks. I can turn it off now. I should be done for the night."

"I wish I could turn it off," he said, his gaze moving over her face, then down her neck to her chest.

Dillon stepped back. She wasn't a fool. She was a virgin and trustworthy, but she wasn't a fool. "I'm going now. My brothers are expecting me."

He grabbed her arm, and when he did, Gray felt Dillon—the one beside him in the bed—grab his arm too.

"Your brothers are tearing into a deer carcass right now, sweetheart," he hissed, his fangs descending as he yanked her to him. "I can't stop myself. You are just too sweet, too damn ripe."

Terrified now, Dillon tried to push him away. "Let me go."

The male grinned, reached for the split in her blouse and tore it all the way to her navel. "Fight me all you want. You haven't the strength to deny me yet."

She kicked at him, tried to get her knee up between his legs, but he squeezed her too tight. Panic blurred her vision, and she forced herself to breathe, forced herself to think. Begging didn't work, strength—she did have enough—maybe if she acted above him, reminded him of who he was hurting.

"You dare touch a *veana*, Impure," she rasped, flashing her own set of fangs and lunging for him. "The Order will cage you for just looking at me wrong."

"A *veana*." He laughed as he hauled her up and tossed her on the metal table. "You are a *mutore*, sweetheart—a Beast, little better than an animal."

"You're the only animal in this room!"

He hit her hard across the face. So hard she passed out for a moment. When she came to, her pants were off, her underwear was ripped and hanging at her waist, and the guard was pushing into her. Blinding pain stabbed at her lower half, and she tried to get up, tried to slap and push and get away, but he slammed her back down. Her head hit the metal table and one second after it did, she shifted into her jaguar form.

Gray pulled out of her temple as gently as he could manage, but not before he saw what her tear-heavy cat eyes did: Cruen, standing at the entrance to the laboratory, watching—curious, clinical, as though she were nothing more than a scientific experiment.

His rage barely contained, he gathered Dillon up in his arms and rocked her.

"Baby . . ." he uttered, the urge to kill so ripe within him he could hardly breathe.

"You promised me," she whispered.

Oh, fuck, I don't know if I can keep that promise, he heard his mind scream as his hand burned with the need to hold a blade—the very hand that held her mark. *I don't think the jaguar within us both will let me.*

Blood ran from Alexander's wrist as he moved through the gates of his old *credenti* and headed down the path toward town. He wondered if his blood would still be welcome in this place if the community members had decided to station guards at the entrance.

He imagined not. His mother and her mate had a shitload of pull in here, and there was nothing they despised more than seeing him—being reminded that a son of the Breeding Male had once been forced upon them all.

Darkness ate up the pathway inside the forest, but it was a good thing. Most members of the *credenti* would be inside at blood meal and family reflection.

The scent of the village pushed into his nostrils, and he growled in disgust. "I shouldn't have come," he grumbled. "With Cellie locked up and Sara—"

"Nicky swore he'd contact us the second he has a way in," Lucian said, keeping pace beside him, his white-blond hair reflecting the light of the moon overhead.

"Yeah, I know."

"And with the Eyes doing that bullshit avoidance dance, it could be a while."

"I know," Alex snarled.

Lucian turned to glare at him. "Then stop being a pussy and let's get this done."

"Maybe I misspoke," Alex said, sidestepping a fallen tree. "What I meant to say is, I should've come alone."

Lucian smirked. "Yeah, right. What fun would that be?"

"You keep your nose clean, Luca, seriously."

"Sure, sure." He pointed his chin in the direction of the town, which was only a few yards away now. "Think we'll run into that winner set of parents of yours? I'd love to introduce myself, then introduce them to my fangs."

"We're not here for a reunion," Alex said, though the idea wasn't half bad.

Lucian shrugged. "Just sayin'. If it comes to that."

"If it comes to that," Alex said in a low voice as they maneuvered to the back of one of the shops, "you can't do anything, especially draw blood. Not with how close to the change you are and will always be."

"Shit, Alex," he hissed, annoyed. "It's not meno-pause."

"No, it's a thousand times worse. Bronwyn's blood inside you keeps you sane and moderately calm, but there's no way of knowing if something could set you off. And she isn't here to haul you back." He shrugged. "I'm just sayin', be careful."

A sound drifted over to them then, a soft whistle that could've been a bird in one of the trees overhead if they hadn't planned the signal themselves.

"Over here," came a sharp whisper.

Alexander and Lucian followed the sound and the scent and found the Impure female they'd been told would be meeting them behind a small, dark house a couple of yards down.

When they approached, she retreated from the shadows and met them solidly, her chin raised. She was little more than a girl, maybe nine or ten, and Alexander felt a pinch in his side.

"You're the Roman brothers," she said, her dark eyes large and curious. "Sons of the Breeding Male." She looked at Alex. "I wasn't yet born when you lived here."

Good thing. She would've been visiting him in a cage, not under a star-clad sky. "What can you tell us?" he asked, trying to keep his tone gentle, though he was pretty sure a trace of impatience needled through.

"There is a structure far out in the old pastures," she said, pointing to the right. "It's very hard to get to, and it's abandoned." She paused, chewed her lower lip. "Or they think it is."

Alexander wasn't altogether convinced that Cruen had a hideout here. It was just too irrational, too arrogant. Then again, both attributes ran thickly within that *paven*'s veins.

"You'll show us," Lucian said, no question in his tone.

She nodded. "But payment first."

Alexander took out a small bag. It was filled with *credenti* gold. "Here you are."

She looked at the bag of coins and frowned. "I don't want that."

"Why not?" asked Lucian, confused.

Her voice dropped even lower. "The elders here will know I've done something bad to get that gold. I won't be able to spend it on the one thing I want."

"And what is that?" Alexander asked.

Her large eyes met his. "Blood. Pure blood."

"You get that from the Order. Why would you—"

"Not enough," she interrupted, a sudden passion in her voice. "Never enough. And it has been worse lately. More work, less blood—more being rounded up and taken to the Paleo."

Alexander glanced at Luca, who shook his head and cursed under his breath.

"Take it, whatever you need."

As Alexander put his wrist before the *veana*, felt the unremarkable prick of her young and unsteady fangs, he thought of all that was collapsing within their breed.

Gray Donohue's fight didn't seem trivial anymore. This inequality, overly strict rule, and forced sterilization within the Eternal Breed was wrong and vile, and something Alexander was determined to see changed before his own little Impure entered the world.

20

The small wound in her temple stung, but the one that had just been unleashed inside her threatened to crush her flat. As she stood at the edge of the bed, the darkness of night still coating the room and the scent of sea, blood, and climax in the air, she watched her true mate sleep.

This wasn't running.

She was going to get his mother and bring her back to him. She knew Mondrar well. She could take the risks. As a Pureblood, she wouldn't be detected by the Order.

He shifted his weight, one heavily muscled arm reaching for something across the bed. Her skin prickled. Her mind whispered for her to take off her clothes and get back in bed.

But instead she crept out of the cottage and into the deep night.

This wasn't running, she told herself again as she

flashed away. This was proving that she understood Gray's purpose and that his fights were now hers.

He was weak, so weak that when Cruen called for him, he came without a second thought.

The ancient *paven*'s favored reality was an endless strip of sun-warmed beach. To the untrained and virginal eye it seemed tranquil, harmless, but to anyone who'd ever been there for any length of time, they knew the ocean, sand, and palms beyond were a never-ending trap.

Cruen's fire-blue eyes moved over Titus piteously. "You appear weary, Brother. Hungry." His mouth tipped up at the corners. "How about you tell me what you need and I will tell you what you will give me for it?"

"I cannot revert back to Breeding Male status, Cruen," Titus rasped, looking for something to catch his weight but finding nothing.

Nothing but Cruen's outstretched arm.

He turned so that his pale wrist was exposed. Titus's fangs extended and his mouth watered.

"I cannot become an animal, a rutting monster that is reviled and feared," he continued desperately.

"You will go to Mondrar," Cruen said flatly. "You will make sure the *mutore* female . . ."

My daughter.

". . . finds and removes Celestine Donohue from her cage."

Through his haze of blood lust, Titus tried to make sense of such a request, but it was impossible. Hunger clawed at his insides, roused the Breeding Male.

"Yes, Cruen," he cried out. "Yes."

Only when his fangs were an inch deep within Cruen's vein and suckling down his wondrous, magical blood did Titus recall the evil *paven*'s final words.

"Then bring the mutore to me."

"Hey, sleeping beauty."

Gray opened one eye to the sun pouring in from the skylights. His head was pounding jackhammer style. What the hell? Then he remembered taking Dillon's memories—then he remembered those goddamn memories themselves, and a fresh wave of vitriol battered him.

"Dillon." He reached for her.

"She's gone."

Piper's voice. He sat up, his eyes narrow slits through the slamming of his brain and realized it wasn't the sun at all. It was still night and all three Warriors stood at the end of his bed, one of them holding a flashlight.

"Get that thing out of my face, Rio."

His own face a mask of disgust, the military Impure eyed the bed. "Don't need to ask what you've been doing."

Gray turned his gaze to Piper. "Do you know where she is?"

Piper shook her head.

"I can't fucking believe that *veana*," he grumbled.

"Really?"

Piper jabbed the male in the side with her elbow. "Shut up, Rio."

"So you had one hot night," Rio amended, his tone a little more sympathetic. "It's not like you—"

Gray flattened him with a look. "Love her?"

The male shrugged.

"Love doesn't solve the big problems, G," Vincent said coolly. "Trust me, I know."

Piper sideswiped him with a glare. "No, Gray. Trust *me*. I know."

Gray wasn't in the mood. For their jokes, their bitching, or their advice. Last night had been one of the greatest fucking nights of his life. He'd made love, straight up and real, to the *veana* he loved; he'd heard her tell him that she loved him too; and he'd finally been allowed inside her head, her heart, and her past.

How could he have possibly known she'd regret it all, cancel out everything they'd built together in the last several hours, and bolt?

He got out of bed, nude and head pounding, and went into the closet. He flipped on the lights. "Tell me you have something for me, Pip," he called out. "I need to get my mother out of that bullshit hellhole, bring her here, and then we'll get back to work." He pulled on his clothes with far too much venom, then walked back into the bedroom. "I won't be deterred again after this."

"I'll go with you, if you need a second."

About to pull on his shoes, Gray eyed Rio. "You're serious."

His face contorted with irritation. " 'Course I'm serious. Fuck you."

"Well, I appreciate that, man. I do. But I'm going to go in quick, quiet, and solo, just like at the Paleo." He nodded at the male. "I'll contact you if I get into trouble."

"You do that," he said. "And, you know, I hope your mom's okay."

"All right. All right," Piper said loudly. "One more word from the penis gallery and I think I'm going to stick something sharp in my eye."

Vincent turned to stare at her. "Penis gallery?"

"Yeah, I said it." She nodded at Gray, pulled out a piece of paper. "Finish up with the shoes there, and I'll show you how you're going to get into Mondrar."

Mondrar was truly hell aboveground, which made Dillon feel oddly at peace there.

She had been inside the six-floored domed structure with its open, forget-about-privacy cells and aniselike scent twice. Both times she'd gone undercover as a guard looking for criminals who'd had political connections to her human senator. She'd paid killer bank to learn about the secret tunnel that had been dug by two former inmates over a fifty-five-year span. Granted, it was blocked up with four feet of moss and a metal container, but the thirty-minute dig to get inside was worth it. She would locate the *veana* and get her out, bring her back to her son—to Dillon's true mate.

Prove to him that she loved him.

Jesus, she really had become a pussy.

As the sky outside turned a steely gray, Dillon slipped on one of the sets of Mondrar inmate clothing hidden inside a metal box within the floor, grabbed the other and the heavy broom beside it, and began her search.

She moved quickly and quietly, inspecting one floor after another, careful to keep her eyes down. She acted as if she was just another one of the low-risk prisoners assisting in maintenance. But by the fourth floor she started to grow concerned. She'd been inside Mondrar for thirty minutes and she hadn't found Celestine. The longer she stayed, the more dangerous it became.

Just when she was about to change her plan, head up to the top floor and work her way down, a voice called out to her from one of the cells.

"This way," the male voice hissed. "The one you seek is here."

Dillon couldn't see where the voice was coming from, but she followed it, moving down a long row of open cells, her hackles raised. She wasn't about to trust anyone, but information from a fellow prisoner could yield something new.

"She is at the end of the cell block," the male voice uttered, but from where, Dillon could not see. What the hell was this? And who was this?

But then she spotted the *veana* at the far side of one of the wide hallways, just as the voice had said, and she broke into a relieved grin. She looked around, her eyes darting from cell to cell, searching for the voice, the face. Her jaguar was on edge, claws out, ready to strike. Who was he? And why would he want to help her?

"Go to her," said the voice, strong, older. For a moment she thought she'd heard it somewhere before, but then he uttered more forcefully, "Now, *Veana*. Before they come for the morning meal."

Damn it. Dillon had a choice to make and fast. Still vigilant, she left the mysterious voice and ran down the hallway, straight to Celestine Donohue's cell. Supplied inside the container, she had the key that opened every cage on this floor and she quickly used it to open the door.

The older *veana* was alone and curled up on her pallet. Dillon raced inside and gave her a shake. "Wake up and put these on. We need to go. Now!"

The *veana* looked up, her eyes tired and confused—and startlingly like her son's. "Who are you?"

"A friend of Gray's and Sara's. I've come to take you home."

Cellie's gaze flickered to the open cell door, then the set of work robes Dillon had tossed on her lap. In seconds, she was on her feet, robes on, following Dillon out into the hallway.

"I hope you know what you're doing," she said, her gaze flickering every which way.

"Me too." She handed Celestine the broom, and the two of them kept their heads down and slowly made it to the stairwell. Once inside, they took off, racing down the steps. At the bottom, Dillon motioned for her to follow and they headed toward the metal plug and the moss. But just as they rounded the corner, a figure dressed only in a black robe and hood flashed in front of them.

Dillon shoved Celestine behind her, dropped into fighting stance, and hissed.

"I am not here to stop you," the figure said.

Dillon recognized the voice at once. "It's you. You helped me find her, get her out. Why?"

The robed figure shook his head, raised his arm. Dillon braced herself for something—she wasn't sure what. But once his arm was above his head, he froze.

"What is this?" Dillon demanded, ready to rip the hood right off this male. "What are you doing?"

"I am sorry," he said, dropping his arm. And as he

did, the metal plug opened to reveal the strange blue light of a nearing dawn. "Go. Just go. Quickly."

Dillon didn't ask anything more, didn't even give him a second thought. She grabbed Celestine's hand and ran through the opening.

21

"Holy shit." Lucian let out a low whistle to accompany his curse.

"How many know about this?" Alexander asked, taking in the lavish interior of a cabin that, from the outside, appeared to be falling down.

"Only my father," said the young female. "He assists Master Cruen in exchange for blood and . . . other things."

"Master Cruen?" Lucian uttered with a sneer. "That's what you have to call him?"

The female looked surprised. "It is how many Impures refer to the Purebloods who employ them."

Not my little Impure, Alexander thought blackly as he moved to the far end of the room where a small laboratory was set up.

"When was he here last?" he asked the female as he picked up a glass jar and examined the contents.

"Hasn't been this month at all."

"Does he come frequently?"

"Varies," she said, her nervous gaze continually checking the window. "There's never a pattern to it."

Frustration built within Alex. Without a pattern, it was going to be difficult to lay a trap. It wasn't as though they could camp out here and wait for the *paven* to show up.

He dropped the jar back on the metal table with little care. "How does he manage to get inside the *credenti* without being seen?"

"He is Order." As if that explained it all—and maybe it did. "But he was seen," she added cryptically.

Alexander's brow lifted.

She smiled shyly. "By me. It was how my father found out . . . how he got the job—"

"Alex, get in here." Lucian's call from the other room interrupted their discussion and had Alex on edge.

With the speed gifted to a morphed male, he was by his brother's side in under five seconds. "What is it?"

Lucian's eyes were strained, his mouth grim. "Check out the painting. Over the fireplace."

Alexander turned. For a moment he wasn't exactly sure he was seeing what his brain was telling him he was seeing. "Is that . . . Cellie?"

"Unless she has a twin we don't know about," Lucian said blankly.

"Why would Cruen have a painting of her?"

"No idea. It's fucking creepy, though."

"She's in *swell*."

Lucian neared the canvas, squinted at the bottom right-hand corner. "Look at the date."

Alexander moved beside his brother, leaning close

to the wisp of black scribble, confusion assaulting him. "That can't be right. That's after Sara and Gray were born."

"Unless she had another kid," Lucian uttered.

Before Alexander could respond or even process, the young female burst into the room. "We have to go," she said, panic threading her tone. "Someone's coming, and the light of a new day threatens."

The bargain he'd struck with the Pureblood at his side made Gray fierce with anger, but at least he was inside. The Pureblood, who's name was Jem, had assured Gray that his mother was well and that they would have zero problems getting her out. Sounded great, sounded perfect—hell, it sounded too perfect. After the night he'd had—shit, the year he'd had—Gray wasn't trusting anyone.

Dressed in the uniform of a guard, Gray moved in the same brisk manner as Jem, trying like hell to mute the sound in his head. Like the Paleo, this place was a constant buzz of thought. He had to work hard to sift through the barrage and find the one he'd come for.

"How close are we?" Gray whispered tightly as they passed row after row of cell blocks.

"She's on this floor," the *paven* answered. "Down at the end."

Gray's hands balled into fists, itching for his blades. He sure as hell hoped so. Because if this *paven* was wrong or fucked him in any way, he was as good as dust.

When they came to the end of the hallway, Jem sank back into the shadows and Gray followed. As two guards walked past, Gray tried to pull in the thoughts of the male beside him, but he couldn't grasp on to anything except the chaos of level upon level of inmates.

"This way," Jem whispered, moving out of the shadows and back into the light. "Hurry."

As the din on the floor continued to grow, Gray followed the *paven* to the right, then walked down a length of empty cells.

Finally, the *paven* slowed. "Here it is."

Everything happened fast and furious then. Jem had the door of a cell pulled wide. Inside Gray's mind, he heard the cry of a woman, saw a blanketed figure inside the cell, and rushed at it without listening to his screaming instinct. The cell door slammed shut, the blanket dropped to reveal nothing at all, and the Pureblood who had screwed him was slowly backing up.

But not fast enough.

With a feral growl, Gray shot forward, thrust his arm through the bars, grabbed Jem and yanked him forward, clipping his forehead against the metal bars. "You fucking asshole."

The Pureblood struggled to get free, but Gray had *her* blood inside him, along with a torrent of adrenaline. He was every bit the Beast his mate was.

Jem looked terrified and confused as he tried to turn his head, twitching both ways.

"Looking for help?" Gray asked.

"Please," the male begged. "I'm sorry."

"I'm not," Gray uttered. In one rush of movement, he reached for the blade at his back, slammed it through the bars, and sliced the *paven*'s neck.

When he tossed the body to the ground and stepped

back, he found a *veana* in Order robes standing right behind the dead *paven*, a black circle around her narrowed left eye.

"Thank you," she said with a false smile, her long white hair in two neat plaits behind her back. "Saved us the trouble of doing it. He has betrayed us many times."

Gray wasn't interested. "Where is she?"

The *veana* pretended to look surprised, her clay-colored eyes wide. "You came to find someone? I thought you were here because you finally realized what a bad little Impure you've been and were ready to accept your punishment."

"Where is she?" he repeated, cold violence in his tone.

The smile faded and she walked toward him, the body of the *paven* disappearing with one wave of her hand. "You and your brethren have been trying to break into our frequency for some time. We have felt your push."

Trying to break in. Gray sneered. Who was this *veana* kidding? "And you will continue to feel our push until we have what we want."

Her lip curled. "And what is that?"

"Ending castrations, choice within the Impure breed, equal rights."

A soft, gentle laugh escaped her throat. "The problem, my heart-beating friend, is that Impures are not equal and they never will be."

Gray reached out and grabbed her by the throat with one hand. Had his blade pressed into her temple with the other. Her eyes filled with amusement, and she placed her hand over his and squeezed. Gray felt an electric current run through him, but nothing more severe than that. His surprise was echoed in the *veana's* eyes, now completely stripped of her easy confidence and mirth.

She stared at him as though she were seeing him for the first time. Her eyes narrowed and he pressed the blade a millimeter deeper into her temple.

"Ending my long life won't get you what you're after."

"It's a start," he said aloud.

"It's a start to war."

Just as Dillon had said. He twisted the blade. "We're prepared for that."

"No you're not." She studied him, her gaze serious. "You will never have the army of Impures you'd need for an uprising. Not when they rely on the Order to survive."

The arrogance of that statement, of this *veana* and all who thought like her, made Gray's insides shatter. He was nothing; his father was nothing, Sara . . . No matter what happened to him, he was going down fighting for all of them.

"Impure slaves for eternity—is that it?" he said.

"It is what they excel at." Her eyes connected with his. "Most of them, anyway. Now, you are different. You have gifts, Gray Donohue. Unlike your father."

Gray pressed the blade into her skin. A trickle of blood snaked down the side of her face. "Don't speak of my father, or the rock at your feet will run slick with your blood."

But she didn't heed him. Her gaze traveled down the arm that held her—an Order member. "He was like-minded, yes, but he didn't have your mental gifts. Or this unusual strength you seem to possess." Her eyes lifted, locked with his. "He cried on the table, you know."

Every cell in Gray's body screamed at him to drill his blade deep within her skull and get rid of one more Order member. But his mind flared with warning and with the voices of the cell mates on the floor, some who were overhearing his conversation.

With sharp hatred, Gray drew back his blade and released her. "You want me to attack you."

She grinned broadly. "Not only do you have mental gifts and curious strength, but you have restraint as well."

"I'm done playing with you," Gray uttered. "Come back when you have something interesting to say."

"Like a bargain?" she whispered. "The Order stops the castrations of Impures, gives you equal footing as the Purebloods, equal rule, equal life?"

He sneered. "Yeah, something like that."

"I cannot."

"Then fuck off." He turned and started to walk away, back into the darkness of the cell.

"But *you* can."

Her words stilled him. And even though he knew he was dealing with the devil here, those words she'd just uttered were far too tempting to ignore. He glanced over his shoulder and caught her smug gaze.

She inhaled deeply. "Well, you can try."

"I believe I already am."

Her eyes narrowed and her fangs elongated. "We have a vacant chair on the Order."

His pulse jumped in his veins; his nostrils flared. "And?"

She drew closer to the bars until it almost appeared as though she were a part of them. "If you were to take that chair, you would speak for all Impures."

His heart slammed against the ribs that housed it. In his mind, the very logical place that knew this was at the very least a bluff, thoughts were forming. And possibilities, possibilities he desperately wanted to jump on at the very remote chance she was actually offering something real.

"The Order would never allow an Impure at its table," he said with a grunt of forced humor.

"Not just any Impure," she agreed. "No. But an Impure with gifts? Possible. Granted, solutions to issues raised must be fought for and agreed on by all." She tilted her head and sighed. "But it is a . . . voice."

This was madness. Complete and total insanity, and yet he was hooked like a fucking fish with a worm before him.

Thing was, the worm wanted something too. What was it?

She grinned, knowing exactly where his mind was headed. "Though we don't believe the Impures could manage to win a war against us, the Order does not wish to incur one. There is already enough discord and unrest in the breed." Her brows lifted. "With all these *mutore*s on the loose."

As anger, sudden and deadly, burned within him, Gray feigned ignorance. "What's a *mutore*?"

Her snow-white eyebrows lifted in surprise. "A Beast, a shape-shifting vampire who has no place in this world, in our breed. They are a bad omen, a mistake against nature, and they bring bad luck to anyone who comes in contact with them." The smile that spread on her face was primitively devious. "With the Pureblood circles your sister runs in, I'm surprised you haven't heard of them before."

The true price of a seat on the Order was becoming clear.

Her eyes flashed. "I want the *mutore* you harbor. This animal. *Dillon*."

The way the *veana* said his mate's name nearly sent Gray over the edge. His fingers itched to toss the blade he still held in his hand straight at her head. But that would be foolish.

Instead he wrinkled his brow, shook his head, and said, "Who?"

"Meow." She laughed, her eyes bright. "It is funny that you should protect the very one who has betrayed you."

Something moved inside him, near his heart, but he ignored it. "I have no idea what you're talking about, but clearly you love hearing yourself attempt to be cryptic."

"Why did you come to Mondrar, Gray? Did someone tell you there was something here you might be interested in?"

His entire body flooded with heat, and the true mate mark on his hand burned.

The *veana* looked sympathetic. "Clearly your gifts have not extended into seeing the truth in those you love. Are you so disbelieving that someone like her would sell you out, and the four other *mutores* she is in contact with, just to pay for her freedom?"

No. Gray's nostrils flared. Not possible. She was a nightmare, a hellion, a ruin, and a bolter, but she wouldn't dive that deep into the soul-sucking pool of betrayal.

Even for freedom.

And yet a faint trace of doubt snaked through him.

"No, I see you're not." She reached up to her temple and smoothed the skin with her fingers. The nick, the drops of blood, gone in a heartbeat. "Think of what you could do for 'your' kind with a seat on the Order." Her chin dropped. "You father would be so proud, Gray."

He stood there, still as stone, legs apart like a gunslinger, and just let the chaos inside him reign.

"Think about it: Order Member Gray Donohue," she said. "I will return in an hour for your decision."

She flashed, as he suspected she'd been capable of doing all along—even in his grasp.

Alexander and Lucian arrived at the back door of the house in SoHo just as the sun was coming up. They'd narrowly escaped being seen by the female's father, who had been so surprised to see his daughter there he'd made a thorough sweep of the compound. The poor female had been so shaken up, Alexander had wished for the sun to heel and remain hidden for another few minutes so he could've offered the girl another meal of his blood.

But she'd had to make do with the bag of gold coins

he'd forced into her small hands before they'd raced away.

Alexander heard his family before he saw them. Lucian too, and they both followed the din to the library, where the Romans and the Beasts were congregating. The massive pile of Roman brothers within the bookshelf-lined walls had become a custom as of late, and normally Alexander would've appreciated the warmth of the sight before him. But after being in his *credenti*, after seeing the painting of Celestine, he felt decidedly confused and shaken.

He wanted Sara, in his bed, her arms around him. But it was Sara who needed the comfort now. Nicky hadn't contacted them when they were inside the *credenti*, which meant no Titus, no Eyes, no way into Mondrar, and by the look on his true mate's face, she hadn't received any news either.

Kate and Bron bracketed her on the couch. "Nothing from Gray. Nothing from Dillon," Sara told him, paler than he'd ever seen her.

Alexander crossed to her at once, took her hand and pulled her to him, gathered her in his arms. "If they're not here by dark, I'll go and find them all."

"We will all go," Erion said, and when Alexander glanced over at him and at the Beasts, each one nodded in turn.

"We will invade the Order if we have to," Nicholas said, going to stand behind Kate.

"The Order," Alexander snarled, though he held his mate with a gentle hand. "The puppet masters of us all. Even our father seems to have abandoned us again. I'm beginning to agree with Gray and his movement, this

Resistance. The Order's one-size-fits all, dictatorial, thumb-in-every-bloody-pie rule needs to end."

As the room erupted into a fit of opinions, facts, ideas, and strategy to deal with the Order, Alexander realized no one had asked him and Luca about the bunker, about Cruen. He glanced over at his brother, who at that moment had eyes only for Bronwyn and their child.

Perhaps he'd hold on to this news, he reasoned, tightening his hold on his beloved, especially the painting they'd seen, until he could question Cellie himself.

"You have a tracking device in your leg," Dillon said, her fingers prodding the older *veana*'s skin behind her knee. "We need to remove it before I take you home."

Just like she'd done with Gray, Dillon had flashed Celestine to several locations before sticking the landing. She wasn't exactly sure what had made her choose the one she did. Maybe it gave her strength to sit beside the Eastern Vermont riverbank again; maybe she just wanted to feel close to Gray.

"You know how to do it?" Celestine asked, her eyes sharp as she straightened her leg.

Kneeling beside her, Dillon nodded as she retrieved one of the knives she'd taken from Gray's stash in the cottage. "But you need to hold really still."

She felt the *veana*'s nerves take hold for a moment, but as Dillon made a small incision in Cellestine's skin, Cellie held firm.

"So you are the *mutore* the Order seeks?" she said, her tone a little breathless.

"Guess so." Figures, she mused drily, locating the

small metal disk. Gray's mother would hate her already.

"And your name is Dillon." She jerked a little when she said the name.

"Please hold still," Dillon warned. "I don't want to catch a vein."

She did as Dillon asked, kept quiet for a moment or two, but clearly it was all she could manage. "My son has strong feelings for you."

Why did that statement sound as though it was the worst fate in the world for this *veana*? *Jeez, maybe get to know me, then hate me*, Dillon thought as she applied pressure under the disk, trying to gently pry it free.

"Strong feelings can make us do things," Celestine said almost piously. "Make us choose things that aren't in our best interest."

Dillon popped out the tracking device, tossed it in the water, and blew on the wound. Then she stood up and gave the *veana* before her a dark glare. "You bet your Pureblood ass it does," she snapped. "I should be a thousand miles away from here, from the Order, from Gray." She reached down and grabbed Celestine's hand, pulled her to stand. "But like you said, strong feelings can make us do things that aren't in our best interests."

Celestine's gaze softened. "Like rescuing the mother of the male you care for?"

Dillon sighed and got ready to flash the *veana* home. "No. Like rescuing the mother of the male I love."

22

Gray paced inside the cell, so fucking frustrated he wanted to ram his fist through the brick wall. He couldn't reach out to his warriors, and since the Order member had been there, the other inmates on his floor were suspiciously quiet. He wasn't sure if the white-haired *veana* had shut down the frequency inside the walls of the prison or had just put the fear of the Order's wrath into every one of the prisoners' minds.

Whatever was making the world so soundless around him was also allowing for thoughts of Dillon and the "deal" the Order had made to come through loud and sickeningly clear.

The Impures would have a seat on the Order, a way to bring to light all the changes they wished to make and fight for without actually having to bleed. Seat, voice, issues heard—and all for the low, low price of his true mate.

This time when he reached the brick wall, he did

slam his fist into it. Pain rocketed into his arm, made the mark of the jaguar hiss and sting and bleed.

She's not here to blow on you, he told the thing.

Goddamn it. If she'd betrayed him—if she really had laid those poisonous bread crumbs down for him to follow, then they were dead. She had to know that. She didn't care, didn't love him like she'd claimed to last night.

Fuck, could a lie be told that convincingly? And if so, was her freedom really so vital to her that she would destroy not only what was between them, but her very soul?

He shook his hand, trying to get rid of the sting.

And then there was the flip side of this sizable predicament. If he refused to believe it and told the Order to shove their deal up their collective asses, would he be once again choosing his *veana* over the Cause?

Jesus . . . and after she'd left him, no word, no note, no nothing. True mates—no blessing, only a curse.

He felt the *veana* approach. *Hour's up, ladies and gentlemen.* He growled when she made her appearance at the bars of the cage. "Do you have an answer for me, Gray Donohue?"

"No."

She looked startled. "I gave you sufficient time to think—"

"Wake up, *Veana,*" he snarled, moving toward the bars until he was just inches from her face. "My answer is no."

From startled to combustible in one second flat. "I thought you had intelligence," she spat, her fangs dropping, her eyes turning a deep and menacing red. "But you are just like your father."

"Your flattery makes my balls twitch," he said, pushing his chin at her. "You have my answer."

Her upper lip curled and she leaned in and whispered, "Your balls will do more than twitch when they are laid out on the stone slab inside the Paleo."

With one last snarl, she whirled around and flashed from his sight.

Gray headed straight for the brick wall and, once again, let his fist fly. If blood was going to be spilled for this cause, he'd be drawing it first.

"He went into Mondrar hours ago," Vincent said, his dark brown eyes thick with concern. "We haven't been able to contact him or the Pureblood we've been working with since."

Standing on the exterior steps of the Impure *credenti*'s main hall, Dillon stared at the warrior, unable to process what he was saying for a moment. She'd arrived at the new *credenti* with Celestine barely five minutes ago. Gray's blood still within her, she'd managed to get through the enchantments again and was on her way to his cottage when Vincent and Piper stopped her.

"He should've been back by now," Piper said, the cold November wind picking up around them. "We're going to have to go in."

"I don't understand this," Dillon said, her mind reeling, her jaguar fighting to get out, get to her mate. "He's an Impure. He would've been found out the second he entered that hole. His heartbeat—the Order knows the heartbeats of every inmate."

Piper's face blanched. "Is that true?"

"Goddamn it." Dillon gripped the railing. "I knew he was planning something, trying to find a way to get her out—but I didn't think he was expecting to do it himself!"

"Our Pureblood contact said nothing about this," Piper said, clearly upset. "Would he have known?"

"Known and used it?" Vincent added, his jaw working tight, his eyes hot. "Could that be what we're talking about here? A double cross?"

"I don't know," Dillon said, her brain working. "But either way, he's fucked." Fear crept into her chest, threatened to take apart her ribs and squeeze at her lungs. "We're going to need Purebloods to help get him out. You three remain here and try to work some mental magic, see if there's any way into the Order you haven't tried."

They both nodded.

"I'm going to take Gray's mother to the Romans right now, get all the brothers onboard, and form a plan of attack."

Vincent turned his gaze to Celestine. "You're Gray's mother."

"That's why you left?" Piper asked Dillon, her eyes wide. "Why didn't you tell him?"

"What?" Dillon said, her mind so focused on the task at hand she didn't understand what the female was getting at.

"Why didn't you tell him where you were going?" Piper repeated, harsher this time. "He thought you'd bolted."

Dillon stilled, felt Celestine do the same beside her. Bolted? He'd thought she'd run . . . Oh God. Of course he had. Her mind flew backward to every single time she'd run from him. Oh God. She was such an idiot. Why would she think that saying "I love you" and letting him see the horror of her past would immediately make him trust her?

She despised herself in that moment—her impulsiveness, her ignorance when it came to common courtesy in a relationship. But she would convince him that she could do better. That she would do better.

She just had to find him first.

She looked up at Piper, then Vincent. "I wanted to surprise him."

She felt Celestine's hand on hers, and before she could think of another thing to say, the older *veana* flashed them both away.

Titus had failed him.

And it would be the last time.

Atop the snow-capped mountain, Cruen stood beside Feeyan and affirmed their bargain.

"You will have her," she assured him, her white hair flying in the wind as she stared out to the mountains in the distance.

"When?"

She tipped her chin. "The Paleo at nightfall."

"How can you be so sure she will come?"

"The male she loves is being blood castrated this very eve in front of all the Impures he so desperately wants to save."

Cruen felt a strange pull inside him. "Gray Donohue."

She nodded. "It is a show not to be missed—by either the caged Impures of the Paleo or the poor, lost lover who will never arouse him again."

"You sound almost giddy, Feeyan," he observed. It was a trait he knew well, one he prided himself on. Just not with this male, not with any child of Celestine's.

"I pray it will be an end to this Impure Resistance once and for all," she said. "And to the *mutore*." She said the final word with such disgust in her tone that Cruen had to keep his hands at his sides for fear he might grab her by the throat and bleed her dry right then and there.

But that time was not today. "I will be there," he said calmly, coolly.

Feeyan turned her head to look at him. "But remember, you must make it appear as if you've stolen her from the Order."

It looked as though he wasn't the only rebel within the Order. Power was a greedy *veana*. "They will not be furious at such a loss?" he asked. "Will they not see you as a failure?"

A smile flowered on her lips. "Not when I give them four *mutore* for the one I lost."

The blood inside Cruen, both ancient and demon-kissed, went cold. "What is that?"

"I have blood memories from Celestine Donohue," she said, her eyes alight with the excitement of a predator with her prey already caught and held inside her jaws. "There are more *mutore*. The Roman brothers harbor them."

Cruen's insides quaked. "Have you shared this information with the other Order members?"

"Not yet." Her eyes clouded with a rush of power. "But when I bring them in, before the others, there will be no doubt who is their leader."

Poor Feeyan, he mused, turning his gaze to the white slopes, his mind already planning for the night ahead. She would have no *mutore* to display, and the Order would have no leader to declare.

Dillon burst into the house, and with Celestine at her heels, they ran down the hall toward the main rooms. "Where is everyone? Hello!" Dillon shouted, panic clear in her tone. "Goddamn it! Answer me!"

They turned the corner, and at that very moment, the doors to the library flew open and Alexander and Nicholas came rushing out.

"Are you all right?" Alex asked, his brow strained, as they ushered Cellie and Dillon into the library.

"What the hell happened?" Nicholas asked as the room grew quiet. "Where's Gray?"

"Mom!" Sara was up and in her mother's arms in seconds. "Oh my God. I thought I'd lost you. What happened? Why were you taken?" She noticed Dillon then and forgot all the questions she'd just asked. "Dillon, thank you."

"You might want to hold off on that 'thanks' for a few minutes."

"Why?"

"Gray went into Mondrar to get Celestine too and he never came out." She put her hand up to stave off the questions. "We don't have time. I don't know what's going on in there or if something's happened to him." Her nostrils flared. "I can't scent him, but I don't feel as if he's hurt. Not yet." Her gaze moved around the room. "I need all the Pureblood males and females who can handle a weapon to help me get my mate back."

The words "my mate" reverberated throughout the room, but the *paven*s didn't remain still and seated for long. Both the Romans and the Beasts were on their feet in seconds.

"I need Glocks," Phane said to Alexander.

"And if you have a spare set of blades," Helo added, "that would do well for me."

Erion nodded. "Blades for me too." He nodded in Lycos's direction. "Ly only uses his wolf hardware."

That elicited a grin from the normally stoic *paven*, who seemed to be more than interested in going into the vampire prison.

"Well then," Lucian said, blood lust in his eyes. "Let's go hunting."

But the words were barely out of his mouth when the wall behind them began to shift and sway like waves on the ocean. And rising up from the deep were the words of the Order.

Gray Donohue will be blood castrated this day when the light is stolen by the stars. Spectators are not welcome to attend. Unless they are mutore.

No one said anything for one solid minute; then Lycos growled low and menacing, and Erion turned to them all and said, "They know we exist."

23

Bleeding from the face, hands, and lower back, Gray was led into the Paleo through an entrance he'd never seen before. They were above the arena and the massive circle of cages. He'd been flashed to an exterior platform several stories up by Feeyan, then handed off to four Pureblood guards.

Clearly he had a thing for making trouble with guards. He'd fought them on his way out of Mondrar and fought them on his way into the Paleo.

The thoughts from the guards that surrounded him staged a violent invasion of his head.

"Another animal to be tamed."

"You won't be flashing those fangs for much longer, Impure."

The curious Impures who huddled inside their cages added their thoughts to the already potent cocktail as he was led down to the arena.

"What is it?"

"*Who is it?*"

"*Oh God. Covered in blood and bruises. What did he do?*"

Though his temper remained hot, Gray forced himself to keep a cool head. He had to figure that at this point he was on his own and fighting for his life.

The guards kept him on a short leash as they moved into the arena and walked him to the very center stone slab. Gray saw the dried drops and smears of blood that decorated the stone and hissed. But he cut himself off immediately. They all had to assume he'd given up—the guards and the Impures—that he'd accepted his blood was next, that his would join the blood of his fellow castration victims.

But he wasn't going down nice and easy.

That's right. Not without a fight, assholes.

Gray waited for the very second when the guards shifted their hold to get him onto the slab. When they did, he sprang into action. He jerked down, slammed his fist into one, two, three groins, then rocketed back up to head butt whoever was in his way. Their groans of pain and spurts of blood were his signal to run, but the fourth guard caught him around the neck. Squeezing the air out of Gray's lungs with his side-of-beef-sized arm. Gray sent his elbow back with a grunt. He made contact, but just as he thought he'd gained his freedom, one of the now-recovered guards got in his face. The *paven* slammed one hard and blinding right cross into Gray's temple.

Stars hijacked his vision; then blackness closed in as he heard Feeyan's irritated command. "Do what you will to restrain him, but make sure to leave enough blood for the castration."

*   *   *

Team player, she wasn't. Or hadn't been, before him. But this was a grand mission—bigger than any of them realized or wanted to admit. Gathered inside the abandoned club, heading for the elevator that would take them down to the Paleo were Dillon, Uma, Kate, Celestine, the Impure warriors, the Romans, and the Beasts. The only two not there were Sara, who was in *swell* and had offered to remain home with Ladd, and Bronwyn, who couldn't leave her young *balas* yet.

As the majority of the group piled into the elevator, Piper, Rio, and Vincent stayed where they were.

"This is where we part company," Piper informed them as the other two warriors moved to either side of her. "We have your blood inside us, Dillon. We'll keep in contact and let you know if and when we break through."

Dillon nodded as the metal door closed. "Good luck." Then she stabbed the button to send them all down into the pits of the Paleo.

The three Impure warriors had found a fissure inside the Order's mainframe and were going to attempt to put pressure on it to open as the battle waged. They believed that in the chaos of their attack, the Order's defenses would be down and they might be able to push their way in through that tiny crack. And if they were really at their best? Maybe they could unplug the power grid.

Dillon had shared blood with all three, forging a mental connection. Like a walkie-talkie through the brain.

The metal box hit the ground floor, and as they'd planned, the group surged out, weapons ready—eyes, ears, fists, and fangs ready too as they moved cautiously down the long, dim hallway. They knew they were expected, and they knew the moment they entered the main section of the Paleo, every guard—Pureblood, Impure, and Order member—would be on them.

Up until this point, Dillon had forced Gray to the back of her mind. She needed a clear head for leadership and control, strong instincts and quick thought. But as she neared the secret way into the arena, the thought of him stretched out on that stone, the Order's fangs pricking his thigh, removing all the desire for mating from his beautiful male body, made her jaguar emerge and snarl.

Helo moved along beside her. "Easy, Dilly. Control your shift. Control your mind."

What about my heart? she wanted to ask. *The one no one thought I had, or would ever have?* The one Gray Donohue had given her.

When they hit the door and the tension for battle within the group was palpable, Dillon turned and faced them all. "I want to say one last time that the Order wants me. None of you have reason to risk your lives here."

"None of us?" Erion said, his nostrils flaring, his Beast, his lionlike demon, flickering in and out of his expression.

"The *mutore* have every reason," Phane confirmed with growling heat, his mismatched eyes bright with the fire of battle.

"Yes, my sister." Fangs dropped low, Alexander gave her a grave look. "We all have reason. Family, mates, my Impure *balas* that grows within my true mate."

"My son," said Celestine simply.

"Justice," Nicholas said resolutely, Glocks heavy at his sides.

"Freedom," Lucian said. "For all who want it. For all who have ever felt as though they had to fucking run to get it." He grunted, held up his blade and Glock. "No more."

Dillon stared at them all, truly understanding for the first time that this was about far more than just answering the call to battle. Each one who stood before her had conviction, drive, and a desperate need to prove their worth that maybe they'd been holding on to forever—until this day could pull it from them.

She grinned broadly, flashed them a quick growl from her jaguar, and raised her weapons. "Let's go get my true mate."

When Gray came to he was staring at a ceiling—broad, curved, and lit with hundreds of candles. It was only when he felt the wet burn of wax hit his face that he realized where he was—and why. With a grunt, he bolted upright, but got only about a foot high. He was stretched out on the stone slab, arms and legs strapped down by heavy, thick ropes. His entire body ached with the pain of his wounds, both open and internal, but he didn't give a shit. This wasn't about him.

It was about them.

All around him, Impures were flattened against the bars of their cages, eyes wide, staring into the center of the arena, watching him. No Order members, no guards. He was alone—an example. For a moment, he wondered if his father had been privy to the same view. What had he done? What had he thought, said?

He felt the pressure of the surrounding Impures' thoughts and opened his mind to allow them all to enter, allow their fears, questions, and prayers to rain down on him. His nostrils flared at the sudden onslaught. So many of them wondered who he was and why he was being singled out—some even thought they recognized him from the rescue missions.

His gaze took in each one as far as his neck could stretch. Maybe it was time to tell them.

"I am Impure warrior Gray Donohue," he shouted into the din, then waited a moment for the space and the minds around him to quiet. "The Order wants to kill my voice by castrating my body, but I will never stop fighting."

A sudden menacing heat moved through him, stealing his breath for a moment. The Order? Had they heard him? From wherever they were?

He inhaled, heavy and purposeful. "Remember, you choose!" he shouted. "All of you! You make the decision to lie down and have your blood stripped."

"Return to the arena. Muzzle him."

"They're coming to strip my voice from me now! But they can't take it from all of us! Don't you see? Only together, with one mind, can we defeat them!"

"Move, you idiots! He is rousing them!"

Fuck! They were near. His eyes wild, Gray cried out into the frenzied air, "Look around you! At one another! You are powerful! Together, you are power—"

It was all he could say before the pressure in his throat

silenced him. But even though his words were taken, they were echoed in his mind by the Impures around him. Louder and louder, more and more, until their thoughts gave way to actual sound.

Feeyan flashed to his side then, her face a mask of disgust and fury as she leaned in close to his ear. "They may be ready to fight," she whispered. "But all it will take to break them again is more castrations, more blood spilled."

For one moment, Gray felt the true depth of that statement. Fear, pain, it was a powerful motivator, especially to a group that had been held down under the thumb of the Order for so long—no, forever. They didn't know what freedom looked like, what it felt like.

"Your father was castrated on this very table. Did you know that?" she whispered, an eager smile in her tone.

Ire slammed into Gray, and in one sweeping movement, he jerked his head up, bared his fangs, and sliced into her ear.

Feeyan bolted up, her eyes white hot. "Bastard." She hit him hard across the face, splitting his lip.

Gray lapped at the blood and for a split second tasted Dillon.

"It was useless to fight back then," Feeyan hissed, "and it is useless to fight now."

"Don't listen to her, Gray."

Gray froze, every muscle in his body on sudden alert. That voice, among all the others inside his head. He closed his eyes, sifting through all the voices until one floated to the top.

Alexander.

"*We're all here, Gray. Ready to fight.*"

Gray's eyes opened. He glanced up at Feeyan, who was healing her torn ear, wondering if she'd heard it too. But she gave no sign that she had.

"*You will not be castrated today,*" Alexander continued, and Gray could practically hear the grin on his face. "*And if all goes as planned, neither will anyone else in this hellhole.*"

And then came the words that made it all right, made the bruises and the blood heal in their way, made his heart swell and ache with belief.

"*Your jaguar won't allow it.*"

24

Above the arena, coiled over the silver-draped balcony, the remaining eight Order members watched the scene below. The *paven* called Drued spoke to his neighbor Titus, his tone thick with apprehension.

"What does she think to prove with this?" he said, the black circle around his left eye creasing within his strained features.

"Our everlasting, impenetrable, and supreme power," Titus offered, watching his daughter's mate receive another blow to the head from Feeyan. His fangs twitched.

"The Impures are enraged," Drued said. "I fear they will not be contained this time."

"I fear you're right," Titus said. Nothing would remain contained, he added silently. Including himself, his Breeding Male gene. His blood was already growing weak and he had not followed Cruen's instructions, but assisted the escape of Dillon and Celestine. He feared that the day of reckoning that was clearly coming for the Order from down below was also coming for him from the Supreme One.

"Is this the Order you set out to join, Brother?" Drued asked, his blue-black eyes resting on Titus's face.

"What is that?" cried the *veana* Order member at the end of the row, yanking both Titus and his neighbor from their discussion. "What moves below like a tidal wave?"

Titus looked down and gasped as the figures of many he recognized and many he had given life to surged into the Paleo, weapons drawn, cries of battle on their tongues.

"No . . ." uttered Drued, his voice laced with terror and dread. "We do not want a war here."

"And yet," Titus whispered, "they have come to fight."

He heard them. All around him. It was like a great waterfall of sound pushing into the space, echoing off the walls. In his mind he heard the Impures' excitement and cheering. In his ears he heard a battle cry.

Feeyan flashed from his side and Gray lifted his head. Through his bloodstained vision, he saw them all rushing into the Paleo—the Romans, the Beasts, his mother, Kate, and Dillon. His heart stuttered in his chest at the sight of her. Fierce, beautiful, the jaguar behind her eyes. Goddamn it, he'd doubted her. He'd actually considered the words of the Order over the *veana* he loved. He'd spend much time making amends for that mistake—a mistake he'd never make again.

While the Beasts smashed the locks on cage after cage and the Romans battled the guards, Dillon, Kate, and Celestine rushed toward him. Their eyes were wide and horrified as they caught sight of his injuries, but they quickly pushed themselves to focus on locating all of his bindings. They worked fast, knives through rope, back and forth until each snapped free. Dillon leaned near to his face and stilled for one second. She locked eyes with him; then she dropped her head and kissed him. It was quick, fierce, and said all they could in that moment before they headed back into the fray.

Gray sprang from the stone, caught the blades that Dillon tossed his way, and quickly assessed the battle. Thanks to the Beasts, the cages were open and Impures flooded into the arena. They carried anything they could use as a weapon and were advancing in almost military-style rows on guards.

Gray caught sight of something in his peripheral vision. It was Feeyan and several other Order members being pressed into the group of fighting guards. The Impures on the other side of the Paleo must've wrapped around and pushed them into the chaos.

Suddenly an overwhelming sense of pressure ran through Gray's body, then straight up into his face and his mind. What the hell? The Order?

"Flash!" one Order member shouted.

Feeyan's eyes were wide with shock and fear. "I cannot."

"I am immobile as well," said another.

"It's those warriors," Feeyan cried. "They've got in again. They're blocking us from flashing, blocking our power! We must find them."

The surge of pressure was a mystery no more. Piper,

Rio, and Vincent, Gray thought, his slashed mouth turning up in a prideful grin. They'd done it. And here, in this great bloodletting nightmare of a place, the Impures had done it. The Beasts, the Romans, brandishing their weapons and taking out one guard after the next—a great change was upon them all.

"We will not give up the Order. No matter what parlor tricks you play on us."

In the very center of the chaotic battle, Feeyan stood before him, her eyes demonic, her bloodred fangs fully extended over her lower lip. Gray's hands twitched against the handles of his blade.

"There's no trick," he called out, "but the talents of a 'race' you believe less than your own."

There was a sudden shift in the crowd and a group of Impures who had heard her overconfident reply descended and grabbed the *veana*.

"Get off me!" she screamed, struggling like a rat in a trap.

But the Impures held her firm. There were too many, and in short order Feeyan began to deflate.

"Tell me what you want," she uttered with bitterness.

"Yes, please," came another Order member, a *paven* who was also being held. "Tell us what you want."

The Impures grew quiet and contained. They all looked at Gray, who thought in that very moment that his father was with him, inside him.

"I want only what was offered," Gray said, his eyes level with Feeyan. "We will have a seat on the Order. One for Impures and one for *mutore*."

There was a collective gasp as all the eyes of the Order widened with shock as they processed the fact that Feeyan had offered something so outrageous.

"Make your choice," Gray said to them. "Chaos, dissent, death to both sides—that is what is promised if you refuse us this step into equality."

The Impures roared their agreement, and the Order members, for the first time in their very long lives, felt a true crack in their framework.

They looked around, then at one another; then Feeyan uttered blackly, "It seems as though we have little choice."

Gray walked up to her, his own fangs extended. "Welcome to our world."

Her lip curled.

"Now say it," he commanded. "Loud, so everyone can hear."

Through gritted teeth, she cried out, "Two seats on the Order will now be granted to an Impure and a . . ." She shook her head, nostrils flaring.

Gray placed his blade tight at her throat. "You wanna make it three seats?"

"A *mutore*," she finished.

The Impures released the Order members and eased back. A celebratory whoop went through the crowd. Gray walked away from his nemesis, but as he did, his gaze caught on something behind her—something that made his brain squeeze and his fingers dig into the handles of his blade.

Someone had Dillon and was pulling her toward the door that led to the secret tunnel.

*   *   *

"We are going home, my daughter."

Dillon couldn't believe the hands that had wrapped around her within the crowd and pulled her away with such impossible strength belonged to Cruen.

"Home?" she said bitterly, struggling against him. "Is that what you call your laboratory?"

"You called it that once," he said. "And you will again."

Gray had taught her what home truly meant. She'd never mistake that lab of cold cruelty as home. Gray was her home now.

"Why?" she asked. "What you could you possibly want from me now?"

The *paven*'s ice-blue eyes flashed possession. "You are my child. And if you come, the others will follow."

"My brothers. That's what you really want, isn't it?"

He didn't answer her.

"Not a chance, Pops," she snapped. "I'll never be your bait, just as I'll never be your daughter."

For the second time, she shifted into her jaguar form before Cruen. But this time, it wasn't to protect herself from pain—it was to rip the *paven* in front of her to shreds.

Cruen took a step back, his eyes narrowing, and Dillon unsheathed her claws. But before she even had a chance to spring, Gray appeared from behind Cruen. He rushed at the *paven* and struck fast, sinking his twin blades directly into the ex-Order member's back. Cruen screamed and dropped forward. Not giving him a moment to recover, Gray ripped out one of the blades and went to slice Cruen's throat.

But Dillon's growl arrested him. "You promised, Gray."

He glanced up. Looking into her green cat eyes, he remembered what he'd said after viewing her memories last night.

Offering her his full trust, he nodded and stepped back. A move that gave Cruen enough time to yank the remaining blade from his back, flip over, and scramble to his feet.

But the cat was faster than the ex-Order member.

Dillon's jaguar leaped at his chest, sending him back and down upon the stone floor. She hovered above him, her jaws wide, razor teeth millimeters from his throat.

Cruen winced.

"You look scared, Dad," Dillon hissed. "I would think the sight of me shifting would bring you as much pleasure and interest as it did back then—back when you were watching me be raped by your guard."

The world stopped, stilled, froze as Dillon breathed hard and fast into Cruen face.

There was a moment—so brief Dillon later wondered if she had seen it at all—where Cruen's eyes flashed with pain-laced regret. But it was gone in an instant and replaced by demon eyes so similar to Erion's she pulled back a foot.

Beneath her, Cruen started to move, his body humming. Then suddenly, he shifted. He shifted into a Beast so grotesque, so unrecognizable, that Dillon scrambled off of him and dropped into a crouch.

"You're *mutore*!" she cried.

Silence filled the Paleo, and Dillon felt the eyes of hundreds on them—Impure, Pureblood, *mutore*, and Order.

And so did Cruen. He looked up, eyed the Order first, then someone or something behind them that Dillon couldn't see, and then he flashed, leaving the entire breed in stunned silence.

25

"I want the truth now," Sara said, looking first at her brother, then her mother. "From both of you."

After leaving the Paleo to the Impures to dismantle brick by brick, the entire family had flashed back to the Romans' compound. But only the three who had unfinished business remained outside to watch the sunrise.

Celestine didn't ask what information Sara did have. She just started from the beginning. "Your father and I met after I ran from my *credenti* and after I met the Romans." She smiled to herself as the memories made pictures in her mind. "He was a passionate male, an Impure bent on defeating the Order and their rule. Our relationship was taboo, as you know, but we hardly cared. We were very much in love. We ran away together and built a life, lived as humans. Jeremy worked in secret to bring about the uprising." She focused on Sara and Gray. "And then you two came along, and we had to make sure you weren't detected by the Order."

"How did you do that?" Sara asked.

"We fed you human blood."

Sara gasped.

"Everything we did was to protect you," Celestine said quickly. "You will know how that feels, Sara."

"But he was never able to see that uprising," said Gray, who had been relatively silent up until then.

"No." Celestine's shoulders drooped a little. "He was taken as Gray was today to the Paleo for castration."

"Oh God," Sara said, a sudden flash of fierceness within her blue eyes. "I pray the Order will never have this kind of power again."

"Your brother will see to it," Celestine said with a broad, proud smile. "It won't be easy, but it's a beginning—it's something."

"Tell us what happened after Dad was castrated," Gray prompted as the sun began to rise golden and shiny.

Celestine swallowed the memory. "Afterward, he returned home a changed male. He didn't want me, didn't want to be near me. It was very hard. As I said, we had started out very much in love."

As she watched her children process what she'd said, what it meant, how it brought things together in their minds, Celestine held her breath and prayed there would be no more questions, no more digging. She couldn't bear it.

"And that's it?" Sara said, looking sad and as though she missed her father.

Celestine nodded. She knew exactly what her daughter was feeling because she'd felt it too. More times than she could count.

"I'm so sorry we didn't tell you," Cellie said. "That I didn't tell you. It is the choice you make sometimes as a parent. Protection at the risk of losing trust from the ones you're protecting."

Gray's bruised and battered face studied hers for a moment, and then he leaned in and kissed her cheek.

Celestine felt as if the world had been removed from her shoulders in that moment. She'd borne the weight of her secrets for so long, and now that they were free—the brunt of them at any rate—and her children had seemed forgiving, she could finally be the mother to them that she had once been and wanted so much to be again.

And then Alexander, from wherever he stood inside his home, spoke within her mind.

"He had a painting of you, done after Sara and Gray were born. You looked as though you were in swell, *Cellie. Were you? Shit, I pray not. I pray you didn't have a* balas *with that mad* paven. *If you did and I find out, I will have to tell my true mate. She will never forgive you. And perhaps neither will I."*

She was *veana.*

She was jaguar too.

And, she mused, swimming toward him through the steam, she was his.

After a little Roman family feast of blood and seed-cake, Dillon had flashed herself, her true mate, and the warriors back to the Impure *credenti.* It was going to be her home now. Because in her heart, the one Gray had given her—or maybe he had just helped her find the one that had been lost inside her, crushed by the weight of something so terrible—she knew that wherever he was, that's where she wanted to be.

Rock cave, Impure *credenti*, beneath the heated water of a hot spring—didn't matter as long as they were together.

Leaning back against one side of the bank, Gray opened his arms to her, and without hesitation, she swam into them. With her eyes locked on his and her legs wrapped around his waist, Dillon blew her *veana*'s healing breath over his face until each bruise, each cut vanished.

"Thank you," he said, his steel-gray eyes triumphant and happy, the happiest she'd ever seen them.

"No," she said, inching herself closer. "Thank you."

A slow, easy smile touched his mouth, and he trailed one hand up her spine until he cupped her neck. Dillon shivered, every inch of her skin anxious for more. And it would come, she knew. She didn't have to beg for it or pretend it meant nothing, all to keep her sad, dusty unbeating heart protected. No. With this male she could be who she was, good or bad, *veana* or cat, and he would ever care for her with such tenderness, passion, and true love.

"Your head is full of thought," he said, studying her, his hand coming around to cup her face. "I wish I could hear."

She grinned playfully. "Then you'd know all my secrets."

His eyes grew suddenly serious at her words, and the scent of his regret met her nostrils. She breathed it in, trying to ease it, take it away.

But it held fast.

"D," he said, his eyes moving over her face, his mouth grim. "There's something I have to say to you, something I need to tell you. When I was inside Mondrar, in that cell with the Order *veana* attempting to bargain with me, telling me my mother had never been there and that you had betrayed me. There was a moment of doubt—" He shook his head, his hand dropping from her face. "Shit, this is hard."

She stopped him. "Of course there was."

His gaze lifted to hers.

"I'm surprised there was only a moment." She wrapped her arms around his neck and pulled herself closer, her gaze clinging to his. "Ever since that horrible day when I was a young *veana* . . . I have been running—from everything, everyone, and God, especially from feeling anything remotely close to emotional connection." She gave a little smile then. "When you came along, back when we were lying across from each other in those sickbeds in the Romans' house"—she watched as he caught the memory too and smiled—"something inside me sparked to life. It scared the shit out of me, Gray. I didn't know what it was, but I sure didn't want to feel it. I guess I didn't want to want someone like that. And I did everything I could to push you away." Her throat tightened then. She tilted her head. "But you never gave up. You got mad, you got frustrated and dictatorial—you told me I was being an idiot." She laughed. "But you never gave up. On us. On me."

A deep and unshakable yearning crossed his features. "Fool in love."

"No," she said vehemently. "I was the fool. You had the love." She shook her head. "And even with all of that offered to me, I kept running away. So I get why you had a moment of doubt." She shrugged gently. "Why would you think that this last one was any different?"

"Because you loved me enough to not only tell me so, but to show me," he said simply.

Tears welled in her eyes and this time she didn't swipe them away. She wasn't a pussy for feeling. She was healed.

He leaned toward her until his mouth was an inch away from hers. "Even through your fear, you trusted me to keep you safe, your heart safe." He gave her a kiss, then found her gaze again. "Your eyes on mine the whole time, remember?"

How could she ever forget? It was the moment of her rebirth. She nodded, one renegade tear making its way down her cheek.

"So, no more running?" he asked, catching that tear with the pad of his thumb and easing it away.

She shook her head, titled her chin, and brushed her lips against his. "Not unless you're by my side."

He growled softly. "I like that. Don't know if I can keep up with the jag though."

She laughed. "Oh, you can keep up, Male. In fact, I'll let you take the lead. After all, you're so good at it. And you're going to need the practice for your new job." She shook her head. "Oh my God, Gray. You on the Order. I can't imagine it."

"I can't either," he agreed, pulling back so he could find her gaze. "That's why I'm not taking the job."

Dillon couldn't control her shock. "What?"

As the mist rose around them and the November

sun played hide-and-seek in the sky, Gray explained. "I belong inside the fight, D, using my mind and my fists. My blades. And trust me when I say that there is much fight ahead. I will lead on the ground."

"Then who?"

"I think Rio will do well as Order." He started to laugh. "They'll despise it quickly and fear him in their way." Then he caught her gaze and his grin widened. "Between him and you, the Impures and the *mutore* will gain equality and respect slowly but steadily."

Dillon froze. "Wait, what?"

He cleared his throat. "Order Member Dillon." Then he inclined his head and whispered, "Can I kiss you?"

"No!" she shouted. "Hell no!"

"I can't kiss you?" he said with a mocking smile.

"I'm not serving on the Order!"

He pulled her in and kissed her neck. "Of course you are, baby. It utilizes your skill set. Arguing, quick thinking, bossing people around. You'll rule that table of eleven before long."

His kisses to her neck were growing hungry and her insides were heating up, but she managed to mutter a terse, "I would rather eat my own eyeballs than sit at the table with those bastards."

His lips moved to her ear. "The jaguar loves the idea."

Without thought, she started to purr. Goddamn it. It was as if the animal was ruled by him. "That's because she has the possibility of biting heads off at work."

"Exactly," he whispered, raking his fangs down her neck. "Dream job."

Her belly clenched with heat, and an ache of need spread down over her pelvic bone and into her cunt.

"So, in this scenario you've dreamed up in your head," she murmured as he gripped her backside and pressed her closer. "You go off to fight and rescue and all that shit, and I go to work all day with the red-fanged asshole committee. Then we come home . . ."

"And make babies."

Her eyes popped.

"All day, all night," he whispered huskily.

"Slow down, true mate of mine."

"Fine, fine. We'll start with one and see how we do." With a possessive growl, he lifted her up and placed her down on his shaft.

Dillon gasped at the delectable feeling of being filled by the male she loved more than anything. She gripped his shoulders and started to move. "Oh, shit, that's all I need. Little jaguars running around."

Gray groaned as his hands raked up her back and into her hair. "Sounds like heaven on earth. You, me, and a litter make three."

Dillon leaned in and nipped at his lower lip.

He pulled in a breath and she felt his cock pulse inside her. "You'll never truly be a good little kitty cat, right, D?" he asked.

Grinning, she shook her head.

"Oh, thank God," he uttered.

He moved inside her then, slow and easy and languid until her breathing changed, until she could barely keep a thought in her head.

But there was one she had to hold on to, one she had to share before she sank under the delectable waves of orgasm and drowned in his touch.

"I know why your gift was deaf to me," she said, heat coursing through her.

His brows came together. "What do you mean?"

"You never needed to hear my thoughts, Gray, because you always listened to my heart."

His eyes locked on hers and his expression grew tense with emotion, just as his body grew tense with nearly debilitating desire. Then he started to thrust, deeper and deeper into her, marking her and her jaguar with his seed, with his heart, and with his undying love.

Epilogue

"What do you think?"

Erion led the Beasts and the Romans into the first floor of the empty building. It was a massive space, perfect for their new home and their new family dynamic. "A *mutore* compound," he said.

"Right next door?" Lucian said with a sharply raised eyebrow that contrasted with the softness of the *balas* who was strapped to his chest by some strange contraption.

"It was available," Erion said simply. "And it's big enough for the four of us, plus guests, a training room—"

"We'll need to put in a pool," Helo said, looking around the warehouse-like space with its brick walls and thick pillars. "I've got to have my water."

"And some type of aviary," Phane put in. "Doesn't have to be big, just somewhere for the hawk to stretch its wings."

Over near the window, Lycos snorted. "I suppose I'll have to go up north to hunt."

Phane chuckled. "Unless you want to find prey on the New York City streets."

"Don't tempt him," Helo said tightly.

"And we'll need to break down this wall."

All four *mutore* turned to look at Alexander, who stood in the doorway and took in the great space before him.

Erion raised one black eyebrow in his direction. "You want to have us all together? Think hard on that, Brother."

But Alexander didn't have to. Or maybe he already had, because he seemed so confident. "It is how family should be."

"Would be more convenient," Nicholas agreed with a grin. "As we keep expanding this Roman clan."

As Lucian held an example of this growth close to his chest, all eyes shifted to him. He hadn't noticed and was doing a sort of jig with his body and a shushing sound with his mouth. It was the last thing in the world a near animal like a Breeding Male would be doing, and laughter broke out among all the brothers, sending Lucian's head up and his fangs down.

He sneered at the lot of them and flipped them off.

"You look like a *tegga*," Erion remarked, using the ancient vampire word for "nanny," as he continued to chuckle.

"Well, you look like a demon-faced bitch," Lucian returned, though his hands cradled his child's head with nothing but extreme care.

The juxtaposition of harsh *paven* and soft, doting father had Erion sobering for a moment. "This *balas*," he said, nodding at Lucy. "You are pleased with it?"

Lucian looked at the Beast as though he were crazy, and Erion rephrased his question. "Being its father. You enjoy that role?"

"It's pretty fucking great, yeah," Lucian said, then gave the male a hard stare. "And call her an 'it' again and I'll be forced to demonstrate how parental I and my five friends here are." He made a fist.

Behind Erion, the Romans and the Beasts laughed heartily.

"I meant no disrespect," he told Lucian. "It is how we were always referred to."

A shot of reality, or maybe it was a reminder of the past and all they'd seen and been exposed to, but it commanded the room and caused both the Romans' and the Beasts' laughter to cease. Lucian walked over to Erion and regarded the demon-eyed male. "What's got your *mutore* panties in a bunch, E? For a *paven* who is pretty terrifying to look at when you got the Beast mask on, you look terrified."

It wasn't something he was used to or comfortable with—allowing his insecurity to be seen. Especially not by one as unsympathetic as Lucian Roman, and yet Erion knew the *paven* would be honest with him. His voice dropped to a harsh whisper, "I have my concerns with this role."

"Are we talking about the role of Daddy Demon?" Lucian asked, his eyes glittering with amusement.

Erion growled low in his throat, but the defensive reaction died off quickly and he asked, "What if you drop her? Hurt her?" His voice grew tense with worry. "And doesn't it worry you that she might see you as . . ."

"An asshole?" Lucian interrupted with a grin.

Erion shrugged. "Asshole. Monster. Take your pick."

"Her mother has seen me as an asshole and as a monster," Lucian said, "and she still loves me. I'm hoping for the best from my little bloodsucker here."

"But a *balas* that has already grown," Erion said tightly. "He already has beliefs and opinions."

"And? You think that Ladd won't accept you if you decide to kill this fear thing you're holding on to and tell him the truth?"

"Something like that," Erion admitted, a strange sensation coursing through him. It felt oddly like fear, but no fear he'd ever felt before.

Lucian dropped his chin. "Talk to him."

"What?"

"Just start something. Let him get to know you—you get to know him. Find out what he likes, what he doesn't."

"What if the thing he doesn't like is me?"

Lucian grinned, then dropped a kiss on the top of Lucy's head. "The chance we all take, Brother."

Erion's gaze moved over Lucy's sleeping face, and for one brief moment he wondered what Ladd had looked like at that age. "She's very small. But strong and beautiful. You are fortunate."

"I tell myself that every fucking day," Lucian said.

As if he'd been waiting outside until they'd finished their conversation, Ladd burst through the front door,

Kate behind him. His grin wide, his eyes bright with excitement, he held something high in the air. A piece of paper. He waved it around, showing it off to all the brothers.

"I have it," he announced, nearly singing the words. "My letter to Santa."

Frowning, Erion stared at the paper. He wasn't familiar with this person, Santa, but perhaps this was a place to begin with the young *paven*.

"Is this a friend of yours?" he asked the boy. "Another vampire *balas*?"

The three Roman brothers burst out laughing, and Ladd gave Erion a huge, sweet smile. "Oh, Uncle Erion. Santa's not a friend. He's a toy maker. He rides on his sleigh with reindeer and drops down people's chimneys and puts presents under their trees."

It was like a new language. Erion glanced at his Roman brothers. "Is this true? Is it some sort of magic?"

But before Alex, Nicholas, or Lucian could answer, Ladd nodded. "The best magic ever. I'll show you my letter, if you want?"

Erion nodded, and Ladd started toward him, happy and brimming with excitement. But just a few feet from Erion, he stopped. His face bunched up and he glanced down at his middle. "Something's wrong," he said, his voice frightened.

"Ladd," said Erion as the fear in the boy's voice clawed at his chest.

The boy whimpered. "I feel . . ." His gaze flipped up to Erion's and held. "Help me."

It was all he said, for he was gone in an instant.

His letter drifted to the floor.

The floor that was being carved into with an unseen hand.

When I have my *children back, you will have yours.*

Erion shifted into his Beast and roared as around him the room erupted into chaos.

Don't miss the next exciting novel in the
Mark of the Vampire series,

ETERNAL DEMON

Coming in May 2013 from Signet Eclipse.

"**A**re you listening to me, Your Highness?"

Hellen drew back her bow, aimed it at the streaking ball of pale yellow light ten feet in front of her, and let the arrow fly. She waited for impact, for the impish little rogue demon to drop, but it didn't. It ran away, cackling.

She turned and glared at Eberny. "You must cease talking while I hunt."

The ancient demon, a male-female hybrid, was undaunted. "You will be leaving us very soon, Your Highness. Your father has instructed me to make certain you understand your duties."

Under the haze of auburn daylight, Hellen grabbed another arrow from her quiver and said in a dangerous voice, "My duties."

"Indeed," said Eberny, following Hellen as the young female demon suddenly took off, jogging along the perimeter of the Rain Fields. "How you are to conduct yourself."

That little bastard, thought Hellen, her eyes searching for the lost rogue. Ah! There. It was ducking in and out of a cloud, grinning its toothless grin, toying with her.

With one easy movement, Hellen drew back her arrow and sent it straight for the cloud. It whizzed through the Rain Fields like a bolt of lightning.

Flash! A hit.

Hellen grinned as the rogue demon exploded.

"A worthy shot, Your Highness," said Eberny in a contained voice before picking up the topic of discussion from a moment ago. "It would be wise to recall the lessons learned in the Academy. The ones stressing a female's obligations to her male counterpart."

Scanning the Rain Fields for more rogues, Hellen snorted. "Unfortunately, I do not recall them. A much-needed nap was taken during that bout of instruction, I believe."

Eberny's mud brown eyes narrowed with disapproval. "Your highness, that is not at all amusing."

And yet girlish laughter sounded behind them. Hellen looked up to see her two younger sisters skipping down the black-earthed hillock toward them, yards of fuchsia and gold skirt trailing behind. Levia and Polly looked like a painting, so demure, so female. Perfect demon royalty. While she—if not for her long red coils of hair—looked like their brother.

"Hellen, dear."

"Pray, don't shoot at us. We come in peace."

Each female gave her a kiss on the cheek. They

smelled of fireflower, the only flower allowed to grow in the underworld. It was most rare, picked and bottled the moment it bloomed, then made into a perfume oil for the daughters of the Demon King.

Hellen preferred the scent of ashes, of the black soot beneath her feet—of the death of each rogue demon.

She was strange that way.

She had been told many times that she was named for her place of birth.

Hell.

But over the years she had come to wonder if her mother had known what grew inside her womb, what she would be unleashing into the underworld. A true hellion. Had the female demon had a premonition about a fiery gust of flaming hair and a defiant disposition? Then come to a quick decision about the name?

A sudden flash of light, bright blue and practically spitting off rogue energy, caught her peripheral vision, and she whirled around, grabbing for an arrow.

"Your Highness, please," Eberny implored. "Listen to me."

Hellen shifted the bow and arrow, tracking the muted blue light deep in the Rain Fields before her. "My eyes may be on my target, Eberny, but my ears are open. What is it you think I need to know?"

"The male you are to be given to will expect certain behaviors."

"Indeed. I spread my legs when instructed, yes?"

Behind her, Levia and Polly gasped. Hellen drew back her bow and grinned. She could practically see the girls' wide eyes and gloved hands covering their mouths. She would miss them terribly, miss their sweet ways and perpetually outraged reactions. But, then again, she was glad to be going. Her sacrifice would be their safeguard, always.

Eberny's voice dropped to a whisper. "Sexual relations are only a small part of being a submissive partner, Your Highness."

Submissive.

Hellen's urge to kill amplified and she narrowed her eyes on the acres upon acres of Rain Fields, where the rogue demons who hunted her family loved to hide.

"Do not look him in the eyes when he speaks to you," Eberny continued.

"Where shall I look, then?" Hellen asked with an emotionless tone. "Between his legs?"

Again, her sisters gasped. "Oh, Hellen, you are wicked," said Levia, her voice muffled through her gloved hand.

Eberny turned to them and sniffed. "She enjoys giving me pains in my head."

Very true. Hellen chuckled and drew back an arrow, waited for the flash of blue, and sent the arrow flying. It missed by a good ten feet. The little bastard's subsequent cackling killed her laughter.

"If you could just be more like your sisters," Eberny said on a sigh.

Hellen glanced back at the lovely specimens of female demon and shook her head, her gaze affectionate in the extreme. Yes, she would miss them terribly. "I know. It would be easier all round."

Levia and Polly laughed, rushed forward, and embraced her.

"You are perfect as you are, Hellen," Levia crooned.

"Yes, indeed," agreed Polly. "Except for the hunter attire . . . Perhaps if we had something made in a pale shade of pink—"

The mute button was pressed on Polly's appraisal of her clothing as Hellen spotted the blue rogue staring at her through a thin layer of cloud. It grinned. Hellen's blood heated and she gripped her bow tightly. She had been hunting demon rogues ever since she could hold a bow, and they knew how to play with her. They weren't afraid to die or to be hunted. On the contrary. They loved it.

And so did Hellen.

Sir Ugly and Blue widened his yellow eyes and made a disgusting noise at the lot of them, then took off.

Hellen smirked. "I'll be back."

"No, Hellen, wait," Levia called.

But Hellen raced into the Rain Fields. Drops of water as hot as ash fell from gray clouds only feet off the ground. She'd been inside the Fields hundreds of times, and knew how to maneuver through them without getting burned. Bow and arrow at the ready, she kept her quick pace, her eyes narrowing each time she lost sight of the blue flash of light.

It came as sudden as a breath; a rush of intensity, a familiar scent. Hatred and disappointment, sadness and intense power.

Hellen stopped short and dropped her weaponry. A forced and familiar action. A tornado ripped through the Rain Fields, came straight for her, and stopped a foot away. The blood of excitement, of chase that had been rushing through Hellen's veins a moment ago turned to black ice.

He was before her.

The Devil himself.

The Demon King, Abbadon.

Hellen looked up. "Hello, Father."

In his present state Abbadon looked the very essence of a demon. Ten feet tall, red skin pulled tight over heavy, impervious muscle, eyes the color of the clouds that only moments ago parted for him. As Hellen stared up at her sire, she saw nothing of herself in him and yet knew that she of all her sisters was the most like him.

"What are you doing?" he asked in a voice unworldly and growlingly low.

Unlike her sisters, Hellen felt no fear when standing in her father's presence. Only a desperation within her mind to be cautious and thoughtful with the words that came out of her mouth.

"Preparing myself for wedded bliss."

His scaly-skinned eyebrow lifted. "With a longbow?"

"Perhaps this male you have sold me to will appreciate my hunting skills."

There was a flicker in his gaze, a momentary flash of fury, but he contained it. "I allow you to hunt the rogue demons for me because, frankly, you are far superior a shot than any of the male hunters I possess, but it stops the moment you leave my underworld. Do you understand that?"

Hellen nodded.

"You will not shame me."

"I am rather good at it though, Father."

Again the flash of fury clouded his already pale eyes. "Yes," he hissed. "But after today, the consequences will be dire."

Hellen's muscles tensed. "Today?"

The Devil's grin made the black, scorched earth below her feet tremble. "The time has come, daughter. You will leave us and take your place aboveground—"

"With the bloodsucker," Hellen finished for him.

Abbadon's nostrils flared, and he coiled over her like a snake. The air went silent and the rain ceased to fall. It was his attempt at intimidation. There was nothing the Demon King appreciated more than fear in his offspring. Especially in the one before him.

But Hellen remained cool under his taut, red-faced glare. This was never the way to get her to cower, get her on her knees, eyes down and shoulders trembling. Unfortunately, over the past few years, Abbadon had found the way into her fear center.

He cocked his head to one side. "Is that your sisters' carefree laughter I hear?"

Hellen heard nothing but the deadly silence and the threat that hovered next on her father's thin, reptilian-like lips.

"I will do as I am instructed," she said in a quiet voice.

In a shock of movement and hot wind, he rushed toward her. Matching her height now, his face the color of rich, thick blood, he placed one long finger under her chin and lifted. "You had better."

Or the two lovely demon females on the bank of the Rain Fields back there will feel my true wrath, he didn't say.

He didn't have to say it.

Hellen pulled her chin from his touch and said in a firm voice, "I will be the perfect little demon."

Abbadon grinned and gave a wave of his hand to the fields around them. "You will be the perfect little female."

The clouds instantly released a torrent of hot rain, sound returned to the air, and out of the corner of her eye, Hellen saw a flash of blue light.

"Now," Abbadon said, his gaze sweeping over her. "Get back to the Dwelling. You leave within the hour, and you must be bathed, combed, dressed, and prepared."

Prepared.

Hellen clung to the word as the Devil turned and dissolved into the hot, misty air. She had sacrificed herself, would give herself to this bloodsucker who her father had sold her to, but that's where it would end. And her most important bit of preparation would make it so.

The flash of demon blue hit her peripheral once more, and without taking another breath, she had stretched her bow back and released. The arrow hit the target, and Hellen reveled in her final kill as she walked out of the Rain Fields and toward her sisters for the last time.

Erion's lip curled as beneath his feet, the earth rumbled. It was a soft, uncomplicated movement, just a hint of warning to the animals thereabouts. *Flee, little ones. Get out of the way before you're run down by an ill-fated traveling party.*

And a mutore paven who would kill anything and anyone who gets in his way.

The earth's easy shudder intensified. Was this it? he mused, his fangs descending. The parcel he'd come to steal?

The *bride.*

Cruen's bride.

For a moment, Erion stood his ground, his gaze narrowing on the length of dirt road ahead. But when the shudder escalated to a shake, reverberating up through his feet and calves to his gut, into his chest and all the way to his jaw, making his teeth rattle inside his mouth, Erion dropped into a fighting stance and unsheathed his blade.

This was no wedding party approaching, he thought blackly, circling slowly so he could see in every direction. This wasn't Cruen's bride. Couldn't be. This was nature's doing, inconvenient though it was, a cry of—

The thought died inside his mind. Before him the earth suddenly cracked in one long seam, splitting apart with a jarring lurch. *Christ!* Erion jumped back as the plaintive wail of breaking rock and shifting plates stole the forest's air. What the hell was happening? An earthquake? He was on California land after all.

A few feet away, a megablast of dirt shot into the air, raining down sharp black pellets onto his face and body. He should flash. Get out of this particular line of fire. Return to France and demand a new location from the shifter who'd given him this disastrous one.

He was on his way, his cells nearly transferred when, suddenly, from inside the dust geyser came a wail, a shriek so intense Erion felt it deep within his bones. Like a wave crashing against the shore, he heard it again and again. The sound boomed through the forest, pinging against trees, then slamming back into Erion's ears. He shook his head, attempting to clear the sound. As he did, his gaze caught on the crack in the earth. The sound seemed to emanate from the very center. Though any sane *paven* would've drawn back at that point, Erion moved closer. He saw something.

What was it? What the hell was he seeing?

His blood pounded in his veins, every muscle inside him tense and ready.

But for what?

Then he saw it fully, saw *them* fully—two horses, pale as paper, with see-through skin, emerging from the ground. They were snorting and sighing. They were pulling something.

Steeled and ready for a fight, Erion stared unblinking at the scene before him, nearly thinking himself mad as a gleaming, bride white, pumpkin-shaped carriage crawled out of the hole in the earth, its legs moving like a gigantic white spider.

Erion's mind squeezed.

No.

Impossible. Perhaps even insane. This couldn't be Cruen's bride. Inside this Cinderella's carriage from hell?

As the ghostly team cleared the split in the earth and found solid ground, the carriage came to a halt. One of the horses turned its head and eyed Erion. Its nostrils flared in warning and it pawed the ground.

Erion's hand tightened around his blade, and in that moment he remembered what he was doing there.

Who he came to steal—and why.

As if they sensed it too, the transparent beasts shifted their gazes and took off, bolting into the woods, dirt kicking up around them.

Erion followed, his blood fueling his pace. This female, whatever she was, belonged to him. She was his bargaining chip—the ransom he would keep at his side until Ladd, the *balas* he'd created and had not known existed for so long, was returned. Returned to the ones who knew how to love.

He ran through the cool black woods, keeping pace with the carriage until it burst forth into an open field. Moonlight poured down from overhead, spreading its ethereal glow over the overgrown expanse.

In a burst of speed, Erion shot forward, made a quick right, and stopped dead in front of the horses. The beasts screamed as they came to a halt, rearing up, nearly braining him with their massive hooves. The demon inside of Erion pulsed to get out, to tame what was snorting and hissing in front of him—muzzle what was letting loose a cacophony of terrified screams inside the bride white carriage.

He smiled grimly. The terror was only beginning for his parcel.

He leapt onto the footrest near the carriage door and gripped the handle. A flexible wall of dark magic pushed at him, tried to buck him off, tried to convince his mind that he was seeing a mirage, but Erion mentally shoved back at the sensation and yanked at the door.

It wouldn't budge.

Not a problem. He enjoyed tearing off the gift wrap on a parcel.

Reaching up, he grabbed the metal bar on the roof of the carriage, swung back, and crashed his feet into the carriage door. It went down with a thud. Another feminine scream, and the horses panicked and took off across the field. Erion's gaze was razor-sharp now, but all he saw was a blur with electric green eyes before he was hit in the chest and thrown backward.

He landed on the ground with a teeth-shattering slam, something fierce and flooded with layers of skirt on top of him. He heard the horses scream and snort, saw out of his peripheral vision the coach clattering past, leaving the meadow for the dark woods beyond.

"Before I kill you, I want to know just who the hell you are!"

The Layers of Skirt spoke.

Erion's brows descended over his narrowed gaze. The female sat astride him, had his arms pinned to his sides as though she were under the impression she had some kind of control in the situation. In truth, he could not only flick her off like a bothersome fly, but stretch her arms over her head and slit her throat with one fang all within a breath. But then he wouldn't be able to feel her weight atop him. So, for a moment, he let her remain where she was.

Miles and miles of pale red hair, illuminated by the moon overhead, draped either side of his shoulders, and those inhuman eyes, the color of emeralds in the brightest sunlight, gazed down at him with equal parts scorn and I-want-to-rip-your-head-off.

This female, Erion mused, the organ between his legs pulsing with curiosity, may be sixty-five inches of soft, round, sexual pleasure wrapped up in a hundred irritating layers of creamy white wedding costume, but she was clearly one fierce bitch.

He had no doubt that she would kill him if he gave her the chance.

If he gave her even an inch.

With one smooth, swift roll, Erion reversed their positions. On her back, her arms now pinned above her head, her hair splayed like a sunrise around her face, and her eyes flashing in the moon's light, she hissed at him—struggled against him like a caged animal.

"You have made a grave mistake, male," she said, her voice as deathly as her gaze.

"We shall see," Erion answered, his tone smooth and resolute as he slipped his free hand around her waist.

She kicked at him, tried to get her knee up between his legs. "I am to be mated this night, you fool!"

"I know."

"My betrothed will not look kindly on having his bride accosted," she said through gritted teeth.

"I am counting on it," Erion said, tightening his hold on her, his gaze traversing the landscape one last time. "Let us hope that Cruen cares enough to come after you. For if he does not . . . well, we are both dead."

And from the cold, moonlit ground, Erion flashed away, his parcel still struggling like a feral cat at his side.